Winner of the Spur Award for Best Western Historical Novel

"The grandeur of vision, the sweep of history, the inevitable clash of race and time . . . *The Snowblind Moon*, in fact, delivers all that and more."
—*New York Daily News*

"Rich narration . . . highly believable . . . a gem."
—*St. Louis Post-Dispatch*

"An enormous and vital story, resoundingly told. The struggle for the Plains—the last great conflict between whites and Indians—requires a book of great expeditionary detail and length to do justice to the . . . ways of life that met there, and Cooke's novel succeeds with honors."
—*Publishers Weekly*

"An intensely readable story crammed with authentic Western lore."
—*The Washington Post*

"An epic canvas created with sure, masterful strokes. Bravo!"
—John Jakes

"Breath-holding . . . brilliantly executed."
—Ruth Beebe Hill, author of *Hanta Yo*

THE SNOWBLIND MOON by John Byrne Cooke

PART ONE: BETWEEN THE WORLDS
PART TWO: THE PIPE CARRIERS
PART THREE: HOOP OF THE NATION

HOOP
OF THE
NATION

THE
SNOWBLIND
MOON
JOHN BYRNE COOKE

TOR

A TOM DOHERTY ASSOCIATES BOOK

THE SNOWBLIND MOON PART THREE:
HOOP OF THE NATION

Copyright © 1984 by John Byrne Cooke

Reprinted by arrangement with Simon and Schuster

First Tor printing: September 1986

A TOR Book

Published by Tom Doherty Associates
49 West 24 Street
New York, N.Y. 10010

ISBN: 0-812-58154-7
CAN. ED.: 0-812-58155-5

Library of Congress Catalog Card Number: 84-14009

Printed in the United States

0 9 8 7 6 5 4 3 2 1

For my father, who helped to instill in me a love of books, which was easy, and of history, which took somewhat longer.

When I was a boy the Sioux owned the world; the sun rose and set in their lands; they sent ten thousand horsemen to battle. Where are the warriors today? Who slew them? Where are our lands? Who owns them?
—SITTING BULL

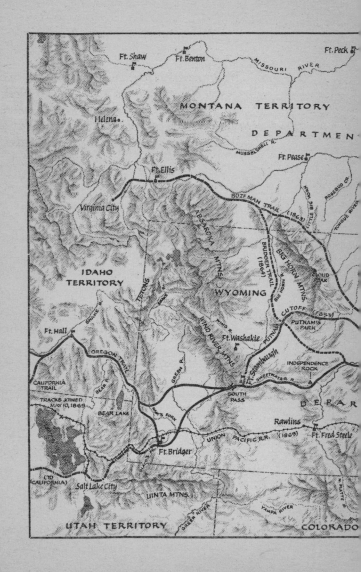

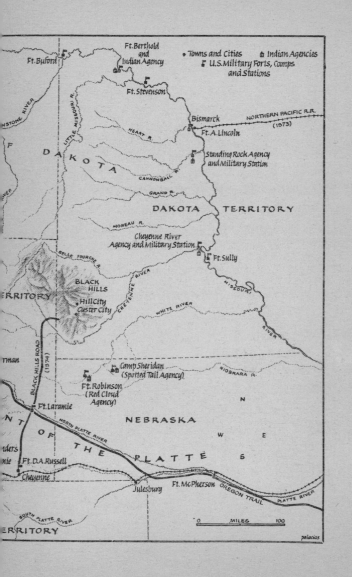

• Towns and Cities   🏛 Indian Agencies
𝔉 U.S.Military Forts, Camps and Stations

Ft.Berthold and Indian Agency

Ft.Buford

Ft.Stevenson

NORTHERN PACIFIC R.R.
(1973)

Bismarck

Ft.A.Lincoln

HEART R.

LITTLE MISSOURI R.

YELLOWSTONE RIVER

Standing Rock Agency and Military Station

DAKOTA

CANNONBALL

GRAND R.

DAKOTA   TERRITORY

MOREAU R.

Cheyenne River Agency and Military Station

Ft.Sully

BELLE FOURCHE R.

BLACK HILLS

Hillcity
Custer City

MISSOURI

WHITE RIVER

RIVER

CHEYENNE RIVER

RRITORY

BLACK HILLS ROAD
(1974)

rman

Camp Sheridan
(Spotted Tail Agency)

NIOBRARA R.

Ft.Robinson
(Red Cloud Agency)

N

Ft.Laramie

NEBRASKA

W   E

NORTH PLATTE RIVER

OF   THE   PLATTE   S

anders

nie

Ft.D.A.Russell

Cheyenne

Julesburg

Ft.McPherson   OREGON TRAIL   PLATTE RIVER

SOUTH PLATTE RIVER

0   MILES   100

ERRITORY

palacios

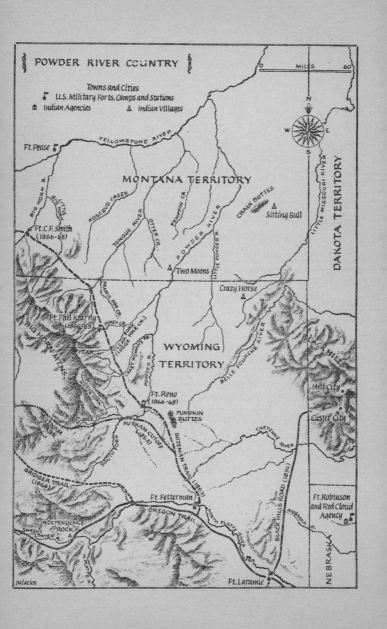

What has gone before in *Between the Worlds* and *The Pipe Carriers*, Parts One and Two of *The Snowblind Moon* . . .

In the winter of 1876, war clouds gather over the Powder River country of Wyoming Territory as the government moves to confine the last free-roaming bands of Sioux and Cheyenne on the Dakota reservation. A military column under General George Crook starts north from Fort Fetterman, but they are preceded into the troubled region by two riders: Chris Hardeman, a former army scout, and Johnny Smoker, a young white man captured by the Cheyenne when he was an infant and raised by them. Hardeman saved Johnny's life at the Battle of the Washita, where Johnny's Indian parents were killed, and the two have been together ever since. With Crook's blessing they have come seeking the Sioux chief Sun Horse, hoping to convince him he must surrender, and thereby to influence other hostile headmen to give in without fighting. Johnny's Indian father was Sioux, not Cheyenne, and he was Sun Horse's eldest son. Hardeman too knows Sun Horse indirectly: as a youth, Hardeman was trained in scouting by Jedediah Putnam, a former mountain man who later settled in the Big Horn foothills and has turned to raising cattle. Jed and Sun Horse have long been friends; Jed's brother Bat married Sun Horse's daughter and lives with Sun Horse's people—the Sun Band—who winter just a few miles from Putnam's Park, where Jed's settlement is located. Hardeman hopes Jed will help persuade Sun Horse to surrender, heading off a new Indian war.

But when Hardeman and Johnny arrive in Putnam's Park, they learn that Jed Putnam died six months ago and the little ranch is now in the hands of his daughter Lisa, a woman in her early thirties, and his black partner Julius Ingram, a former slave and cavalryman. The news of the approaching army shocks Lisa. She is concerned for Sun Horse's safety and wants to help him remain free, but she can see no choice for him other than the one Hardeman brings: fight or surrender.

Nor can Sun Horse, when Hardeman, Lisa and Johnny bring the news to his village, although he sees a good omen in the return of the grandson he believed to be dead. Old Hears Twice, the band's prophet, recently foretold the coming of a power that might help the band—a power that stems from the meeting of two people. Sun Horse is certain that Johnny is one of the two, but who is the other? Even by himself, the youth might bring good fortune to the Sun Band. When the boy was eight years old, he had a powerful medicine dream. In it he was told that he stood between the world of the Indians and that of the whites, and he would not choose between them until he was about to become a man. Sun Horse made Johnny promise that when he chose between the worlds, he would tell Sun Horse of his decision. Has he come now because he has chosen? If he chooses the Indian world, he may bring great power to help the people, the dream said. Sun Horse ponders these dilemmas, but he can see no way to delay giving in to the white soldiers, and when the Sun Band's council meets to decide what to do, Sun Horse is silent. Without his voice to lead them in another direction, the councillors choose surrender.

Sun Horse goes to Putnam's Park to tell Hardeman of the band's decision, but his arrival coincides with that of a traveling circus, lost in the winter snows. There is brief gunplay when the panicked circus men fire on the Indian delegation, but tragedy is averted by Lisa, Hardeman and Julius, who draw on the circus men and force them to lay down their arms. A clown performs for the crowd, helping to dispel the lingering tension. His cap falls off, revealing long brown hair, and Sun Horse sees that it is a young woman, not a man. Johnny Smoker is smitten by the girl, and in that moment Sun Horse is certain these are the two the prophet heard. Will their power help the Sun Band? Sun Horse doesn't know, but now he finds a way to avoid surrender, at least for the time being. He will send pipes of peace to General Crook and to his cousin Sitting Bull, asking them both to keep the peace until summer, and he will promise to speak for peace to the hostile leaders. He will send Hardeman with the pipe carriers, to persuade the white general, but Hardeman will not know the full extent of the message for Sitting Bull: Sun Horse will ask his cousin to call for a great gathering of the bands in summertime, so the people can decide for themselves the momentous issues of peace and war. Sun Horse feels new hope that he may finally fulfill a promise of power that was given to him years before in a medicine dream: to understand the whites and to lead his people to live in peace beside them. But it must be a peace without surrender.

Hardeman sees in Sun Horse's willingness to speak for peace to the hostile chiefs an increased chance of ending the new war before it starts, and he agrees to the headman's plan. With due ceremony the pipes are prepared, and the pipe carriers set out for the north.

Hoping to see more of the clown, Amanda Spencer, Johnny agrees to guide the circus to the main trail. But as the wagons thread their way through the narrow river canyon below the park, an avalanche of snow comes crashing down, wiping out the circus's cook wagons and supplies, but sparing the people, who are now trapped in the mountain valley. Lisa sees at once that she will have to sacrifice some of her cows to feed the circus people, but her greater concern is for Sun Horse. What if the pipe carriers fail? What if the war begins? With Julius's help she devises a plan: Hunt with us, she asks Sun Horse. With your help we may bring in enough meat to save my cows and help your people as well. She offers gunpowder and grain to the Indians, knowing that if the hunt is successful and the Sun Band's horses are strengthened by her grain, the band will be strong enough to move if the soldiers come near.

But the winter has been harsh and game is scarce, and the best efforts of Sioux and white hunters bring in only a little meat, not enough to make the kind of difference Lisa hoped for. Sun Horse sees in this failure a sign that the spirit powers have turned away from the Sun Band; he retreats to his lodge and begins a fast, seeking within himself to know the reason.

In Putnam's Park, Johnny Smoker spends much of his time with Amanda, and she seems to return his interest in her. Like Johnny, Amanda is an orphan; her parents were killed in a circus tent fire years ago and she was raised by Hachaliah Tatum, the circus's owner, as his ward. But Lisa Putnam knows something that Johnny does not: Amanda and Tatum are lovers.

Meanwhile, the pipe carriers are traveling as quickly as

they can in the face of bitter winter weather. They find that Crook has separated his cavalry from the wagons and infantry, and is moving up-country surprisingly quickly. The pipe carriers press on to overtake him, but disaster strikes when a Crow hunting party attacks them in the night, wounding Sun Horse's grandson Blackbird badly. The little band turns off Crook's trail and finds shelter in the village of Two Moons, a Cheyenne, on the Powder River. Two Moons sends riders to Sitting Bull, and to Crazy Horse, who is also camped nearby, and when the great war leaders arrive, a council is held. Sitting Bull accepts Sun Horse's pipe and agrees to keep the peace until summer, but only if Crook will leave the country at once. The council sets forth further conditions as well: Crook must return in the summer with a peace delegation to hear the Indians' demands for a reservation in the Powder River country and an agency here. They will not give up this land and go to Dakota. As soon as the council ends, Crazy Horse and Sitting Bull leave to return to their own villages.

Hardeman fears that the council's conditions mean certain war. When Cheyenne hunters bring word late that evening of Crook's whereabouts, Hardeman leaves the village alone in the night to find the soldiers, planning to lead them to Sitting Bull's village and force the war leader to surrender, thus showing the futility of resistance. He is willing to do anything, even betray the trust that Sun Horse put in him, to prevent a new war.

But during the time it has taken the pipe carriers to reach Two Moons' village and gather the council, Crook's expedition has been on the move. Despite the harsh weather the soldiers seem to grow stronger as the march progresses, and they cover more ground each day. Last to join the command was Second Lieutenant Hamilton Whitcomb, a recent graduate of West Point, son of a Virginia family that fought on the losing side of the Civil War. He is assigned to Company E, Second Cavalry, where his troop commander is Brevet Major Francis "Boots" Corwin, an embittered Union Army veteran who sees in this campaign his last chance to win recognition and promotion on the battlefield. Corwin resents Whitcomb's youth and his Southern heritage, and the relations between the two men are strained.

The soldiers are beginning to fear that the country is deserted when at last they spy two Indian hunters and give chase. The Indians slip away as dusk falls, but the column's scouts find their tracks. Crook divides the command, sending six companies, including Corwin and Whitcomb's E Troop, off through the night on the trail of the hostiles. As dawn approaches, the scouts find a village ahead, on the Powder.

The soldiers attack Two Moons' camp, surprising the Indians, who nevertheless manage to fight an effective withdrawal from the tipis. Captain Moore's company was ordered to take the high bluff overlooking the village, but he fails; soon the Indians gain the heights and now the soldiers find themselves on the defensive. On the forward line, Whitcomb performs well under fire, but Corwin is badly wounded in the leg.

Hardeman enters the battle alone, on horseback, trying to find Reynolds, to stop the fighting. He rode through the night only to come upon the soldiers' tracks heading south; he turned back at once, but too late to stop the attack. Wounded by the soldiers, who take him for a renegade, he is carried by two warriors to a sheltered position held by the Indians. He sees Blackbird wounded again, charging the soldiers, and rides to save the boy, followed by Hawk Chaser, another of the Sun Band's pipe carriers. Hardeman is shot from his horse, but he manages to drive back the first of two cavalrymen who come riding to finish off the wounded boy. Hawk Chaser stops the other, but he is killed, and then, just when Hardeman is sure that the soldiers will advance to finish the job, a bugle sounds and the soldiers withdraw from the village.

Hardeman passes out from the effects of his wound and wakens later that evening to find that the Cheyenne have abandoned the smoking village site and only the pipe carriers remain, together with a few Sioux who were in Two Moons' camp and have now decided to join the Sun Band. Little Hand, who carried the pipe for Sitting Bull, and Standing Eagle, Blackbird's father and war leader of the Sun Band, are torturing a soldier who was taken alive. Hardeman stops the torture by shooting the soldier, infuriating the Indians. As they surround him, he loses consciousness again.

HOOP
OF THE
NATION

LISA PUTNAM'S JOURNAL

Tuesday, March 21st. 5:50 a.m.

With the two heifer calves born yesterday we now have twenty-eight all told; there are thirteen bulls and fifteen heifers. Except for two that are weakly, all are fine specimens. We have lost five. Scours persist among the newborn but my father's remedy of beef broth, pectin and honey has served at least as well as the patent medicine, which is now exhausted.

This is the sixth day of Sun Horse's fast. Since Johnny rode over to the village two days ago and returned with news of this quest for spiritual guidance, worry about Sun Horse has been added to my increasing concern for the safety of Uncle Bat and Mr. Hardeman. It seems they have been gone forever.

Yesterday evening Mr. Tatum informed me that he believes it may be possible to clear a way through the avalanche in another week. The halfway mark was only passed yesterday, but progress is much faster now, aided

*by the warmer weather, the greater care the men are using
with the blasting powder, and most of all the participation
of Rama. Mr. Tatum berates himself for not thinking of
Rama sooner. The old barnyard scoop, fitted with iron
rings for the harness Harry made to fit the elephant,
enables Rama to move a great deal of snow and debris in
much less time than men with shovels. They now apply all
their energies to loading the wagons, and the remaining
portion of blocked roadway diminishes daily at a hearten-
ing rate.*

*There is much I would like to say to Mr. Tatum but I
have held my tongue. It is best not to let enmity and
recriminations out into the open when people are confined
together as we are, and he will be gone soon enough.
Good riddance, I would say. I have come to share his
impatience for the road to be clear and the circus to be on
its way. Certainly their early departure will be the best
thing for Johnny, and perhaps Amanda herself has realized this. Less than a week ago she was almost throwing
herself at him, but for the past several days she has been
much more reserved. He still spends what time he can with
her, but he is so shy that I doubt there will be any open
expression of his feelings, which is just as well. What
would he do if he learned the truth about her? I believe it
would break his heart. When he is not with her or off
working with Hutch, he spends his time with the Waldheims.
He has not given them a definite reply to their offer of
employment. When the circus leaves he will remain here to
await Mr. Hardeman, and I hope that when he is at last
ready to set off on his own, Johnny will have given up the
romantic notion of chasing after the circus, and Amanda.*

*It is her I worry about the most. What is to become of
her. Things cannot go on forever as they are.*

She will be in the kitchen by now and I must go.

CHAPTER ONE

After the noon meal Lisa saddled her horse and led him from the barn, preparing to ride down through the meadows for her daily look at the calves, but she hesitated when she saw Alfred Chalmers approaching alone.

It was a blustery day, typical of early spring in the mountains. The snow was soft underfoot. Sunlight and clouds swept across the valley with the wind. Julius had turned three new mothers and their calves out of the heifer lot and he was hazing them down to join the herd. The clowns and acrobats were already at work in the barn and just now the yard was deserted except for Lisa and the Englishman.

"Mr. Chalmers, may I have a moment of your time?"

Chalmers raised a hand and changed course to join her.

For five days Lisa had said nothing of what she had seen that morning in the second-floor hallway, not to Hachaliah Tatum, not to Amanda, not to anyone else.

Amanda had turned, her hand still resting on the latch of Tatum's bedroom door, and she had discovered Lisa watching her. For a moment neither of them had spoken, and then Lisa had invited Amanda to come to the kitchen for a cup of coffee. Together they had made the fire and the coffee, and when Harry Wo brought word that Ling had decided to remain in bed a while longer, Amanda had helped Lisa and Joe Kitchen make breakfast. She had little experience at domestic tasks, but she was a willing pupil and Joe had assigned her to making the breakfast biscuits. They had been widely praised as the best ever, much to Amanda's delight. Since then she had joined Lisa in the kitchen each morning before dawn and they had an hour or more together before Joe and Monty arrived. They had exchanged confidences and become close friends; they had talked of their lives, but never of Hachaliah Tatum.

"Miss Putnam. Another splendid luncheon. Ah, dinner, I should say. I can't get used to calling it dinner in midday. I do try. When in Rome, you know."

"Mr. Chalmers, you must be aware that Mr. Tatum and Amanda are, that is—I don't know just how to put it: They are not simply . . ." She was at a loss.

Chalmers grew serious. The wind whipped his straw-colored mane about his head. "I am aware, Miss Putnam, if I, ah, take your meaning correctly. We are all aware, of course."

"Has this situation existed for long?"

"For several years."

Lisa was shocked. "But then why, I mean how can you . . ."

"Permit it?"

"Yes. Thank you for making this easier for me."

The wind gusted so hard that Lisa held on to her hat to keep it from blowing away. Chalmers shifted position and raised one arm, extending his cape like a protecting wing to shelter her. "Miss Putnam, we in the circus live in a small world that is closed to society at large, both because of its disregard for us and our consequent disregard for it. Ordinary people will allow us to entertain them but they will not have us sit at the same table, if you see what I mean. Within our own small world we live in intimate contiguity with one another. We have no home except the circus itself. It's rather as if many families lived beneath a single roof; there is little privacy except that granted by common consent. Because of this we have developed our own customs, and the most strictly observed of these is that one does not interfere in the affairs of another unless there is a call for help."

"And there has been no such call?"

"There has not."

"But you can't take her compliance at face value, certainly not in the beginning? She was so young!"

Chalmers looked at his huge feet. "The, ah, situation had existed for some time before we were aware of it. Amanda was in no danger; no harm was being done to her. She made no objection."

"Sometimes the harm is not easy to see."

Chalmers said nothing.

"No one has talked to her, then? None of the women?"

"Perhaps. But I am not aware of it."

Lisa touched his arm. "Mightn't you encourage her to—"

"To what, Miss Putnam?"

Lisa shook her head and dropped her hand. "I don't know. At the very least she should know that her friends care for her. She should know that you would support her if she ever decided to change the situation. To end it."

Again Chalmers made no reply. Lisa gathered up her reins and mounted her horse. "I'm sorry. I have no right to meddle."

"You are not meddling, Miss Putnam. You have made us feel at home here. That means more to us than I can say. We are all very grateful. Amanda respects you and she has accepted you as her friend. You are only expressing your concerns, and believe me, I will think about what you have said."

"Thank you." She gave him a brief smile and rode away.

Her worries for Amanda unsettled Chalmers, coming as they did on top of his own. Ever since Lydia's warning he had watched the girl closely and he had seen the change, too sudden to be genuine. Overnight Amanda had ceased to flaunt her affection for Johnny Smoker. She ate her meals with Tatum and exchanged only pleasantries with the boy in the presence of the circus master, but she was playing a role.

I see it more clearly than the others, Chalmers thought, because I know the theater and they do not. When Hachaliah is about, Amanda is on stage. She plays the young innocent for all the world to see; she is Hachaliah's faithful companion now, with not another thought on her mind, but she overplays the part. Underneath it all, what is she thinking? What does she intend? Can she imagine that she has pulled the wool over Hachaliah's eyes?

The final act of the drama would be played out soon, once the river road was open, and Chalmers' conversation with Lisa Putnam had left him with the feeling that he too would have to take part in the action before it was done.

He spent the rest of the afternoon helping Harry Wo replace a cracked skid on the hay sled. He and Harry had become frequent companions since the arm-wrestling match. Harry usually delighted in teasing the strongman about the opponents he would have to face for years to come in Putnam's Park, but today Harry was quiet, full of concern for his pregnant wife, who kept to her bed for half of each day now, and the two men worked together in silence save for the few words needed to coordinate their labors.

Chalmers found the hard work far more satisfying than practicing with his bell weights and iron bars. Like the rest of the performers he had felt the strain of growing boredom. He was anxious to resume the accustomed routine of daily performances, breaking the tent down and setting it up, moving on to the next town and the next show. Practice served a purpose, but it took performing before an audience to keep the acts honed to a fine edge.

He missed the hunting that had been such a welcome diversion for a time. No one had gone out for several days. The warmer weather made getting around difficult in the mountains; horses and men on foot broke through the surface of the snow and the going was slow, but it was more than this that kept the hunters home. "You cain't whistle up game where there ain't none," Julius had said when Chalmers suggested the two of them go off on snowshoes. "Perhaps it's true that evil spirits have taken the game away," Chalmers had replied in jest, but Julius had answered him perfectly seriously. "Cain't say. I'll leave that to Sun Horse."

Chalmers perceived that the Indians' refusal to hunt had had a greater effect on Julius than the Negro admitted. It seemed that Lisa as well, indeed each of those that lived in Putnam's Park, had grown quieter in recent days, ever since the old chief had undertaken his fast. Only Hutch was unaffected. His infatuation for Maria Abbruzzi kept him intoxicated throughout his waking hours; he remained untouched by the moods of the others and seemed to take great delight in even the foulest day, and Chalmers suspected that in company with the young ranch worker Maria had found ways to relieve her own boredom. If Carmelo

Abbruzzi came to share Chalmers' suspicions, there could be trouble.

Hutch was out of harm's way today. He and Johnny Smoker had gone with Chatur to help with the work at the avalanche, and they would not return until suppertime.

When the new skid was fitted to its iron runner and bolted to the sled, Harry thanked Chalmers and went off to the house to assure himself that all was well with Ling. The sun had fallen behind the western ridge and the wind had died away, and already there was a new crust on the snow as the temperature dropped below freezing. Chalmers perched himself on the corral fence to wait for Lydia and the others to emerge from the barn, and he marveled at how soon he had become accustomed to the wintry climate. Wrapped in his cape, he enjoyed the view of the peaceful valley much as he might have enjoyed a pleasant Dorset afternoon. Overhead, the swift low clouds of midday had given way to wispy brushstrokes tinged with pink and red. "Mares'-tails" the circus teamsters called these delicate forms, and claimed they were portents of stormy weather. There had been a ring around the sun that morning and this too was said to presage an end to the warmth that had lasted for four days now. "Never trust a chinook," the wagon drivers said. "It'll snow by Sunday." But Lisa Putnam had scoffed at their predictions. "Oh, it may snow," she had said when Chalmers asked her opinion, "but we have another saying in the mountains: only fools and newcomers predict the weather." And so Chalmers' new interest in mares'-tails and rings around the sun was tempered with caution. To know what the weather would do, one waited until it did it. Perhaps it would be as well to adopt a similar attitude about all things, instead of worrying about what Amanda or Hachaliah Tatum or

Carmelo Abbruzzi might do to interrupt the tranquillity of this place.

"I could knit a sweater with the wool you're gathering."

He looked down to find Lydia standing beside him, her black eyes probing his face.

"Just thinking, my dear." He got down from the fence.

"Yes, and I know what troubles you. It's that girl. You know Hachaliah has his eye on her."

"We'll be gone soon enough and it will be over," Chalmers said, hoping it was so.

Others were coming out of the barn now. Lydia took his arm and guided him toward the house, away from ears that might overhear. "Perhaps," she said. "But I think Hachaliah smells a mouse."

"A rat, dear. He smells a rat."

"That too. Can't you see? She is different. Where is all that flirting she likes so much? She is a regular trollop when she knows she'll be gone the next day and some young fellow's heart broken behind her. But look at her here. Quiet and polite, and her eyes everywhere but on that boy when Hachaliah is nearby. I have not seen her this way before, and it worries me. You always said someday she will break away from him, as a child breaks away from the parents."

"Yes. I didn't think it would come so soon. You think that's what it is, then?"

Lydia shrugged. "If it is, what do we do?"

"Perhaps I should have a word with her."

"I will speak to her if you like. The woman's touch might be best."

"No, my dear, this is something I must do. It may be something I have put off for too long."

With his mind made up, he took the first opportunity that presented itself. The supper gong rang before Tatum and the teamsters had returned from the avalanche and Chalmers intercepted Amanda as she entered the saloon.

"May I have a word with you?" He took her by the arm and led her to a table by the windows, far from the line forming at the serving tables. "I have seen no more of that new routine we all liked so well," he said as he seated her. "I hope you won't abandon it."

"No, it's just that, well, Hachaliah wants us to make some changes and we can't agree on them." She looked out the window. The wagons full of men were approaching on the road; as usual Tatum rode in the lead on his white stallion.

"And Sam and Carlos? Do they side with Hachaliah or you?"

"Oh, we all know how we want it to be. It's Hachaliah who wants to change it."

"Often an instructor does not see when his pupil's abilities outstrip his own, my dear. You have come to that point and you mustn't let him stifle you. I think perhaps because I have known you all my life I have taken your abilities somewhat for granted myself. You really have an exceptional talent, you know. Old Sam was saying much the same thing the other day."

"Was he really?" Amanda was both pleased and flustered by this praise.

"Indeed he was. You know, it's possible that a time may come when you will wish to rise beyond the confines of this show. Not that we take second place to anyone, you understand. It's just that sometimes a change is necessary for further growth, if you, ah, see what I mean. Others would be glad to have you, I'm sure. Perhaps even Barnum. And if the day should come when you decide to leave us, your friends will understand." He took her hand in his own. She was looking at him solemnly and in her eyes he saw a maturity beyond her years. It was not the first time he had noticed this quality in her, the ability to be a child one moment and a woman the next, and it encouraged him to discover it again. "We believe in you and we wish you only the best, always. If there is anything we can ever do for you, you have only to let us know. That is really all I wanted to say."

"Thank you, Alfred." It seemed that she might say something more, but then she spied Julius coming through the kitchen door and she jumped to her feet. "There's Julius. I want to ask him if we can play music after supper." She kissed Chalmers quickly on the cheek and skipped away, a child once more.

As Chalmers watched her go he wondered if he should have been more direct. He had planted the seed; when it might grow or whether it would grow at all remained to be seen. He had tried to tell her that when and if she decided to make a break with Tatum her friends would stand by her, but he had done it in his own roundabout way. Directness in personal matters was not in his temperament.

Lydia rejoined him then and together they went to the serving line. The teamsters arrived, hurrying as if the food might be all gone before they reached the tables. Chalmers noted that Henry Kinnean had discarded his sling altogether. Since he had resumed his position as overseer of the unruly teamsters, Kinnean ate and drank by himself and he no longer gambled with the other men.

"I think it would be nice if we sat with Amanda tonight, don't you, dear?" Lydia said as they received their plates. When Hachaliah Tatum arrived at last he found an empty seat kept for him between Lydia and Amanda. Gunther and Greta Waldheim were at the same table and Lisa and Joe Kitchen arrived soon after, leaving the last few diners to serve themselves. Throughout the meal the talk was pleasant and inconsequential, but as Amanda rose to go, Tatum put a hand on her arm.

"You look a little tired. This might be a good night for you to go to bed early."

Amanda slipped from his grasp and stood behind Lisa's chair. From a nearby table Johnny Smoker was watching her. "I feel fine. Anyway, Julius and I are going to play music tonight."

"Mr. Ingram will understand if you ask him to put it off until another time."

"He might, but I won't ask him. He's very busy and I will play with him when it suits him. Besides, you said we'll be gone in a few days and there are more tunes I want to learn from him."

Tatum ceased his resistance but he could not conceal his annoyance. "Very well, but don't be too late."

As the meal was cleared away the two fiddlers sat by the potbellied stove. They played reels and waltzes and traded tunes back and forth. Johnny came to sit with them and soon there was a circle of listeners. Hutch brought his banjo and Papa Waldheim his accordion, and the cheerful quartet repeatedly won applause from the small audience.

It seemed to those present that Amanda's music shone with a special brilliance. She played tirelessly, choosing fast tunes and happy ones, and when she followed Julius's lead she appeared to know instinctively where he was going, even when the tunes were new to her. For the most part the onlookers were content to sit and tap their feet, sometimes singing the words to a song they all knew, but a few dancers rose to move among the tables from time to time. Alfred Chalmers took Lydia in his arms and guided her to the darkened corners of the room and twice Johnny offered his hand to Lisa.

In a pause between tunes Hachaliah Tatum cleared his

throat; he drew his watch from his waistcoat pocket and looked at it meaningfully. Oblivious to this reminder, Amanda began a new song. Tatum opened his mouth as if to speak, then closed it and stalked from the room.

Others were leaving too, for the hour was late. The weary teamsters had gone long ago, some to their rooms in the house, the rest to the tents. The fiddlers turned to gentle tunes now, ballads and slow waltzes and Negro gospel songs. Maria Abbruzzi whispered in Hutch's ear and soon the two of them went off together. Papa Waldheim squeezed a final chord from his accordion and latched it shut, leaving the fiddles to play for just a handful of listeners, sending their notes across the saloon like birds paired in flight, swooping and dipping and rising together. At last Julius found himself nodding.

"I best get myself to bed," he said, getting to his feet.

Amanda relieved the tension in her bow. "Thank you," she said.

"I should be thankin' you. You put new life in this old fiddle. We'll see you tomorrow."

With Julius gone only Alfred and Lydia and Johnny remained. Lydia's head rested on Alfred's shoulder and her eyes were closed. He patted her gently on the arm.

"Hmm?" She looked up. "Oh, my goodness. Come along, Alfred." With a smile at Johnny and Amanda, they were gone.

"We're all alone," she said.

"I guess we should go to bed too." He didn't move.

How could he even think of sleep? she wondered. Couldn't he feel her excitement? Didn't he sense that she had planned for the two of them to be alone tonight?

"Oh, let's stay a little longer. I haven't even had one dance with you."

"There's no one to play for us."

"I'll play." She stood up and retightened her bow. "Here. You just have to stand a little farther away from me." She raised the fiddle and Johnny put his hands at her waist as she started to play the slow waltz she had played on the night of the circus's arrival, and again on the tightrope. "I've given my waltz a name. It's called Johnny's Waltz now."

"For me?"

"Of course for you. Who else would I name it for?" She could see that he was pleased and she quickened the tempo a bit as they twirled among the tables. She felt that she was gliding on air.

It was all going to come about, now that she had found the way to free herself! She and Johnny would be free together! How could she have been such an idiot? For days she had been close to despair. As soon as she had determined to break free of Hachaliah, he had tightened his grip on her. She had been too brazen in encouraging Johnny, and Hachaliah had demanded repayment in kind. She had been with him every night since then and he kept a closer watch on her during the day, whenever he was in the settlement. He spent an hour or more each day watching the clowns rehearse, and it had taken Amanda only a short while to realize that so long as she remained within his reach he would never relinquish his dominion over her.

Leaving the circus was unthinkable. It was her home and her life. She had imagined herself alone, cut off from her friends, unable to perform, and she had recoiled from the prospect. For a time her determination had waned and she had all but given up hope, and then Alfred, gentle Alfred, in his own bumbling way, had provided the answer.

You have an exceptional talent, he had said, and the very earnestness of his expression had made her see this praise in a new light. The other performers had always complimented her and she knew they genuinely enjoyed her performances, but she had never considered the meaning of those compliments beyond the boundaries of Tatum's Combined Shows, until now. *Sometimes a change is necessary for further growth*, Alfred had said, and the answer to her problems had exploded in her mind. She could have both her clowning and her freedom! Other circus owners would appreciate her talent, and she need not be on her own! Johnny Smoker would be her guide and protector, but unlike Hachaliah he would not control her. Instead she would control him, but he would never dream that her velvet reins rested on his shoulders. He could find work anywhere and he was not afraid to set out for places he had never seen. To him that was the heart of living, making your way in the world and seeing as much of it as you could. It would not be difficult to persuade him to visit the eastern states, and while they were there she could approach another show. Where there was a circus, there were horses, and Johnny had magic with horses. The Waldheims had seen it and others would see it too. She and Johnny would find work together, and who was to say that some of her old friends could not join her later on? When she rose to a position of prominence in the new show she would send for Sam and Carlos, and perhaps Alfred and Lydia would come as well!

Suddenly there was no limit to what she could do. She felt that she scarcely knew the person she had been before she arrived in this snowbound wilderness, for here she had seen how to free herself of her fetters. Not just in her art but in all other things as well she would decide her own destiny. It was Johnny who had awakened this resolve in her and with Johnny's help she had a chance to loose Hachaliah's grip on her until she might slip away and be free of him forever.

She would set her sights high. The Bailey and Cooper circus was going to California this summer and Aaron Cooper might be glad to have her back. There was even talk that Cooper and Bailey planned a European tour. And beyond Cooper and Bailey there was Barnum. Wouldn't Hachaliah turn green if she got a job with Barnum!

Hachaliah was waiting for her now. He expected her to creep to his bedroom when the house was asleep, as she had done so often in recent days. But tonight he would be disappointed. She needed time to gather her strength for the final step. Somehow she must keep away from him for a few days, away from his attempts to hold her by every means at his command. And she needed time with Johnny.

The first step was to make Johnny declare himself. He was so shy! Sometimes Amanda wanted to shake him out of the almost reverential attitude he displayed toward her, as if she were a sainted virgin to be placed in a shrine. But she must be careful. She must not disturb the pure image he had of her. She must kindle a fire in him. He must make the first move. Men needed that. They had to believe that they created a woman's desire and compelled her to submit to them by the force of their will. Allowing them to believe this was a gift women made to men, and the means by which a woman could control any man she chose.

Of one thing she was certain: she would pacify Hachaliah Tatum no more. She must proceed cautiously with Johnny, but time was short and she was ready to dare anything to effect the break now. When the circus left, it would go without her. She would stay behind with Johnny here in Lisa Putnam's comforting home, and when Chris Hardeman was back and Johnny knew his friend was safe, she and Johnny would start out together.

She brought the waltz to an end and curtsied to Johnny. "Thank you, sir. You dance beautifully, as always."

Johnny shifted from one foot to the other, and even in that simple movement she could discern the unevenness caused by his old wound, the trace of a limp that disappeared so miraculously when he danced.

"It is late," she said. "I suppose we should go to bed." She looked him in the eye to see if he suspected her veiled meaning, but she saw no hint of it. "Will you be a gentleman and see me to my room?"

"I don't guess it'd be proper for me to go upstairs with you."

"See me to the stairs then. Is that proper?" She was teasing him now. She took his arm in hers and together they left the saloon and made their way along the darkened hallway to the foot of the stairs. A coal-oil lamp hung at the upstairs landing, its wick turned low. Amanda stood close to Johnny, still holding his arm. "You're worried about Chris, aren't you?"

"He'll be all right. I'd feel better if I was with him, though. It's good to have someone watch your back."

"Shouldn't you go to the Indian village soon to see if there's any news?"

"I thought I might go up tomorrow."

"Take me with you?"

"Sure. You want to go? We won't see Sun Horse, not if he's still shut away by himself."

"That's all right. Hears Twice will be glad to see us and maybe I'll get to see the *heyokas* perform. We could stay overnight, the way we did before."

"What about Tatum? He said you couldn't go off without his say-so."

"He'll be down at the avalanche. Besides, I can go where I like. We can stay with Penelope! She'd be glad to have visitors."

Johnny smiled. "I'd like that."

She pressed herself against him. "It will be fun, just the two of us. Thanks for saying you'll take me."

"That's not much." Johnny seemed embarrassed. "I'd do more for you than that. A lot more."

"Would you really?" Her chin tilted up ever so slightly and she shifted her body toward him. His arm found its way around her, so tentatively it barely touched her. Her free hand slipped up to his shoulder. She wasn't sure if the slight pressure she applied there pulled him to her or if he bent of his own will, but she felt his breath on her face as she closed her eyes.

Their lips met. Seldom was a kiss more chaste, and yet Amanda became aware of nothing beyond that place where their flesh touched, and she felt a warmth that remained when they parted and she climbed the stairs alone.

She had thought she might lure him upstairs after all, leading him on with one kiss and then another, but that could wait until tomorrow in the Indian village, far from Hachaliah's sight and hearing.

She took the lamp from the landing, and once in her room with the door carefully bolted behind her, she sat at the delicate veneered dressing table and set the lamp so it shone on her face. She peered at herself and placed a finger on her parted lips. They felt unnaturally warm to the touch. In the moments when they had touched Johnny's, she had discovered something new about him, something that excited her and fueled her hopes. There was a strength behind his tenderness, one she wasn't sure Johnny himself even suspected.

He was different from the others, the young men whose attentions she encouraged in every place where Tatum's Combined Shows made an appearance. He was so different that she was pressing her attentions on him, although they were concealed in the guise of a young lady's modesty. She stared at herself, eyes wide in the warm yellow light of the lamp. It was true. She was pursuing him. She had never done anything like it before. Always she had simply let herself be seen and the young men flocked around her. She led them on and sometimes let them find the pleasure they sought, and she felt renewed by their adoration. But she didn't want them.

She wanted Johnny.

Her eyes and mouth opened wide in mock astonishment and she covered her mouth with the fingers of one hand, the picture of shocked modesty. She dropped her hand and smiled at herself. Could she control him as easily as the others? It would take more than whims to move him. She would have to know what she wanted, and to know that she would have to be unafraid. In the Indian village she would take him. He would think it was he that had taken her and he would be hers forever. Or for as long as she wanted him.

The doorknob turned. She started and looked fearfully over her shoulder. Damn the lamp! The light beneath the door had betrayed her presence.

"Amanda?"

The voice was soft but she knew it at once and it confirmed her fears.

"Amanda." Again the knob turned and the door creaked as it strained against the bolt.

She arose and crossed the room, her bearing erect and her face calm. She paused to unbutton her bodice halfway down.

"You took your time," Tatum muttered as she stood aside to admit him. She closed the door quickly and silently behind him. He wore a satin dressing gown and soft calfskin slippers.

"I'm tired, Hachaliah. We worked hard today. I'm getting ready for bed."

"Ah yes. Somehow I imagined you would be tired now after playing music until all hours." The edge of sarcasm was cloaked less carefully than usual. His face was placid but the voice was hard. His eyes dropped to her bosom where the petticoat showed through the open dress. She wished she had left the buttons fastened.

He reached for her but she stepped back. "Not tonight."

"Oh yes, tonight. And any night I wish."

"What about my wishes?" Amanda felt the anger growing within her. "Do you think about what I wish?"

"Of course I do. That is why I'm here." He slipped out of his dressing gown and set it aside. His flannel pajamas were dark blue, with white piping. He sat on the bed and began to unbutton the shirt. The hair on his chest was turning gray. On his head he used a pomade that kept the hair there shiny black.

His muscles flexed as he took off the pajama top. His abdomen was firm and flat. He sat back against the headboard wearing only the blue pajama trousers. He was proud of his body and the sight of it caused a familiar quickening of breath in Amanda's breast. She clenched her hands and dug her thumbnail into the flesh of her forefinger, smiling as she felt the pain. "You're so sure about what I want, aren't you?"

"Reasonably so." He smiled too, pleased with himself.

"My teacher."

"Yes. And you have learned well. There's little more I can show you, except my appreciation."

"You're right. I have nothing more to learn from you." She felt a sudden bravado. It was true she needed him no more. The realization made her almost giddy. "Whatever else I have to learn, I'll learn somewhere else."

"From someone else, is that what you mean?"

"Yes!"

In an instant he was off the bed and moving to her side. He seized her arm so tightly that she gasped. "You dare talk to me that way? After all I have done for you? Do you know where you would be without me? In a workhouse with snot dribbling from your nose! Or someplace worse!"

"In a whorehouse?" she suggested defiantly.

"Yes! But I suppose you would take it in stride!"

"Lower your voice!" she hissed.

"Ah!" Tatum's eyes gleamed. "So you would rather the whole world didn't know? Perhaps young Johnny Smoker would no longer follow you about like a lovesick puppy if he knew the truth about us?"

"You wouldn't tell him!" Amanda's tone was brave but she felt a sharp fear deep within her. How would Johnny's feelings change if he knew? Worse yet, what would he do if he should learn that she, and not Hachaliah Tatum, had been the one to initiate their physical relations?

It was true.

For eight years following her parents' death, Hachaliah had cared for her unselfishly, with a genuinely parental affection that never overstepped the normal bounds. And then in a moment of crisis Amanda had changed everything. She was sixteen, feeling the first strength of her womanhood, when she fell in love for the first time. He was a youth of fair appearance and some wealth, four years her senior. He seduced her expertly and she did not resist, for he held up before her a promised life beyond the circus, a life filled with gleaming carriages and liveried servants and gala balls beneath crystal chandeliers. For two weeks while the circus remained in Baltimore he showered her with gifts and promised that the secret romance would be proclaimed to the world on the day before

Tatum and the rest departed for the nation's capital. But when the day came, Amanda's swain was conspicuous by his absence. He sent a single rose and a note of farewell. Alas, his parents had made another match for him, he said, and he would be disinherited if he defied them. In a fit of grief, jealousy and rage, Amanda had fled to the comfort of Hachaliah's arms. Through the night she had clung to him, and as the dawn broke and he kissed away fresh tears, she had returned his kisses. At first he had resisted, but she had learned much from her faithless suitor in a short time, and already she knew how to release a man's primal urges. In joining her flesh with Hachaliah's she had sought to guarantee that he would never leave her as the callous youth had done, that she would always find comfort and protection—and pleasure—by his side. It had never once occurred to her that she might one day wish to leave him and that the new bonds she had created might hold her back.

Hachaliah still had hold of her arm. "Wouldn't I? Do you really want to know?" His expression was almost pleading. He relaxed his grasp and stroked her arm lightly. "But there's really no need for us to quarrel, is there? You'll never leave me. I know you too well. I know your needs. And your desires." His voice was low and earnest and his eyes had softened as the anger left him. They were dark and liquid and they held her in his grip even when he released her arm.

"I won't respond," she said, unable to look away. "I won't move."

"You'll move." It was barely a whisper. One by one he unfastened the remaining buttons on her dress until it was open to the waist. He pushed it off her shoulder and slipped the sleeves off her arms, and the dress fell to the floor. She stood absolutely still. He pushed the straps of her petticoat from her shoulders and soon it too lay in a soft heap about her feet. He placed a hand on her midriff and moved it slowly upward. She felt a surge of blood beneath his palm. Her nipples hardened.

"Ah. You see?" His eyes were still locked on hers.

"It's the cold." She pressed her nails into her palms with all her might.

He knelt before her and hooked his fingers into the waistband of her woolen tights. He pulled slowly downward, taking her only other undergarment, that one of silk, with the tights, leaving her naked before him. She stood like a statue; the clothes about her feet were the drapings of the sculptor's pedestal. Her eyes were closed.

Tatum lifted her easily and deposited her on the bed. His arms left her and she heard a movement, then felt his weight descend onto the bed beside her. When he moved against her she felt his nakedness and his desire. She lay rigid. His lips touched hers and moved down to her breasts, touching each one briefly. His hands roamed her skin, stroking and caressing. One moved to her thighs. "Tell me to go," he said softly.

Her mouth opened and she made a small sound that was not a word.

He leaned over her and his breath warmed her face. Somewhere far below he was touching her. "Tell me to go," he said again, and his lips grazed hers.

She fought to keep from responding. This was not the way she wanted it to be. She had planned her escape. He could not hold her any longer. Tomorrow she and Johnny would be off to the Indian village and there they would stay until the gulf between her and Hachaliah Tatum grew so wide he could no longer reach across it.

His lips were at her ear, catching the lobe and teasing it. But he couldn't reach her even now, not unless she let him. And yet so long as he was near her she must give him no cause for alarm, for he could be dangerous if his suspicions were aroused. He must suspect nothing until he saw that the door of her cage stood open and she had flown to safety. She must fool him completely.

As his mouth returned to hers she caught his lower lip between her teeth and held him captive as her arms went around him to pull him down against her. Below, she let herself go, rising to meet his hand, ending the contest of refusal and persuasion they had played out so often before.

When he slept, Amanda lay beside him for a time, matching the rhythm of her breathing to his own, but her eyes were open. At last she lifted the covers and arose, making no sudden motion. The fire in the stove had burned low and the room was cool. She wrapped herself in her gown and sat at the dressing table, where the lamp still glowed. She reached for the jars that contained her clown makeup. First she applied the white, covering every inch of skin, even the insides of her ears. Her movements were careful and controlled, as if she were preparing for a performance of special importance. Next she drew black lines that radiated from her eyes like the rays of the sun. Close to the corners of her eyes the work was made more difficult by the salty drops that ran down her cheeks, but she dabbed them away with a kerchief of Egyptian cotton and applied the last pointed lines to her satisfaction. She inspected her work and smiled. Slowly the smile faded and her countenance fell into the very picture of grief. Then a hand came up, passing before the sorrowful visage, and in its wake the smile shone brightly once more.

She arose and began to dress.

CHAPTER TWO

For seven days and nights the sticks had remained crossed before the entrance to Sun Horse's lodge, proclaiming that the one within would be left undisturbed. Sings His Daughter had gone to live with relatives in the camp. Elk Calf Woman came and went with wood and water but she took her meals with Mist and Hears Twice and there was no cooking fire in Sun Horse's lodge.

The people glimpsed the headman when he went to relieve himself, but that was rarely now: he ate nothing and had no need to move his bowels. He made *inipi* daily, accompanied always by Sees Beyond. The people paused as Sun Horse passed by. Sometimes he smiled but more often he scarcely seemed to see them.

"He has decided to die," some said, but others disagreed.

"He seeks power for the people," said one.

"He is praying for the *pte* to come help the two-leggeds," said another.

"When the grass is up I will go to the soldier town," said Elk Leggings, pondering what event from the winter

47

moons he would choose to paint on the winter-count robe. How to show that the band had lost its power and fallen away from the Lakota spirit? Unless Sun Horse offered guidance soon, the band would scatter in the spring. Elk Leggings had heard the talk around the lodge fires at night, the men speaking their thoughts softly, none trying to dissuade those who would go to the northern bands, or the others who would turn their ponies toward the place where the sun rose and go to the Dakota reservation. Perhaps this is what he would paint—the tipis of the Sun Band scattering, the camp circle broken and its sacred power lost.

In Sun Horse's lodge, Sees Beyond remained a while after the *inipi* this day. Outside, the sun was shining and the people moved about, smelling spring in the air. Sees Beyond felt Sun Horse slipping away to a place he could not follow. He tried not to show his concern; the old man was wise and knew the dangers of the spirit world. It was for each man to seek power as he knew how. *Wakán Tanka* touched each one in a different way and each must follow his own path.

But he must speak. "Do not leave this world, *Tunká-shila*," he said, and wondered if the old man even heard his words. "Your power is here. Use it for the people."

Sees Beyond was afraid. As Sun Horse became more remote, he felt his own power waning. We are tied together, he thought. Our hands touch. He stands in the world of men, one hand reaching into the spirit world; I stand there, but I see also the world of men, and my hand touches his, keeping me in this life. If he dies, I will die as well.

"My power?" Sun Horse's voice croaked. He took the drinking bladder from the place where it hung behind him and let a little water trickle into his mouth. He swallowed and seemed to grow stronger. "My power is no more than a promise, and I have failed."

Sees Beyond's hand found the stick he used to guide himself when he walked alone, and he rose. "You have led the people for twenty snows and more," he said. "You can guide them still." He tried to sound confident and reassuring.

"Perhaps," was all that Sun Horse said. Sees Beyond found his way around the fire to the entrance, but as he bent to step through the opening, Sun Horse spoke again.

"I would speak to Hears Twice. Find him for me and send him here."

When Sees Beyond was gone, Sun Horse sat in silence for a time. Suddenly he raised his eyes toward the peak of the lodge and cried out, "Oh, Grandfathers! If I may still use my power for the people, give me a sign!"

He heard a wind coming, far off in the tops of the trees beyond the camp circle. He liked to go among the trees and listen to the different voices of the wind. The sound it made in the tops of the trees was his favorite song. He could hear it moving there although it did not touch him on the ground below.

The wind drew nearer and flapped the lodgeskins as it passed. It came from the north, *Waziya*'s breath. The weather was changing. All life was changing. Did this wind bring the power to cleanse and heal, or did it come to fight against the life-giving force? It was true that the cold and snow seemed to hold life in abeyance for a time, but even in winter there was life everywhere. There were few creatures about, but those were the ones in which the life-force was strongest, the hardy ones that neither burrowed deep in the earth nor went south to stay warm. There were ravens and woodpeckers and chickadees and eagles, squirrels in the trees and deer and elk and *pte* in the wooded draws, beavers that came out when warm winds let the ice melt, ermine and foxes and wolves, and the snow-shoe hare, who grew his own white coat to blend with the snow. The day before, Sun Horse had walked on the mountainside, and he had followed the tracks of a hare, finding where it had stopped to nibble at the seeds from a pine cone and the place where it had rested beneath a snow-laden bough. All this he saw from the tracks. And then the tracks had stopped. In the middle of an open place the tracks simply disappeared. Sun Horse had been puzzled for a moment, until he saw the other signs, the sweeping marks of the wings on the snow as they flapped to rise into the air again with their burden of struggling hare clutched in the claws that even then were crushing the life away. One life had ended that another might continue. Always there was life and death, but winter was truly when life began. Each creature to be born in the spring was in its mother now, biding its time, as if it knew that all too soon it would be flung into chaos to care for itself.

Sun Horse knew that he too should bide his time, but he was impatient. He sensed that this spring would bring chaos to the Sun Band as well, disrupting the pattern of years, and whether or not it would survive the disruption was up to him. But he was no closer to knowing what to do than when he began his fast. For seven days he had cleansed himself in the *ini ti* and for seven days he had eaten nothing, to cleanse his flesh as well as his spirit. Yet he seemed to draw farther away from understanding what he had done wrong, why he had failed to realize the power that *wamblí* had promised when the young Snowblind Moon still had horns.

Over and over again he came back to the *washíchun*, and each time confusion was the result of his ponderings. His power was to understand the whites, but he could find no way around the central puzzle: *washíchun*, a people not at peace with themselves. How then to make peace with them? How to accommodate their power-without-limit to the power of the Lakota so both peoples might live within the same circle of life? How to assure that the Lakota might still walk the good red road that led to an understanding of the spirit? Sometimes it seemed to Sun Horse that the whites were *wakán*, a mystery, and yet they were not like the other mysteries he had studied all his life. They moved beyond the patterns he knew. It was as if they stood apart from the circle of life. There was a proper place for everything in the wholeness that enveloped both the physical and spirit worlds of the Lakota, but where was the place for the whites?

He did not lack for questions, only answers.

There was a soft cough outside the lodge and Sun Horse bid Hears Twice enter. He invited him to sit and together they smoked a solemn pipe, each offering it to the directions, before Sun Horse told the old seer why he had asked him to come.

"I do not know which way to lead my people," he said when the pipe was done. "Perhaps if you listen and hear the sounds of things to come, that will help me decide."

Hears Twice nodded, agreeing to the headman's request, and he left without having spoken a word.

Sun Horse felt powerless. His strength as a leader had been his power to decide, and it had flowed from the power of his vision—the power of the sun, the power to grow—giving him an ability that had rarely faltered, the power to guide his people toward a path of growth both as a band and as part of the Lakota nation. Yet now he felt no direction beckoning him. The power to grow was the power to change, even to make fundamental changes in the way a people lived; in the time of the Ancient Ones the

Lakota had lived among forests and lakes in the Land of
the Pines, but then some had moved out onto the plains;
they hunted the buffalo and made houses of skin, and in
time they tamed the horse. They were called *Títonwan*—
the ones who camp on the plains—and they were now the
last remaining strength of the Lakota nation. All the other
bands had been subdued by the whites.

From the first, Sun Horse had seen that the coming of
the whiteman would bring great changes and he had dedi-
cated his life to preparing his people for those changes.
Now a turning point had been reached and change was
demanded, but which way to turn, and how to change
without losing touch with the center? Everything depended
on making peace with the whites, a peace that would leave
the spiritual strength of the Lakota intact.

But the whites did not make war as the Lakota and their
neighbors did, and so they could not make peace in the
same way. A new way would have to be found.

The Lakota fought to test the bravery of the young men.
War was a young man's task, and his teacher. The greatest
honor was not in killing but in the degree of risk to which
a warrior exposed himself. The trials of the warpath, the
risk of going deep into the enemy's land to raid him and
steal his horses, to stand before dangerous odds, these
taught the young Lakota fortitude as well. Raid the enemy,
steal his horses and women, learn bravery and fortitude;
treat the women well and give the horses to those in need,
and learn the honor that comes with generosity. Bravery,
fortitude and generosity; these were the qualities a young
man learned, and above all he learned to use them for the
people. He found honor not by thinking of himself but by
showing great courage for the people.

But in time even the bravest warrior might give up war
and gain still more honor, for to experience war was to

learn the value of peace, and none were honored more than the peacemakers. A man laid down the shield and lance if he wished, and from these men came the most trusted councillors, the old-man chiefs who thought constantly of the good of the people.

Among the whites too, such things were known. Sun Horse had heard that the Great Father in *Washing-ton* had been a war leader once, but now no longer wore the warrior's clothes. But there were few other similarities, and many differences, in the way the whites made war. When the plains people fought one another, some died, but never as many as when they fought the *washíchun*, or when the whites fought among themselves. Sun Horse had been astounded to learn that during the whiteman's war between brothers sometimes more men had died in a single day than were numbered among all the bands of Lakota. And the whites preferred to kill at a distance, with little risk. What honor was there in that? None. Worse, they did not go home after a day's fighting and wait until another day, once the honors had been sung and the scalps danced. They fought every day and they fought for the complete conquest of their enemy. Did they not see that war could bring honor to both sides, that neither side need be crushed? It was even said that some whites had traveled far across great waters to fight people of other lands; they fought until they destroyed the camp circles of the enemy, it was said; they kept the enemy in chains for many years, never making them members of the white tribe. Fought on such a scale, how could war teach the young? How could people learn of individual honors and bravery? Surely such a war could teach nothing but shame and sorrow to the loser, and what arrogance might come from winning such a victory? To win over an entire people would make the winner think he was a better man, his people a better people. Only more trouble could come of that.

It seemed that the whites fought to change the life of the enemy forever. . . .

Sun Horse drank again from the water bladder, frightened by what he saw now. It was not only in war that the whites behaved this way. . . . They sought to change beliefs as well.

From his first contact with the black-robe priests Sun Horse had seen the similarities between the beliefs of the whites and those of the Lakota, but the whites saw only the differences. Wherever they went they wanted the plains people to put away their old beliefs forever. They saw the Mystery and called it *God,* but they did not see that the Lakota prayed to the same force, because his prayers took unfamiliar forms. They said the Lakota worshiped heathen gods and prayed to animals, and they dismissed his beliefs as "superstition," revealing in their use of the word their own fear of the unknown. They hid away in wooden buildings to pray, cut off from the touch of sun and wind, and they worshiped a cross made of wood; they said *God* lived in these places, but they did not see God, the Great Mystery, in all things and so could not understand how the buffalo or coyote or softly running rabbit could be worthy of prayer. The black-robes came only to "teach," never to listen; they talked of their *God* and denied the spirit power in a thunderhead or the winter wind.

Sun Horse's head ached and he felt dizzy. Not since the early days of his fast had he felt this debilitated. His power seemed far away, beyond his grasp. Perhaps he had been wrong to wait. Perhaps he should have sent Hardeman to tell Three Stars that the people would accept his spotted-*pte* meat and his blankets, and go with him to the soldier town. Perhaps that would have been best.

Outside the lodge the sun emerged from behind a cloud and the dark interior of the tipi brightened somewhat. Sun Horse heard a child scream in play and a mother's voice scolding. Do not disturb Sun Horse, she said, and Sun Horse shook his head. It was good that the little children should play. Even at the time of the Sun Dance, the most sacred ritual of the Lakota, the little children were encouraged to play and shout all they wished, and when someone made *inipi*, a child could put his head in the door and ask questions, for everyone knew that little children were very pure and were favored by *Wakán Tanka*.

How would the child eat today? How could Sun Horse protect the child tomorrow? These were the questions he should be pondering, not the mysteries of the *washíchun*, which made his head spin.

There was a commotion on the far side of the camp circle and several voices were raised, and for a moment Sun Horse felt a chill of alarm, but there was no alarm in the voices, nor the cries of joy that would have sounded if the pipe carriers were seen returning.

Strangers approached the camp. He knew the sounds of his village as well as he knew the sounds of his own lodge. There was a quickening when strangers approached, like the quickened flow of blood in a man when he felt excitement or danger.

Who could it be? Sun Horse found it difficult to return his thoughts to the world outside his lodge. He felt removed, distant, as if it didn't really matter who the strangers might be.

It seemed that his son and grandson and the other pipe carriers had been gone forever. Where were they now? And where were the soldiers? Several days before, a signal had been seen, far off. *Soldiers have attacked a village.* . . . That and no more, as the wind and clouds returned.

Had Three Stars refused the pipe? The pipe carriers might be captives in the hands of the soldiers. Or they might be dead.

Perhaps there could be no accommodation but surrender.

The entrance flap was opened and Sings His Daughter put her head through the opening. "Lisaputnam and the black whiteman are here. There are some of the Strange-Animal People with them."

Sun Horse nodded but made no move. She withdrew. The councillors could meet the whites and hear what they had to say. Sun Horse could do nothing for them now.

There was movement around the camp as men and women went to see the visitors, and then, before these movements had died away, he heard the voice of Dust, the crier, moving around the camp to announce the news. Dust's voice was high and shrill, a tone he used only for important tidings. "The white *heyoka* girl is lost! She left the settlement in the night! The whites ask our help to find her!"

Amanda watched the buildings impatiently as the first rays of sun touched the valley. She saw the first people moving about, walking among the wagons, flowing like chips of wood in a stream toward the Big House for breakfast. She smiled when the tiny figures began running out of the house, to the barn and the wagons, darting here and there. She had been missed.

She wore the buffalo coat Lisa had given her, but beneath the coat she had on only her clown costume, and she had taken a chill in the predawn cold. She moved higher on the ridge to a sheltered spot among a bunch of rocks from which she could catch the warmth of the sun and still watch the settlement. She saw the figures converge on the barn and then larger figures emerging, some going off in various directions up and down the valley and a group riding together up the trail to the Indian village.

"Here I am!" she shouted, but the ants scurrying hither and yon below her couldn't hear.

Her flight had been impulsive, unthinking. It was her own inability to refuse Hachaliah from which she had run. She realized now that she had put herself in real danger by wandering off alone into the hills to the west of the park. Dawn had been hours away when she left the settlement, but the waning crescent moon had helped her to find her way. Higher and higher she had climbed, driven at first by a kind of strange elation. She was making the break at last. She had been badly frightened by an owl that had leaped into the air from a branch above her head, showering her with snow as she shrieked in terror. *Hooo! Hooo-hooo-hooo-hoo,* he had called back to her, each *hoo* softer than the one before. He had flapped away on silent wings and she had seen the tufted horns against the moon.

She had been relieved when the eastern sky began to brighten, and the appearance of the sun had banished the last of her nighttime fears.

She knew that if she started downhill now one of the searchers would find her soon, but it occurred to her that there was some advantage to be gained by putting off her discovery a while longer.

Let them worry about me, she thought. Let them all worry, Hachaliah most of all. He'll think twice before he forces himself on me again.

But Johnny would worry too and she did not want to hurt him. Maybe he would be the one to find her! She could hide from the others! If Johnny came along she would let herself be seen, and seducing him would be easy in the aftermath of a dramatic rescue.

Satisfied that the search was begun in earnest, she left

her watching place and climbed higher still, until she stood atop the ridge that separated Putnam's Park from the rising peaks to the west. Of course if she did not see Johnny she must still allow herself to be found before nightfall. She knew where the trail was that led to the Indian village. She would move in that direction and as the day wore on she would find the trail and follow it toward Putnam's Park until the searchers found her. But there was no hurry just yet. She walked along the ridge until she found a place where the sun and wind had cleared a rocky ledge of snow and there she stopped to rest as the sun rose higher. The ledge was sheltered and warm and soon the warmth lulled her to sleep.

When she awoke the sun was at the zenith. She sat up, searching the glistening slopes around her for moving figures.

Whatever could have made her run away? they would wonder. They must be frantic with worry by now.

She gasped aloud as the idea struck her. If ever again Hachaliah threatened to tell Johnny the truth about the two of them, Amanda could silence him with a threat of her own! She would threaten to tell everyone that Hachaliah took advantage of her all those years ago and she kept silent out of fear! She would tell them that at last she had tried to break it off but Hachaliah flew into a rage and took her by force! He raped her cruelly and so she had run away! And they would believe her no matter what Hachaliah said! Why else would she have run away into the wild mountains unless something truly terrible had happened to her? It was a desperate resort; if Hachaliah called her bluff and she had to use the story, Johnny would be shocked. But he would pity her, as the rest of them would, all her friends in the circus and the settlement, for no one but she and Hachaliah knew the truth. When Hachaliah had been dealt with, Johnny's desire to heal and protect her would overcome his shock and she would play the injured innocent to perfection.

Made light-headed by the power of her idea, she clambered down from the ledge and set off over the snow. The crust was soft now and the going was difficult as she broke through every few steps. She found a drifted crest of hard-packed snow at the edge of a steep slope and she walked along the peak, imagining it was a tightrope stretched from one rocky promontory to the next. In the natural amphitheater below her, an imaginary audience watched. She played an invisible violin, slowing her steps to the time of the silent waltz. It was Johnny's Waltz; she would play it for him when they were together again.

She reached the end of the snowy ridge. Her eyes stung and they were beginning to water. She closed them as she bowed elaborately to her admirers. She lost her balance and fell forward.

She cried out as she hit the snow, but fortunately the slope was not long. She tumbled and rolled and came to a stop at the bottom. Above her the slope began to move, breaking into sections that slid at different speeds before slowing and stopping. Amanda scrambled out of the way of the small avalanche. She saw now that streaks and folds in the snow showed where other slides had occurred, all running down into the little amphitheater. She remembered the frightening force of the avalanche that had almost destroyed the circus on the river trail, and as she climbed back up the slope she followed a scattering of rocks that provided a natural ladder out of the bowl. She would have to be more careful of slopes from now on.

She set off for a stand of dark green pines, squinting hard against the glare, which seemed to have grown stronger. Her eyes were watering steadily now and she blinked to clear them. The tears brimmed over and ran down her cheeks. She dabbed at them with her hand, and her glove came away smeared with white paint and a touch of gray where she had smudged one of the thin black star-points around her eyes. She wished she had brought her silver compact with its powder and small mirror. She wanted her makeup to be perfect. No harm could come to her as Joey. Joey always emerged unhurt in the end. Joey was the one who stood in the center of the ring at the end of the performance and accepted the applause alone, before beckoning the rest of the performers to join her.

But the compact had been given to her by Hachaliah and so she had left it behind.

She staggered and nearly lost her balance. She stopped for a moment to shield her eyes with a hand. Not even closing them offered any relief. The light was softer but her eyelids smarted as if her eyes were full of sand. She pulled her clown hat low on her forehead and stumbled on. When she gained the trees she stopped in the cool shade. She swept the snow off a fallen trunk and sat for a while, until the chill underfoot began to penetrate her fur-lined boots and she was forced to set off again to warm herself.

She moved north and a little east, keeping track of Putnam's Park and the position of the sun behind her, making for the trail connecting the park with the Indian village. It helped a little to be moving away from the sun.

But by mid-afternoon she could barely see. Her eyes were swollen and painful and they watered constantly, blurring her vision. When she tried to follow her own tracks to retrace her steps, the sunlight on the snow blinded her completely, and she found herself wandering aimlessly, crossing her own trail. She broke through the crust with almost every step now and the struggle was exhausting her.

She stopped to think, fighting off panic. She knew there must be fifty riders out looking for her. If she just went in the right direction she would find help, but her vision was failing. She could still make out the general form of objects close at hand and the shape of the land around her, but no detail. The sun was an awesome glare that filled half the sky; it was lower now, moving toward the west. Putting it behind her she started off downhill, but cliffs fell away before her and she was forced farther to the north. Beyond the cliffs were steep slopes covered with snow and she skirted these too, fearing an avalanche. Finally she found a wooded hillside that seemed to offer a safe descent. She moved through the trees with her hands in front of her to ward off the branches, falling often and sometimes bumping into the tree trunks when she fell, emerging at last in a small meadow.

By peering through her fingers from the shadows at the edge of the trees she saw that the meadow was the bottom of a small valley. Around her, the land rose on all sides. Overhead, clouds covered the sky and she could no longer locate the sun.

She was lost, and night was coming on. A sob escaped her and then another, and she gave in to them, sinking to her knees in the snow. Her head ached and the pain seemed to be spreading to the rest of her body. Her stomach churned and she tasted the bile rising to her throat. Quite without warning she doubled over and vomited violently.

When the spasm passed she wiped her chin and spat to expel the bitter taste from her mouth, and then she became aware of a sound close at hand. It was the sound of a large animal breathing, a whuffling, snorting sound that caused her to go rigid with fear. The hunters had spoken of bears and wolves in the mountains. Why had she forgotten this until now? What had she been thinking of to go off by herself? She managed to turn her head and she let out a stifled cry of terror as she made out a dark shape looming close at hand. She scrambled away on all fours, seeking the shelter of the tree trunks, and when she turned again she saw that the huge shape was moving past her, unconcerned. Curving horns crowned a massive head that hung from great humped shoulders. She knew the beast now. She had seen a buffalo once before, in another circus. Beyond the first there were others. A dozen, two dozen or more of the blurred shapes with the high humps and small hindquarters, all moving in the same direction across the snowy meadow.

CHAPTER THREE

A shot startled Whitcomb out of a sound sleep. His legs jerked spastically as he awoke; his horse shied at the sudden movement and Whitcomb fell. He hit the muddy ground as other shots rang out.

"Get him, for Christ's sake!"

The men were shooting at a deer, but the animal leaped

a small gully and vanished into a patch of pine trees a hundred yards away as a final fusillade failed to bring him down.

Whitcomb got to his feet and moved his shoulder painfully, but he judged that no permanent damage had been done by the fall. He brushed some wet snow and mud from his buffalo coat.

The day was fair. A gentle breeze from the south was warm on his face. The sun shone brightly and small clouds dotted the sky.

First Sergeant Dupré returned Whitcomb's horse, handing him the reins. "It was Rogers who saw the deer first, sair. He fired without permission."

"It doesn't matter, Sergeant. If he had killed it he'd be a hero. We can't punish him for missing." They had seen no Indians for three days and the men were becoming careless, but no more careless than he for allowing himself to sleep in the saddle. The men were looking around anxiously now, but nothing moved anywhere in sight. They were alone, eighteen men and thirteen horses. Lieutenant Corwin lay on a travois, unconscious. Close to the west, foothills and mountains rose above them. To the east, the plains lay somnolent and deserted.

It was the fifth day since the battle, the third since they had seen another living soul. Two hours ago they had left Clear Fork, the upper portion of Lodgepole Creek, and now they were making their way south along the Big Horn foothills, west of the old wagon road, keeping to cover as best they could. The jerky McCaslin had gathered in the village was almost gone and the deer was the first game they had seen; fresh meat would have cheered the men more than anything except the sight of Crook's column, but Crook was far away, somewhere on the Powder.

"Mr. Reb! Where the hell are you?" Whitcomb turned to

see that Corwin had raised himself up on one elbow. He moved to the troop commander's travois, followed by Dupré. "Why have we stopped?" Corwin asked. His face was ashen and the skin was stretched tightly over his cheekbones. There were dark hollows beneath his eyes.

"Private Rogers saw a deer, sir, but we didn't bring him down."

Corwin shook his head as if he had trouble understanding the words.

"There's a grove of trees ahead, sir. There might be some water there. It looks like a good place to rest for a while."

Corwin frowned. "Follow my orders, Mr. Reb."

"Excuse me, sir, but which orders are those?"

"We'll stop as usual when we find a suitable place." Corwin slumped back on the travois. He heaved a long sigh and closed his eyes.

Whitcomb turned to Dupré. "You heard him, Sergeant. That place is good enough. We'll tether the horses in the grove and let the men get some rest."

With Whitcomb and Dupré in the lead the little band got under way again. Although they dared build fires at night now, the men slept better in a patch of sunshine with pickets keeping watch. Hostiles could spring from anywhere and at night the men slept fitfully if at all.

They had had no rest on the night following the battle and the next few days had been little better.

It was only through Corwin's foresight that the abandoned remnant of E Troop had escaped annihilation at the hands of the Indians as the battle ended. Whitcomb had brought his flanking party back to the troop's defensive line in the brush to find that Corwin had sent Sergeant Dupré for the horses and was moving his remaining men to the thickest stand of trees near the river. There was no sign of Polachek and his platoon; Corwin guessed they were pinned down by the renewed barrage of fire from the Indians on the bluffs.

Dupré and his two men had come along the ice moments later, but they brought only thirteen mounts. They had reached the horses to find the animals tethered, E Troop's horse handlers gone, and fighting taking place on the south side of the village as a group of Indians tried to intercept Captain Mills's horses, which were being brought down from the mountain. Fire was coming from the full length of the bluff face above the battlefield, and Indians were once more infiltrating the village, moving out from the base of the hillside. The soldiers still in the village were giving ground and it seemed to Dupré that the situation was precarious. He and his men grabbed fifteen horses, intending to return at once with more men to get the rest, but two of those they took had broken away and bolted when a burning tipi exploded close to the riverbank.

Corwin had ordered Dupré to remain on the line then, sending Sergeant Duggan and Corporal Stiegler with four men to get the rest of the horses. He sent Sergeant Rossi to contact Polachek if he could, but when Rossi had been gone only a few minutes, a group of mounted troopers galloped through the village to where Polachek and Lieutenant Paul had taken position, apparently to save them from being cut off. At the same moment, three Indian boys had brought a dozen or more horses to the warriors in the redoubt. One of the boys was shot, and this had provoked an abortive charge, which was driven back. Corwin could not see the action well from where he lay in the brush, but he could see the mounted troopers withdrawing hastily once the Indians were repulsed, and he saw that they had Polachek, Paul and Rossi with them, together with all the men from that end of the line, the riders screening the men on foot from the continuing fire that came from the bluffs. "It looks like retreat is the better part of valor, boys," Corwin had said, and he prepared the men to mount. But the first bugle call had come then, ordering a withdrawal, and when the Indians saw the troopers in retreat they had burst from cover and poured into the village, cutting off E Troop's escape in that direction and making it impossible for Duggan and Stiegler to return with more horses. With the Indians' attention on Reynolds' column, which was forming up and moving off to the south, Corwin had led his men across the river and they had taken cover in the thick brush there, where Whitcomb had been with his flankers just a short time before.

By a miracle they were not discovered. They had huddled together in their hiding place, weapons at the ready, hands on the horses' nostrils to keep them quiet, and Sergeant Dupré had whispered a prayer in French. The Indians had combed the village to see what could be salvaged and evidently found very little, judging by how soon they had begun to trudge off downstream along the trail on the western bank, the one the women and children had taken earlier. By dusk they were all gone except for a few that plainly intended to remain the night, and the handful of soldiers had dared to move a little farther downstream.

But they couldn't go far. There was no telling how near the main body of hostiles might have camped and they couldn't risk stumbling on the angry warriors in the night. They had found a new hiding place in a larger copse of trees and there they remained, kept warm only by the horses and the foresight of Sergeant Dupré, who had brought several extra greatcoats when he fetched the horses. Each man in the little band had a coat, and the coats had kept them alive through the fireless night.

That night had been a torment. At the first screams from the village the men had wanted to come out of hiding to rescue the poor wretch that had fallen into the hands of the savages, but Corwin had held them back, knowing that the platoon's only chance of survival lay in escaping detection. Some of the men had been near rebellion, but then a single shot had stopped the screams and in the morning the Indians were gone.

The reduced command consisted of Lieutenant Corwin, Whitcomb, Sergeant Dupré, Corporals McCaslin and Atherton, and thirteen private soldiers. Four of the men had serious frostbite; two were unable to walk. Apart from Corwin, none was wounded.

They had crept past the still-smoking village and started off upstream, hoping against hope that they would be able to overtake Reynolds and the rest of the attack force at the juncture of the Powder and Lodgepole Creek, where they were to await Crook, but they had been forced to take cover several times during that first day to avoid small bands of Indians moving up and down the river valley, and by nightfall they had made only eleven or twelve miles. The next morning they had been elated to discover the tracks of Crook's four companies entering the valley from the west. The clouds had descended and it had begun to snow in earnest, and the little band had pressed on under cover of the weather, with McCaslin and Private Gray a hundred yards to the front to watch for Indians. The valley had broadened steadily and the growth of cottonwoods along the stream grew denser, and the soldiers had kept to the trees.

They had halted when Gray appeared suddenly before them, motioning them frantically to take cover. McCaslin had returned a short while later with the disheartening news—they had reached the mouth of Lodgepole Creek but Crook and the reunited command had already gone off up the Powder and the rendezvous site was swarming with hostiles. From the number of mounted Indians it was apparent that the refugees from the burned village had found help somewhere near at hand. Most of the Indians were moving upriver after the soldiers while another group was heading downstream with a herd of horses that included a few cavalry mounts, apparently stolen from the command during the night.

Corwin and his men had kept hidden until the snow thinned and they saw that the wide valley was deserted, and it was then that Corwin had announced his decision: they would make no further attempts to rejoin Crook. The Indians posed too great a risk, he said. There was little chance that such a small force could get safely through the savages. They would do best to stay away from both Crook and the hostiles and make their way alone. They would go up Lodgepole and turn south along the Big Horn foothills. When they neared Fort Reno they would send a patrol to see if the supply train or any part of Crook's force was still there. If not, they would have to continue to Fetterman on their own.

And so they had pushed on with Corwin in the lead, reeling in his saddle. Since leaving the Powder they had seen no one, red or white. On reaching the Bozeman road they found no tracks more recent than their own, made on the march up country, and Corwin, confined to a travois by then, had decided that they would stay away from the old wagon road, keeping closer to the foothills where the terrain offered better cover.

Whitcomb watched the men as the tiny column reached the grove of pines and halted once more. Without being told what to do some of the troopers gathered the horses and took them into the grove to be tethered while others began to gather firewood, but their movements were slow and listless. Two of the men had bandaged hands that were all but useless. One trooper's eyes were completely covered against the glare of the sun and everyone was affected to some degree with snowblindness. Whitcomb still wore his green goggles but few of the others had them.

We're the walking wounded, he thought. Scarcely better than refugees.

"Excuse me, sir, 'e's asking for you." It was Corporal Atherton. He had taken on himself the chore of caring for Lieutenant Corwin. For two days after receiving his wound, Corwin had complained of no pain, although his face was gray and drawn and the effort it took for him to remain on his horse could be seen by all. On the third day he had been unable to keep in his saddle. After he had fallen twice they had built the travois and covered him with a buffalo robe.

"What time do you make it, Corporal?" Whitcomb's gold watch had been smashed in the battle. He didn't know when. Probably when he threw himself on the ground to defend the line against the charge from the Indians' breastwork.

Atherton glanced at the sun.

"Oh, about midday, I should think, sir. It's a nice enough day, isn't it?"

Whitcomb followed Atherton to Corwin's litter. Corwin was singing softly to himself.

> *"Heave away you ruling kings,*
> *Heave away, haul away,*
> *Heave away my bully boys,*
> *We're bound for South Australia.*
>
> *Oh, a sailor's life is a hell of a life,*
> *Heave away, haul away,*
> *Without any money, without any wife—"*

" 'ere's Mr. Rcb, sir. Excuse me, Leftenant, but that's 'ow 'e asked for you.''

"It's all right."

"Ahoy, Mr. Reb! Stand fast, bo'sun! We'll run up the colors when she comes about!" Corwin grinned grotesquely. The troopers were keeping an eye on their commander, watching but not watching. It was plain that his raving made them uneasy.

" 'e's like that off and on, sir," Atherton informed Whitcomb in a low voice. " 'e'll be like that for a time and then 'e's quite 'imself again."

So far, Corwin had been fit to make each important decision when it came along, but his condition was worsening steadily. What would happen when a decision was demanded and Corwin could not make it? Whitcomb wondered.

"Ask Sergeant Dupré to come over here, will you?"

Whitcomb knelt to untie the bandanna that held Corwin's trouser in place over the wound. He pulled the trouser aside and drew back at the stench.

"You didn't know I was a sailor, did you, Ham me boy?" Corwin was looking at him with steady eyes.

"How are you feeling, sir?"

"Like shit, Mr. Reb. Like the bottom of the post latrine. Damn you, be careful!"

Whitcomb was untying the bandage. "Sorry."

"What sort of progress have we made?"

"Quite good today, sir. I think we've come about ten miles this morning."

"That's good. That's good. Jesus, that hurts! Yes, by God, I was a sailor once. Not the fancy kind, just a working seaman. Christ, I was seasick the whole voyage. No more of that, I said. But I'll tell you something, Ham.

The seafaring life has got the songs. The cavalry should have songs half as good as those. Listen to this:

> *"Farewell and adieu to you Spanish ladies,*
> *Farewell and adieu to you ladies of Spain,*
> *For we've received orders to sail for old England,*
> *And we hope in a short time to see you again."*

He sang in a pleasing baritone but with none of the gusto of a sailor leaning to his work on a pitching deck. Instead he raised his head and sang the air softly, like a lullaby or a courting song.

"Well, I didn't have the stomach for it, anyway. The war was just getting started and I joined the Volunteers. Made lieutenant in three months. Hard up for officer material, I'll tell you. General Crook started out as a captain, regular army. By the fall of '62 he was brevetted lieutenant colonel and appointed brigadier general of Volunteers. All he had to do was wait for his permanent rank to catch up with him. But he deserves it, no question about that. He's a hardworking son of a bitch. I'm still waiting. Look here." He tapped Whitcomb on the shoulder. "I may lose track from time to time, but I'm not as far out of it as I seem. The singing and all that—it's just to help me forget the pain."

"You need your rest when you can get it, sir. That's the best thing for you." Whitcomb removed the last wrappings of bandage and tried to hide his reaction at the sight of the wound.

Dupré joined them then and he inspected the wound as Corwin began to sing again.

> *"Me boots and clothes are all in pawn,*
> *Go down, ye blood red roses, go down!*

The whalefish swims around Cape Horn,
Go down, ye blood red roses, go down!
Oh, ye pinks and poseys—Good Christ!''

Dupré had gingerly touched the livid flesh beyond the edges of the wound. The skin was dark and mottled. Corwin pushed his hand away and lay back on his litter, breathing hard.

Dupré turned to Whitcomb. "A word, sair, if you will."

They withdrew a short way. Around them the men lay scattered within the shelter of the trees, each in a patch of the warm sunlight. Small fires were burning and a few of the men were making a weak broth by boiling strips of jerky in cups of water. The horses were tethered in good grass, well back in the trees. From a distance any inquiring eyes would see the trees but not those sheltered there. Whitcomb was pleased to see that the faint white smoke from the fires dispersed quickly and was not visible above the treetops. They had all learned a good deal about making smokeless fires in the past few days. Dry willow wood was best and the dead branches of cedar and pine were safe too.

"We did not loosen the tourniquet in time, sair."

"Hmm?" He returned his attention to Dupré.

"We did not loosen the tourniquet in time."

During the second frigid night after the battle, Corwin's leg had swollen, which had the effect of tightening the tourniquet and shutting off the slight flow of blood Dupré had permitted to continue. When the limb was next inspected, the foot had shown signs of frostbite, but a more serious affliction had taken hold in the wound.

"Is it gangrene?" Whitcomb felt obliged to ask the

question, but even to his inexperienced eyes the putrid state of the wound was apparent.

"I am afraid so. Without medicines, we can do nothing."

Whitcomb noticed for the first time that the ends of Dupré's mustache were no longer waxed and curled. Instead they drooped on either side of his mouth, giving him an almost Oriental appearance. He realized that Dupré was waiting for him to speak, and he pulled himself together. I mustn't let my attention wander, he thought.

"And if we leave it alone, the gangrene will continue to spread."

"Yes, sair."

Whitcomb felt helpless. What would happen if Corwin lapsed into unconsciousness? Who would make the decisions then? "I have heard that sunshine sometimes has a good effect on morbid conditions. We'll leave the wound uncovered today while we rest. It may do no good, but it can't make things worse, can it?"

"No, sair, it cannot make it worse. I have posted pickets, sair. Gwynn and Gray to begin with. I will have them relieved in two hours if you wish to stay longer."

"You should make your report to Major Corwin, Sergeant. He's in command, not me."

"Forgive me, sair, but you should be."

Whitcomb was taken aback. "You're not serious."

"Your superior officer is wounded, sair. Most of the time he is not himself. On campaign an officer must use his judgment in a case like this one."

"You should think twice before you counsel mutiny, Sergeant."

Dupré gave a Gallic shrug that could have meant anything. "You must prepare yourself for the eventuality, sair. What will you do when he gives orders that make no sense?"

"I'll cross that bridge when I come to it. Right now let's see if we can't make him eat something."

With Atherton's help they made Corwin drink some of the jerky broth and eat a few pieces of the dried meat. Afterward, Whitcomb sat with his back to a tree trunk and watched over the little encampment as the men slept.

We're not much of a fighting force, he thought. Not even a full platoon. One first lieutenant, badly wounded; one very junior second lieutenant with less than a month of field duty; a handful of soldiers in varying stages of disrepair—we're the lost platoon of Company E. Thank God for Dupré and Atherton and McCaslin. They're the ones who should be in command if Corwin's unable, not me.

A hand shook his shoulder and he realized that he had fallen asleep. He was surprised to see that the sun had moved around to the west. Sergeant Dupré stood over him.

"I imagined that you might wish to be getting along, sair."

"How is Major Corwin?"

"Resting comfortably."

A few hours of exposure to sunshine and fresh air had dried Corwin's wound but the flesh surrounding the mottled area was still livid and tender. As Atherton replaced the bandage, Corwin awoke and groaned.

"We'll be getting along now, sir. With your permission," Whitcomb said.

"Weigh anchor, Mr. Reb." Corwin's voice was weak and his eyes seemed dead.

The little group moved slowly, despite the efforts of Whitcomb and the non-commissioned officers to keep up a better pace. After a time, Whitcomb relaxed his efforts and permitted himself to doze in the saddle, jerking awake every few minutes. Each time he raised his head it seemed they hadn't moved since the last time he looked, but the horses and men plodded on. They moved, but nothing changed; the same looming mountains stood on their right and the same desolate vastness to the left. Even the sunlight couldn't warm the empty landscape.

Where would Crook be by now? he wondered. Once he had resupplied himself from the wagons at Fort Reno he could turn on his pursuers, if they followed him that far. The cavalry would become the hounds once again and the Indians would revert to their natural role as foxes. Crook might bring the wagons up-country this time, along the Powder. Sooner or later he was bound to join forces with Terry and Gibbon and together they would round up the hostiles, but Ham Whitcomb would miss it. His career would get no leg up from this campaign.

There was no help for it. Just now the remnants of E Troop were confronting the soldier's eternal task—survival—in a new and more fundamental form.

He had no more illusions left to be shattered. At West Point he had imagined himself going into battle as part of an army bent on a common goal, with objectives to be taken and lines to be held. Never in his most fearful dreams had he imagined anything like this, being cut off and alone in a land so huge it seemed to be without limit.

We keep moving but we never arrive at our destination. There is no front and no rear; the enemy is everywhere and nowhere. This is what Purgatory must be like for soldiers. We're the Lost Platoon of the Foreign Legion, condemned to wander through Purgatory, forever alert, forever afraid. Is this what all the Indian wars are like?

He found the notion so discouraging that he drew his horse aside and dismounted. He would walk for a while and think of other things. As the rear of the column passed him he fell in beside Corporal McCaslin, who marched there as file closer. The wiry corporal walked a good deal of the time, often giving up his turn on horseback to one of the other men. He seemed to feel the lack of adequate food less than the rest of them.

"How's the snowblindness today, Corporal?"

McCaslin's eyes were red-rimmed and bloodshot.

"Oh, not so bad, sorr. There's some of the boys have it much worse."

Whitcomb removed his green Arizona goggles. "Someone else can use these for a while. Give them to whoever's in the worst shape."

"Thank you, sorr." McCaslin accepted the offering. "Corporal Atherton has a pair as well, and the major won't be needin' his, not while he's restin'. We'll trade them off and make do." He lowered his voice. "Beggin' yer pahrdon, sorr. Did Sahrgint Dupree have a word wid yez about takin' command?"

"Not you too. I thought you told me the men would follow Major Corwin to hell and back."

"That they would, sorr, when himself is himself. But he's not been himself for some days now, and he'll not be gettin' better until we get him to a doctor."

They walked for a time in silence. McCaslin sensed Whitcomb's troubled thoughts and when he spoke again his voice was cheerful.

"If we had some grease, sorr, we could mix it wid a bit of charcoal from a fire and smudge it on our cheeks. Cuts the glare, y' see. We'd look like a lot of haythen Indians, but it'd be a blessin' for the eyes."

Whitcomb considered this. They had no grease and no prospects of getting any unless they brought down some game. McCaslin was watching him expectantly but he could think of nothing else to suggest. He found it difficult to concentrate on anything but his hunger and fatigue.

"I was thinkin' of the horses, sorr," McCaslin said at last. "There's one or two won't go much farther. We could have fresh meat for the boys and a bit o' grease too."

Whitcomb shook his head. "Is that what we've come to? Eating horsemeat? My God, Mac, I never thought it would be like this."

"We're not so bad off, sorr. Except for poor Peter Dowdy, rest his soul. And the major, of course. But we've come through it wid no one else wounded. Just a bit of frostbite here and there. We'll do all right."

McCaslin's good spirits cheered Whitcomb and he felt a little better. He picked up his pace and moved up the column, looking at the horses with new interest. Gwynn's mount walked with an unsteady gait and its eyes were listless. It wouldn't make it to Fetterman, perhaps not even to Reno. Whitcomb was surprised to find the juices running in his mouth at the thought of fresh meat, no matter what the source. Maybe McCaslin's suggestion wasn't such a bad one. He would speak to Corwin about it when they stopped for the night.

Shadows were reaching out from the mountains now, and when they covered the travelers, Whitcomb allowed himself to relax a little. Even if hostile eyes were watching from somewhere out on the plains they would never see the small group of horses and men moving against the dark mass of the Big Horns. Cloud Peak, toward which they had steered until today, lay on the right now. Tomorrow or the next day they would cross Crazy Woman's Fork and from there it was only another day or two to Reno. If they kept up the pace.

He resolved that one way or another he would keep them going. If they had to eat horseflesh, so be it, but they would march every day. At the end of the trail there was rest and proper food, and care for the injured. He prayed Crook had left the wagons at Reno.

The darkness gathered slowly and he realized that the equinox was at hand. What was the date? The twenty-first? No, the twenty-second. The battle had been on the seventeenth; St. Patrick's Day, as John Bourke had reminded him. It was spring, but there was scant evidence of the changing season hereabouts, save for the longer days.

As the dusk thickened he looked about for a place to spend the night. The platoon crested a rounded toe of the foothills and he spied a depression ahead. There was a trickle of water and some brush off to the left where the depression became a gully. He mounted his horse and overtook Sergeant Dupré in the lead. "We better make camp here while there's still some light to find wood," he said.

They moved into the gully where the brush was thickest. A small fire here wouldn't be seen.

Atherton reported that Corwin had mumbled and dozed through the evening march. He had not known Atherton when the corporal gave him water. Together, Whitcomb and Atherton inspected the wound and found that the mottled area had spread. Neither commented on the obvious, but Whitcomb showed the leg to Dupré when he returned with the wood detail, and the Frenchman nodded.

"It must come off, sair. If the bad blood goes above the knee, he will lose the whole leg."

Field amputation was not a specialty taught at West Point but Whitcomb had heard of it often enough. It was the preferred treatment for any serious wound in a limb. A serious wound elsewhere on the body usually resulted in death. Further fatalities were caused by amputations, but if the patient survived he received a pension and a discharge. Some preferred death.

Corwin opened his eyes and looked at them. "Where is the wind, mister?" The voice was not his own.

"The wind, sir?"

"We'll take in a reef if it blows up." Corwin's eyes closed and his breathing became deeper.

"You must take command, sair." Dupré spoke softly. Whitcomb looked at him briefly and then looked away. It was easy enough for him to say; the top sergeant proposed and the officer disposed. What would Dupré do if Whitcomb weren't there? Would he take command or take in a reef?

Whitcomb chuckled and Dupré looked at him strangely. "I'm all right, Sergeant. The leg . . . Should it be done soon?"

"The sooner the better, sair."

Whitcomb shook his head. Throughout the afternoon he had shut the possibility of an amputation from his mind as resolutely as he might have rejected the thought of his own death. "Leave me alone with him for a while," he said, and he sat cross-legged on the ground beside the travois.

Corwin looked up and smiled. "Well, Ham, we gave them the slip, eh?"

"Sir?"

"The Indians, boy. We gave them the slip."

"Yes, sir."

"You know, I never thought I would want to be back in Arizona, but I could stand it a bit warmer right now. I can't seem to get warm enough. Did I ever tell you about Arizona, Ham?"

"I'll get you another robe, sir. Then you can tell me." When he returned with the robe Corwin was looking up at the heavens, where the stars were winking on one by one. Whitcomb spread the robe over the supine form and tucked it in at the edges.

"There's heaven and hell in Arizona, Ham. All tucked

away hundreds of miles from nowhere. Heaven was called Jennifer. God she was beautiful! She was my wife. Did you know I was married?'' He looked at Whitcomb and Whitcomb saw that his eyes were brimming with tears.

''No, sir.''

''Of course you didn't. I forget that I don't speak of it anymore. But she was beautiful, Ham. We were stationed at Camp McDowell. Then I was transferred and I let her go alone in the ambulance, her and the baby. Things had been quiet and they had just one squad as escort . . .'' He wiped his eyes with an unsteady hand and coughed to clear his throat. ''They didn't give 'em the slip that day. Apaches, Ham. God I hate them!''

Whitcomb was shocked. ''You lost them, sir? Your wife and baby were killed?''

Corwin waved his hand to brush the memory away. ''It was a long time ago.''

''I'm sorry, sir. I had no idea.'' The words were trivial and inadequate, but he could find no way to express the heartfelt sympathy that Corwin's revelation had aroused in him.

Corwin grinned oddly. ''I drank a good deal, but it doesn't make you forget, not really. You remember that when you've got something to forget.'' He lay back and closed his eyes. ''There was another girl once. Just as beautiful. If I'd married her everything would have been different.'' His eyes opened again. ''It's all a matter of choices, Ham. You pick your direction and you go, otherwise you stand at the crossroads forever.'' The eyes closed and it occurred to Whitcomb that he might as well be looking at a cadaver, for all the life that was left in the face. Corwin began to hum a tune and then he whispered the words.

"Farewell and adieu to you Spanish ladies,
Farewell and adieu to you ladies of Spain,
For we've received orders to sail for old England,
And we hope in a short time to see you again.
We'll rant and we'll roar like true British sailors,
We'll rant and we'll roar, all on the high seas . . ."

His voice trailed off and he slept.

Whitcomb got stiffly to his feet and he saw that the men were gathered in a circle around a fire nearby. Overhead the sky was dark. He hadn't been aware of the fire being built or the passing of the last light in the west. Time seemed to be proceeding in jumps, flitting past him when he wasn't watching.

"There's coffee, sir." Atherton held a steaming cup out to him. Sergeant Dupré had found a sack containing three pounds of coffee during the battle, in one of the lodges he had inspected. He had appropriated the coffee without hesitation and it was this precious reserve, as much as the jerky, that kept the men going.

Whitcomb took the cup. He held it tightly in his gloved hands and stood with his back to the fire. Someone handed him some jerky. He chewed each bite of the dried buffalo meat thoroughly and washed it down with coffee, and when he had consumed his share he felt as contented as if he had eaten a full meal. He dropped down on his hocks and let his head droop forward, enjoying the warmth and crackle of the fire.

"That's the last of the jerky, sir."

"Hmm?" He looked up and blinked. He could fall asleep in an instant now. That was what he needed. A good night's sleep. Maybe Corwin's wound would show some improvement in the morning. Wake up early and perhaps find some game at dawn. What had Dupré said about Corwin's leg? It had to come off? Surely that could wait. There was time to decide about that later on.

"It can wait," he said aloud, and realized that they were all looking at him. Sixteen pairs of eyes focused on him.

I'm the youngest here, for God's sake! Why does it have to be me? He searched the faces and he didn't like what he saw. Hope fading, confidence waning. Uncertainty. And questions too, directed at him. What are you made of, Mr. Reb? Now's the time to show us all.

What made it possible for an army to win was the belief that it would win. So simple, until that belief failed. At some indefinable moment the will faltered, first in one man, then in the others, and then defeat followed as certainly as night followed day. "You can see it in their eyes," Cleland Whitcomb had told his son. He had taken Ham to see Lee's surrender because he wanted the boy to glimpse the great man at least once, even in defeat. When the short ceremony was over and Lee emerged from the farmhouse, Cleland Whitcomb held Ham by the shoulders and thrust him forward, and Robert Edward Lee, United States Military Academy Class of 1829, had looked Ham Whitcomb straight in the eye for a moment before passing on.

He saw Lee's eyes before him now, sixteen pairs of them.

"What are your orders, sir?" It was Private Gray who spoke. Whitcomb saw that the gray-haired soldier was regarding him kindly. When Whitcomb had taken his dozen men to flank the Indians behind their breastwork during the battle, it had been Private Gray who showed Whitcomb how to withdraw from his position across the river, making it look as if the line was still held. Gray had been the last man on the line and he had retreated in quick darts, firing from each place he stopped. What would you do now, Private Gray? You helped me then and I could use your help again. What would Captain John Wesley of the Army of Northern Virginia do in my place? You fought your war and you came out of it alive, even though you lost.

But he couldn't ask for help, not of Gray or Dupré or anyone else. The gold band on his hand was his badge of office, and the West Point seal conferred on him a great burden.

"How is your horse, Gwynn?"

"Poorly, sorr. He won't go beyond a walk."

"Very well. We'll slaughter him tonight and pack as much of the meat as we can. Sergeant, how much coffee is left?"

"Enough for four days, sair, maybe five."

"All right. Meat and coffee will keep us going. We should be at Fort Reno in three or four days, but we'll have to march all day from now on. There will be a nooning stop but no time for sleeping." He paused. The burden seemed bearable so far. "We have to protect our eyes. You're no good to anyone if you can't see. The men with goggles will take turns sharing them with the others."

"Excuse me, sir." It was Gray again. "I've heard somewhere that a bit of cloth tied across the eyes is a makeshift sort of goggle. You cut small holes in it. I don't know why I didn't think of it sooner."

Whitcomb was shocked by the simplicity of the suggestion. Why hadn't he himself thought of it sooner? Or why hadn't Dupré or McCaslin or Atherton thought of it, with all their experience on the frontier? Because the first few days after the battle were stormy, and when the sun appeared, he and everyone else had welcomed it. They had squinted and marched on, and now most of the men were affected in some degree by snowblindness. It was the commanding officer's responsibility to foresee such dangers and prevent them.

"We're none of us thinking too clearly, I guess," he said. "All right then, the flankers and pickets will use the goggles and the rest of us will make do with cloth."

"Are you taking command, sir?"

The voice came from somewhere in the circle, but Whitcomb was not sure just where. It didn't matter. The voice asked for all of them. Why did he have to ask? Must there be a formal declaration? Wasn't it enough that Whitcomb was deciding the things that needed deciding now? He took a deep breath. "In view of Major Corwin's condition, I am taking command temporarily until he recovers."

"He won't be recoverin', sorr, not with that leg."

"I agree, Corporal. I'm afraid the leg will have to come off." He set his cup aside and stood up. "There's no sense in further delay. I'll need a sharp knife. Who has one?"

"Use mine, sir." Donnelly offered a long blade, handle first. Whitcomb accepted it and thumbed the edge. It was razor-sharp. He realized that it was the knife Donnelly had used to unman the wounded Indian during the battle, but that didn't seem to matter. Perhaps there was even some poetic justice in using it now; the Indian would have a small measure of revenge on the cavalry from beyond the grave.

"Some of you men bring the major close to the fire," he said. "If anyone has any spirits, I want to know it now."

It was Dupré who reached into his coat and brought out a nickel-plated flask encased in tooled leather. "Cognac, sair. Not the best, but he will not know the difference."

Gentle hands carried Corwin from his resting place and

set him before the fire. The movement caused him to grimace and open his eyes suddenly.

"My God damn leg's on fire. Do something, for God's sake!"

"We're going to do what we can for you, Major. I hope you're feeling a little better." Whitcomb felt ridiculous for mouthing such pleasantries. He knelt beside Corwin and placed a blanket under the injured leg. He peeled back the uniform trouser and sliced off the woolen underwear above the knee. Corwin grunted each time the leg was moved. Dupré passed the flask to Corwin, who sniffed it and managed a smile.

"You're a souse, Dupré, you French son of a bitch. Here's to the French." He raised the flask and drank deeply, and then he saw the knife that McCaslin was passing through the flames of the fire. "Oh, I see it now! You bastards want to take my leg! I'm damned if you will!"

He drew back fearfully but Atherton restrained him. "Easy, sir. It's for your own good. That leg is killin' you as sure as an Indian would if 'e got the chance."

Corwin's eyes were wide with alarm and they found Whitcomb now. "It's you, you Rebel son of a bitch! Don't think I don't know what you're up to! You want my command! Well you won't get it! Each of you men is my witness. I'm still in command here! If this Rebel tries to take over, I'll file charges of mutiny. The same goes for any man who helps him."

"Don't be hard on Mr. Whitcomb, sair," said Dupré soothingly. "He is doing what he must do."

"He's a God damn Johnny Reb!" Corwin was agitated and fearful.

"That he is, sorr," said McCaslin. "And so is Private

Gray, but he serves you well, just like Mr. Whitcomb here.''

Corwin looked at Whitcomb again. "You might as well cut my throat as chop off my leg! I'll go home with two legs or not at all!''

"Lie still, sir, if you please. Private Gray, I'll need you and four others to hold him. Arms, legs and shoulders.''

"All right, you bastards,'' Corwin said as their hands took hold of him. Rather than have them proceed against his will he gave in. "Have at it. I'll get a peg leg and I'll still kick your sorry asses 'round the parade ground. Give me a minute, boys. Let the brandy take hold.'' He drank again, and paused to come up for air.

> *"Oh they call me Hanging Johnny,*
> *Away, boys, away,*
> *But I only hang for money,*
> *So hang, boys, hang.*
> *Me father was a sailor,*
> *Away, boys, away.*
> *He should ha' been a tailor,*
> *So hang, boys, hang!''*

He drained the flask and threw it from him. "Lay on, Macduff, and shoot the son of a whore that first cries 'Hold, enough!' '' He laughed feverishly.

It seemed to Whitcomb that the amputation took forever. Dupré offered to perform the surgery but something compelled Whitcomb to take the ugly task on himself, and so with occasional advice from Dupré and McCaslin and Private Gray, who held Corwin's shoulders, he proceeded. The leg was cut at the knee; without a bone saw it was impossible to sever it elsewhere. Dupré placed a stick of willow in Corwin's mouth for him to bite on but he bit through it and screamed as the knife severed the first tendon. After that Whitcomb closed his ears to the screams and he breathed a prayer of thanks when Corwin slumped back unconscious.

When the leg was severed he cauterized the stump by heating the knife red-hot in the fire and applying it to the open flesh until the bleeding stopped, choking on the smell. At last he turned away and let the knife fall from his fingers, forcing himself to breathe deeply. He was soaked with sweat. Several times during the operation he had thought he might be sick; he was grateful that he had come through it without that humiliation.

Gwynn and another man, Private Heiss, had slaughtered Gwynn's exhausted horse and there was meat already cooking on the fire. Bile rose in Whitcomb's throat at the thought of eating, but he choked it back. He turned away from the fire and saw the lower part of Corwin's leg lying where he had set it, lifeless and abandoned, and he vomited violently then, falling to his knees and heaving again and again until there was nothing to come up. A canteen was offered and he heard Private Gray's voice. "Have a little water, sir."

He rinsed his mouth and spat and got shakily to his feet, wiping his mouth with the back of his glove. "Someone will have to bury that." He gestured at the leg without looking at it. "I want two pickets posted now. One-hour shifts. Each man to be sure the other stays awake. I'll take the first watch."

"No, sair."

Whitcomb looked sharply at Dupré. Damn it, were they going to turn on him now? Why were they all staring at him? Their faces were different; the look of defeat had gone and it was replaced by something new. What was it? A new sense of purpose, it seemed. Probably all scared to death of Corwin's threats, and they would stand against him now, just when he had his mind made up to take charge. Corwin was right. He had been too familiar with the men, too lenient. He had allowed the Mr. Reb nickname to gain currency. He hadn't reprimanded Rogers for firing at the deer and risking all their lives. He hadn't pushed any of them hard enough and now they thought they could oppose him freely.

He turned on Dupré and his voice was harsh. "I'm in command now, Sergeant, and I said I will take the first watch."

"And with respect, I say no, sair. You must rest."

"Sahrgint Dupree is right, sorr," McCaslin offered. "Ye'll be needin' yer rest. The boys'll post a guard."

"I'll take the first watch, sir," said Private Gray.

"Me too, sir" came from Donnelly, who was rubbing clean the blade of his knife with a handful of sandy soil. Already the others were pairing up, sharing blankets and robes, bedding down near the fire.

Whitcomb nodded dumbly. "Very well. Sergeant Dupré, I'll leave the picket duty in your hands."

He saw that Corwin had been covered with several robes. What else must be done before he went to sleep? There didn't seem to be anything. He spread his own robe by the fire and wrapped it around him like a cocoon.

He felt foolish for ever doubting the men. They hadn't turned on him after all. So he and Corwin were both wrong; Corwin for thinking a commander must be distant and stern, he himself for believing that truly caring about the welfare of the men was all that mattered, when there was something far more important at stake in earning the troopers' loyalty. If they were to believe in you they had to be certain of just one thing—your willingness to lead them. Most men didn't want that responsibility and they looked up to those who were willing to take it on, no matter if they were kindhearted souls or hardassed bastards.

The last thing he heard before his exhaustion claimed him was a voice that called out softly from the darkness, "Good night, Mr. Reb."

CHAPTER FOUR

Johnny Smoker sat on a rock and watched the shadows lengthen. The sun moved without moving. The space between the fiery ball and the mountain peaks narrowed and vanished and the jagged summits pierced the disk. The snow glowed with reddish fire and the shadows of the lodgepole pines were dark blue. The mountain slopes were vast, still and trackless.

Johnny had been atop the large boulder for more than an hour, watching all around him. Sometimes the tracker found his quarry best by remaining in one place and letting his eyes do the searching, but Johnny had seen nothing. His horse was tethered twenty yards away in a stand of trees.

Was it possible that she had already been found? He was

within sight of Putnam's Park and he had heard no shots, seen no riders reconverging on the settlement. Today even he carried a gun, a Remington Army .44 that had belonged to Jed Putnam. The weight was strange and unfamiliar at his waist. The first of the searchers to find Amanda would fire three shots, repeating them at intervals as he brought her in, until the signal was picked up by the others and everyone had heard it.

It had been Lisa Putnam who discovered that Amanda was missing. When Amanda failed to appear as usual in the kitchen while Lisa was making breakfast, she had thought that Amanda must be sleeping late because of the long evening of music, but when the circus people came to eat and there was still no sign of the girl, Lisa had gone upstairs to wake her and found her gone. Tatum professed to know nothing and no one else had seen her.

Johnny had left the park on his own, not waiting for the others to organize the search. He had moved quickly on horseback while the morning was still cold, but luck had not been with him and he had found no tracks. Amanda had left the settlement on a frozen crust that bore her weight easily. In winter the faint marks she made might have remained for a time, if the day was calm, but today the sun had warmed the surface of the snow and wiped out the nighttime tracks of rodents and other small animals as cleanly as if they were swept away with a broom. Johnny had moved in ever-widening arcs, searching to the west for reasons he couldn't name, but he had learned long ago to follow his instincts when hunting in the wild.

He could remain still no longer. He climbed down and made his way to the horse and his feet crackled on the new crust that was already forming on the surface of the snow. The night would be cold. If Amanda did not find shelter before darkness fell, she would die.

Why had she run away? Was it something he had done? He remembered the kiss of the night before, a magic moment when he had wanted only to hold her and never let go. But he had hesitated. She had offered herself; not merely her flesh but her spirit. She had offered him a chance to say something, do something, to reveal his feelings. But he had let the chance slip by.

He must find her. It was up to him. He had let her get away. Whether or not she had run because of him didn't matter. All that mattered was finding her and never letting go of her again. She belonged with him and he would tell her so.

The horse was nervous. As Johnny untied the reins the animal looked this way and that, its ears shifting about, the nostrils flaring. It heard or smelled something, but its actions lacked the element of stark fear that would have been plain if it sensed a predator near at hand. Johnny had seen no large animals all day, nor any tracks, only squirrels and woodpeckers and a few smaller birds, and three ravens that had dived and swooped as if performing for him alone while he sat on the rock.

As he mounted the horse it tossed its head and whickered. It perceived a distant movement and shied away, and Johnny saw the buffalo.

It was an old bull, standing atop a gentle slope a hundred yards distant, silhouetted against the amber light of the western sky. *Hunh!* it snorted, and the sound reached Johnny clearly in the silence. The head moved, the snout was raised, and again came the *hunh!* The bull turned and walked off, disappearing behind the ridge.

Johnny started up the slope at once. Something had brought the animal to this high place, away from the sheltered valleys where the buffalo preferred to browse for forage. A person on foot or horseback could disrupt the habits of wild animals. . . .

Watch the animals and learn from them, the Cheyenne instructed their children. Johnny sought the bull now as a helper and a guide. It was grasping at straws, a white man might say, but Johnny made his decision with no conscious thought and he accepted the rightness of it without question.

From the top of the slope the tracks of the bull led across a broad meadow into the trees. Johnny followed, wondering that the lone animal should move so fast. A grazing buffalo did not walk as if it had a destination; it wandered, the search for food never far from its thoughts. Only in herds did the buffalo go far and fast, for reasons known only to them.

Johnny followed the bull's trail easily, keeping an eye out for other tracks as well. When he emerged from the trees onto another open hillside, the bull was waiting. It set off again, as if satisfied that he would follow. The animal's behavior was unnatural, and Johnny felt a sudden chill, almost a premonition. It was a feeling he had not known in many years. He had experienced it first in a dream, when a white buffalo cow had spoken to him without words and had predicted the course his life would follow.

He kicked his horse into a trot to overtake the bull and he circled the animal as a hunter or a wolf might circle a herd of buffalo, but the bull did not take alarm. Instead it stopped in its tracks and only the great head moved to keep horse and rider in sight as they rode around him. Johnny felt the chill again, stronger now, and a heightening of all his senses. This was a bull, not a cow; it was the same dusty browns of ordinary buffalo, not white, and yet the animal was anything but ordinary. It allowed him to satisfy his curiosity, and when it started off again, Johnny was content to follow at a distance, almost fearful of approaching too close to this beast that behaved so strangely. He could hear the bull's breathing and the sound of its hooves in the snow, both abnormally loud. The crunching of his own horse's hooves seemed deafening. He felt as if he had crossed some invisible line and moved beyond the normal world, leaving behind him everything he had learned in seven years.

Do not be afraid of the power that comes to you, Sun Horse had said to a young boy very afraid of a vivid dream he had had during the night. The dream had filled him with an overpowering awe and he had struggled to wake up, seeking the familiar world of his parents' lodge. He had told his mother of the dream and she had called for his father to listen, and White Smoke had grown solemn as the boy repeated his words. "Go and tell this to your grandfather, just as you have told it to me," his father said, and he took the young boy out of the lodge and pointed to the horns of the camp where the tipis of the Sun Band stood in a place of honor. The boy had wanted his father to lead him, but White Smoke laid a hand on the boy's shoulder. "There is nothing to fear," he said, and the boy went on his own, sure that all eyes followed him. Through the great encampment he walked, paying no attention to the children playing all around. *"Hunhé!"* one man exclaimed. "The White Boy of the Shahíyela has his heart on the ground. Has a young woman sent back your ponies?" But the boy ignored the teasing and kept on. At last he had reached the tipi with the yellow sun painted near the entrance and very timidly he had scratched on the lodgeskins and coughed politely. Sun Horse had listened to the tale of his dream and told him not to be afraid. Little Warrior was a child of the *Tsistsístas* and not a cowardly boy, and after hc had talked with his Lakota grandfather for a time he felt proud of the dream and awed by its power, but he was no longer afraid.

So long ago, and even then a vision that came in his sleep, not on the vision quest as part of reaching for manhood. "Do not be afraid of the power," his grandfather had said, and he had accepted it then. But he was no longer that boy; he was a young man who had chosen the white world, in which there were no dreams of power, no visions of buffalo that became young women. A world in which *Ptésanwin* did not exist.

And yet he followed the bull as if it led him by a rope. He followed it higher into the hills, along the top of a steep escarpment and then down again, moving to the north. The sun, which earlier had only dropped behind the mountain peaks in the west, was falling behind the true horizon now, and the light was failing. The bull descended a wooded slope, meandering among the trees as if searching for something, and Johnny's heart leaped as he saw other tracks mingled with the bull's, the small tracks of a human being.

At the bottom of the hillside the bull stepped out of the trees into a small meadow. There were still more tracks spread across the flat expanse of snow but Johnny paid them no attention. He had eyes only for the human footprints, and he followed them quickly, urging the horse forward. At the foot of the valley the tracks ended where a small brown shape lay curled in the snow. It could have been a buffalo calf asleep, or a small deer, but Johnny saw the red clown's hat and the light brown hair, and he was already off the horse and running the last few steps, calling Amanda's name.

Her face was warm to the touch and she moaned as he rolled her over and took her into his arms. "Amanda?"

She seemed to come out of a deep sleep. "Johnny?" She reached up and touched his face. Her own face was streaked with tears, the clown makeup blotched and smeared. The lids of her eyes were almost swollen shut. "Johnny? Is that you?"

"It's me."

"Johnny, I can't see!" A sob escaped her and her body shook.

"It's all right. Everything's all right now," he said holding her tightly.

Night was falling quickly and there was a little breeze. He could hear the wind in the trees, the sound of his own breathing and Amanda's, the creaking of the snow beneath him as he rocked her in his arms. But something had changed. . . . The sights and sounds around him were normal once more; the heightened awareness that had come over him when he first saw the buffalo bull was missing now. He looked around and saw that the bull was gone.

The inside of Sun Horse's lodge was silent save for the sounds of the fire. Hears Twice bent over Amanda's still form, which lay on a pallet near the fire. He had one ear against her chest, listening. At last he straightened up and made a few signs—*I hear no death*.

Sun Horse nodded. Johnny Smoker sat beside him, watching everything that passed between the two men. The Lakota village was much closer than Putnam's Park to where he had found Amanda and so he had brought her here, firing shots occasionally as he rode. He had been within half a mile of the village before the Lakota scouts found him in the dark. Amanda had lapsed into unconsciousness on the journey to the Indian camp and she had not wakened since.

Elk Calf Woman handed Sun Horse a twist of dried

grass. He touched it to the fire and blew out the flame at once. He passed the smoking twist along Amanda's body and the pleasant scent of sweetgrass filled the lodge. With his free hand he scooped the smoke from the air and stroked the small form, passing the purifying scent everywhere, finishing with the face and head.

Amanda was still dressed in her clown costume, but her buffalo coat had been removed. Sun Horse spread the coat over her now and pulled a robe atop it, covering her from toes to chin.

From outside came the sound of hoofbeats. Lakota messengers had been sent to the settlement to tell the whites that the girl was found; they were returning now, and by the number of horses he heard, Sun Horse guessed that some of the whites had come to see for themselves that the girl was well.

He spoke to Sings His Daughter and she stepped through the entrance. There was a moment's conversation outside the lodge and then Lisa Putnam entered.

"Is she all right?" she asked in Lakota.

"She is snowblind. If she wakes again, she will live." He had instructed Sings His Daughter to allow only Lisaputnam into the lodge. The others would have to wait.

Lisa bent over Amanda and touched the unconscious girl's cheek and forehead with her hand. She smiled at Johnny. "I'm glad it was you that found her." She stepped back out of the lodge and there was more talk, then the sound of horses leaving. After a few moments, Lisa returned. She sat by the fire near Amanda.

"Mr. Tatum wanted to come in but I said that was against the doctor's orders," she said to Johnny. "You should have seen his face." She smiled. "I told him that Sun Horse had cured more snowblindness than any white doctor. Alfred and Joe were with him. They'll see he doesn't try to come back until she's ready to see him.''

Johnny nodded, not sure why he found this news so welcome, except that Amanda was never quite herself when the circus master was near.

Sings His Daughter entered the lodge and set a bowl of snow beside Sun Horse before taking her seat next to Elk Calf. Sun Horse began to sing a curing chant. He took snow from the bowl and sprinkled it on Amanda's eyes. The paint on her face had not been touched, except to wipe clean the eyelids. The paint was her power and Sun Horse had ordered that it be left as it was.

Again and again he reached to the bowl, sprinkling the snow in small piles that gradually covered Amanda's eyes and grew slowly as the flakes continued to fall from Sun Horse's hands. The snow had taken her sight and now it would restore it to her. So gently did he handle the snow, so carefully had Sings His Daughter gathered the powdery flakes, they seemed to fall on Amanda's face as from a cloud, settling in their own way as they might have settled in a quiet patch of woods.

When the bowl was empty he lit the sweetgrass again and passed the smoking twist along Amanda's body, spreading the smoke with his hand, and he followed the sweetgrass with sage smoke this time, to drive away all but the friendly spirits. When the herbs were extinguished and set aside, he took his ceremonial bag from around his neck and opened it. He held the bag over his palm and shook it gently, and a little dust fell into his hand. He set the bag down and rubbed his palms together quickly, then blew the dust away. The small cloud puffed into the air over Amanda and settled slowly.

It was the last trace of earth from his vision-hill. The

symbols of his vision were gone now. He was looking beyond the symbols.

He began to chant the curing song again and now his voice was joined by a second, softer and higher. Elk Calf Woman beat lightly on a small drum in her lap as she sang, and Sings His Daughter shook a rattle made from the dried scrotum of a buffalo bull. It was rare for women to take part in a healing ceremony, but as holy man and healer, Sun Horse had the power to change the ceremonies if he wished, and he sometimes called on his wives to assist him. The healing power of woman was great, and he wanted to summon all that power today. As always, he prayed to the directions and to all living things, each one a separate manifestation of *Wakán Tanka,* and he prayed not just for the clown girl but for himself as well.

Here in his lodge were the two people who had met when the Snowblind Moon was young, when *wamblí gleshka* had spoken to him and he had felt the movement of power all around him. The *heyoka* girl lay before him, her spirit far away. If she died, the promise of power would be broken and his hopes would be gone like the symbols of his vision. When he had heard Dust's voice announcing that the clown girl was lost, Sun Horse had come out of his lodge and he had directed every able-bodied man in the village to join the search. He had sensed then, as he did now, that the solution to his dilemma was still within his reach, but only if the girl lived. If she recovered, he would continue his search for peace.

The warmth of Amanda's face began to melt the mounds of snow that covered her eyes and the water ran down her white cheeks like tears. Sun Horse ended the chant. His wives set the drum and rattle aside and began to prepare sleeping robes on an extra pallet. Elk Calf said a few words to Lisa, inviting her to sleep there, and Lisa readily agreed. She was dull with fatigue after a long day in the saddle.

Sun Horse raised the robe covering Amanda and motioned Johnny to lie beside the girl. "Sleep here with her," the old man said in Cheyenne. "Keep her warm."

Fully clothed, Johnny lay down beside Amanda. Sun Horse covered them both and resumed his seat by the fire. As the others dropped to sleep one by one he remained awake, keeping watch over his grandson and the clown girl. The night was calm and the village quiet. Sun Horse let his mind drift, touching here and there on the separate aspects of his dilemma, and he prayed he would have one more chance to fulfill the promise he had been given so many years ago, atop the small hill overlooking Fort Laramie.

It was dawn when Amanda stirred. She opened her eyes and raised her head, and the slight movement awakened Johnny.

"Johnny?" she said, looking at him as if in a dream. "Good, you're here." She lay back and closed her eyes again.

Johnny slipped from under the covers and knelt beside her. "How do you feel?"

She opened her eyes and looked around her. "Where am I?"

"We're in Sun Horse's lodge."

"Oh." She let her head fall back.

"Can you see?" Sun Horse asked in English, rising from his robes.

"Of course I can see." Her eyes suddenly opened wide. "I was lost! Oh, Johnny! You found me and I couldn't see!"

Lisa was awake now and she came to kneel beside

Johnny. "You were snowblind," she told the girl. "Do your eyes still hurt?"

Amanda nodded. "They're sore. But I can see! I thought I was blind."

Lisa smiled. "You won't stand much bright light for a day or two, but your eyes will be as good as new."

On the other side of the lodge Elk Calf left her pallet and moved to the cooking fire, where an iron pot had sat on the coals throughout the night. She spoke in Lakota to Lisa.

Lisa nodded and turned to Amanda. "Can you drink a little soup? You should eat something if you can."

"I guess I am hungry."

Elk Calf passed a wooden bowl and a horn spoon to Lisa, who helped Amanda raise herself to a half-sitting position.

"Oh, that's good," Amanda said as she tasted the broth. Lisa fed it to her a spoonful at a time until it was all gone. The girl lay back gratefully on the soft robes, tired by the small effort of eating and soothed by the warm soup inside her. "I remember now," she said, frowning as she tried to make the memory complete. "I was trying to find the trail between the Indian village and Putnam's Park. I went downhill, but my eyes got worse and worse and I fell down in the trees. And then I was in a field with some buffalo. That's the last thing I remember until Johnny found me. It's all like a bad dream. Except the ending." She smiled at Johnny.

Sun Horse leaned forward and spoke again in English. "It is a spirit animal you see. It led my grandson to you." It had not been *Ptésanwin*, of that he was sure; one such vision in a lifetime was more than all but a handful of men had ever experienced. But he was just as sure that the bull was the spirit of *pte* sent to guide his grandson.

"But it was long before Johnny found me," Amanda protested. "The sun was still up and there were lots of them, all walking past me. They stopped to look at me. I know I saw them."

"There were other tracks," Johnny said slowly, remembering. He closed his eyes to bring back the scene. Even when he was not paying full attention, the number and direction of tracks he saw did not escape his notice. With his eyes still closed he spoke again, moving his hands to show his own movements and where the tracks had been. "I came out of the trees and the bull stopped here. Amanda's tracks went off to the right. The others were in the middle of the meadow, going up the valley." He opened his eyes and looked at Sun Horse, speaking now in Cheyenne. "They were there, Grandfather. They could have been the tracks of buffalo."

Before the day had fully brightened, the scouts and hunters were gathered hastily and Sun Horse addressed them with his white grandson by his side. *Akíchita* were named to control the hunt; no one would be permitted to jeopardize its success; the survival of the people might be at stake.

"My grandson will take you to a small valley surrounded by trees," said the headman, "and there you will find the tracks of *pte*."

"There are no tracks," a young scout said arrogantly. "We have looked every day and we would have seen the tracks if any *pte* were near."

Sun Horse did a strange thing then. He lowered his head and made the *hunh!* snort of *tatanka*. He shuffled around the scout, sniffing the air. "If I see you first, will I leave my tracks for you to follow? Do not forget that *pte* is the most holy of the four-leggeds, and wise in ways that men are not. Shall there not perhaps be a small band of *pte* like the Sun Band? Might they not choose to stay low in the mountains in some sheltered place where the grass grows tall and thick in the summer moons? Where they can forage in the winter while others go hungry? Follow my grandson and you will find them as I have told you.''

''If they are there, we will find them,'' said Walks Bent Over, the hunchbacked young man who was head scout of the band. He was given heart by Sun Horse's words and he felt a burden lifting from him. Until the news of the clown girl's disappearance had been brought to the village yesterday, Walks Bent Over had been the only leader to guide the actions of the young men for many days. With Standing Eagle away and Sun Horse retreating into what some said would be his death fast, Walks Bent Over had seen eyes turned toward him for guidance, and he had sent the scouts out to watch the trails, far enough away to give the people time to break camp and move if bluecoats were seen, but not too far. He had placed the eyes of the Sun Band in a ring to guard the people, as the *pte* formed a ring around the helpless ones when danger threatened the herd, with horns and eyes outward. The horns of the Sun Band were few, and those not sharp enough to ward off the far-shooting guns of the bluecoats, and so the eyes must be all the sharper, Walks Bent Over had told his scouts. He had rejoiced when Sun Horse emerged from his lodge to direct the search for the white *heyoka* girl, and he rejoiced now at the renewed strength of the headman. Sun Horse's tone was confident and his eyes were bright with hope.

With women along to do the butchering and pack horses to bring back the meat, the hunters set out. Sun Horse's grandson guided the band unerringly, although he had come down from the hills in the dark the night before.

When the band entered the little valley surrounded by trees, the tracks were there. They followed the trail up a draw and over the next ridge and there beyond a small stand of trees they saw the breath cloud of the herd.

The hunters waited as Walks Bent Over advanced cautiously, keeping downwind, to scout the best route for the attack.

"A big herd!" whispered one young man.

"Any herd appears big to eyes so young," said an older man who remembered herds so vast that *Ina*, the Mother Earth, shook all day and night under the passing feet of her children, as a woman trembled with pleasure in the arms of her man.

"There are five times ten *pte*," Walks Bent Over announced when he returned, and he made signs to Johnny Smoker. *They say that the buffalo-dreamer shall be a great hunter, and the words are true*. He placed a hand on Johnny's shoulder, expressing his gratitude for a job of scouting well done. Then he smiled and made more signs: *They also say the buffalo-dreamer shall get the woman he wants. Good hunting, my friend!* The other men laughed softly and several stopped to place a hand of approval on Johnny's shoulder before moving off toward the herd.

The surround was made on foot, the hunters and scouts spreading out to take position, the *akíchita* watching the hunters to be sure that none fired too soon. Clad in the skins of wolf and coyote, the scouts crept forward. The herd drew in on itself with the bulls on the outer edges, snorting and pawing the snow, but the buffalo did not take fright. They were used to four-legged predators circling the herd to watch for those too young to move quickly or the old and sick that might be easy prey. A healthy bison had little to fear from wolves and coyotes.

But these predators carried guns. When they were in

position, the scouts shot the old bulls first, the leaders. Then one man wounded a cow so she moved in circles and started the herd milling in confusion, and then the rest of the hunters started to shoot carefully, taking their time. Whenever one animal took the initiative and tried to lead the remaining ones away, the new leader was shot and once again the *pte* milled about until all were dead in the snow and the hillside echoed with the trilling of joy from the watching women.

When the first of the meat reached the village, the fires were built high and the kettles were filled and great cuts of ribs were placed over the flames to roast slowly. Some women cooked in the old way as well, making a soup in the buffalo paunch by dropping hot rocks in with the meat and water. Children and dogs darted here and there, trying to steal a bite of meat from under the watchful eyes of the women.

It was mid-afternoon when Johnny Smoker returned, riding triumphantly at the head of a long string of horses all packed with meat. He was surprised to see Amanda walking with Elk Calf Woman, coming from the creek, where they had made *inipi* together. Amanda's clown makeup was gone and in place of her costume she wore a simple deerskin dress beneath her buffalo coat. With Amanda delivered back to the lodge and tucked once more in her robes, Elk Calf went off to help Sings His Daughter in cutting up the meat. Sun Horse rose from his seat by the fire and took Lisa Putnam by the hand. "Come," he said in Lakota. "Walk with me. We will walk through the camp and see the people happy." They went out of the lodge and the two young people were left by themselves.

"I asked them to leave us alone when you got back," Amanda said a little shyly. "I have something I want to say to you."

It seemed to Johnny that the girl before him was someone he had never seen before. It was Amanda, but she had changed in some indefinable way. The eyes that met his so calmly revealed a new contentment, as if a persistent worry had finally been put to rest.

He remembered his thoughts on the mountainside, and what he had to tell her. Walks Bent Over's words about the buffalo-dreamer came back to him then and they gave him confidence.

She took one of his hands in her own. "First, I want to thank you for saving my life. I guess that should be the most important thing of all, saving my life, but there's something else I want to say and it's even more important to me." She paused, and then said, "I'm leaving the circus."

Johnny was nonplused; he had no idea of how to react to this news, but Amanda smiled. "It's because of you, really. Without you I never would have had the courage to do it. Hachaliah has taken care of me all my life just the way Mr. Hardeman has taken care of you. But it's time I was on my own. You understand, don't you?"

Johnny nodded. He understood very little except his feelings for Amanda, which were suddenly even stronger than before.

"I don't mean I'm giving up my clowning. I'll look for work with another show. I'm just leaving this circus, and Hachaliah. It's something I have to do."

"Then you won't be going with them when they leave."

Amanda shook her head. "I asked Lisa if I could stay with her until I know where I want to go."

Johnny smiled. "I guess I'll be staying too. I was about set to take that job with the Waldheims, but not anymore. Not now. That was just so I could be near you until I got up my nerve to speak my mind."

She dropped her gaze and her voice was soft. "What were you going to say when you got up your nerve?"

Johnny took a deep breath and plunged on. "I almost lost you yesterday. I don't want that to happen again. I don't know why you took out like that. I don't know that it matters much now. You don't have to say if you don't want to."

"I ran because I didn't know what I wanted. I do now." She raised her eyes to meet his and held his hand even more tightly.

"Does that mean yes?" Hope was plain on Johnny's face.

"Did you ask a question?" She was teasing him, but he was very serious.

"I got nothing to offer you really, just me and a few things you could pack on one horse. But I'll try to make whatever kind of life you want, wherever you want it. I figured I better speak my piece and let you make up your mind before you went off somewhere else." He paused, hoping she might say something, but she kept silent, regarding him solemnly. "I know I'm not making a very good job of this, but I ain't had a whole lot of practice. Come to think of it, I don't guess anyone gets much practice at this sort of thing. It's something you only do one time if you do it right. That's how I'd like it to be."

He asked her to marry him then, and she said yes, and she was surprised to find tears of joy coming to her eyes.

Until today Amanda had had no intention of revealing that she was leaving Hachaliah and the circus, not until she had drawn Johnny out first, making him declare his need for her, his wish for them to be together. That had always been her way, letting her young men think that every action of hers was their doing. But today when she had awakened for the second time, in mid-morning, she had found Lisa and Sun Horse watching over her. She had realized in that moment that she was utterly safe from Hachaliah Tatum, and the feeling had changed her. She was in a world where Hachaliah could not control her; he could not reach her here and if necessary she could remain here until he was far away. For the first time in her life she knew what it was to be free.

And then to her astonishment she had discovered something else. When she learned that Johnny had gone off with the hunters she found that his absence made an emptiness in her. She felt incomplete without him and she was impatient for him to return. It was a feeling she had never known before, and she realized that she did not want Johnny merely as a guide to help her make the break with Hachaliah nor as a paramour to use for a time and then discard. She wanted him as a companion. She wanted to share her life with him.

The discovery had left her dumbfounded and strangely pleased with herself, as if she had wrought this change by her own hand. Her immediate goals had not changed—finding work for the two of them in another circus, adding to her reputation and fame—but this was something she wanted now for Johnny as well as herself. As he had shown her how to stand on her own so she would show him the way to a new life, an exciting life that would take them together wherever they wanted to go.

She had grown impatient for Johnny to come back. At any sound from outside the lodge she had inquired if it might signal his return from the hunt. When Sun Horse had suggested she take a sweat bath to speed her recovery she had agreed readily enough, hoping it would help to pass the time. She had become restless in her confinement and was glad of a chance to move about. She found the fragrant steam invigorating and even her eyes felt almost normal, although they were still a little sore. And when she stepped out of the sweat lodge she saw the world anew. It was as if the sage-scented steam had washed away her past; she felt reborn.

When Johnny returned at last, her heart had jumped at the sight of him and her acceptance of his proposal was heartfelt and genuine.

He rewarded her with a kiss as chaste and moving as their first. She clung to his hands as if she would never let go, profoundly grateful now that she had not given in to her first impulse and pressed a seduction back in Putnam's Park after that kiss at the foot of the stairs. She should have known that the way to make Johnny hers forever was not to give herself but to withhold herself! He saw her as a tender virgin and she would be as pure as he imagined her. They would stay in the park when the circus was gone, spending their days together and their nights apart, until Chris Hardeman returned. Then the three of them would make their way to some town where there was a minister and she and Johnny would be married, and only then would she give herself to him, proudly, as a virgin might, with nothing to hide. It was the way he assumed it would be and she wanted it that way too, to please him, and because the intervening time would allow the memory of Hachaliah's touch to fade until it could be forgotten.

When Lisa returned to the lodge with Sun Horse, she saw the joy on the faces of the two young people. It was a joy she had known once herself, when the cavalry lieutenant had first touched her heart. But when she tried to remember the lieutenant's face she could see only Chris Hardeman. She had very nearly said something to reveal her feelings to him on the day he left, something to say that she was concerned for his safety and would feel his absence until he returned. But she had hesitated, and he had gone.

She had long been aware that in the sparsely populated western territories the paths of separate lives often crossed briefly, never to cross again. At the moment when two paths met, sometimes a chance flared and burned brightly for a short time. But caution was best thrown to the winds at those times, and only boldness reaped the possible rewards. Lisa had honed her awareness of such moments, but with Hardeman she had let the moment pass without speaking. She felt a sudden anger at her timidity. Johnny and Amanda had nearly lost each other because they had not spoken their feelings sooner. If Johnny had not found the girl she might well have died. Lisa resolved not to hesitate again when Hardeman and her uncle Bat returned. If they returned. Hardeman might leave anyway, but he would go knowing how she felt.

She stood with the fire at her back and she did not remove her goatskin coat. "It's time for me to be getting home," she said after they had told her their news. "I've got to see to my calves. And I'll announce your engagement." She looked at Amanda. "Mr. Tatum expects to have the road clear in a few more days and there's a lot of talk about the farewell performance. They'll want to know if you'll be part of it."

Amanda brightened. "I forgot! Oh, Johnny, you'll get to see the show!" She turned to Lisa. "Of course I'll perform. Please tell them I'll come down as soon as I can."

"I think it would be just as well if you don't come down right away. It will give everyone a little time to get used to the idea of your leaving them. Anyway, you need another day or two of rest. I'll be back up tomorrow with pack horses for some of this meat. Sun Horse says he's got to repay me for the grain and gunpowder I gave him, even though the Indians made the hunt by themselves. We'll see how you're doing then." She was thinking of Hachaliah Tatum, whose first reaction to the news of Amanda's engagement she couldn't imagine. She hoped that with a few days to consider it, he would see that nothing he could do would change how matters stood.

With scarcely an hour left before sunset, Lisa did not delay her departure. She kissed Amanda, and Johnny too, to his embarrassment, and with a promise to bring Hutch and Chatur back with her on the morrow, she was gone.

That night the Sun Band feasted. Men and women visited from lodge to lodge and invited the needy ones to eat with them, and wood was brought for a bonfire in the middle of the camp circle. Even while many were still eating, the drumming began and the dancers gathered. When the sound of drums and chanting voices grew loud, Amanda and Johnny came out of the lodge and sat with Sun Horse, wrapped in their robes, the young man looking at Amanda as often as he looked at the dancers circling the fire.

Between the dances the *heyoka* performed for the people, often doing their tricks and antics close in front of the white girl so she could see them well. Both drums and voices fell silent and the sounds of wonder came from many throats as the two *heyoka* presented Amanda with sacred presents. She had brought the news of the *pte* herd, which she had seen clearly even with her snowblind eyes. She had brought the life-giving power to the band and the special gifts were made in appreciation. Talks Fast, the elder *heyoka*, painted a jagged bolt of lightning on each of Amanda's cheeks, and then he gave her a wooden cup and *heyoka* bow, the cup representing the water that came from the west, the power to make things live, and the bow the Thunder Beings' power to destroy.

When the first light of dawn appeared in the east, the wind began to gust and clouds moved in to cover the sky. Some of the people turned to their robes for a little sleep, but many remained awake, extending new invitations for others to come and share the meat from their fires. There was a new spirit in the village, one that had not been felt since the autumn moons. The people were strong again and the camp circle was reunited in hope. Yet still Sun Horse had not eaten. He had moved among the people, smiling to see them happy and strong once again, exchanging a few words here and there, but no morsel of *pte* meat had passed his lips. He seeks the path that leads to a lasting peace between Lakota and *washíchun,* the oldest of the councillors said; he seeks to unite the power of the two worlds. He takes too much on himself, others said; the band is strong again and we have nothing to fear. Perhaps Standing Eagle is right and we should fight the bluecoats if they come. Sun Horse should eat now, so he will be strong to lead us whatever may happen.

Before the dawn, Sun Horse had gone back to his lodge and the clown girl and his white grandson went with him.

As the morning brightened, the camp grew quiet. Few moved about now; most who were still awake contented themselves with resting in the comfort of a warm lodge and a full belly. A few women resumed the butchering of the meat, which would take days, and some others began to work at a few of the hides. One man who still moved among the tipis was old Dust, the crier. When a family wished to invite another to eat, they might give him a piece of rib roast to pay for his services in announcing the invitation. Already he had eaten more than enough, but until the last vestiges of the celebration died away he would perform his duty and carry any message he might be asked to carry from one lodge to another, or throughout the entire village. He paused in his wanderings to look up and down the valley and he was surprised to see a small group of men and horses moving slowly toward the village from the northern trail.

Surely none of the scouts were still out? All had taken part in the hunt and none had been sent off again. Then who . . . ?

Two of the horses pulled pony drags bearing burdens that looked like men and he saw now that there were some women with the little band. And then he recognized the man who rode in the lead. It was something in his movements, his bearing in the saddle or the way he raised a hand in greeting, for Dust's eyes were no longer sharp enough to discern a face at such a distance. But he was sure now, and he placed a hand over his mouth in wonder.

Could such an honor be his? Usually someone called his name and he went where he was summoned, there to learn what he must announce. This time he was the first to know the news! And it was news all the village had long awaited.

He took a deep breath and faced the camp, his head held high. As he began to announce the glad tidings he walked with stately steps around the circle, moving as the sun moved through the sky and as a man moved when he entered a lodge, calling out in the high penetrating tones he reserved for the most important events. "The pipe carriers return! They are coming now! The pipe carriers return!"

CHAPTER FIVE

Within moments the camp circle was alive again. Those who had so recently gone to their robes were awakened by the crier's news and they poured from the lodges. The women working the hides dropped their scrapers to join the gathering crowd. Coming so close on the heels of the successful hunt, the long-awaited return of the pipe carri ers seemed providential, and the news of their coming banished fatigue and raised the spirits of the people to new heights. Joyfully the children ran forth, trailed by barking dogs, but as they drew near the riders their cries of greet ing died away. They saw the pony drags, one bearing a long bundle, one carrying Blackbird. They saw the strangers, and some smiles from the women and children, but the expressions of relief at finally reaching a place of shelter were overshadowed with weariness and sorrow. They saw the faces of the men daubed black with paint, and even ones so young knew that the black face-paint signified great intensity of emotion about some serious matter. In war, it could indicate either victory or defeat,

113

and often it was a sign of mourning. The children looked from face to face, seeing the tired eyes and bitter expressions, and they saw that one face was missing. Like a flock of birds they turned as one and ran back to the village, silently now. They found their parents in the crowd, clutching the grown-ups' arms and hands as they whispered the sad news, and from some of the women came cries of apprehension.

Sees Beyond went quickly to Sun Horse's lodge, guiding himself with his stick, and he coughed at the entrance. When Elk Calf opened the flap he spoke loudly enough to be heard within. "The pipe carriers return, and their faces are painted black."

Sun Horse had heard Dust's announcement and he had already donned his robe. He stepped out now, followed by Johnny and Amanda and his wives. Penelope came running from her own lodge. She joined her father and clutched his hand.

The travelers entered the village through the horns of the circle and turned left, moving in the ceremonial fashion. The people watched silently and gathered behind them as they advanced. Standing Eagle and Little Hand rode at the head of the band, their blackened faces set and solemn. Behind them rode Lodgepole, who always had a smile for the children and a cheerful word for the women, but he was unsmiling now. His wife ran to his side and touched his leg to assure herself that he was well. He took her hand in his and she walked along beside him. Next to Lodgepole was the *washíchun* Hardeman, and he was wounded. Beneath his coat of waterproof cloth, which hung open, a ragged bandage was visible, binding his left arm against his body. He slumped in the saddle and looked as though he might fall, but now he gripped the saddle horn and drew himself up, raising his head. His face was painted too, and the people wondered at this, for they knew it was not the *washíchun* custom. Next in line were the strangers, the Oglalas. The villagers saw the short hair of the women, the arms gashed in mourning, and the weak condition of the children, but they did not dwell on these things, for their eyes passed quickly to the two pony drags that came last of all, led by the Oglala men. On one was a long bundle, well wrapped and securely lashed down; on the other lay Blackbird, covered with two buffalo robes. His face was no longer that of a young boy ignorant of all manly concerns.

Something very bad had happened, that much was plain. Has there been a fight? If so, with whom? And where was Hawk Chaser? Was it his body in the covered bundle on the pony drag? No one voiced the questions. The answers, and everything that had happened to the messengers since they had left the village, were things of great importance to the people, to be told formally to Sun Horse and the councillors after a pipe had reunited the travelers in the spirit of the band.

The wife of Hawk Chaser stood by Elk Calf, clutching the older woman's hand. Her eyes searched in vain among the horsemen, and when she saw the pony drags she let out a low moan and closed her eyes. Her daughter Yellow Leaf cried out, a long wail of anguish, and as the riders stopped before the headman's lodge the girl ran forward, dodging among the horses and startling them, stopping abruptly as she reached the rear of the little procession. She looked from Blackbird to the long bundle so like the shape of a man, and back at Blackbird again. She saw the tears brimming in his eyes, and she threw herself on the ground beside him, bursting into a torrent of sobs.

The pipe carriers dismounted and stood before Sun Horse. Johnny made a small sign to Hardeman, wanting to know if he was all right. In return he got an almost imperceptible nod that did little to calm his fears.

Sun Horse looked in the faces of the men and he knew they had failed. He turned to those gathered around him. "Help these relatives," he said, gesturing toward the Oglala families. The women were so exhausted they could barely stand. Women of the Sun Band moved forward at once to take the refugees to their lodges, where they could eat and rest. "Those who have robes or clothing to spare, give it to them," Sun Horse said, and others went to fetch what they had. The Oglala men remained behind as the women and children were led away.

Sun Horse motioned the travelers toward his own lodge. "Come and eat," he said. "Then we will talk." But Standing Eagle made a sign of negation.

"We have traveled for six days," the war leader said, "and we have been hungry all the while. We shared our *wasná* with the Oglala until it was gone. My brother Lodgepole killed an antelope with his far-shooting gun and we ate that, but for the last three days we have eaten nothing, and slept very little. Food will make us tired. We will talk now, while our hunger is sharp to remind us of our difficulties. It will help us to tell them clearly, so the people will hear. Later we will eat and sleep. First we must talk."

"The people must hear what we have to say, Father," Bat added.

Sun Horse looked from one man to the other and then he moved forward to the pony drags, helping himself along with a twisted stick of oakwood that he used as a cane. Bat had never seen his father-in-law use a cane before. Sun Horse appeared much older now than he had when the pipe carriers left the village, just eighteen days and nights before. The old man was very thin and his strength seemed to be failing.

Sun Horse stopped beside Blackbird. The boy had one hand on Yellow Leaf's shoulder and the girl had stopped crying.

"You are tired, Grandfather," Blackbird said.

Sun Horse nodded. "I have not eaten. I have been searching for . . . something. I do not know what it is." With the successful hunt he had thought that the answer to his quest was close at hand; now it seemed more distant than ever. If the peace were broken already, what hope could remain? Was it broken?

"I'm tired too," said Blackbird. "Let the people hear us now and then I will sleep until the grass is green."

Sun Horse felt a stab of fear for his grandson's life. He turned to Standing Eagle. "The wound . . . ?"

"There are two, Father. One in the leg and the other in the side. They will heal. The boy was treated by Ice, the Shahíyela healer, and by Iron Necklace." Here he indicated one of the Oglala men. "He is a bear medicine man."

Sun Horse nodded, greatly relieved. "We will hear what the pipe carriers have to say."

During the time it had taken to receive the travelers into the village, the sky had darkened above the mountains. The wind was gathering strength, gusting among the lodges, and a little snow was beginning to fall. Even as the fire was built in the council lodge the men began to take their seats, and Johnny Smoker found a place beside Hardeman. The youth came alone; Amanda had gone back into Sun Horse's lodge to await him there. He saw his friend's hollow cheeks and sallow complexion and he didn't know what to say. He had never seen Hardeman so tired. His fatigue seemed to be rooted somewhere deep inside him.

The scout put a hand on Johnny's arm in greeting and there was no strength in the grip.

"You all right?" the bearded man asked.

Johnny nodded. "Amanda got lost. She was snowblind. I found her and brought her here. She's still getting her strength back, but she'll be all right."

It was just like Johnny to tell a big story in so few words. Hardeman was glad to see his companion again after having been apart from him for what seemed a lifetime. He had noticed the way Amanda stood close beside Johnny, holding his arm, as if that was the only place she felt safe. What he had seen between them before he went away had grown, that was plain, and the knowledge gave him comfort. Whatever ties might help to keep the boy in the white world were all to the better.

"It seems like you've been on a hard trail," Johnny said. It was a term the two of them used to mean a difficult journey or bad trouble, or both.

"Didn't have much luck," Hardeman admitted. "We made pretty good time on the way back, everything considered." His eyes were on Blackbird, who was being carried into the council lodge on a litter. The lodge was filling rapidly now, the councillors talking softly among themselves as they took their places. The scene reminded Hardeman of the council in Two Moons' village and the hopes that were raised there.

"These folks made meat," he observed. He had seen the hides and carcasses.

"When Amanda was lost she saw some buffalo," Johnny explained. "The scouts found them. The hunt was yesterday."

"You and the girl getting on?"

Johnny blushed. "Amanda and I— She's leaving the circus. We're—" He hesitated, not sure he should bring this up just now. The pipe carriers' news was far more important.

"Making plans?" Hardeman offered.

"Just one so far. We're getting married."

There was life in Hardeman's smile and renewed strength in his grip as he put his hand on Johnny's arm once more. "That's good news," he said.

"We ain't got much else worked out just yet. We've got some talking to do."

"Well, you're a pretty good talker when you set your mind to it. You'll get it worked out."

Johnny smiled, feeling uncertain and grateful at the same time. Chris always knew how to lift his spirits, but he had meant it to be the other way around. If anything, Chris was the one who needed to have his spirits raised, but there was no more time for talk now. The lodge was full, the entrance flap secured, and the flames leaped high as buffalo fat was added to the fire to make a bright light. Sun Horse was loading a pipe.

The pipe was lit, and as it was passed around the inner circle the sounds of horses entering the village were heard in the silent council lodge. A moment later Dust put his head into the entrance to say that Lisaputnam was here, and Sun Horse motioned that she might enter. Scarcely had Dust withdrawn when Lisa stepped into the lodge, her eyes darting this way and that until they found first Bat and then Hardeman seated there, and it was difficult to tell which man she was the most glad to see. Her mountain goatskin coat was covered with a dusting of new snow. She accepted a place that was made for her at the bottom of the inner circle.

Lisa and Hutch had come with pack horses as she had promised, and they had brought Chatur to see Amanda. Hutch and Chatur were with the girl in Sun Horse's lodge now. As the three riders approached the village they had seen the clouds that were gathering in the north and felt the strength of the storm that was imminent. They had intended to stay only a short time, but when Lisa was told that the pipe carriers had returned, she had dropped her reins and made straight for the council lodge, and she would stay until the council was done. She might be stranded by the storm but nothing would move her from this spot.

She looked at Bat and was grateful for the smile he gave her. Her eyes moved on to Hardeman, who met her gaze once and then looked away. The brief contact chilled her. She saw a man who was at the end of his resources, both in body and mind, a man who was defeated.

When the pipe had returned to Sun Horse, Standing Eagle was the first to speak. He told of the journey north, of finding the cavalry tracks and seeing the army wagons, and the encounter with the Crow war party at Prairie Dog Creek. He recounted the night attack, and here he invited Blackbird to tell what had happened when he went off alone to try to recover the stolen horses. As always in council, each man told only what he knew from his own personal experience.

Blackbird spoke from his litter. He related how he had overtaken the Crow warrior and been wounded, and how Hardeman had saved his life with the far-shooting buffalo gun. The councillors raised their voices in praise when they heard this, and all eyes turned to the white scout, who sat stone-faced and unmoved, as if he neither heard nor saw what took place around him. But as always Bat was translating the proceedings for Hardeman, and when Blackbird said he had no more to tell, Hardeman spoke up, adding a few words of his own, saying that Blackbird had counted coup on the dead Crow, as was his right. Again the voices of praise swelled loud and Blackbird blushed with pride.

The listeners fell silent as Standing Eagle told of leaving the cavalry's trail and finally coming on the Cheyenne village on the Powder. The smoking pipes grew cool as he spoke of the council held there, and the arrival first of Sitting Bull and then Crazy Horse. There were murmurs of wonder from the councillors then, to hear of these great men gathered to hear the message from Sun Horse. Standing Eagle told of the peace terms that grew from the council, what was to be offered to the whites and what demanded in return. Crazy Horse had agreed to these terms, he said, and in the end even Sitting Bull had given his approval and he had smoked the pipe of peace. There was an outburst of joy in the lodge at this news, but it died away quickly as the men gathered there remembered that the pipe carriers had a man dead and they did not yet know how that came to be, or why the messengers' expressions and bearing told unmistakably of failure.

Standing Eagle moved along now to the night following the council and Bat watched his brother-in-law closely, but the war leader said only that the pipe carriers had left the Cheyenne village before dawn to find Crook, Hardeman going ahead of the others, and when Standing Eagle turned to introduce the Oglalas, who would tell how the battle began, Bat knew the war leader would keep the bargain the two of them had made in private on the journey home. Bat had wrested from his brother-in-law the promise to tell the story this way in exchange for Bat's silence about Standing Eagle's outburst in the council with Sitting Bull and Crazy Horse. " 'Tain't like you'd be lyin'," Bat had said, pressing the point in English although the two of them had been riding beyond the hearing of the others. "You jest hold back on a piece o' the truth. What's important is, Christopher saved your boy's life; twice, mebbe. And when the lead got to flyin', he sided with us and fought agin' the bluecoats. Mebbe he was figurin' t' bring the soldiers to the village when he lit out, mebbe not. Mebbe he jest figgered he could do better talkin' t' Three Stars on his own first. I dunno and you don't neither. So you tell it like I say or there's gonna be a heap o' folks hear how you made a fool o' yerself up there in front o' them big fellers.''

Taking turns, the Oglalas related how the soldiers had been among the lodges before the alarm was sounded and how the people had fled to the bluffs and fought hard to repel the attackers. One of the men had seen Hardeman enter the battle. He described how the white man had tried to stop the fighting, only to be shot by the soldiers and rescued by two Shahíyela.

Now Bat took over the tale and there was no one to translate for Hardeman, but Bat added enough signs to his narration so that Hardeman was able to follow the gist of it. Bat told how the three youths had brought horses to the stranded Indians, how Blackbird had been wounded while charging the soldiers, and of Hardeman's attempt to save the boy. Bat described how the scout had shot at the troopers, unhorsing one man, and once again Hardeman heard voices raised in praise of his actions, followed by the *ahhh-h*'s of sorrow as the listeners learned at last how Hawk Chaser had died. They understood now why the white scout's face was painted in the Lakota way, and he saw the acceptance in their expressions. Lisa favored him with a kind look and Johnny's face shone with pride for his friend.

They thought they knew it all.

As Bat continued, telling briefly of the return journey, Hardeman readied himself for the moment when he would have an opportunity to speak. He was bone-weary, although his wounds were healing well enough; the persistent exhaustion depleted his spirit as much as it weakened his flesh, but he knew he must gather himself for one last effort before he could give in to the fatigue and let go completely. It was in preparation for this moment that he had risen from his pony drag to enter the Sun Band's village on horseback, and he had thought long and hard about what he wished to say.

On the morning after the battle he had awakened on a jouncing travois. For a time he had not known where he was or how he had been wounded, but the pain in his shoulder had convinced him that he was alive and awake, not dreaming or already beyond the cares of the flesh and its place in the earthly realm. Before long a Sioux squaw had come into sight, looking down on him from horseback, and he had recognized the woman who had cut the soldier's private parts. It had come back to him then, the screams and the scene of torture and his shot that had ended it. Oddly enough, the woman had smiled at him. She urged her horse forward and rode out of sight, and a short while later Bat Putnam came into view, wheeling his horse to ride close behind Hardeman's pony drag. "Reckoned we might lose you, pilgrim," Bat said, and he too smiled. Hardeman had been too weak to make any response and Bat rode near the pony drag in silence for a time. "Well," he said at last, "I reckon you'll be needin' yer rest." And then he had added, "By the by, we give that young feller a proper restin' place; the soldier feller. Built him a scaffold on the benchland. Wrapped him in a cavalry horse blanket. Laid a pistol and a carbine by his side. Wasn't much, but we done what we could fer him." And then he had ridden off to leave Hardeman alone.

Hardeman had been unable to fathom Bat's good will

and the absence of recriminations, but he had lacked the strength to unravel those mysteries just then. Soon afterward, he had dozed off again. For much of that first day he had slept, and when he was not sleeping he had lain on the pony drag, letting it take him where it might, while he allowed his mind to drift freely, empty of thoughts and plans. All his thoughts and plans of recent weeks had failed him and brought him nothing, and he was content to do no more than simply exist, leaving his fate in the hands of others.

But as the journey lengthened and his strength began to return under the care of the Oglala healer, Iron Necklace, one by one the men came to see him, almost as if these visits were some kind of ritual, and each man in his own way had made it understood that he had Hardeman's welfare at heart and wished the white man a full recovery. Little Hand had surprised him by delivering his saddlebags, which he had thought lost for good, into his hands. The warrior had made signs to say that he had found them in the village, in the wreckage of Kills Fox's tipi. One of the bags was scorched on the outside but the contents were unharmed.

Standing Eagle was the last to pay his respects, but he too came, and he too brought a gift, which he held up for Hardeman to see before laying it on the pony drag beside the saddlebags. It was the remains of the scout's Sharps rifle. Kills Fox's lodge must have contained gunpowder, for the buffalo gun had been near the source of a powerful explosion. The stock was blown completely away and the barrel was bent. "Ain't much use in it now," Standing Eagle said, "but I reckoned you might want it. This gun saved my boy's life, and I'm beholden for that. Didn't say so before." The war leader's countenance had not been entirely free of suspicion and distrust of the white man.

The expression of gratitude seemed to discomfort him and as soon as he had delivered it he took his leave.

The attitude of the Indians had perplexed Hardeman all the more. Why did they no longer blame him for shooting the wounded trooper? And beyond that, surely they suspected why he had left the Cheyenne village in the dark of night, before the battle. Bat himself had said as much. Was it possible that his attempt to save Blackbird from death at the hands of the soldiers had wiped out any blame for what had gone before, and even for his robbing them of their torture victim later? He was sure that could not be the full explanation for their generous treatment of him now, but he had no inkling of their true reasons until one evening when the little band was making camp on the south fork of Crazy Woman's Creek after a long day's march. They had traveled for five days since leaving the battle site, making fair time despite the pony drags, and there was talk that they might reach the Sun Band's village the next evening, or the morning after that. While the men and women went about making fires and small shelters for the night camp, Hardeman's pony drag was placed close to Blackbird's. The travois bearing Hawk Chaser's body was left some distance away. The first two days after the battle had been bitterly cold and transporting the body had presented no problems, but as the weather warmed, the warrior's corpse thawed in the daytime and at night it was unwrapped to refreeze quickly and slow its decay. Removing their dead and wounded from the field of battle was a point of honor among the Sioux and they were taking special pains in Hawk Chaser's case.

Hardeman and Blackbird had seen each other several times during the journey, at one resting place or another, but Blackbird had been as much weakened by his wounds as Hardeman and they had spoken little, other than to inquire about each other's progress.

"You are well today?" Blackbird asked on this occasion, as he had done before, practicing his English on the white scout.

"I'm some better," Hardeman acknowledged. "Iron Necklace has a way with wounds. Dunno why he makes such a fuss over me."

Blackbird was surprised at the white man's tone. "You are one of us," he said. "Iron Necklace is *wapíye*, a healer. He would care for any of us the same."

"I'm not one of you, boy," Hardeman said, more harshly than he had intended. "You best understand that. Everything I did, I had my own reasons, and they're not the same as yours."

Blackbird nodded. "My uncle Lodgepole explained this to us on the night of the fight—the battle, you call it? Your shot made me awake and I looked out of the little hut, the healing lodge. I saw the dead *washíchun* soldier and the men around you like wolves. Then you fell, and my uncle Lodgepole caught you. He brought you—carried you—to the healing lodge. He asked Iron Necklace to care for you. Little Hand said that when you are well he will torture you because you shot the soldier, and my father . . ." Blackbird hesitated and dropped his gaze. "My father said the same. My uncle Lodgepole stood before the healing lodge and he spoke to them. 'My friends,' he said, 'the *washíchun* do not think as we do. Their soldiers are not taught to die bravely in the way we understand. Some die well in battle, but they do not understand the chance a warrior is given when he is taken by the enemy. The white scout has told our way to the bluecoat and you have seen that the bluecoat was brave then.' 'The white scout shot the bluecoat,' said Little Hand. He is very angry still. 'Yes,' said

Lodgepole. 'He knew what we did to the bluecoat, but our way is not his. When the *washíchun* take an enemy alive they put him away in the iron house. Spotted Tail, the uncle of Crazy Horse, was in the whiteman's iron house for many years and you know how he changed. The *washíchun* think it is good to change a man like that, breaking his spirit. They do not understand our way, giving a man a chance to die bravely, with a strong spirit.'

"Then my father said . . ." Again the young man hesitated, but he forced himself to look Hardeman in the eye as he continued. "My father said, 'Let him die. He is *washíchun*, and no longer a pipe carrier.' 'That is true,' Lodgepole said, 'but he saved your son's life. A warrior died to save him, and he is a guest in our camp.' And then my uncle told them a story of Sitting Bull when he was a young man. He killed a *Kanghí* woman with an arrow, they say. She was a captive of the Lakota, but she was a woman who gave herself to many men, not clean enough to be taken into the band. 'Adopted' is the word? The women wanted to burn her, and they started a fire, but Sitting Bull did not wish to see the torture, so he shot the *Kanghí* woman with an arrow and the people accepted this. Lodgepole told the story and he said to my father and the other men, 'A man does what he must. It is for other men to understand and accept, the Ancient Ones have said so.' "

Hardeman saw how the simple tale had made it impossible for Standing Eagle and the other men to judge him any differently than they would have judged one of their own kind who had killed a captive in similar circumstances, and, beyond that, how it compelled a broader acceptance of the white man's different ways and customs. He was well aware of Bat's crucial role in guiding this response. Without the mountain man's thoughtful words to calm their passions, the warriors would have acted on instinct, and Hardeman's body would have been rotting on a scaffold beside the dead soldier, or it might simply have been left on the battlefield for the wolves and coyotes. His life had been saved by Bat's friendship, which he had cast away like an old boot on the night after the battle, and he saw that his willingness to discard that friendship, and any further concern for the Indians along with it, had been born of despair—a despair that arose from his own failure.

On the journey back he had been raised from despair by men who had every reason to regard him as a mortal enemy.

A man does what he must. It is for other men to understand and accept. Was it possible that any people could embrace that simple principle as completely as the Lakotas appeared to do? Hardeman had gone off to find Crook, intending to lead the soldiers to Sitting Bull and force a surrender; he had hoped it could be done without bloodshed, but if the attempt had gone awry he might easily have been the instrument of more deaths than were caused by Crook's troopers in the Cheyenne village. His traveling companions did not know the details of his intentions, but they suspected, and yet they had continued to accept his presence among them and they had sustained him in his time of need. If they had known the whole truth, would they have been so understanding? Would Bat still have spoken in his defense? He had no way of knowing. But they had treated him more than fairly, and as the little band's journey neared its end he had resolved to repay their generosity as best he could. There was little enough he could do now. With Crook no doubt pursuing the campaign against the hostiles, there was scant hope that any of the terms reached at the council in Two Moons' village could be salvaged. The simple question now was, could the Sun Band be kept out of the fighting?

Bat brought his narrative to an end and there was a thoughtful silence in the lodge as the men considered all they had heard. Hardeman saw how some of the councillors glanced at him, to all appearances kindly disposed toward this stranger in their midst. Sun Horse kept his gaze on the white scout for several long moments, nodding thoughtfully. Hardeman looked at Blackbird, resting on his litter, and the boy smiled at him. As much as by the tale the youth had told him, Hardeman had been impressed by the boy's ability to tell it in English. Clearly, Bat Putnam had been taking pains for some time to instruct Blackbird in the white man's tongue. Was it because the mountain man knew that the boy would grow to manhood in a world dominated by the whites? Did Sun Horse realize this as well? Hardeman hoped so. The sooner the Sun Band came to accept that fact, however unpleasant it seemed to them, the sooner they would accept the only course left to them now.

Standing Eagle reached into his robes and drew forth a beaded pipe bag similar to the one in which Little Hand had carried the pipe for Sitting Bull. Without opening the bag he handed it to Sun Horse, and then he spoke.

"My friends, this was the pipe for Three Stars. I have returned it to my father and I am a pipe carrier no longer. I speak now as war leader of Sun Horse's camp." He drew himself up and looked around the gathering, and it seemed he was glad to be rid of the burden he had carried for so long. "When the bluecoats had destroyed the Shahíyela village, there were none who spoke of peace. 'Now it is war,' He Dog said. He has gone to join his *hunká*-brother Crazy Horse, and all the Oglala went with him, save these men and their families, who have relatives here." He

gestured at Iron Necklace and the two other Oglala men.
"Two Moons also spoke of war. 'The Shahíyela were at
peace with the whites,' he said. 'Now we will fight beside
our brothers the Lakota. It is better to leave our bones on
the prairie than to surrender to men who make war on the
helpless ones.' He sent his young men on the bluecoats'
trail to try to recapture the horses the bluecoats stole, and I
wished to go with them! I wanted to chase the bluecoats
and fight them again to punish them for what they did!"
He looked around him, seeking approval, and he saw some
men nodding in agreement, their faces dark with anger.
But others turned away. They had heard the pipe carriers'
tale and they knew Standing Eagle had fought in the battle.
Even while he carried a pipe of peace the war leader had
taken up arms, and so the power of the pipe was broken. It
would seem that Standing Eagle had never believed in his
mission, and perhaps that was why it had failed.

Standing Eagle continued, his voice calmer, but still
proud. "On the day after the fight we started upstream
along the Powder and we met the Shahíyela warriors returning. They had taken back many of the horses and the
bluecoats did not come after them!" The men who sided
with Standing Eagle voiced their delight on hearing this
news, and Standing Eagle smiled. "It seems that Three
Stars does not like to fight when the warriors come against
him and there are no helpless ones to hinder them. Perhaps
he has already gone from our country. I do not know
where he is now, but I know this: if we stand strong
against him, we can whip him!" His manner grew more
serious now. "My friends, before you sent us with the
pipes, you said that if we failed, you would take the
people to Dakota to make peace with the whites. Well, my
friends, the Shahíyela were at peace with the *washíchun*
and you have heard what the bluecoats did to them! The

Shahíyela lodges are burned and the helpless ones are homeless. They go to Crazy Horse, asking for food and clothing and shelter. Will you still make peace with the men who have done this? Will you have us become beggars who must go from place to place with our hands out?'' He looked at his listeners, demanding an answer with his eyes, and then he gave his own reply. ''No, my friends, there can be no talk of peace with the *washíchun* now. We are Lakota! Let us live as the Lakota have always lived! Let us prepare to fight! Let us show the bluecoats we are men!''

There were some *hau*'s of approval now, but many men remained silent, and the division in the lodge became more plain to see when Elk Leggings spoke next.

''I am a councillor of Sun Horse's camp,'' he began, formally stating his right to speak. ''I am father of the *wichasha wakán* Sees Beyond, who prepared the pipes of peace with Sun Horse. I have the right to advise our people, but I do not speak now to tell others what to do. Each must decide for himself. I will go to Dakota when the snows melt. If the *washíchun* want war, there will be war. If we fight the whites, our power as a band is broken. Our power is to understand the *washíchun*, not fight them, and by understanding them, to find the way to peace.''

There were murmurs of agreement, and before they had died away the scout Walks Bent Over straightened his head on his misshapen shoulders and began to speak.

''My friends,'' he said, ''Standing Eagle has reminded us that before we sent the pipe carriers we agreed to surrender if they failed. Well, my friends, they have failed and war has begun. Have you changed your minds? Do you see some way to avoid surrender and still keep our power as a band? If so, tell me what it is! I wish to know!

For myself, I see only two ways: we must surrender or we must fight.''

From the back of the lodge came a voice. "To fight the *washíchun* is to fight the whirlwind! Sun Horse has said so himself!''

The sounds of agreement were loud now and all eyes turned toward the headman to see if he would confirm his own words, but Sun Horse made no reply and it was Hardeman who finally spoke. He cleared his throat and got slowly to his feet so all could see him, even those in the back. He glanced at Bat Putnam and then he began to talk, and Bat put his words into Lakota.

"You asked me to go with Standing Eagle and Lodgepole and the others, and I went with them because I wanted peace between our peoples, just as you did. In Two Moons' village I saw great men meet to decide on peace or war, and they chose peace. They were willing to give up much, and I believe Three Stars would have accepted the terms. On both sides there are good men who want peace, men like Sun Horse and Three Stars, and Little Wolf and Two Moons. Even Crazy Horse and Sitting Bull, who have fought hard to defend their people, agreed to the council's terms because they saw a chance for peace with honor, without surrender.'' Hardeman struggled to keep hold of the thoughts he had marshaled so carefully, which threatened to desert him now as his tired mind tried to place one after the next for greatest effect. He was painfully aware of the need to speak well if he hoped to make an impression on these men. "I hoped that the good men could sit down together and talk quietly, and I hoped they could prevent this war. But General Crook found us before we found him. His soldiers attacked the village and now the fighting has started.''

Some of the listeners made soft sounds of agreement.

They shared the whiteman's disappointment. They too had hoped for peace and had seen their hopes dashed. But the white scout had done his best, as had all of the pipe carriers; it was not his fault the fighting had begun.

Hardeman heard the sympathy in their voices and he knew they were not prepared for what he would say next.

"Even if the soldiers hadn't come, even if we had found Three Stars in time and he had gone from the country now, there would still have been war."

This surprised the councillors. What did the whiteman mean? He himself had supported the terms in Two Moons' council and had said they might keep the peace. What was this new talk of war?

Hardeman looked at Sun Horse, and he directed his next words to the old man. "You know that the whites fear any gathering of the bands, but still you called for all the Lakotas to come together in the summertime. I know you did this because you believe that peace as well as war can come from strength, but the white man fear your strength. They wouldn't wait to see if you spoke of peace or war. They would look at a gathering like that and they would be afraid; when a white man is afraid, he fights." He raised his eyes and looked around at the other councillors. "Elk Leggings has said that when the white men want war, there will be war, and he's right. But it's not only the whites who love war." His eyes stopped on Standing Eagle and then moved on. "There are many Lakotas who talk of fighting instead of peace."

There were a few soft *hau*'s from those who opposed the war leader's fiery talk.

Hardeman was glad that some, at least, could admit the truth of what he said, and he moved along quickly to press his advantage. "In a great summer gathering the warriors would see the lodges filling the valley bottoms and the pony herds covering the hillsides''—he was caught up in his speechmaking now and he made broad gestures with his one good hand to indicate the extent of the huge encampment—''and they would think that nothing could break the strength of the Lakota nation. Some men would still speak for peace, but would the others listen? Would the warriors accept the terms from Two Moons' council?''

From Sun Horse's expression, he saw that the old man had had these same doubts himself. He waited a moment to let the headman ponder them again, and then he continued.

''One way or another, the summer gathering would have meant war. I knew this the same way a man knows that the sun will rise in the east, and so I tried to prevent it. I left the village alone and no one knew where I had gone. I went to find Three Stars. If I had found him, I would have led him to Chalk Buttes, to the camp of Sitting Bull.''

The councillors reacted to this news with surprise and anger, and Hardeman raised his voice to make himself heard above the hubbub. ''Not to fight him! To surround him and make him surrender, so there would be no summer gathering! It was the only way to save the peace terms!''

Bat too had raised his voice to make the translation heard, and when the councillors understood Hardeman's last words, they quieted their protests, willing to listen again, but there was no kindness now in the faces that watched him, except, strangely, in the expression of Sun Horse. His look was so benevolent and vague that Hardeman was not sure the old man had all his wits about him.

''With Sitting Bull taken captive, and no gathering of the bands, the whites would think they had won a great victory,'' he told the councillors. ''They would no longer fear you. They might have let you keep this country here, or a part of it. They might even have given you the agency you've always wanted. To keep that hope alive, I would have betrayed Sitting Bull to Three Stars. But I never got a chance. I found the soldiers' tracks and I followed them, but it was too late. The fighting had started and I couldn't stop it.''

The hostility that had greeted his confession of what he had planned to do when he went off alone had dwindled. The men who sided with Standing Eagle still looked at Hardeman with dark faces but the others now revealed something akin to despair, as if they understood what he had done and why, and saw his failure as yet one more chance for peace snatched away by an unkind fate. These men were in the majority, and it was to them that Hardeman spoke now.

''There is no more chance for peace without surrender. You know we met Three Stars' wagons when we were on his trail. There were eighty wagons, all carrying the things he needs to make war. He sent them back to wait for him somewhere.'' He looked at Standing Eagle again. ''That's why Three Stars went upstream. He wasn't running away. He went to his wagons. With new supplies he'll turn back to fight again. He'll keep after the war leaders until he catches them. If he doesn't find them now, he'll keep on through the summer and the fall and winter, if that's what it takes. The war may be long and the men on both sides will fight hard, but in the end it won't matter how many warriors you send against Three Stars, because he will win. Even if you kill a hundred or a thousand soldiers, there will be another hundred or another thousand to take their places, and Three Stars won't give up. That's not his way of making war and it's not the white man's way. When the white man starts fighting, he keeps on fighting until his enemy surrenders.''

Hardeman felt his strength failing, but he had little more to say. He turned to Sun Horse. "You wanted to make peace not only for your own people but for all the Lakotas. Now it's too late to save the Sioux nation. You can only save yourselves, and there's just one way to do that. You'll have to surrender."

He sat down, glad it was over. He had done what he could. He had told them the whole truth as he knew it; it was all he had left to give, to repay the Sun Band for trusting him. They knew everything now, and they could judge him however they wished. Like Sun Horse, he too had hoped to make a far-reaching peace, one that would embrace not only the Sioux but the Cheyenne and Arapaho and all the whites as well, and bring an end to war in the northern territories. But he had failed. If the Sun Band would heed his advice and remove themselves to a place of safety, that would be a small achievement, hardly noticeable in the bloodshed that was sure to come, but it would be something.

No one spoke at once to contradict his words, and his hopes rose. Maybe they would see that he had spoken the truth and there was no other way left to the Sun Band. Bat was looking at him, and Lisa and Johnny too. Later he would talk to them and make them understand, if they didn't already. First he would have to sleep. Right now, he could barely remain upright.

The only sounds in the lodge were the crackling of the fire, where the strips of buffalo fat had melted into pools that occasionally spat and hissed beneath the flames, and the noise of men blowing softly through their empty smoking pipes as they waited to see who would speak. Gradually their attention came to rest on Sun Horse. His was the one voice they all wished to hear, the one voice that could change whatever decisions the councillors had reached in their own minds, if his words were persuasive.

Sun Horse was aware of the attention and he knew he must speak now, but still he did not know what to advise. It was as if nothing had changed since the Snowblind Moon was young, when the white scout and the One Who Stands Between the Worlds had first come to the Sun Band's village. The choice remained the same: surrender or fight. Could there be any other path left open now? Walks Bent Over had said not, and Hardeman believed there was only one choice—surrender. The pipe carriers had failed, the war had begun, and by the council's previous decision the Sun Band should go to Dakota and surrender. But the whole band would not go; those who favored fighting would go north with Standing Eagle and Little Hand and the band would be broken. Sun Horse knew his son would never surrender now; he would rather die, and there were others like him.

Yet the pipe carriers had not failed entirely. Unless Three Stars found each of the Powder River bands and defeated them all in turn, there would still be a great council in the Moon of Fat Calves; even now Sitting Bull's news riders might be spreading the word. Many would heed the call, hoping that in the strength of the Lakota nation they would be safe. In his heart, Sun Horse wished to go too, for he knew it might be the last time the nation's hoop was raised. And still he wished to address the council. *Will the warriors accept the peace terms from Two Moons' council?* Hardeman had asked. Sun Horse did not know the answer, but he did know that no man or group of men could deny the people the right to come together to talk and listen. It was for the people to decide such great issues, each man deciding for himself. That was the Lakota way. But Sun Horse knew that if he counseled the Sun

Band to stay out now, hoping to avoid the soldiers and reach the great gathering unharmed, some like Elk Leggings would go to Dakota soon, unwilling to take their families where there might be further fighting, and still the band would be broken.

Sun Horse clung to a stubborn hope that there must be another way, some way to keep the band together and the chance for peace alive. It was more than a hope, it was a suspicion that gnawed at him, causing a pain almost as troubling as a wound in the body. It seemed to him that the answer to his dilemma was closer than ever before, as if it lay in something he had heard here today. Yet it hid from him still, as a young man hid in his robe and waited along the river trail until a young woman came for water. The solution was simple, Sun Horse felt certain. Perhaps so simple that he had overlooked it all this time. What could it be? Somewhere lay the path to his power, but he could not find it.

Another pain troubled him too—the constant knot of hunger that had twisted his belly all day. He had not felt it in many days, not since the first period of fasting. The body grew accustomed to the lack of food and the spirit grew light, rising to the place Sun Horse sought, a place free from the limits of the flesh where he might see clearly, but the hunt and the meat it had brought to the village offered him too many reminders of food, the smells of *pte,* both raw and cooked, and the sounds of happy people who for a time at least were well fed. His stomach growled at him now, reminding him of his flesh and its frailty, making it even harder for him to bring some order to the conflicting thoughts that troubled him. The meat posed another puzzle: all was not as it had been when the Snowblind Moon was young; *pte* had returned, a good sign; the village was strong again, but how was that strength

to be used? Could it provide a solution to the most immediate challenge—how to assure that the band would remain
united? Throughout his fast Sun Horse had felt his people
slipping away from him, and he had despaired. That was
what he must prevent above all.

He placed a hand on Standing Eagle's shoulder to brace
himself and he struggled to his feet. He moved his free
hand in an arc that took in Standing Eagle and Little Hand,
Blackbird where he lay on his litter, Hardeman and
Lodgepole and the Oglalas. "These travelers are tired,"
he said. "They must eat and rest now. We have heard
their words and we have much to think on. We too must
rest before we decide what to do. My grandson will come
with me to my lodge and I will care for his wounds.
Sometimes the young see more clearly than older men and
I would hear him tell everything he has seen." Sun Horse
did not know whence came the sudden desire to hear
Blackbird's version of the journey, but he knew that he
wanted to speak with the boy beyond Standing Eagle's
hearing, particularly to know what he had to say about
Hardeman and the council at the Shahíyela village.

"Let those who have much meat take some to the
lodges of these men, who were not here for the hunt. The
pte have returned to the Sun Band, and *pte* is the source of
life. We will eat, warm in our lodges, and tonight we will
sleep well. Tomorrow we will meet again." The thought
of food sent an insistent rumble through his stomach. He
would have to eat soon. He had passed the point at which
fasting helped to clear his mind.

He remained standing, and now others rose. Those near
the entrance began to file out of the lodge. The men would
return to their own tipis where they would eat again, and
then they would visit among themselves to talk. Some
would come to see Sun Horse, if the crossed sticks were

removed from the entrance to his lodge. Tonight the councillors would enjoy their wives and sleep the contented sleep of a full belly, and tomorrow they would return to the council lodge. They would be strong in their opinions but they would not agree on what to do. As never before the band needed a leader to guide it. Once again, Sun Horse had managed to delay committing himself to one course or another, but he knew he could not delay much longer, not if he wished to guide the destiny of his band and keep it whole.

As Standing Eagle rose he handed Sun Horse his oakwood cane. The old man gripped it firmly and turned his back to the fire to store up some warmth before going out into the wind and snow. Standing Eagle pulled Blackbird's buffalo robe up about the boy's chin in preparation for carrying him across the camp to Sun Horse's lodge, where the pipe carriers would eat soon.

Bat got stiffly to his feet. For once, he hoped the welcoming meal would not take long. He and Standing Eagle and Little Hand all had families waiting, but custom decreed that the travelers should accept the hospitality of the headman's lodge after a long journey made on the band's behalf. Bat was glad to be home and he wanted nothing more than to retire to his own lodge and be alone with Penelope. But she understood and she would wait for him. She had always waited for him, from the beginning.

Lisa moved to Bat's side and she took one of his hands, squeezing it with both of her own. "I'm glad you're back. I've missed you."

He put a long arm around her. "You heard how it went. Could of been better, but we're safe and sound. All but one." She hugged him close and they were quiet for a moment. "We heard about the avalanche afore we put out. Looks like you're stuck with them circus folks."

"They're digging out the river road. It will be clear in a few more days."

Bat's eyebrows went up. "That so? That's a piece o' work." He looked at the councillors filing out of the lodge, then back at Lisa. "You'll stay fer sump'n to eat?"

"I think we better not. Hutch and I came to pack some meat from the hunt. We should be getting on before the storm breaks."

"We'll send word what the council decides. Might be I'll bring it over myself in a day or two." He didn't say that he might bring Penelope as well, and their lodge, and that he might be leaving the Sun Band for good if they decided to go to Dakota.

"I'd take it kindly if you'd wait long enough for me to grab a bite or two, Miss Putnam." Hardeman had managed to get to his feet unaided. "My fire's just about gone out and I better stoke it up before I head on. That is, if I can impose on your hospitality again."

"Of course," she replied uncertainly.

"Well, time's a-wastin'," Bat said, and he moved to help Standing Eagle with Blackbird's litter. Each man took hold of one end and they rose in unison, holding the litter between them. Bat was in the lead and he was about to step out of the lodge when Hutch and Chatur entered, looking around for Johnny Smoker.

Bat smiled at Hutch. "You gettin' any work done, or you spendin' all yer time with them circus girls?"

Hutch blushed at the accuracy of Bat's guess. "Oh, Julius keeps a person busy, what with calving and feeding and all. We're looking after the circus stock too."

Bat grinned. "I reckon them fillies need lookin' after."

"What spare time I got, Johnny's been learnin' me to rope."

"He's a good learner, too," Johnny put in, slipping into

his blanket coat, which he had removed when the council lodge grew warm. "He already knows most everything I do."

"He's gonna learn me about horses next," Hutch added.

"Hmmp. Take you some time to learn all he knows 'bout them," said Bat. With that he bent over and stepped through the entrance, being careful to keep the litter level.

By now all the councillors were gone from the lodge. Sun Horse moved close to Lisa and took her arm. He spoke briefly and she heard him out before translating for Hardeman.

"Sun Horse says there is no need for you to ride any farther today. He invites you to stay here, in his lodge. He says you have traveled far enough and you need to rest." Hardeman's painted face unnerved her. She felt that she was talking to a stranger.

Hardeman looked at the old man and shook his head. "You thank him for me, if you would. Tell him I've got a mind to sleep in a real bed for a change."

He did not give his true reason for refusing. Tired as he was, he felt compelled to go on until he had left behind Sun Horse and the Indians and all the reminders of his failure. He had started his fruitless journey in Putnam's Park and he wished to end it there, where he could disappear into a back room and sleep until the events of recent weeks seemed no more than a troubling dream. "Tell him one more thing," he said. "Tell him he can't stay here forever. He's running out of time."

Lisa and Sun Horse spoke back and forth and Lisa turned back to Hardeman. "He says when the day comes for the Sun Band to leave this place, they will leave."

Hardeman addressed Sun Horse directly now. "If the army finds you they won't sit down to talk, not now that the fighting's started." He turned to Lisa, losing patience.

"Can't you make him see that? He's got to understand that there's no more time!"

She kept silent, unable to add her voice to Hardeman's plea but no longer able to oppose him. There seemed to be little enough hope for the Sun Band and yet now at least they had meat. The Snowblind Moon was gone and soon they could safely move. What did Sun Horse intend to do? She knew that he had purposely delayed a council decision today, but why? If he hoped to avoid surrender, why didn't he tell his people what he had in mind?

Sun Horse looked up at the peak of the council lodge where the wind buffeted the smoke flaps. Flakes of snow swirled into the smoke hole and evaporated in the warm air. He smiled benignly at Hardeman and spoke to him.

"He says the winter spirit is not ready to go back to his lodge," Lisa explained. "He saw the new moon last night for the first time. They call it the Moon When the Ducks Come Back. He says the ducks will be late this year. As long as the cold winds blow, the Sun Band will stay here. He invites you to return here when you're rested. He says Blackbird will be glad to see you. He says the true man of peace is always welcome in his lodge."

To Hardeman it seemed that Lisa was not certain he deserved this title or the invitation that accompanied it.

Sun Horse moved toward the entrance, motioning them to follow, saying a few words over his shoulder.

"We must come and eat now," said Lisa. "He says we all need the strength of the buffalo. I gather they attach some spiritual significance to this hunt. They credit Johnny and Amanda with bringing the buffalo back to the Sun Band."

Hardeman nodded, too tired to protest further. There it was again, the talk of spirit power coming from Johnny. No doubt Sun Horse was praying daily to the buffalo or the north wind or the snow gods, or whatever spirits he still hoped might offer some help to the band. But in the end all the prayers and dreams and spirits and imagined manifestations of heavenly intervention would only serve to assure the band's eventual destruction if false hopes delayed their surrender. Hardeman had expended the last measure of his reason in an effort to make Sun Horse see that he must admit defeat, and still the old man was stalling for time. Hardeman could do no more. If the Sun Band sought an early entry at the gates of Perdition, they would have to find their way alone.

Sun Horse stepped out of the lodge and waited for the others beside the entrance. They gathered around him and moved along in a group, Sun Horse leaning on Lisa's arm. Snow was falling thickly. The sky was as dark as dusk although it was midday. The wind was gentle but the occasional strong gusts hinted that the storm was still gathering force on the mountain slopes and would descend in its fury before long.

"You want me to ride over to the park with you?" Johnny asked Hardeman. He pulled his hat down low to keep the snow out of his eyes.

"There's no need. You stay here and take care of that girl. Get that talking done."

Johnny seemed relieved. "You'll be there for a few days? Amanda and I will come over when the storm's done. The circus is going to give a performance before they go. I know she'd like you to see it."

"I'll be there."

"They'll still want a guide when they head out. You think you might go with them?"

"Me? No idea, Johnny, none at all." It was the simple truth. Until this moment, Hardeman had never given a particle of thought to what he might do once the pipe carriers' journey ended. Just now, putting one foot in front of the other was about the extent of his abilities. He needed no further puzzles to solve. Anything beyond the day at hand was untouchably remote.

He stumbled and caught himself and Johnny took his arm.

"Are you sure you're all right?"

"We'll look after him," Lisa said.

"Between the three of us, we'll get him back home," said Hutch.

Chatur smiled at Johnny. "He will be in good care."

"Oh, I'll be all right," Hardeman grumbled, shaking off Johnny's hand. It annoyed him to be discussed as if he were an invalid, although privately he knew he was not far removed from that condition.

"You're a stubborn man, Mr. Hardeman," Lisa said, and he merely nodded. Her tone managed to convey both a solicitous care for his well-being and a repressed anger. She was probably riled about his plan to betray Sitting Bull to the soldiers, but it couldn't be helped. She had been in the council and she had heard it all.

He realized that he had secretly hoped to return to her with a promise of peace for the Sioux, or at least a future free of warfare for the Sun Band. He had imagined her joy and gratitude and had allowed himself to think that such a deed might win him a place in her affections. But he had failed and she knew the details of his defeat.

The meal in Sun Horse's lodge was quiet. Amanda had fallen asleep again and Sun Horse sat near her in the back of the lodge while his guests ate. He himself took nothing. Elk Calf and Sings His Daughter kept the bowls and platters full, but the food and warmth made Hardeman so drowsy that he could barely hold his head up, and long before he had eaten his fill he rose, preparing to go before he fell sound asleep over his food.

Lisa was quick to follow his example. She cast a meaningful glance at Hutch, who hid his disappointment at having his first meal in an Indian lodge cut short. He was less obvious in his fascination with the Indians and their ways than Chatur, who was still looking about goggle-eyed, but Hutch took it all in with a boyish wonder.

"Well, hoss, you keep yer powder dry," Bat said as Hardeman buttoned his St. Paul coat.

"I'll be seeing you" was all the reply Hardeman could muster.

"More'n likely."

It was a simple exchange, but as Hardeman stepped out of the lodge after a nod to Blackbird and a farewell smile to Johnny, he felt a pleasant satisfaction, as if by those few words he and the mountain man had reaffirmed their friendship. Bat was much like his late brother, and in the understanding that had grown between himself and Bat, Hardeman saw a chance to redeem that other friendship, which he had neglected until it was lost to him. It didn't do to cast friends carelessly aside. Hardeman had wished to do just that after the battle, but Bat had refused to let go and Hardeman was grateful to him.

He followed Lisa to the horses and he saw that a mount had been brought there for him, a pinto from the Sun Band's herd, provided with a saddle. He wondered what had become of his roan after the battle. Probably some Indian had him now, unless the soldiers had taken the roan away with the Cheyenne ponies. The pinto looked small beside the large American horses. While the guests ate, the pack horses had been laden with cuts of buffalo.

Lisa started off in the lead, setting a brisk pace, and Hardeman kept close behind her while Hutch and Chatur brought up the rear with the pack horses. The wind had found its stride now, and the snow flew across the ground. As the riders crossed the divide that separated the Indian valley from Putnam's Park they had to cling to their hats, but as they descended the far slope the wind grew less severe. The snow thickened, obscuring all but the closest patches of trees and revealing nothing at all of the hills and mountains above. Hardeman had thought that he remembered the trail well, but he realized that in his present state he could easily have become lost without Lisa Putnam to guide him. It discomforted him to feel so helpless, but he gave up trying to determine where he was and allowed his head to nod while the pinto plodded along after Lisa's horse.

He felt a hand on his arm and he jerked awake to find Hutch riding beside him, supporting him by his elbow. He had gone to sleep and had very nearly fallen.

After that one of the others rode next to him, talking to him occasionally to be sure he was awake. He forced himself to breathe deeply and sit straight in the saddle. He was determined to make it under his own steam to the Big House and whatever bed he first set eyes on. He rolled his left shoulder and felt the pain start again. He had almost forgotten the wound. He willed the pain to keep him awake, but even that trick threatened to fail him now. Like a horse that had run for too long, his will was growing winded and had begun to slow down. With no hands at the reins it would soon come to a halt of its own accord.

Just a little while longer, he told himself, but his body seemed to belong to someone else. Even the snowflakes that stung his face could not hold his attention.

This time he did fall, landing on the wounded shoulder. Lisa was off her horse and beside him in an instant, helping him to his feet. "He'll have to ride with you," she told Hutch. "You hold on to him. I'll lead his horse."

"I'm all right," Hardeman insisted. He commanded his body to mount the pinto and it obeyed. The pain in his shoulder was sharp now. He started off at once, trusting the horse to find a path through the trees. He heard the others coming along behind him, but he did not look back.

The snow thinned a little and the surroundings seemed more familiar. He came out of the trees suddenly and saw the settlement before him and he reined the pinto to a halt to take in the sight. The storm clouds covered the valley solidly, supported by the ridges. The circus wagons and tents were arranged in rows near the barn, their peaked roofs covered with snow. There were footpaths among the wagons, more paths leading to the house and barn. There was a sense of permanence about it all; the circus was part of the settlement now. Lights shone in many windows, where lamps had been lit against the gloom of the day. Smoke came from a dozen chimneys, large and small. The scene was peaceful and welcoming, and Hardeman smiled. The feeling that arose in him was one he had almost forgotten, one he had not experienced since he was a boy back in Pennsylvania, before he got the urge to wander. Here in this small valley where Jed Putnam had planted his dream and made it grow, Hardeman felt at home.

He knew he was slipping from the saddle again but he didn't care. Here at last he could rest.

CHAPTER SIX

While those in his lodge slept, Sun Horse stepped out into the storm and walked around the camp circle, aided by his oakwood cane. Night had fallen and the wind was strong. It tugged at his robe. He pulled the old buffalo hide over his head and held it close beneath his chin to shelter his face from the driving snow. He moved around the circle as the sun moved around the sky, pausing at the cardinal points. His own lodge stood in the west, opposite the entrance to the camp; the power of the west was to make live and destroy, and resolving this paradox lay at the heart of his search. Would the band be destroyed or would it live? The north was the region of cold and death, but it was also the power of the north to cleanse and heal, and it was for this power that he prayed tonight. At the horns of the camp he stopped to chant a short prayer to the east, praying for the power of true understanding, the under-standing that led to peace. The south offered the power to grow and he needed that power too, so his people could

149

grow and change and remain strong through whatever was to come.

When he reached his lodge again he passed it by, stabbing the ground with his cane and hastening himself along impatiently, careless of the cold and wind. He had no more time to retreat into reflections and prayers, no more time to ponder his life and the elusive nature of the *washíchun*. He must decide what to do! Tomorrow the council would meet again and they would demand to know his decision. There could be no more delays.

Your power is in this world. Use it for the people. You can guide them still. Sees Beyond had said this not long ago, just before the whites had arrived in the village with the news that the clown girl was lost.

But how to guide them? Surrender or fight? Nothing had changed.

Everything had changed. Soldiers had attacked a village. The fighting he had hoped to prevent had begun. The pipe carriers had returned. Hawk Chaser was dead.

Just before learning that the clown girl was lost, Sun Horse had cried out to the Great Mystery, asking for a sign that he still had the power to help the people. He had heard a mother quiet a child and he had wondered how that child would eat.

Now there was meat. Were the *pte* the sign he had prayed for? The band was strong again, but how was that strength to be used without leadership to guide it? Which way to turn? To Dakota or to the summer council? And above all, how to keep the band intact?!

Sun Horse continued around the circle until he came once again to the horns of the camp. There he turned and walked straight across the circle to his lodge. The camp circle represented the hoop of the world, and from east to west stretched the black road of worldly troubles. With his troubles heavy upon him, Sun Horse prayed for the power that entered the camp from the east: Oh, *Wakán Tanka*, help me to understand.

If the *pte* were the sign he had asked for, why then was he still at a loss? Why could he not see the meaning of the sign?

Pte, the most sacred of the four-leggeds. The greatest gift to man, for *pte* provided the essentials of life.

In the lodge they all slept on, his white grandson and the clown girl, Blackbird, and his wives. The fire was built up high. The wind buffeted the lodgeskins; it hummed among the lodgepoles where their naked ends rose above the peak into the breath of the storm. Occasionally a few flakes of snow gusted into the smoke hole, only to vanish before they reached the ground.

The lodge shuddered from a strong gust and it seemed to Sun Horse that even the storm was impatient with him. It blew to urge him onward. It brought the air and the village alive. The world was alive around him, howling its impatience. He imagined the men and women of the village awake and gathered in a ring around his lodge, all blowing with the storm, impatient to hear what he would do.

As he sat down by the fire Blackbird raised his head.

"*Hau, Tunkáshila.*" The boy had fallen asleep after Hardeman and Lisaputnam had gone, while the other pipe carriers were still eating. "I didn't mean to sleep," he said. "I wanted to speak with you."

"But you were very tired and so you slept. Now you have rested and we can talk." Sun Horse moved to the boy's side and unwrapped the dressings on his leg. The Shahíyela healer Ice had used his powers well. Soon Blackbird would have the full use of his leg. The newer wound on his side was still angry and swollen but it too would heal well. The soldier's bullet had glanced off a rib, breaking it, but Iron Necklace had bound the youth's midsection tightly and the rib would mend. Either wound could have been fatal without proper care.

"Will I limp, Grandfather?" the boy asked.

Sun Horse smiled. "Perhaps, but you will not be crippled. You will still grow up to be a strong man."

Blackbird looked at the pallet where Johnny Smoker lay asleep. "Your other grandson limps, but he is strong. Before I went away with my father you said something about the strength of the warrior who does not fight."

Sun Horse nodded. "You wished to hear nothing of such strength then."

"Tell me about it now."

"Such a warrior does not conquer by fighting but by the strength he keeps inside himself."

Blackbird knitted his brow and pondered this for a time, and then he said, "I would tell you of our journey, Grandfather. There is something I have learned, but I don't yet know what it is."

Sun Horse felt a small surge of excitement. The boy's words described his own feeling as well. Stronger and stronger within him grew the certainty that he had already learned what he needed to know to make his choice. It lurked somewhere inside him, hiding. Perhaps if he listened to the boy . . . He settled himself and prepared to hear his grandson's tale.

Blackbird began by telling of finding the cavalry's trail and following it, and how the *washíchun* scout Hardeman had wanted to move along quickly while Standing Eagle had seemed to hold back. He told the other events of the trip, each in turn, always being careful to say what he knew from his own experience and what he had learned from others. He passed along quickly to the arrival in Two Moons' village; he spoke of the strength of the Shahíyela camp, the people happy there, and the honor he had felt to be included in the council. And then for the first time Sun Horse heard of Standing Eagle's shocking interruption in the council, speaking loudly for war with the bluecoats even as he carried the pipe of peace. Blackbird left nothing out, telling of He Dog's rebuke and the way Crazy Horse had smoothed away the trouble and made the hearts of the council good again. Blackbird was plainly troubled by what had taken place. He sensed that his father's actions were not those of a man who thought first of the good of the people.

It saddened Sun Horse to hear of these things, but he was not surprised. From the start it seemed that the war leader had not believed in the mission of peace. Why else would he hold back? Could it be that he had actually wished for the bluecoats to find a village and start the war before the pipe carriers could reach them? And once in Two Moons' village, in council with two great Lakota leaders, he had tried to rally them for war, not peace.

Standing Eagle was angry at the whites for all the wrongs they had done to the Lakota, but his anger hurt his own people. It filled his lodge; it filled the councils, no matter if he sat silent or if he spoke. A man should not bring such anger to his people. He should go far away to some place where he could release his anger, and not come among his people again until it was gone. But it was not Standing Eagle's nature to set aside his own passions and think only of the people. Sun Horse had hoped that his only remaining son would change with age, but he saw now that Standing Eagle would not be one of those who chose to set aside the shield and lance and take up the greater burden of leadership. Where then would come the wisdom to guide the Sun Band when he, Sun Horse, was gone?

He took his smoking pipe from the pouch that hung at the back of the lodge and stoked it slowly as he listened to Blackbird tell of waking in the dawn to find his father and uncle gone, catching his horse and seeing the soldiers come riding all in a line, the warning of the blackbirds, and of his part in the battle that followed.

"I was foolish, Grandfather," the boy said, averting his eyes. "When the soldiers passed me without shooting, I thought I would survive the day no matter what I did. But the blackbirds had warned me. 'Fly away!' they said. 'Fly away from the whites!' I didn't listen to them. I forgot that wisdom is more important than strength, and so I charged the soldiers." He looked at Sun Horse, pleading for understanding. "I was the moccasin carrier! My friends and I had some good horses. I wanted to bring them to my father so he would see I was not afraid. Did I do wrong?"

"You did not do wrong."

"A man died because of me," Blackbird said, unwilling to speak Hawk Chaser's name. "Perhaps it was not wrong of me to bring the horses to where the men were fighting. I wanted to help the women get away. But I charged the bluecoats because they killed my friend and I thought they could not hurt me. And because of me the white scout was wounded and a great man died, a man of the people. He rode into the guns of the bluecoats with only a lance! He was strong and wise, and he spoke always of the good of the people. He died for me, but he could have done so much more for them than I can."

"He died that you might live."

"But I am not one of the helpless ones, to be protected by the warriors!"

"You are the future of the people," Sun Horse said, and he felt a sudden chill. It was as if the words had been spoken by another. He heard the truth in the words and he felt the chill of his power moving around him. The feeling reminded him of the day when the Strange-Animal People had arrived in Putnam's Park, the day *wamblí* spoke to him. . . .

"I will miss him, the one who died," Blackbird said. "He used to tell me tales of the people, and I learned from him."

Sun Horse nodded. Hawk Chaser was a storyteller. As an old man he would have entranced the children. But he would never be an old man.

"Who will tell the stories now that he is gone?" the boy asked.

"Others tell the tales."

"But they are the old people."

"In each generation there are those among the young who learn the tales better than the others, those who have the ear to tell them and a way of telling that will make others listen."

"I would like to learn them."

"You know the tales."

Blackbird nodded. "I know them, and I have even told the little children a story sometimes, but I want to be good at it, as he was. I want to be like him, Grandfather."

"Perhaps you shall be."

Blackbird was silent for a time, but then he looked at Sun Horse again. "Another man helped to save me. A *washíchun* came to help me. I do not understand the whitemen, Grandfather. Among the whites there are men as different from one another as the Lakota and the *Kanghí*. I do not understand them!"

"They are very difficult to understand," Sun Horse agreed. "All my life I have tried to understand them and still I know only a little."

"I want to understand them," said Blackbird. "Is it true

that they are without number? And that they will never go away?''

Sun Horse nodded. He had told the boy these things too many times to deny them now.

''In the council at Two Moons' village, Sitting Buffalo Bull and Crazy Horse said that the Lakota and the *washíchun* cannot walk the same path. Their feet cannot touch the same earth, they said. If this is so, how can we survive? If they are so many, surely they will win over us some day?''

''We must survive by making peace,'' said Sun Horse. He felt the chill again, and new hope, born of the change in his grandson.

''If I understood my power better, a man would not have died,'' Blackbird said glumly. ''I thought nothing could hurt me, and I was wrong.''

''You heard the warning of the blackbirds and you flew away as they told you. You did survive the day, and you did nothing wrong. Go to sleep now.'' Sun Horse needed to be alone to put his thoughts in order, but Blackbird was still troubled.

''I have been foolish in another way, Grandfather. One that is even worse. I didn't see it until now.'' The youth was very solemn. ''I thought I had only to be a little older, a little taller, and I would be a man. I wanted to be a warrior like my father so the people would raise their voices when I came back from a fight, and I was angry with the *washíchun* because it seemed they would change the world before I could become a man.''

''And now?'' Sun Horse felt his skin tighten and tingle all over.

''I see that I wanted to be a man and still play as a child plays, thinking only of myself. I am still a child, Grandfather. I have much more to learn.'' He sighed and closed his eyes. ''There is so much to learn about being a man.''

Before long the furrows of worry left his brow and he slept while Sun Horse watched over him.

The old man's stomach rumbled loudly and he became aware of the smells of the welcoming feast, which still lingered in the lodge. There was meat in the pot over the cooking fire. He felt the juices flow in his mouth and he struggled to turn his thoughts away from his hunger. Why had it returned to him now to distract him from his quest for power? His search was no closer to its goal than when he started. . . . Or was it? When he was curing the clown girl he had thrown away the last specks of dust from his vision-hill in an effort to look beyond the symbols of his power, trying to grasp its essence . . . and the clown girl had recovered. His curing power was still strong. What of his power to lead? Perhaps it too was as strong as ever, lacking only the understanding of how to use it. . . .

Even his grandson spoke of power and understanding. It seemed that a power had truly come to Blackbird on the morning of the battle. The helper from his becoming-a-man vision had returned to give him a warning. *Fly away from the whites!* the birds said, *and you will survive the day.* The boy had charged the bluecoats' guns, but his first thoughts had been of the people. Only after he had called a warning to the sleeping village, only after he had taken the horses to a place where they were needed most, did he fling himself into the fight to avenge a fallen comrade. And despite being wounded again, he had survived.

Twice on his journey the boy had been badly wounded. He had been close to death, and he was changed by the experience. He wished to learn the true meaning of manhood now; he wished to learn responsibility for the people. . . .

Sun Horse felt his hopes rise.

Two men had ridden to save the boy from the soldiers.

One Lakota and one white, united in a common purpose. . . .
Why?

Hawk Chaser had died because he was the boy's *hunká*-
father, and one *hunká* would do anything to save another.

And what of the other who rode to save him? Hardeman
had risked his life twice in a single day. He had tried to
stop the fighting and he had failed, but he had been
successful in saving Blackbird. And he had saved another
boy, long ago. It was in his nature to save a boy in trouble
just as it was in his nature to try to make peace. He knew
war and he understood the need for peace. He had been
willing to do anything to achieve it, even betray the trust
that Sun Horse had put in him when he sent him with the
pipe carriers. . . .

But it was not only Sun Horse he would have betrayed if
he had led the soldiers to Sitting Bull! That was plain from
his words here in the council today. He was ashamed of
what he had thought to do. *He would have betrayed himself!*
The action went against his nature. It was not his nature to
betray a trust.

He would have betrayed himself, and of course he had
failed, for a man could not go against his own nature.

It was not in Standing Eagle's nature to make peace
with the whites, and so he had failed when he carried a
pipe of peace. . . .

Sun Horse trembled with the force of the chill that took
him now. Outside, the wind gained force; around him the
lodge trembled; beneath him the earth trembled; the uni-
verse was pregnant with power.

A man cannot go against his nature, neither Lakota nor
washichun. . . .

Three Stars won't give up, Hardeman had told the council. *That's not his way of making war and it's not the*

whiteman's way. When the whiteman starts fighting, he keeps on until his enemy surrenders.

Could it be that Hardeman was right after all and the only possible end was surrender? In the end the whites would be true to their nature; if only conquest would satisfy them, then they would destroy the hoop of the Lakota nation forever and there would be no accommodation, no joining, no living together protected by the sacred tree that stood at the center of the world, where the red and black roads came together.

If this were true, then Sun Horse's quest, his days and nights of searching for the path to peace, had been in vain. If this were true, then *wamblí*'s promise was false, Hears Twice's prophecy was false, his own vision from the butte overlooking the Laramie fort was false, and that could not be! Had not his vision led the people here? Had they not lived in peace for twenty-five snows? Had not Hears Twice's prophecy come true, with the life-giving power of *pte* returned to the band?

The visions and the signs could not be false! They must be true, and they must have a purpose! Had not Blackbird been saved by his vision, his spirit helpers coming to guide him safely through the battle? The boy had nearly died and yet he lived. He had grown a great deal in a short time and his thoughts turned to the good of the people. Why?!

Sun Horse looked at the sleeping youth beside him and he recalled his own words—*You are the future of the people. . . .*

He gasped, and his eyes opened wide in astonishment. For a long moment he remained motionless and then he covered his eyes with his hands and bowed forward where he sat.

He had been blind. As surely as the clown girl, he had been snowblind, made sightless from casting about on all sides, even when the *pte* were found, even when the answer to his search came into his very lodge.

He straightened and opened his eyes, and it seemed to him that he saw for the first time. The sleeping forms around him, the furnishings of the lodge, the fire, even the most familiar objects, appeared newly created and full of hope.

He inhaled deeply, tasting the odor of cooked meat that filled the lodge, the flesh of *pte,* the most sacred of the four-leggeds, and then he began to laugh silently. He shook until he had to hold his sides and he laughed until the tears ran down his cheeks. Except for his broad smile, he might have been crying. His stomach growled and he laughed harder.

Finally the quiet shaking stopped and Sun Horse wiped the tears from his leathery cheeks. He sat looking at Blackbird, smiling still, wishing he could wake the boy to share his good spirits, but his grandson needed to rest and grow strong. When Blackbird awoke in the morning, he would be hungry. Sun Horse would see that he ate well. He would need all his strength for what lay ahead of him.

Blackbird shifted position slightly and began to snore softly, as Standing Eagle had snored when he was a boy, and Sun Horse finally stirred himself. He moved around the fire on his hands and knees, pausing when he reached the sleeping forms of Johnny Smoker and Amanda. He dropped his head low and pawed the ground with one hand, and a new fit of silent laughing overtook him, but he quelled his laughter and grew serious. "Oh, *Tatanka*, thank you for leading my grandson to the clown girl," he whispered. "Truly they have brought a power to help the Sun Band!"

He moved on to where Elk Calf slept and he sat back on his thin shanks when he reached her side. With one wrinkled hand he stroked her face until she opened her eyes. "I will have some broth," he said, smiling, and she looked at him in surprise, coming fully awake in an instant. Tomorrow he would have some roasted meat, but for now just the broth, the life force of *pte*. "And a little liver," he added as Elk Calf sat up. "With gall."

Filled with wonder at the sudden change in her husband, Elk Calf moved the kettle to the center fire and soon the broth was hot. Sun Horse drank one bowl slowly, until his rumbling stomach subsided, and then another, more quickly. With his skinning knife he cut small bites off the liver and dipped them in gall. The yellow gall dripped on his chin and he wiped it away and licked the finger clean. All the time he smiled and said nothing to Elk Calf, but she asked for no explanations. She watched him eat as if she had never seen such a thing before, and when his bowl was placed to show that he wanted nothing more, she returned to her robes. Just as she fell asleep again, she was aware that Sun Horse had left the fire and was slipping beneath Sings His Daughter's robes. Elk Calf smiled. Truly, he was himself once more. When he was ready, he would tell her what he had learned when he was beyond his body and its demands.

Sun Horse fitted himself closely to Sings His Daughter's sleeping form and he felt the smoothness of her skin. His manhood stirred and grew strong and it was this movement that awakened her. She made a sigh of pleasure and moved her buttocks against him, making a place for him between her legs, but he did not take her right away. For a long time he lay close to her, his hands moving very slowly over her body, showing her the peace he felt within him. Finally, when she had nearly gone back to sleep, he enjoyed her gently from the rear and dropped asleep himself, still inside her.

LISA PUTNAM'S JOURNAL

Saturday, March 25th. 12:40 p.m.

Hutch and Julius and I have just returned from feeding. It is blowing a proper blizzard today, although the temperatures remain fairly mild, and the sled got stuck twice in soft drifts. The cattle have taken shelter in the willows. They have survived worse, but I worry about them nevertheless.

The pipe carriers have returned and the war is begun. I am overwhelmed by all that has changed, or I should say by all I have learned, since I sat here to write early yesterday morning. General Crook's soldiers attacked a Cheyenne village on the Powder a week ago and the pipe carriers were there. Mr. Hardeman was wounded in the battle and we have brought him here to recover. (We put him in my bedroom because it is the quietest and most comfortable.) I shall save for another time a detailed account of yesterday's events, the council at Sun Horse's village in which the pipe carriers told their tale, and all I heard there. Today I am full of concern for Sun Horse once more, wondering what he and his advisers will de-cide. They may be meeting even as I write. I fear that with General Crook still in the country they may not be safe even if they decide to surrender. Will he still offer them safe passage if he encounters them now? Sun Horse sug-gested that whatever course they choose they will be in no hurry to leave so long as the wintry weather continues, and now I must admit that I have come to share Mr. Hardeman's impatience. Indians do not experience time in the same manner as a white man. They do not mark its passing as we do, with clocks and calendars, nor are they much given to contemplating what tomorrow may bring until tomorrow itself is here. They pack up and move on not according to any long-standing plan but because the day seems right for it. "When the day comes for the Sun Band to leave this place, we will leave," Sun Horse said. Our way is very different and I am not certain it leads to a better understanding of the world and its doings, but I fear that in the present instance Sun Horse's attitude may endanger his people.

So much uncertainty. I try to go about my work and occupy my mind with the tasks at hand. In that regard the storm is some help, as it makes the world beyond the park seem very remote.

Mr. Tatum is pacing about the saloon, fretting. He fears that his long days of work will be erased by drifting snow. I told him that the river canyon is sheltered and there is not much drifting there, but still he worries and is impa-tient for the storm to end so his men can get back to work. The prospect of imminent departure has created a new excitement among the circus folk, heightened all the more by the preparations for the farewell performance. They all want the show to be top-notch for Amanda's sake. As for

Mr. Tatum, he has not said a word about her to me or anyone else, so far as I can determine. Mr. Chalmers took him aside yesterday and told him of Amanda's intentions, and he got no visible reaction. What can Mr. Tatum be thinking? If it were simply a matter of losing his star performer, I should say he was accepting this turn of events with an admirable stoicism, but because I know the truth about his relationship with Amanda, I find myself awaiting her return with some apprehension. After almost a month of living in close quarters with Mr. Tatum I see a certain unpredictability beneath his polished exterior.

As for Amanda and Johnny's future, I see no reason why they cannot make a successful life together. Johnny has been under Mr. Hardeman's protection and guidance ever since he left the Cheyenne, but he has self-confidence and an independence of mind, and he had already determined to make his own way in the world from now on. With Hutch he has shown an ability to teach, and since finding Amanda in the mountains, he demonstrates a natural tendency to take responsibility for her and to protect her. Perhaps I am prejudiced in his favor because he knows the western territories and understands what is needed for survival here, and I believe those qualities will stand him in good stead wherever he and Amanda may go. They will find no surroundings more demanding than these.

Julius just came to tell me that he looked in on Mr. Hardeman and found him still asleep. He redressed Mr. Hardeman's wound yesterday evening once we had him settled. If the bullet had struck the bone, I believe he would have lost the arm. He has not regained consciousness since he fell from his horse.

CHAPTER SEVEN

Hardeman dreamed. He was in the battle again and the soldiers were shooting at him. Bullets were ripping the air, missing him by inches, and he couldn't seem to run. He was carrying a young boy in his arms. He thought it was Johnny Smoker, but when he looked down he saw it was Blackbird. He had to get the boy to safety.

A bullet slammed into his shoulder and he left the dream behind, struggling toward wakefulness. He realized that he was lying down. He was warm and comfortable. He must be on the pony drag, but why had it stopped? He had to reach Sun Horse and tell him to surrender.

He heard the gunfire again and he opened his eyes. He was in a bed. The gunfire was the rattling of a shutter, latched closed against the storm outside. Through the slats of the shutters he could see daylight. A lamp turned low burned on the small bedside table.

He remembered now. He had reached the council and he had told them to surrender. It seemed like another dream. How had he come to be here? And where was he?

He tried to raise himself on his elbows and then he remembered his wound. His left arm was bound against his body. He was wearing a man's flannel nightshirt and nothing else. He explored his wounded shoulder with his free hand and found a clean linen bandage there. There was a small bandage on his head as well, but that wound was no longer tender to the touch.

He propped himself up with his good arm and looked around the room. The bed was a mahogany four-poster with a simple gingham canopy. The curtains at the room's two windows had a small fringe of lace. On the dressing table there was a framed tintype of Jed Putnam and another of a woman Hardeman didn't know. A spray of dried flowers and leaves stood in a vase on the chest of drawers against the far wall. A cedar blanket chest at the foot of the bed lent the room a subtle sylvan fragrance. The dressing table had a skirt of blue chintz, and a few ribbons hung from the corner of the mirror. He looked at the tintypes again and saw that the woman had Lisa's hair and the same fullness in the lips. She must be Lisa's mother. This was Lisa's room. It was like her, neat and sensible, yet attractively feminine, delicately scented, and so different from the rooms of the most "respectable" whores in Ellsworth, all frills and satins and perfumes that clung to a man for days.

His buckskins were folded and laid across a chair but he saw no sign of the rest of his clothes, although his saddlebags were hung over the back of the chair.

Beyond the bedside table was a rocking chair with a crocheted shawl laid across one arm and an open book on the seat. She had sat there to read and watch over him. How long ago had she left, and how long had he slept?

He needed to urinate. He swung his legs over the edge of the bed and sat up, then hung his head and held it in his right hand until his vision stopped swimming. He got out of bed and looked beneath it. There was a chamber pot there. He emptied his bladder and climbed gratefully back beneath the covers, tired by the small effort. He leaned back against the feather pillows and gave in to the clean sheets and the warmth of the down comforter, allowing his eyes to close. He drifted for a time, half awake and half asleep. The wind shook the shutters again and he remembered the ride down to the park then, and the storm gaining strength. He remembered too the sense of belonging here that had swept away the last of his reserves once he found himself back in the settlement, and he wished for a moment that Putnam's Park might be his. Ever since Jed had set him to thinking about the day when he would want to find some land of his own, he had imagined a place just like this one, a home in the mountains.

Outside, the wind howled, but it couldn't reach him here. He pulled the comforter up close around his chin. It was almost April and still winter wouldn't give up. Spring was fickle in the mountains, not a season to rely on, as any man who had guided wagons on the Oregon road knew all too well. Set out too early and lose half your stock in a blizzard. Set out too late and find the grass brown and worthless along the trail. Today the snow was falling but in six or seven weeks the grass would be green. What would they be doing here in Putnam's Park then? The feeding sled would be put away and the draft horses turned out for summer, unless there was ditching or plowing to do, and Julius and Hutch would turn to new chores. With the branding done and the cattle gone from the park, irrigating would occupy much of their time. They would spill water from the two long ditches that flanked the eastern and western sides of the meadows, damming and diverting in the smaller channels, spreading the water until it covered every patch of ground, smelling the grass and water, walking in fields that were bright with flowers.

Down in Texas many of the cowhands disdained any work they couldn't do from the back of a horse, but Hardeman had irrigated there one spring. The rancher had wanted hay to feed the dairy cows he was raising along with his beeves. With Johnny's help, Hardeman had seen the irrigation started and the hay crop beginning to grow before they set off for the roundup and the long drive to Kansas. He had enjoyed walking in the hayfields where everything was so quiet and peaceful, the water sparkling in the sun as it rippled among the tender green stalks of grass. What would it be like to see that same grass cut in the fall and fed in the winter, and watch the calves you helped into the world grow to size and be shipped off to market?

He tried to imagine himself on his own land, looking at his own cattle, but the picture in his mind's eye became Putnam's Park in summer. He felt the warmth of the sun on his back and saw the valley all green, with perhaps just a trace of snow still in sight on the western ridge. He saw the lesser ridges that curved around the park like arms, meeting at the bottom of the valley where the river slipped between the fingers. A woman stood at his side, and somewhere down in the fields Julius and Hutch were walking with shovels on their shoulders. And then in the conjured vision other figures appeared; Johnny was there too, and Sun Horse and Blackbird, and the Putnam brothers, Bat and Jed. Hardeman imagined he could hear Jed laugh at him for taking so long to settle down.

He opened his eyes and the image vanished. It was a pleasant dream but he wouldn't be here when summer came. He had tried to lead them all, red and white, to a peaceful settlement, but they would not be led. They would have their war, with each side clamoring for honor and vengeance and the triumph of right, despite the best efforts of good men on both sides. But he would have no part of it. He no longer led men to war.

Perhaps it had been useless from the start. Perhaps the races were simply too different to live together in peace. The whites kept pushing the Indians until they fought back or gave in, and as for the Indians, was it so surprising that they should resist now and again? After all, they only wanted a piece of land to call their own. Now, pushed from all sides, they clung to the last of their domain. They would fight to keep it, but in the end the land they were allowed to keep would be to the east, in Dakota Territory, in country less attractive to the white man.

When the end came for the Sioux, Hardeman would be gone from the northern plains. There was nothing to keep him here now. He had tried to make a peace and he had failed. Johnny Smoker was on his own, and as for Lisa Putnam, she had heard his confession in the Sun Band council. She knew he had planned to betray the Sioux to the soldiers. She had hoped they could remain free and she knew now that he had worked against her hopes every step of the way. All that remained was to be gone as soon as he could sit a horse.

The thought of moving on again wearied him. For seven years he and Johnny had moved on whenever there was no reason to stay in one place any longer, and they had always found something new to try, another territory to see. But this time Johnny would not be riding with him.

The door opened softly and Lisa Putnam entered the room on tiptoes.

"Well," she said when she saw that he was awake. "How do you feel?"

"What time is it?"

"It's afternoon. You have slept for almost a full day. We have had dinner already. Do you think you could eat something?"

"About half a horse, I imagine." He raised himself on his good elbow and once again his head swam, but he tried to hide the weakness from her. "If you'll give me some clothes, I'll get dressed."

"You will do nothing of the kind. I promised Johnny I would look after you and that is exactly what I intend to do. You will have your meal in bed and you will stay here until we see how you feel tomorrow." She moved to his side and touched his brow with a hand that was cool and dry.

"There seems to be no fever."

"At least let me go to my own room."

"If you intend to resist me every step of the way, I shall be forced to take stern measures, Mr. Hardeman. I put you here because this is where I prefer to care for you. I am quite comfortable in your room. It was my bedroom when I was a little girl." As she spoke, she was adjusting the pillows and supporting his upper body with one arm while she propped them beneath him so he could sit up comfortably. He was surprised by the hidden strength in her slender form until he remembered that she was accustomed to doing every chore on the ranch, out of doors as well as in, and only wore a dress in the house. Today she wore the simple gray one. Her skin smelled of soap and cooking, but her hair, incongruously, smelled of sunshine.

"You'll have to settle for buffalo stew," she said when she had him arranged to her satisfaction. "I'm not going to kill a perfectly good horse just to suit the whims of an invalid." She smiled. "I'm glad you have an appetite. My mother always said that was a good sign."

"So did mine."

"Is she alive?"

"Not for twenty years. It was typhoid. She and my father both."

"I was young when my mother died. Here, let me give you some light." She turned up the lamp by the bed and then knelt by the small potbellied stove to add a pair of short logs. "It's not very cold outside, but it's blowing a gale. The room stays warmer with the shutters closed when the wind's like this. There." She shut the stove and rose. "Well, I won't be long."

When she had gone, he looked about the room from his new elevated perspective and found it much the same. His eyes fell on the book on the seat of the rocker and he saw that the leather cover was bare of any printing. He leaned out of bed, supporting himself on the small table. He nearly fell, but he managed to grasp the book. When he opened it he was surprised to find that the pages were filled with handwriting. He leafed to the front and saw that he held in his hand a journal written by Jedediah Putnam for the year 1853. He allowed it to fall open to the page marked by the thin strip of silk cloth that was bound into the binding, the page Lisa had been reading. The entry was dated April eighteenth, written at eight-twenty in the evening:

Today the men and I set the roof beam, and the dream of building my own home is becoming a reality. I am fifty years old this month, and about to have my first real home. A trifle late in the day, I imagine. The place in Lexington was never _mine_, not the way this place will be. I will count myself lucky if I have a few years to enjoy it with Eleanor and little Elizabeth. That dream too is within reach. In another month I will go to St. Louis to fetch them here, and if they do not recoil in horror from this wild place, by the first snow in autumn we should be snug enough.

Sun Horse was down today to see how things are coming along. Just a few more weeks and he'll be taking his people off on the summer hunt. I shall miss them, and Bat too. "Big tipi" was Sun Horse's remark when he saw the house. He thinks white man's houses are a pretty good joke. Bat got in a few digs about this one. Too hard to move, he said, and Sun Horse agreed. The two of them are like peas in a pod, happiest out under the sky and ready to move on whenever the wind blows from a new direction. I know the feeling, but from the minute my axe bit into the first tree we felled, I knew I was ready to plant my roots here. They will live out their days in the nomadic life and think me a fool for abandoning it; meanwhile, I, who have wandered with the best of them (and that's truth!), will get the feel of a different life. If I find I have made a mistake, I can always set fire to the house and pull up stakes again, but I don't think it will come to that. A man's got to make his choices, even if they're wrong, but I've seldom been more certain of one of mine. The day I sold my share in Putnam & Sons to Jacob was like the day I started upriver with Ashley and the Major. (Henry, for you poor souls who live in a time when these men are unknown. Lord, I'm glad I won't live to see that.) If the damn boat had sunk right there I would have swum to another one. There was no going back, not until I had seen what lay ahead. And it's the same now. I imagine each generation must make the same decision (those who have the wits to wonder at all about their destiny and so take a hand in guiding it)—whether to build something new, to maintain what has been built before, or to allow even that to crumble and decay. My relatives in Boston maintain the family's busi-

ness and its homes; I am cursed or blessed, I'm not dead
sure which, with the need to start from scratch.

Hardeman raised his eyes from the journal and cast his
mind back across the years. April of '53. Who was he
scouting for that year? Lem Finch again. And by the
eighteenth they might have pulled out of Independence
already, but he couldn't remember for certain. By autumn
in the Big Horns, when Jed had hoped to have his wife and
child all snugly settled in with him in Putnam's Park,
Hardeman had reached Sacramento and delivered his emigrants and turned his horse back toward the rising sun,
hoping to get over the Sierra Nevadas before the first snows.
What would have happened if he had come up here then,
to make his promised visit? Jed might have offered him
work and he might have stayed to help the mountain man
build Putnam's Park.

Hardeman smiled. Jed would have offered, all right, but
he would not have stayed. The wanderfoot was strong in
him still, back then, and as the years passed by, it had
continued to hold off the dream of finding a place of his
own. That had seemed a notion for a later time, one he
could not easily imagine—a time when he would be as old
as Jed Putnam, and ready to settle down. During the years
when he and Johnny were in Texas he had seen that beef
was the coming thing, and he had seen how the men with
eastern and British capital set the pattern for the boom,
grazing huge herds on public lands, gathering them once a
year to be branded and driven to the railheads, and he
knew that his own capital reserve, which had sat for so
long in the St. Louis bank, biding its time, could never
even buy a share in such an enterprise, and so the thought
of finding his own place had been left to gather dust in the
attic of his imagination. Meantime, here in the Big Horns,

Jed had conducted regular spring cleanings on his own imaginings, and without any help from Britishers he might just have hit on the right way to do the thing—a small piece of land and a small herd, just enough that a man could hold it all in his hands and care for it. Beyond that, what else did a man need?

He closed the journal and rested his hand on top of it, scarcely aware of the action, for the realization was dawning within him that the time had come to find his home. There was nothing to hold him back any longer. There was no scouting left, except for the army, and he would not go back to the towns to become like Hickok, all tired and old before his time, convinced that the great adventures were gone forever. A man made his own adventures.

So Jed was right after all. *Wanderfoot's a young man's disease*, he had said. *When it comes your time to stop, you'll know*. At last the time had come. And like Jed he was one of those who needed to start from scratch, building from the ground up with his own hands.

Hardeman smiled. It comforted him to have a new goal. And strangely, knowing what he would do when he left Putnam's Park diminished his urgency to be gone. He needed time to recover from the journey, the battle, and his wound. Time to regain his strength.

His eyes closed. Given the chance, he might sleep the clock around again. How long had it been since he spent a full day in bed? Not since childhood. He felt as weak as a child now. There was time enough for journeying on when he felt stronger. Lisa Putnam seemed to bear him no malice. He would rest here for a while if she would let him remain.

The door opened and Lisa entered, smiling, with a tray in her hands. Hardeman realized then that he was still holding Jed's journal.

"I didn't mean to pry." He set the leather volume on the bedside table.

"It's quite all right. The Putnam family journals are meant to be read by others. Usually only relatives are sufficiently interested." The tray had legs and she set it astride his lap. He remembered his hunger as the aroma from the steaming bowl of stew reached him. In addition to the stew there were fresh rolls and butter and a glass of milk, and canned pears and hot gingerbread, and a small china pitcher of thick yellow cream.

She shook out the linen napkin and tucked it beneath his chin as if he were a child down with mumps. "I'll leave you to eat. I never could stand being watched while I ate in bed. I'll come back a little later."

Hardeman ate quickly, wolfing the stew as soon as it was cool enough. It was much the same as stews he had eaten in the Indian camps, with potatoes and carrots instead of prairie turnips, but there had been no butter among the Indians and no raised bread. It was odd how such small things could do so much to make a man feel at home. He found it difficult to butter the rolls with only one hand, so he slapped on great chunks of butter and ate the bread in large bites, and he was glad Lisa had not stayed to watch.

The food acted as a soporific. Even as he finished the last bite of gingerbread and washed it down with the last of the cream and the juice from the dish of pears, he was nodding. With much care, he lifted the tray off his lap with his one good hand and set it on the floor beside the bed. He lay back against the pillows and closed his eyes and thought he had never been quite so comfortable before.

When he awoke again, the tray was gone and the light outside the windows was fading. The cat Rufus was sleeping on the foot of the bed, apparently not caring that someone other than his mistress lay there. Hardeman was sorry he hadn't heard Lisa return for the tray. The supper gong rang then, the sound of one stroke loud and the next whipped away by the wind, and he knew that she would be busy feeding the circus crowd. He slept again, and when he next awoke the cat was gone and Lisa was sitting in the rocking chair beside his bed, reading her father's journal. The creaking of the rockers had wakened him.

"I'm sorry," she said, "I didn't mean to disturb you. No, that's not true." She smiled at her own embarrassment. "I hoped you weren't sleeping very soundly, because I brought you some soup. Would you like it? It's still warm."

"I haven't done a thing to work off that dinner you gave me, but it seems to have gone away just the same."

She gave him the soup, and buttered bread to go with it, and while he ate she read, not watching him. When he was done she removed the tray and set it aside.

He gestured at Jed's journal. "He writes well."

She seemed pleased. "Yes, he does, doesn't he? And yet other than his journals and letters to members of the family, he wrote not at all. I have sometimes wondered if he might not have become a man of letters if he had been born in different circumstances. What might he have been if he had found no great frontier to explore?"

"He would have been the poorer for it."

She smiled. "You're right, of course. He led a rich life, and he would not have traded it for any other. He was glad to have lived when he did, and perhaps glad that he wouldn't see the changes he knew were coming." She closed the journal and set it aside. "He said that when he first came to the mountains the Indians were the lords of creation. Those were his words. They accepted the white man—the trappers—among them. They taught them what they knew, and they accepted that the whites were different in many ways.''

"And they killed one or two," Hardeman added.

"Yes, more than a few. Believe me, I don't harbor many romantic notions about Indians. They are neither the noble children of nature portrayed by the poet nor the bloodthirsty beasts described in popular fiction. As usual, the truth lies somewhere between the extremes. They live a life very different from our own. They have different notions of death, and the meaning of life, and if I live to be a hundred I will never think as they do. But it was those very differences my father cherished. He called theirs a more 'fundamental' life. Part of its fundamental nature was the immediacy of death. It could come at any moment.''

She paused, as if unsure whether or not to speak the thought that had come to her. "There is a story he used to tell. He would listen to some passing emigrant or drummer or soldier tell tall tales of the mountains and the Indians and all the fights he had seen and the scalps he had taken. When a man brags like that it's mostly hogwash, as you know. My father couldn't abide such men. So when the fellow ran out of wind for a moment, my father would say, 'Imagine this, if you will, sir. Just for a moment, to show these other good people what life in the mountains means to us.' You'll have to imagine his voice telling it. I'm not very good at storytelling. It's in the life, not in the blood, I guess. 'You are traveling alone and you make camp for the night,' he would say. 'You've eaten your supper, such as it is, when you hear another horse, or maybe you don't hear anything, because it's an Indian who's coming up on you. You look up and there's a man in your firelight. Tell these folks what happens next.' Well, as you can imagine, most of them couldn't think of a thing to say." She looked at Hardeman. "What would you answer?''

He thought for a moment, and shrugged. "Anything could happen. With luck you might make a friend. By morning one of you might be dead, or both of you."

She straightened in her chair, plainly delighted by this reply. "Exactly! A man could step into your firelight and he might be your murderer. Or the two of you might winter together. But no matter what happened, the world would go on, none the wiser. That was what my father liked best of all. You stood on your own and lived and died by your wits, and if you were foolish and died a fool's death, the world went on without you." She sat back and moved the rocker gently to and fro, gazing at Hardeman thoughtfully. "You understand this because you have lived much of your own life under those same conditions, but it was something my relatives could never grasp. My relations on my mother's side, that is. They thought my father shirked responsibility. They saw him pass up the chance to take over the direction of Putnam and Sons. They could not imagine why he would do such a thing and so they mistrusted him." She leaned forward now and there was passion in her voice as she continued. "They could never understand that he took on a far greater responsibility. He chose to live beyond the fabric of civilized society. Most men wrap themselves in that cloth and feel naked without it, but my father found it stifling. He chose to live where a man lived or died by his own actions, without recourse to law, often without recourse to men of his own race in case of trouble. He relished that responsibility and he believed that no one who had not experienced that kind of life could lay claim to the title of free man."

Hardeman nodded thoughtfully. "When you first met him, you wouldn't in a month of Sundays think to find such notions in his head. He'd give you his hooraw and do his best to scare you out of your wits with his stories, but all the time he was taking the measure of you."

"And after you knew him for a time he did talk to you. About the other things, I mean."

Again Hardeman nodded. "He was the damndest talker. If he liked you, he'd talk your ear off. Your uncle Bat's a lot the same."

She smiled. "It hardly seems fair that you knew my father so well and I know nothing at all of yours."

Now it was Hardeman's turn to pause and consider whether to bring forth his memories. When he spoke his voice was softer than before. "My father educated himself while he was apprenticed to a blacksmith. He became a lawyer, like Mr. Lincoln. He admired Mr. Lincoln. While Mr. Lincoln was in Congress, my father sat in the Pennsylvania legislature. He bettered himself and he wished still better for me. I was a disappointment to him."

"I find that hard to credit."

"Oh, it's true enough. He had his own particular ideas about a man's responsibility. He believed that in a free nation each man had a duty to help his fellow man along. 'Bear the common burden,' he put it. He used to say that democracy was not a free ride. He believed in the law and he thought the best way a man could do his duty was to serve in the government, to see that the laws were just, and fairly administered." He remembered what Lisa had said about Jed: *He chose to live where a man lived or died by his own actions, without recourse to law,* and he realized that his own father would have found such a notion frightening.

"He sounds quite a remarkable man," Lisa said. "Surely if he were alive today he would see that you have done your part, although you chose a very different life. During the time of the gold rush, my father knew very well that guiding the emigrants had a part to play in the progress of the nation."

"I know," Hardeman conceded. "He told me all about the sweep of westward progress and those other fancy notions, and I believed it all, back then. Maybe I believed it a little too well. I thought leading the way was a pretty fine thing, and then one day I looked back and saw who I'd been leading. That was seven years ago."

"At the Washita," she said, and he nodded. "And so you left scouting behind you."

"Sometimes leaving off isn't enough. You look for a way to make amends."

She sat gazing at him, rocking slowly, and he became aware that he was stroking the scar on his cheek with his fingers. He dropped the arm to his side.

"You must be tired," she said.

"I haven't done much but sleep all day."

"It's past midnight, I should think." She rose. "I have strict orders to look at your shoulder. Julius will be angry if I forget." She turned her back. "You'll have to get out of that nightshirt so I can undo the bandages. It belonged to my father, by the way. You can keep it if you like."

He wondered what she imagined he would do with a gentleman's flannel nightshirt once he was out on the trail, but he could think of no way to refuse the gift so he said nothing.

"All right," he said shortly, and she turned to see that he had the covers pulled up to his armpits, leaving only the top of his chest and his shoulders exposed. She sat on the bed beside him and began to unwind the bandage.

"I was wondering who did the doctoring," he said.

"Julius's first job as a free man was in a Union Army field hospital. He was just an orderly, but he had plenty of opportunity to watch the surgeons at work. Eventually they let him bandage the simple wounds. There." She lifted the dressing away. "It's doing quite well, I think. There is no inflammation; that's what I was to look for particularly."

To Hardeman, the wound looked ugly enough, but he could see where new flesh was already forming at the edges to cover the damage the bullet had done.

Lisa rose and went to her dressing table where she found a pair of scissors and cut away the soiled portion of the dressing. Returning to his side, she refolded the cloth neatly and applied it once again to the wound and placed his right hand over it to hold it in place while she began to bandage his shoulder.

"I'm going to leave your arm free, but you are to wear a sling when you get out of bed."

"Yes, ma'am," he said obediently.

She smiled, then paused in her work as she noticed a twist of scar tissue on his other shoulder. She touched it lightly.

"How remarkable. It's so similar. Where did you get it?"

"At the Washita."

"And this?" She touched his cheek, the tips of her fingers tracing the small scar there, then brushing his beard as she dropped her hand.

"Same day, same place."

"I see." She returned to her bandaging.

"I suppose I should have learned my lesson the first time."

"Hold still, please. There." She tied the bandage off and looked at him. "But you didn't, did you? Once again you were willing to lead a troop of cavalry to a peaceful village. Was it to make amends?"

"To keep the peace, Miss Putnam."

She met his gaze with steady blue eyes that reminded

Hardeman of her father. "I know that's what you hoped to do, but was it really the only way?"

"It was the only way I saw just then. That's what I told Sun Horse, and that's the truth. Anyway, I didn't get the chance."

"I knew Hawk Chaser," she said, taking him by surprise. "When I was a young girl he taught me to ride bareback. He always took an interest in children, telling them stories and making them things. He said the children are the spirit of the Lakota."

"He showed what he was made of, all right." He shook his head. "It was a stupid thing to do."

"Stupid! He saved your life! Yours and Blackbird's."

"We'd have been killed anyway, all three of us, if the soldiers hadn't pulled out just then."

"Perhaps. But that wouldn't have made any difference to Hawk Chaser. He would still have behaved just the same."

"That's why it was stupid. What hope did he have with an iron lance against Springfield carbines?"

"There is always hope! There has to be. I believe in the human spirit. With a strong will, it can find a way. And even if every event in our lives were predetermined by fate, we would still try to change things, wouldn't we?"

"I imagine so. Sometimes we don't get much done for all the trying. I set out to save a people and I ended up saving one boy, and needed help doing that."

"Is it such a small thing to save one boy?"

"I had a chance to make peace and I failed."

"You were not the only one who failed! General Crook failed. Sun Horse failed. Two Moons and Sitting Bull and Crazy Horse failed as well! You cannot place the blame only on yourself!"

"Each of those men did what he could. It's not for me to judge them."

"Nor is it for you to decide for them! You have no right to make a peace by having one band led away in chains in the hope that others will follow! Even if you were successful, what gives you the right to force it on them?"

"That's the way it will end, sooner or later. It's the end of the road for the Sioux."

"Perhaps it is! But they must walk the last few steps as they decide for themselves!"

"And how many dead in the meantime, Miss Putnam?"

"That's not for us to say! Some may choose to die rather than go to the reservation, and they wouldn't be the first people to choose death over the loss of freedom!" She stood suddenly. "Oh, you are a stubborn man!" She turned her back on him and crossed to the window.

"So you said. I didn't argue." He gave her a moment to calm herself and then he said, "Wouldn't you stop the dying if you could?"

She spun to face him and her eyes sparked with anger. "I don't want them to die! But I cannot choose for those people, and neither can you, any more than you could choose for Hawk Chaser or prevent him from doing what he did. You haven't the right!"

He said nothing, and as her anger dwindled she looked away. She moved to the rocking chair and sat down.

"I did not intend that we should quarrel. I would prefer it if we could be friends."

"That was my preference from the start, Miss Putnam."

"Don't you see, if you take too much on yourself, you take away someone else's choice. We must each choose and act for ourselves."

It struck Hardeman that he had heard almost exactly the same words more than once in recent weeks, from the mouths of Indians. *Each man must choose for himself,* Crazy Horse had said in Two Moons' council, and in the Sun Band's village Elk Leggings had repeated the same injunction. The Indians, who were governed by customs rather than laws, accorded certain customs the force of law, and that was one of them.

"I have something to confess," Lisa said now, and her voice was hard, as if she spoke an unpleasant truth. "I had no right to speak to you as I did. You see, I tried to influence them as well. I didn't want Sun Horse to surrender, and so while you were gone I proposed that we should hunt together, Julius and myself and the men from the circus with Sun Horse and his hunters. I thought that if they had enough meat to feed themselves, they would stay free. But the hunt was a failure. Then when Amanda was lost she saw the buffalo and it seemed like a miracle. Now they have more than enough meat. But you see, now I have changed my mind. I believe they will have to surrender if they hope to survive." She was looking at her hands, folded together in her lap, but now she raised her eyes. "What will they do?"

"They will do what they have to do." *A man does what he must. It is for other men to understand and accept.* In the end the fate of the Sioux nation would be governed by their own customs and the choices each man made for himself, no matter how their friends or enemies tried to sway them. Hardeman recalled the leaders with whom he had sat in Two Moons' council: Crazy Horse and Sitting Bull and Little Wolf and Two Moons and Old Bear, men of the people, sober men who took the welfare of their people to heart; they would defend themselves if attacked, and they would urge the warriors to fight for the people. Now it was certain that they would be attacked wherever they were found.

"It seems that all our efforts have failed," Lisa said. "But at least you saved a life. Surely that must go a long way toward making amends, if there is some fateful ledger in which these things are recorded. Blackbird is alive because of you. And Johnny Smoker."

"That was an accident."

"I don't understand."

He met the blue eyes and saw the trust in them. "I didn't mean to save Johnny's life. That was an accident. I came within a whisker of killing him before I even knew he was white."

She waited for him to continue, and the silence lengthened. Hardeman lay back against the pillows and his gaze came to rest on the dried flowers and leaves in the vase atop the bureau. He began to speak then, and he told her the tale he had told to no one else in seven years, starting with how he had come to be at the Washita with Custer's command. He told her of the meeting with Hickok and the hope of making peace with the aid of Agent Wynkoop and Black Kettle, of finding the Indians' trail and how he had circled around the sleeping Indian camp before dawn and learned that the trail continued on to the villages downstream, of arriving at the battle too late to stop it.

"After Black Kettle was shot, I found Custer in the village," he said, and here for the first time he turned to face her again. "I told him the war party had gone on downriver. I told him these were the wrong Indians and he laughed out loud. He said 'They seem willing enough to fight,' and he rode off and left me there. I was right in the middle of the village with men fighting all around me, and I didn't know what to do. I was sitting there on my horse like a Goddamn statue, and then I saw an Indian boy charge one of the officers—Captain Benteen. The boy couldn't have been more than fourteen or so and he had a pistol that looked about as long as his arm. He could barely lift it. Benteen didn't want to shoot the boy. He waved him off. He made signs that if the boy would surrender to him, he wouldn't hurt him. But the boy kept coming. He was on a little pony. He guided it with his knees and he held that pistol in both hands and he shot at Benteen. The first shot missed, but the second one killed Benteen's horse. I guess Benteen thought two chances was plenty. When he got up off the ground he dropped that boy with one shot. The body fell right at his feet.''

He looked again at the flowers in their vase and wondered how they had managed to keep so much color during the long winter months.

''I decided I'd go back upstream and wait with the wagons, maybe. I didn't have much of an idea just where I was going but I knew I wasn't staying there. I started out of the village, but I hadn't gone very far when someone took a shot at me and grazed my cheek.'' He touched the scar on his face and looked at his fingers. ''I saw blood and I looked around to see who was shooting at me, and the next shot hit me in the shoulder. Along about then I understood that someone was trying to kill me. I tried to help them and they wanted to kill me! It made me angry. I don't think I've ever been that angry. The shot knocked me off my horse but I don't even remember falling. The next thing I knew I was on my feet with my pistol in my hand and I had an idea that the shots had come from a lodge nearby. I emptied my pistol into the lodge and then I pulled my knife and went in ready to finish the job. There was Johnny with a hole in his leg.''

He turned on her suddenly and his voice was harsh. ''You see, I gave him that limp, Miss Putnam, and I damn near killed him. In that first moment, even when I saw I'd wounded him, I wanted to finish him off. If he'd been standing or if he'd tried to run, I would have cut him open without a how-de-do. But he was holding his mother. She was dead and so was the man. They were his parents and he was holding on to his mother to protect her from the soldiers even though she was dead.''

"But you didn't kill him. You saved him instead.''

"I saw he was a white boy. Maybe it was just because of that, or because his folks were dead. I thought I'd killed the two of them. He told me later they were dead before I came along, but it doesn't matter much.''

"It doesn't matter? How can you say that?''

"Because I wanted to kill them! I was ready to kill every mother's son in that village, man, woman or child! That's how angry I was!'' He saw the fear in her eyes and he softened his voice. "It's like a madness, Miss Putnam. That's what war does to men. Once you've felt it, you don't forget.''

He was suddenly very tired. He lay back and closed his eyes, wishing to remember nothing more, but he had summoned the images of the Washita and they were still strong before him. He saw the burning lodges once more and smelled the carnage.

He heard the rockers creak and felt a weight rest on the bed beside him. A hand, cool and comforting, rested on his cheek, and then Lisa spoke.

"And yet if you hadn't been there, if you hadn't been shot and if you had never entered that lodge, Johnny might have died that same day. Would you change the events if you could?'' He made no reply and she answered for him. "I don't think you would. Nor would you change what you did for Blackbird.''

"Blackbird will do everything he can to get another chance at the soldiers,'' he said without opening his eyes. All he wanted now was to sleep. "He'll remember Hawk

Chaser and most likely run smack into the guns again to
show he's not afraid to die for the people. They put great
stock in dying for the people." His voice was bitter.
"They're all like Hawk Chaser, the bunch of them. The
whole damn Sioux nation would do the same thing if they
got the chance, run straight into the guns and die for the
people, only there wouldn't be any people left when it was
over."

Lisa took his right hand between her own. "Listen to
me," she said. "If Blackbird dies fighting the soldiers, it
will not be your doing. You have done what you could,
and you took on more than any one man should attempt. It
is no sin to fail; what's worse is not to try."

She was quiet then, and the room was silent. Outside,
the wind had dropped to nothing.

Her weight shifted and he felt her breath on his cheek,
and then her lips touched his, dry and quick, as gentle as
the touch of a butterfly's wings. He felt her hands withdraw from his own and her weight rise from the bed, and
he opened his eyes.

For a long moment she regarded him coolly with an
expression he could not fathom, and then she cupped her
hand around the frosted chimney of the bedside lamp and
with a puff of breath she blew out the flame.

"Why did you do that?" he said into the sudden dark.

"We're running low on coal oil." Her voice came from
close beside him.

Even when his eyes grew accustomed to the loss of the
lamplight he could see nothing, for the shutters blocked
out any faint illumination from the moonless night. There
were sounds of wool against silk, silk against skin, and
then a hand lifted the bedcovers and Lisa slipped in beside
him. She burrowed her face deep in the curve of his neck,
and when his good arm went around her, she fitted herself

close against him and he felt the smooth warmth of her skin, except for her hands and feet and the tips of her breasts, which were cool at first. She was trembling. He held her still and close and he thought that he comforted her, but it was she who comforted him, she who moved so his lips could find hers, she who guided him without seeming to lead, she who remembered to safeguard his wounded shoulder when he had passed beyond such caution. She gave herself freely and without guile, and when they lay still again, he could feel her heart against him, gradually slowing until its beating was barely perceptible, like the muted ticking of a small clock.

LISA PUTNAM'S JOURNAL

Sunday, March 26th. 6:30 a.m.

I have spent the last hour going through my father's old letters, trying to find one I read sometime during the winter, one that has new meaning for me now, and I have just found it. It was written in April of 1851 and was the last letter he mailed before he and his train of wagons left

Independence for Sacramento. He says, "I have taken on a boy this summer, Eleanor. He'll be my assistant scout, or maybe apprentice would be more accurate. He's got a lot to learn but I've a feeling he's one of the ones who'll stick it out. He reminds me of myself, many years ago. His name is Christopher Hardeman and he was born in Pennsylvania. His father's a lawyer and legislator, but young Christopher has got his sights set on the West. He is just about a year younger than I was when I set out up that big river with Ashley and Henry, just as full of spunk and unafraid. When I look at him I think of all I've been through since then; a couple of lifetimes, it seems, and I'm only now fixing to settle down for good. No thought could be farther from young Christopher's mind than that one. What will he go through before he reaches my age? What lands will he see and what people will he come to know? All I know for certain is that he's going to see just about everything there is to see before he slows down enough to plant roots somewhere. He's got wandering feet and a far look in his eye."

Yesterday for a time I allowed myself to hope that Mr. Hardeman might stay on here, but I had forgotten that look, which I noted myself when he first arrived. It is with him still. I imagine I can see it in his face even when he is sleeping. I will not try to hold him against his will.

CHAPTER EIGHT

Hardeman awoke slowly, as he did only when he was enclosed by four walls and a roof, and he became aware that the bed beside him was empty and the sheets there were cool. Her faint scent lingered on the pillow. He opened his eyes. The wind was blowing and the shutters rattled but the light from outside seemed brighter than it had been the day before.

Cautiously he sat up in bed. His vision remained steady and the dullness that had clouded his perceptions ever since the battle was gone. He could feel the cool air on his skin, hear the friendly crackle of the fire in the small stove, see the minutest details of each article in the room despite the limited amount of light admitted by the shutters. His clothing had reappeared, folded neatly atop his buckskins.

He swung his feet to the floor and stood up, and was surprised to discover that he felt quite himself. His first few steps were unsteady, but more on account of stiffness from his long rest than any lingering debility. He used the chamber pot and then turned to the windows to open the shutters. Only when he raised the sash did a sharp pain in his shoulder remind him that he was not to use his left arm.

The shutters swung back to reveal a world bathed in sunlight. Shadows swept across the yard as the wind urged the clouds along. A few flakes of snow were falling still, but the storm had left only four or five inches behind, for all its huffing and puffing.

He saw that the feeding sled was not in its accustomed place in the barnyard. The morning was well advanced and no one had wakened him for breakfast. The thought of food made him aware of his hunger, which was as strong as if he had eaten nothing in days.

A woman passing among the circus wagons saw him and waved, smiling, and he ducked back as he realized that he was stark naked.

In the mirror atop Lisa's dressing table he was greeted by a stranger. He had not seen himself in a glass since setting out with the pipe carriers. His hair and beard were long and unkempt and there seemed to be more gray hairs than he recalled. With his good hand he removed the small bandage from his forehead and he saw that the scab there was well formed. He touched the old scar on his cheek and he remembered then the black paint he had applied to his face with that same hand. Bat Putnam had given him the paint. Bat and each of the Lakota men carried their paints with them, the vegetable colorings and animal fat kept separate until they were mixed together for use. The paint was gone from Hardeman's face now. Someone had washed him as he slept, most likely when they had first put him to bed. Was there supposed to be some ceremony connected with the removal of mourning paint? He had no idea. It all seemed a long time ago, the battle and the journey back, even the council in Sun Horse's village, which he remembered only vaguely. Two days of rest had removed him farther from those events than could be accounted for solely by the number of hours that had passed while he slept. It was as if he had gone to sleep at the moment when he was wounded in the battle and had only now finally awakened from a long period of broken dreams to find himself miraculously healed, or almost so, and transported far from the scene by means he could not imagine.

He was eager to be out and about, wanting to try the feeling of life, as if it were all new to him. He dressed himself in his woolen shirt and pants, which were fresh and clean. All of his clothing had been washed while he lay abed. The bullet hole in the shoulder of his buckskin jacket had been patched with a fresh piece of deerskin and most of the blood had been washed away. The shirt had been similarly repaired. A pair of boots stood on the floor by the chair; they might have belonged to Jed or they might be Julius's, but they fit him well enough. He rolled up the heavy winter moccasins he had worn on the journey back and set them atop his deerskins.

With a brush and comb from the dressing table he imposed some order on his hair and beard. The cutting of his hair would have to wait until he reached a settlement, and although he often trimmed his own beard he left it now as it was. The wild look he saw in the glass rather pleased him. He resembled a mountain man dressed up to go to town.

When his toilet was complete, he cleaned the brush with the tortoise-shell comb and gathered the loose hairs to throw in the stove, noticing as he did so that a few of Lisa'a fine strands were mixed with his own coarser curls, and he remembered the night before.

Far from blaming him for his intentions toward the

Sioux it seemed that she understood what had motivated his efforts and sympathized with his failure. *You have done what you could,* she had said, *and you took on more than one man should attempt.* She had consoled him and she had made it plain that he would be welcome to stay on for a while. But she had sought to be reassured as well, and he recognized now that in his weakened state he had thought only of his own future, the abandoning of one goal and fixing on another, and he had forgotten the threat to Putnam's Park, which was still very real. So long as Crook remained in the field, the war might come here, and when the war was over, the future of the little ranch was far from secure.

Now his weakness of yesterday was miraculously gone. He would need no prolonged period of convalescence. He was strengthened and revitalized and he could sit a horse today, if need be, but there was more he could do here. Perhaps he could even salvage some good from the wreckage of his hopes. The time had come to find his own land, his own home, but there was no rush to be off. He hadn't even decided where he would begin his search. Meantime, the least he could do was try to help Lisa Putnam keep her ranch. He could stay for a time. If the soldiers came near he would intercept them and see that no fighting touched her home. And he would talk to Crook on her behalf. The general's support could be decisive in assuring her title to the park. He would tell Crook that Lisa had fed and sheltered himself and Johnny and had taken them to see Sun Horse, and that she wished for nothing so much as peace between the Sioux and the whites. He would not say that Lisa opposed Sun Horse's surrender. He would tell only the truth, and it might be enough.

And after that? Had her lovemaking been an invitation to stay for longer than a while? To stay forever? Was he

foolish to go looking far and wide for his home when it
might be right here in front of his eyes? His imaginings of
yesterday could come to pass. He could see the park in
summer, all aflower, with a woman by his side. But
Putnam's Park belonged to Lisa and it would never be his.

Once before in his life Hardeman had thought to stay
somewhere because of a woman. It had been in the summer of '68, before the Washita, before he teamed up with
a young boy who spoke Cheyenne in his dreams. Fed up
with the army and the mulishness of its officers where
Indians were concerned, he had turned his back on the
frontier posts and made his way east along the Kansas
River to the booming town of Abilene, where the talk was
of nothing but cattle. He saw the Longhorns for himself
and the men who herded them. The "cow-boys," as they
were called, for many of the Texas drovers were surprisingly young, had reminded Hardeman of nothing so much
as soldiers turned loose at the end of a long campaign.
They drank both to celebrate and to forget their hardships
and they sought all the luxuries they had been denied for
so long. Their fancies were catered to by whores and
gamblers and confidence men who had flocked to Abilene
as they flocked wherever money flowed freely. Hardeman
had lost himself for a time in the section of town south of
the tracks, called McCoy's Addition by some and the Beer
Garden by others, and it was there that he had encountered
the unexpected—an unlikely woman in that unlikely place,
the first woman he had ever wished to make his own.

She was a woman in business for herself and her business was operating the best house of prostitution in Abilene. It was called the Bluebird Hotel, and her name was
Mary Ellen Tompkins. She was twenty-nine years of age.
Her eyes were green, her hair was black, and her skin was
like porcelain china. When she was dressed to go north of

the tracks on matters of banking or some other business, gentlemen newly arrived in town tipped their hats to this self-possessed beauty and sought to learn where they might call on her. When they learned her true situation they learned as well that she was a solitary woman, unattainable and untouchable; she usually had no trouble diverting their advances and directing them toward one of her girls, who were a cut above the usual run of "soiled doves" and "inhabitants of the *demi-monde*," as the frontier newspapers poetically described the cowtown whores. These young women, whose predecessors had attended the leaves of every army since the world began, now offered themselves to the youthful drovers, giving their masculinity and pride needed recognition after the dusty monotony of the long drives.

Her reputation notwithstanding, Mary Ellen took Hardeman first into her arms and later into her confidence. She let him know at once that she had never lived the life of the girls under her care, and bit by bit, in their private moments together, she had told him her dream until he saw it whole and knew she was offering to share it with him.

Tompkins was not her true surname. She came of good family, a family whose name was known in the society of Boston and New York, and when she came of age she had assessed her prospects and despaired. Her mother had married a man of property, and proposed that as a young lady's highest ambition. She took pains to instill in her only daughter the knowledge that she would need in order to snare the right man. Mary Ellen had been instructed in how to become the guiding force—an invisible force, never to be publicly acknowledged, it was made abundantly clear—behind a powerful man. But Mary Ellen contrived to evade her mother's plans and shake off one wealthy suitor after another, desperately seeking some avenue of escape. It presented itself in the death of an uncle who was regarded as a black sheep in the family. He had gambled and sailed and cared little for the world of financial affairs, and his way with the ladies had caused scandals that never quite managed to tarnish the family name, but there were always raised eyebrows aplenty when he tipped his hat to a married woman. Mary Ellen was his favorite niece and she had returned his affection abundantly. When she was a small girl he called on her when she was sick and read her fairy tales. For Christmas he gave her dresses more suitable for roughhousing and play than for formal dinners with servants in attendance, and she was heartily grateful. When she was older, he gave her presents of jewelry and took her riding in Central Park, and with Mary Ellen at least, his behavior was always impeccable. When they were alone he spoke of the endless opportunities America offered to those with sufficient daring and he debunked the notion that only men should be trusted with the management of money. "Look at you," he said on one occasion. "You've got a head on your shoulders as good as any man's, and a damn sight prettier."

When he died he left Mary Ellen a modest sum of money that was not surprising in itself, for he had been fortunate in investments as well as love and had enjoyed flaunting his money as proof that his wild ways had not led him to the disastrous end his staid relations often predicted. But a close reading of his will failed to reveal any trace of the most common Victorian proviso whenever capital was passed on to a female relative, that she should have access to the interest but not the capital itself. The bequest was without any restrictions whatever. As Mary Ellen was of age, there was nothing her family could do to stop her taking control of her inheritance forthwith. Which she promptly did, and just as promptly disappeared from their lives forever.

She had made her way to the frontier, that land of fabled opportunity, intending in the space of the next five years to make her fortune. She had invested in a business with low overhead and high profits, and in one year she had already deposited in Abilene banks an amount equal to three times her inheritance. At the end of the time she had allotted herself she proposed to sell her business and vanish once again, continuing west under yet another new name. She had her eye set on Colorado, where mining and cattle were creating a new society centered on Denver, or perhaps California, where it was said the weather was always mild. She would let it be known that she was an eastern heiress and when the right man presented himself she would marry. She would seek a man whose dream was as strong as her own, but in their life together she would be his equal; wherever they went, whatever enterprise they undertook together, she intended to be respected and free from want, and she would never surrender her will to a man's whims or weaknesses.

Hardeman had spent seventeen years in the west, half of his life then, and he had not yet tired of leading the way. There was much he had not seen, and although he was not sure where he would stop when the time came, he sensed that his was not to be the settled, respectable life Mary Ellen coveted. Leaving her was like leaving a part of himself behind, but he knew that to remain would mean living her life and not his own, and so he had said goodbye. "I shall be here for four more years," she had said as she kissed him farewell. "Until then I will wait for you."

But he had not gone back for her. Once, years later, he and Johnny had passed through Abilene in wintertime. He had ridden south of the tracks and found the Bluebird

Hotel closed and shuttered; Abilene was no longer the railhead, and McCoy's Addition was as quiet as a Sunday-morning churchyard. On making inquiries regarding the former owner, he was told that she had sold out in '72 and gone away, no one seemed to know where, and he had guessed that Mary Ellen had moved on just as she said she would, following her dream. He had realized then that he had cast a life aside when he left her, one of the lives that might have been his if he had taken a different turn.

Since then he had never met another woman who touched him in the same way, until now. Was Lisa holding out the offer of a life together? He was not used to interpreting the unspoken intentions of well-bred women. The women he knew best made their desires plain in a very few words.

If by giving herself she had invited him to stay forever, was that another life he could afford to cast aside? How many similar chances could he let go by before his allotted share was gone? Maybe this was the one he should take.

But all his instincts cautioned him against staying where the land and the dream were Lisa's alone. Dreams were personal things, each taking its own course like the rivulets of spring runoff finding their way down the mountainsides; sometimes two joined and ran together for a time, but with dreams, such joinings were rare.

He became aware that he had been holding the lid off the stove for several minutes and the air in the room was becoming smoky. He dropped the cluster of hairs into the flames and replaced the lid, remembering his hunger and his need to get out into the world, where others had been awake for hours.

With his clothing there was a large square of indigo-dyed linsey-woolsey, obviously intended as a sling for his arm, but he could not tie it in place with only one hand and so he gathered it up with the rest of his things and after a last look around to be sure he had left nothing behind, he went out of the room and descended the stairs.

He went first to the small room in the back of the house where he and Johnny had been quartered on the day they arrived in Putnam's Park. One of the bunks was unmade and a woman's dressing gown lay across the foot of the bed. Lisa obviously thought he would need to stay in her bedroom a while longer. She would be surprised to see him up and feeling fit. He left his belongings on Johnny's bunk and made his way to the kitchen, where he found Ling Wo alone. She smiled as he entered.

"You hungry? I fix breakfast. Lisa say you must sleep all you want, eat all you want."

"Thanks, Ling. I could do with something."

"Coffee there." She pointed at the speckled enamel pot. "You help yourself." She aimed her huge belly at the pantry.

"I could use some help with this." He held up the sling. "If I don't put it on, she'll be angry."

"Don't matter, I think," Ling said cheerfully. "She plenty angry today. Don't know why, anyhow. You come here, I fix it."

He had to bend over nearly double in order for the short woman to tie the sling behind his neck, and while he was in this awkward position there were footsteps in the entry-way and Harry Wo entered from the outdoors.

"Morning," said the squat blacksmith as Hardeman straightened.

"Morning." Hardeman poured himself a cup of coffee and sat down as Harry and Ling conducted a short conversation in Chinese.

"Sorry." Harry turned to Hardeman. "We should talk American. I'm trying to improve her. You got to improve all the time or you don't get nowhere."

"It's all right. I'm just getting used to American myself after three weeks with the Sioux."

Harry nodded. "Interesting folks. Hears Twice pays me a visit when he's down. Ain't seen him in some time. You reckon Sun Horse will surrender?"

Hardeman shrugged. "I quit guessing what he'll do."

Harry nodded again. "Well, we got us a stuck sled. I'm off to help dig it out. Snow's soft today. Might be spring after all."

Harry left and Hardeman sat back patiently to await his breakfast, smelling the odors of potatoes and buffalo steak and eggs frying on the stove. The Sun Band would have decided what to do by now. Would they surrender? He was surprised to discover that he was almost indifferent to the outcome. It wasn't his concern any longer.

After he ate, he wandered outside. The mercury in the big thermometer on the kitchen stoop hovered near forty degrees and the day felt even warmer in the sun. He strolled across the yard toward the barn. He would have a look at the packs he and Johnny had brought with them. They would have to split the supplies between the two of them, he supposed, the things that didn't already belong to one or the other. But there was no rush about that, not with both of them staying on after the circus left.

Down in the meadow several figures were working around the hay sled, trying to free it from a drift. Harry Wo had taken along a second pair of work horses and they were being hitched up. Nearer at hand men from the circus were going to and from the red-and-white-striped tent, carrying articles of equipment, and in the barn he found the acrobats and tumblers and clowns hard at work. Everywhere in the settlement, people were going about their tasks, all but Hardeman. Today he would take things easy, and as long as he only had the use of one arm, the amount of work he could do would be limited, but he would find work.

The packs were just as he had left them. He was opening them to look over the contents when a voice spoke his name.

"Mr. Hardeman?"

It was the English strongman. Hardeman didn't know his name.

"Chalmers. Alfred Chalmers," the giant introduced himself. "We did not actually meet on the night of our arrival. Many new faces and whatnot, eh? All seems long ago now. Good to see you up and about. We understand you had quite some adventures. Ah, I believe you have seen Amanda recently?"

"Not for very long."

"But she was well?"

"In better shape than I was, just then. Don't worry, Mr. Chalmers, they're taking good care of her. Snowblindness cures itself soon enough. Sun Horse just helps it along. And Johnny's there to look after her."

"Yes, I know." The Englishman looked around to see if they were being overheard. "Miss Putnam has told us of their, ah, plans. She thought it best that we should have some time to accustom ourselves to losing Amanda. I have told Mr. Tatum myself."

"How did he take it?"

"Quietly enough. He is not an easy man to understand, Mr. Hardeman. You may not be aware that he . . . he depends on Amanda, you might say. Losing her cannot be easy for him."

"You think he'll make trouble?"

"I believe not. In any event, nothing we can't deal with. Amanda has many friends in the circus and we will stand by her. I just thought you should know."

Hardeman thanked the Englishman for his concern and spent the next half hour going through the saddlebags while the acrobats worked around him. When he stepped outside again he saw that a thin layer of haze had moved in between the small puffy clouds and the sun, diffusing the sunlight. In the meadow Julius and Hutch were feeding hay from a nearly empty sled now, and two riders were coming up the wagon road, Lisa and Harry by the look of them.

When he got a chance he would take Lisa aside and tell her of his willingness to stay and help out. There was more talking to do after that, too. He didn't find it easy to express his feelings but he could make himself plain if he wasn't rushed. Once the circus was gone the place would be quiet and there would be more than enough time for unhurried talk.

A cloud covered the sun and the wind quickened. The air was turning colder. Hardeman thought to get his buckskin coat but as he turned toward the house a movement in the heifer lot caught his eye. One of the heifers was in the throes of giving birth and Hardeman stopped to watch. It seemed to be going well enough; the calf's nose was already in view, and with the next contraction the head appeared with the forefeet neatly tucked beneath the chin. But as the heifer heaved again and more of the calf's body emerged, Hardeman climbed the fence and jumped into the calving lot, feeling in his pocket for his folding knife.

The umbilical cord was wrapped around the calf's neck. He opened the knife as he knelt in the mud by the cow's hindquarters, and severed the cord with a single stroke of the blade. Tossing the knife aside he used his good hand to take hold of the calf by the shoulder and pull gently, trying to help the mother. The thing now was to get the calf out and breathing.

His hand slipped on the birthing fluids and he lost his grip, falling on his side in the mud. He cursed under his breath and slipped his left arm out of the sling. He took hold of the calf with both hands, ignoring the pain deep in his wounded shoulder, and with a final push from the heifer the calf slipped free. It was a bull calf. Hardeman seized a piece of straw from the mud and stroked the calf's nostrils, first one and then the other. Sometimes just tickling a calf's nose would make it sneeze and start breathing on its own, but the calf remained still, its eyes closed. The mother, a heifer no longer, lurched to her feet and sniffed the calf, then began to lick it clean, but Hardeman brushed her away and tried to lift the little bull by the hind feet to drain its breathing passages. There was a sharp pain in his left shoulder and he lost his grip, and as he bent over to try again he was joined by Lisa and Harry Wo, who appeared suddenly at his side.

"The cord was around his neck," he said.

"We better drain him out," said Harry. He seized the calf by the hind feet and hoisted it into the air as easily as a sack of potatoes. Lisa knelt by the calf's head, her elbows in the mud. With two fingers she scooped the calf's mouth and throat clean, then did the same for each nostril.

"Hold his mouth closed," she instructed Hardeman.

He squatted beside her and clamped his hands over the calf's muzzle. She leaned down, covered one nostril with her hand and placed her mouth over the other. She blew hard and released both nostrils, knocking Hardeman's hands aside. The calf coughed, bleated, and opened its eyes.

Harry set the calf down near its mother and spoke soothingly to her in Chinese, encouraging her as she began to sniff her offspring. The calf was breathing regularly now, panting as if to make up for lost time. Hardeman was struck by how different Harry's voice sounded when he spoke English. In Chinese he seemed to be singing some ancient chant.

"These cows all speak Chinese pretty soon," Harry said to Hardeman, and he grinned.

Hardeman leaned against the fence, drained by his exertions on behalf of the calf. It seemed he didn't have all his strength back just yet.

With huffing and stamping from the horses and the creak of wood against wood, the hay sled entered the yard and pulled to a stop beyond the fence.

"You all been rasslin' in the mud?" Julius inquired as he stepped to the ground.

Hardeman looked down at his clothes, which were covered with mud and streamers of birth fluids from the calf. He glanced at Lisa. "I guess I'm in trouble now. This outfit was clean this morning." She didn't meet his gaze. Except for her few words while they worked over the calf, she had neither spoken to him nor looked him in the eye since arriving in the calving lot.

"You in worse trouble with me," Julius said. "I told that woman to make you wear a sling. I didn't mean just hang it 'round your neck."

"It wasn't her fault. She passed on the orders but I needed both hands."

"He got to that cow first," Harry explained. "Without him we might of lost the calf."

Julius scaled the fence with practiced movements and dropped to the ground beside Hardeman. "It's a wonder to me how three folks can get so messed up just saving one calf."

"You can only save one at a time," Hardeman said. Lisa looked at him strangely, and he remembered what she had said about Blackbird. All right, maybe saving one boy wasn't such a little thing. Maybe you could only save one at a time. But at least calves didn't go running headlong into cavalry guns and resist everything you did to guide them to safety.

Julius took Hardeman's left arm in his hands and raised it slightly. Hardeman winced. "Mm hmm." Julius nodded his head. He began to unbutton Hardeman's shirt. "Two bits says you've gone and—yup, you bust it open."

Hardeman looked down and saw fresh blood soaking the bandage on his shoulder.

"You come on with me," the Negro said curtly. "We best get that stopped up. Hutch! You feed those horses and put them out, if you would." The boy already had the harness mostly undone, going ahead with his work without being told.

In the kitchen Julius helped Hardeman out of his shirt and unwrapped the bandage. When the wound was revealed they saw that the fresh bleeding had mostly stopped of its own accord.

"I appreciate all your trouble," Hardeman said. "I didn't mean to ruin your work."

Julius grunted and made no reply. He had no patience for pleasantries just now. Lisa's moods had gone from dark to bright and back again quicker than day and night ever since Hardeman's return, and Julius had no doubt that the scout was at fault. At first Lisa had been all upset about the news of the war starting and Hawk Chaser's death, and although she didn't say so, Julius knew she was worried about Hardeman's wound as well. And then yesterday, she had hummed to herself through the afternoon and evening, staying near the house and spending most of her time upstairs, fixing Hardeman's supper tray herself with everything arranged just so. This morning the cheerful spirits were gone as if they had never existed and Lisa scarcely had a word for anyone. Julius didn't need to know what Hardeman had done to blame him for it.

"You set there and don't move that arm," he said, and went off to fetch a fresh piece of bandage from the medicine cabinet.

As Julius left the kitchen Hutch came in from the entryway. He nodded to Hardeman and accepted the mug of coffee Ling poured for him without a word.

"I reckon Johnny will be along pretty soon, him and Amanda," he said, more as a question than a statement of fact. He sat down opposite Hardeman at the table and couldn't keep his eyes off the wound. He had never seen a bullet hole in a man before.

"Pretty soon," Hardeman agreed.

"I've learned a right smart lot from him while you were gone, about roping and cattle and such. He says everything he knows he learned from you."

"Johnny has a way of picking things up. He didn't take a whole lot of teaching."

"I'm glad he'll be staying on for a bit, him and Amanda both." He fell silent, thinking of Maria Abbruzzi, who had refused his own offer of marriage. She had laughed at his protestations of undying love and she had soothed his wounded pride with her soft lips and warm body, which was so strong beneath the velvet skin. "You are not Catholic," she had said, as if that settled everything. "Besides, you must never marry the first one you make love with, or you will always wonder what the rest are like. If you tell anyone I have said this, I will kill you!" But she kissed him to show she didn't mean it, and she whispered, "I will remember you forever. I will name a son for you." Hutch knew of the Waldheims' offer to Johnny and he had given some thought to asking around to see if he too might not get a job with the circus, but he knew now that Maria would never change her mind and he knew just as certainly that the circus life was not for him. They spent their time in the cities and towns, and after their summer in San Francisco they would return to the East. Hutch's life was here in the West, where the land was suited for raising cattle and real men.

He took a sudden breath and spoke again. "Mr. Hardeman, there's something I'd like to ask you."

"Ask away."

"Well, last fall I come by here kind of by accident. Miss Lisa, she said I could stay the winter, and I was grateful for that. She's a fair woman and the pay's all right, but this place means more to me than just a place that give me a job. I feel like I owe kind of a debt and I don't see how to pay it off. I was fixin' to move on come spring, but I'd be willin' to stay on here. You reckon that would help her out?"

"I imagine it would," Hardeman said, considering the sober young man before him. Hutch's seriousness reminded him of Johnny. "It's not an easy time for her. She's worried about keeping the park."

Hutch nodded. "That's it. See, like today she hardly says a word, and a body can feel her worryin' all the while. She makes out like it's just Sun Horse she's worryin' on, and she don't say nothin' about losin' Putnam's Park. The fact is, she don't say nothin' about the outfit at all, and that's not like her. Most mornin's when she's riding down there, lookin' at the cattle, she'll stop by the sled and have a word with Julius and me, about how the cows look and how many calves there are and how much hay's left, things of that nature. Today she didn't hardly say a word even when she came over to help us dig the sled out. I was thinkin' maybe if I said I'd stay on that might cheer her up."

"It might at that," Hardeman said, hoping his own intention to do the same thing would improve her spirits further.

But he found it more difficult than he had imagined to have a word with Lisa alone. It was almost as if she was avoiding him. Julius came back with the bandage and before he was done dressing the wound the dinner gong rang. The circus folk flocked to the saloon and Hardeman joined them, ready to eat again just two hours after his last meal. Lisa kept herself busy at the serving tables and she never did sit down to eat. After the meal Hardeman returned to the kitchen, thinking she would take a moment for him when she was done cleaning up. But almost as soon as he made his appearance she asked if Ling felt well enough to finish up the dishes with Monty's help, pleading some work or other that demanded her attention outside, and she went off so quickly that Hardeman felt he had done something to offend her.

She remained outside all afternoon and as suppertime drew near he resolved to wait no longer. He thought he knew what troubled her, and he could set her fears to rest if only she would give him the chance. As usual she went upstairs to change out of her man's clothing before supper, and when she came down again in her indigo dress with her hair piled atop her head, he was waiting for her in the door of the library.

"Miss Putnam—Lisa. There's something I'd like to say if you have a moment." He took her arm and guided her into the library, where he had built a fire to warm the room.

She turned to face him and there was no welcome in her look, no acknowledgment that they were anything more than strangers.

Her manner took him aback but he went on. "Seeing as

Johnny will be staying on here, I thought I might stay on too, just for a while. At least until he and the girl get set to move on. I wouldn't want to miss that wedding." He waited for some sign that his offer pleased her, that her moodiness today had been caused by uncertainty over what he might do and the hope of hearing just such words, but she gave him none. She remained withdrawn, as if shielding herself from an impending hurt. "I wouldn't want to see you get caught up in a war, either. I know the army; it might be I could help, if it comes to that. And I'll do what I can about your deed."

"It may be some time before it's all resolved," she said, offering no encouragement.

"I'm in no hurry to be moving on. I'd like to help."

Lisa sighed. It was time to speak the truth. As she had expected, moving on was the first thought on his mind. He would delay his departure for her but he would not abandon it, and even last night as she fell asleep with his arms around her, she had known somewhere inside her that this was the way it would be. This morning she had awakened and slipped out of bed and looked to the future, and she had felt betrayed by her own impulsiveness. Once again she had permitted herself to care for a man who would soon be gone. Like the cavalry lieutenant he had come to her wounded and she had healed him, restoring to him the strength he needed to leave her. But she would keep to her resolve and do nothing to hold him against his will.

She felt a numbing sorrow and cursed herself for a fool; self-pity was something her father had scorned and she would not give in to it now. But the sorrow was not just for herself. It was for Sun Horse and the Sioux, and for Hardeman too, who was closer to the Indians in habits and ways, if not in social customs, than he was to the people who were already moving west in such numbers to claim the realm that had been secured for them, at what cost they would never know, by mountain men like her father and pathfinders like Hardeman. It had taken the arrival of the circus to make her see just how far things had progressed since her own childhood. A bunch of greenhorns could stumble about the mountains, losing their way, entering the heart of the Sioux hunting grounds without knowing it, and in a few days they would move on without any sense of the dangers they had survived. Twenty years ago such a thing would have been unimaginable. That it was now possible convinced Lisa more than ever that the sun was setting on the roaming ways of the Indians, and all others as well. The time of nomadic freedom was giving way to railroads and farms and fences and traveling entertainments like Tatum's Combined Shows, and it was not only the Indians who would be pushed aside. The trappers were gone and the scouts would soon follow in their footsteps. The West was still a land of many opportunities, but the time was fast approaching when those who did not choose among the opportunities before them would be left behind by the rush of progress, and wonder why only when it was too late. Her father had predicted such a turn of events and she saw it now too, coming sooner than either of them had expected, as if Jed Putnam's passing had somehow hastened the day when he and men of his stature would have to give way to Hachaliah Tatum and his ilk.

She wanted to shout her anger at Hardeman, telling him he was blind not to see how quickly his choices were being narrowed down while he roamed along with the far look her father had noted a quarter century before still in his eyes. Stop looking over the horizon! she wanted to cry out. Look at what's right here! It's good, and I'm holding it out to you! But she could do no more. She had made the offer as plainly as she was able and it remained for Chris

Hardeman to accept the gift or reject it. When a man chose to stay with her in Putnam's Park it would be by his own free choice, not because of any persuasions she used to restrain him.

"I do not expect you to leave until you're fit," she said. "I know you'll want to see Johnny again. But if you're going to go, I would prefer that it be as soon as possible."

She turned on her heel and went from the room. If she had remained, Hardeman would not have known how to frame a reply. If she too doubted that there could be a future for the two of them together, then there was nothing left to say. She clearly regretted what she had done last night and she wished him gone.

There was a festive air in the saloon at suppertime. The teamsters were close to breaking through the last of the avalanche and they had high hopes for the morrow. As the meal was cleared away the fat German horse trainer went to fetch his accordion but Hardeman did not stay for the music. His first day out of bed had tired him and he was in no mood for celebration, so he went to the small room at the back of the house where he found Lisa's dressing gown gone and his bed freshly made.

In the morning a gentle snow was falling. Once again he overslept breakfast and by the time he appeared in the saloon it was empty except for Ling Wo and Joe Kitchen, who were wiping off the tables. Hardeman spent the morning sorting through the packs in the barn, dividing the contents as fairly as he could and repacking those items he intended taking with him when he departed. The wound in his shoulder had recovered from being abused the day before and he was confident that he could handle a horse even with his arm in a sling.

After the noon meal he cast about for some way to pass

the time and he thought to offer his help to Harry Wo or
Julius, but as if in answer to his growing impatience, three
riders appeared on the creek trail and once again Joe
Kitchen pounded on the meal gong, this time to welcome
Amanda and Johnny back to the settlement.

They were accompanied by Bat Putnam, and in no time
the three of them were swallowed in a crowd that gathered
from all quarters and moved along with them until they
reached the barn, where the crowd stopped and would
allow them to go no farther until each and every one who
had been concerned for Amanda's welfare had welcomed
her and congratulated her on her engagement.

"Your eyes, they are well?" Carlos was saying as
Hardeman made his way to the center of the throng. "We
hear you are blind from the snow."

"They're fine," Amanda said. "Sun Horse cured me.
He used a magic chant passed on to him by his grandfather. He told me his grandfather could cure snowblindness
better than any man who ever lived." She was wearing her
own boots and buffalo coat, and a deerskin dress and
rabbit-fur leggings given her by Sings His Daughter. On
her head, incongruously, she wore her red clown's cap.
Johnny Smoker stood protectively close to her and one of
her hands rested on his arm. Lisa Putnam stood at her
other side.

"Imagine that old magician working his spells on you,"
Lydia said, shaking her head. "You must beware of sor-
cerers, child." She made a sign to ward off evil spirits and
addressed herself sternly to Johnny. "You see that you
take good care of her, young man. If harm comes to her I
will know, even if I am far away, and I will put a mortal
curse on your soul."

"When Lydia threatens you, that means she trusts you,"
Chalmers added quickly, and Johnny looked somewhat

relieved as those around him laughed, but Lydia's expression remained serious.

"You mark my words," she said softly, and she drew closer to Chalmers and took his arm.

"So I lose my new assistant before he even comes to vork!" Papa Waldheim exclaimed, clapping Johnny on the back.

"I'm sorry. I would have liked working for you."

"Ach! No sorrys, please. You chust take good care of our Amanda. Someone else vill be fortunate to haff you vork for him."

"You won't give up your clowning?" Sam Higgins asked Amanda, concerned. "Miss Putnam tells us you will go to another show."

Amanda dropped her gaze and nodded, suddenly forlorn. "I don't want to leave any of you."

"Come now, my young lady," Lydia admonished her. "We will have no sadness here today. We all understand."

"Indeed," Chalmers added his support, with a meaningful glance at those around him. "There is no need to discuss it and no need to feel sad. Who is to say that we shall not work together again sometime in the years to come?"

Amanda brightened at once, for this was her secret desire. "Oh, I hope so!"

"We've been workin' hard, Carlos and me," Sam said, all good spirits and encouragement. "We've got that new routine down pat, the fisherman and the swell. We'll go over it with you tomorrow and we'll put it in the performance. Goin' t' be quite a show, this one."

There was a distant shout and heads turned to seek the source. Coming up the wagon road at a run, riders were visible in the thin snowfall. There were more shouts now, and raised arms, and behind the horsemen came two wagons, drawn by mules, with men riding in the boxes. Far to the rear came the rest of the wagons, pulled by slow but powerful oxen.

"Looks like you better get that practicing done this afternoon," said Joe Kitchen. "Something tells me we'll be having our show tomorrow."

A few shots came from pistols in the riders' hands and a moment later they swept into the yard, riding in a circle around the circus wagons and finally coming to a stop in front of the crowd by the barn. When their shouting died down and it was possible to make sense of their words, Joe's guess was confirmed. The last of the avalanche had been removed and the roadway was clear, and Hachaliah Tatum had decreed that the performance would be held on the following day.

The wagons clattered into the yard and a new round of cheers was raised by those men. The teamsters on horseback turned toward the barn now, eager to unsaddle their mounts and make for the saloon, for Tatum had promised to buy drinks all around. Some of the performers moved off to join the celebration but Amanda's friends remained clustered around her, the Waldheims and Abbruzzis, Sam and Carlos, Chalmers and Lydia, Julius, Hutch and Chatur, Lisa and Hardeman and Johnny Smoker and Bat Putnam, and all eyes in this group were on Hachaliah Tatum, who entered the settlement last of all, riding in tandem with the one-armed Kinnean. Kinnean saw Hardeman among those around Amanda and he turned aside, taking a more circuitous route to the barn door, while Tatum slowed his white stallion and approached the little gathering at a walk. Amanda drew back but Johnny held her tightly. Lisa moved a step forward as if to prevent Tatum from approaching too near to the fur-coated girl.

Hardeman noted Amanda's fear and the defiance in

Johnny's expression, and he remembered Alfred Chalmers' veiled warning.

"Well, I must say you seem fit enough," Tatum greeted Amanda. His voice was full of care. "I am glad to see you looking so well." His eyes moved to Johnny. "No words of mine are adequate to thank you for saving her life. You have my profound gratitude."

Johnny gave a short nod and said nothing.

"If there is anything I can do for the two of you . . ." Tatum's voice trailed off and his eyes were on Amanda. Then he seemed to collect himself. "Well, we have a show to prepare. If there is any particular arrangement you wish me to make, any alteration in the order of events, perhaps a special farewell, you have only to ask."

He tipped his hat, backed the stallion three paces, then turned and trotted off toward the circus tent.

"It would seem there is no trouble from that quarter," Chalmers mused after a short silence.

"So it would seem," Lisa agreed, although her tone was cautious. She turned to Amanda. "You mustn't stand about in the cold. Come let me make you a cup of tea while Johnny and Bat see to the horses." She took Amanda by the arm and led her off.

"If ve are to perform tomorrow and leave on the day after, ve must feed the horses double," Papa Waldheim said to his sons. "More hay now and grain in the morning."

"We'll help you," Julius said, including Hutch in the offer of aid. The others remembered that they had set work aside to greet the young couple and they dispersed now to return to their tasks, leaving Hardeman and Johnny and Bat Putnam alone with the three horses.

"Come on," Hardeman said to Johnny. "I'll help you unsaddle these animals."

"Now hold on there." Bat put out a restraining hand.

"I ain't come all this way just to take the air. I reckoned you'd like to know that Sun Horse ain't goin' in."

Hardeman stopped and turned. Bat nodded. "Two mornin's ago, the day after you left, he woke up bright as a new penny and he calls a council. 'I will not go to Dakota,' he says. 'We will live in the Lakota way, my grandson and I. Any who wish to stay with us are welcome.' Had Blackbird right there beside him like he couldn't stand to have the boy out of his sight. He says we'll go north when the snow melts and we'll join the hoop of the nation, if there's gonna be a summer gatherin'. He's got a plan to make peace. Didn't say what it was, just that he knew what to do when the time come. Right now we're gonna stick to the Lakota way, he says. Won't surrender, won't fight, just gonna keep clear o' the trouble. And I'm tellin' you, Christopher, it's the doggondest thing. I never seen such a change in a man in all my born days. He's like a young buck again. Eatin' like a grizzly and struttin' about like he was forty again. Threw that cane o' his plumb away. There was sump'n about him, you jest had to believe what he said. Even old Elk Leggin's, him that said he'd be goin' to Dakota come spring, well he ain't goin' now. He's stayin' with the band and so's the rest. We're all puttin' out together when the grass is up. Till then we got the scouts watchin' all the trails. If'n Three Stars comes this way, we'll know in time to stay a jump ahead of him."

It plainly delighted Bat to convey this news and Johnny too was pleased. "You remember how we felt when we left Cheyenne?" the young man asked, and Hardeman nodded. "You had General Crook's go-ahead and we thought we couldn't lose. With a peace man to persuade the hostiles to go in, there wouldn't be any war. You were so sure of it, I believed you."

"It didn't work out."

"No, it didn't," Johnny agreed. "But there's the same kind of look about Sun Horse now. Like he's got something in mind and it's bound to work."

"That ain't certain," Bat said. "A man gets an idea how to lead his people, folks got to believe in him and help out. Everybody's got to do his share. One man alone can't do it all."

Johnny nodded, still looking at Hardeman. "That's right. He'll need help, and I was thinkin' there might still be something you could do for him."

"I did all I could," Hardeman said. "I can't do any more than that."

"Well, I believed that too, but now I ain't so sure. What I mean is, we came to help him right enough, but it was our idea, not his. Maybe that's why it didn't work. What I'm getting at is, the one thing we never done for him was ask what he wanted."

Hardeman was silent for a long time. Johnny had changed. It was no single thing but an impression of many small differences, in the way he spoke and the way he held himself, as if in the time Hardeman had been gone Johnny had grown, not in height or size but inside, where it was harder to see. He stood on his own now and he spoke his mind.

Hardeman remembered the gratitude he had felt toward Sun Horse when the pipe carriers were on the trail north, for giving Johnny the freedom to choose between the worlds. The boy had chosen and the choice had strengthened him. He had taken the last steps into manhood now, and Sun Horse was to thank for that.

" 'Tain't like what you done was a perfect bust," Bat said. "There's one thing come out'n this whole deal I thought I'd never see. That's the Lakotas ready to settle down and change their ways. That's what it amounts to, don't y' see? Up there in Two Moons' council them fellers seddown and said they'd take the country from Fort Reno to the Yellowstone and give up the rest. That's like you or me livin' on some dogpatch piece o' ground in St. Louie or Denver so small you could pitch a rock clear acrost it. It's a big change for the Sioux, but they'll make it if'n they get the chance. They see which way the wind blows. Right now it blows from the east and sings the white man's tune. They know it ain't gonna change soon. They're lookin' for a way to keep from bein' blowed plumb flat. Even ol' Sittin' Bull sees which way his stick floats. He's an ornery son of a bitch and he'll walk 'round a mountain to fight the *washíchun*, but he ain't stupid. Give him a way to live with his pride and he'll come to water and drink too.''

But would the white man drink with him? Hardeman wondered. He remembered how his hopes had been raised in the council in Two Moons' village. It was there that the plan for peace had become something more than his own idea, and there that he had first seen a chance for peace on terms the Indians worked out for themselves. Did Sun Horse see a way to salvage those terms despite the fighting? Hawk Chaser was dead, Blackbird wounded, the Cheyenne and their Oglala friends attacked and homeless, and Crook's column doubtless still on the trail, strengthened now with fresh provisions from the supply train. And Sun Horse was of good cheer.

''Bat says with his brother Jed gone, Sun Horse needs a friend from the white world,'' Johnny said, looking from Hardeman to the mountain man and back again. ''I don't know anybody else who knows the Indians like you do. I'm askin' you to stay on for a while. Call it a wedding present. I don't want nothin' else if you'll do this for me.''

"Fact is," Bat added, "Sun Horse said he'd be pleased if you'd come by and stay a spell while we're waitin' for this to quit." He made a gesture at the falling snow and the surrounding mountains, meaning the winter itself, which seemed determined to linger on. "Might be he ain't got nothin' special to ask of you. But his power's to understand the *washíchun* and he likes to set 'n' jaw with a feller he can trust. Me, I lived with them folks so long I reckon I think most like them now. But you're fresh from civilized diggin's and you're Johnny's teacher to boot. That's the way he sees it, leastways. Might be he figgers he could learn sump'n from you too."

Even as Bat was speaking, Hardeman knew he would heed the old chief's call. Even without Johnny's plea he would have gone. He had thought to speak with Tatum and offer to guide the circus to Rawlins, but now he was glad he had put off talking to the circus master. Sun Horse was still in danger and he was Johnny's only living relative, and Hardeman's desire to make peace had not been snuffed out by the failure of his efforts, merely pushed aside. And now Johnny had shown him a way to try again. *We never asked him what he wanted,* the boy had said, and he was right. Maybe what Sun Horse had needed all along wasn't someone coming along with his own notions of how to save the Sioux but just a friend willing to listen and do what was asked of him, as one friend helping another. And in Sun Horse's village Hardeman would be close enough to Putnam's Park to watch over Lisa without being in her way. He could see that she was kept safe and with or without her consent he would do what he could about her deed. He would see Johnny and Amanda properly married when the time came. He would do what he could to help Sun Horse. And then he would be free of past obligations and ready to look for his home. He would find a piece of land where he could live or die by his own efforts, as Jed Putnam had done. It was a worthy task, one that could keep a man busy. Maybe even busy enough to forget Jed's daughter, in time.

Bat and Johnny were watching him. "I'll be ridin' back after this here circus show tomorrow," Bat said. "You'd be welcome to bed down in my lodge."

Hardeman repressed a smile. "Oh, I don't know. They're treating me pretty good around here. Three meals a day and a soft bed." Johnny was grinning. The boy knew him too well to be fooled. He knew Hardeman had made up his mind to accept.

Bat snorted indignantly. "We got enough buffler over the hill to keep Rendezvous fed. You ain't lived till you get a bellyful of Penelope's *boudins*, and there ain't no bed in the world softer'n a pallet made o' buffler robes."

Hardeman smiled. "Well, now that's settled, you reckon we could get rid of these horses and go have a drink?" He could think of a dozen reasons to pour himself about half full of good corn whiskey, and his juices ran at the very thought.

A gunshot broke the stillness of the yard. Hardeman's hand found the grip of his Colt as he turned, but he relaxed when he saw Tatum beyond the wagons, standing in a stiff pose with one arm outstretched. Four more times the circus master fired and each time a small block of wood jumped off the railing of the pasture fence a hundred feet away.

From the shelter of the barn door Alfred Chalmers and Lydia were also watching Tatum. They stepped aside as Hardeman and Johnny and Bat led the horses through the door, and they remained standing against the outside wall, two motionless figures on the fringes of a barnyard that was full of comings and goings.

"Hold me, Alfred," Lydia said, and she pressed herself against him.

"With pleasure, my dear." He took her in his arms. "Are you cold?"

"I am frightened."

"Frightened? Whatever for?"

"I don't know," she said, and would say no more. She felt a chill that came from inside, not from without, and it was not the first time she had wondered if her second sight were more a curse than a blessing. In her booth on the circus midway she enjoyed herself, taking the hands of the people who came to have their fortunes told. They were timid or afraid or hopeful, or blustering to show that they did not believe in such things, but they believed, most of them. And Lydia invented fanciful tales, stories that would give a hopeless person hope or make a failure believe he could begin again. But on rare occasions she would take a stranger's hand and feel the frightening chill that overcame her when she saw beyond the present moment and could sense what was to come. On those occasions she closed the curtains to shut away the curious; she concentrated with all her being and she told the stranger what she saw. But even then she told only things that would give hope, for a hopeful person could accomplish much and might even alter fate, while a person told of impending misfortune might bring it upon himself. When she sensed death or calamitous events she kept these things to herself and left the future in the hands of God.

What she felt now was a vague foreboding, as yet unformed.

"Take me to the wagon," she said. "I must rest. But I do not wish to be alone. Stay with me, dear. Stay with me a while."

More gunshots came from beyond the wagons. Tatum

was taking glass balls from his pocket and throwing them into the air. One by one he blew them to smithereens.

The saloon was full before the twilight faded, and Hardeman and Bat were among the first at the bar. When the first glass was downed they called for more, and more again when that was gone. Hardeman slowed his drinking then and sipped the whiskey to savor the pleasure the strong drink gave him after such a long abstinence.

From the moment they entered the saloon Johnny and Amanda were the center of attention. Amanda had changed from her Indian clothes into her fawn-colored silk dress and Johnny too was in his Sunday best. When the supper gong rang, several tables were pushed end to end to make a long banquet board, with Johnny and Amanda seated in the center and their friends arrayed around them. The gathering was boisterous and jovial and glasses were repeatedly raised to the young couple. At the foot of the table Bat conveyed Sun Horse's news to Lisa while the conversation dinned around them. She brightened somewhat but he could see that something else was troubling her and then he noticed that she kept a wary eye on Hardeman. The scout too was aware of Lisa, although he never seemed to watch, and Bat divined that some new difficulty had arisen between them. He noted the stubborn tilt of Lisa's chin and wondered if her prideful Putnam nature was at the root of the trouble.

Even before the meal was done the calls for music began. It was to be the full circus band again, complete with tuba, and they wanted Amanda to lead them. "Come on, now," said the circus's second fiddler. "It's the last time we'll all be together. I put your fiddle in the barn, in the clown trunk."

"Tonight ve say goodbye mit music," Papa Waldheim

announced. "Happy tunes I vant to hear, so ve can dance the night avay."

Amanda turned to Julius but he shook his head. "We've got time, you and me. Tonight you play for your friends."

But Amanda would have none of it. "We'll play together or I won't play at all." She pouted, and Julius relented.

"All right. You go fetch your fiddle and I'll see if I cain't find mine."

As the others began clearing the dance floor and preparing the bandstand, Amanda kissed Johnny quickly on the cheek. "I'll be a little while," she said. "I want to get my things from the barn now, while no one is there. I couldn't stand to do it after the performance tomorrow, when everyone is packing up to leave."

Outside, a few flakes of snow were still falling to earth but stars glittered among the clouds and Amanda caught a glimpse of the slender crescent moon setting in the west. In the barn she found the matches that were kept on a beam near the door and lit the lamp that hung there. Her tightrope and the aerialists' equipment had been moved to the tent. Tomorrow the performers would dress here in the place where they had rehearsed for so long; after the show they would pack up and then even the trunks and costumes would be gone.

Amanda fought off a sense of loss that threatened to overwhelm her. She would not be left alone. Johnny would be with her and she felt that they belonged together. In the spring they would go east and she would show him so many places he had never seen, and once they were there the new jobs with another circus and her own triumphant return to the ring would follow inevitably. Together they could do anything! And hadn't Alfred said that some day

she would work with her old friends again? If only she
were brave enough now, all her dreams would come true.

She found her violin inside the clowns' trunk in the
dressing-room stall. It seemed like something she had last
seen in another lifetime. She opened the case and tightened
the bow, then set the instrument beneath her chin and
plucked the strings one by one, adjusting the pegs. When
it was tuned to her satisfaction she began to play Johnny's
Waltz to the empty barn, taking stately steps across the
floor as if she were walking a tightrope. A barn cat
stepped out onto the floor and sat down, watching her
curiously.

"You don't have to give it up, you know."

The voice from the dark startled her so badly that the
bow flew out of her hand and clattered to the floor. The
cat vanished in the blink of an eye. Hachaliah Tatum
emerged from the shadows by the door and advanced into
the lamplight.

"You don't have to give it up," he repeated. She
backed away from him as he approached. He bent to
retrieve her bow.

"I didn't hear you come in," she managed to say.

He made a gesture that sought to reassure her and
stopped his advance, holding the bow out to her. She came
forward cautiously to take it and then stepped quickly
back. She returned the violin and bow to the case and
picked it up, preparing to leave. She could come back later
for the rest of her things.

"Please stay, just for a moment." His voice was soft
and confidential. It was a tone he reserved for their times
alone together, when he was at his most reassuring. With
this voice he had comforted a hysterical child after her
parents died in a fire.

She waited.

"I realize it took a great deal of courage for you to take this step. The fact is, I always knew someday you would need to go off on your own and I tried to prepare myself for this moment." He paused and brushed awkwardly at a smudge of dust on the sleeve of his coat. "I'm afraid I haven't done a very good job of it. Perhaps it's not possible. At any rate, I want you to know that I understand what you're doing and I won't try to stop you. You're free to go, of course. But there is something I must ask of you. It's a proposal I have to make for the sake of my business, and perhaps for your career as well. I want to ask that you remain with us just temporarily"—he held up a hand to still the protest that rose to her lips—"on whatever terms you choose. This may seem like asking you to go back on your decision, but believe me, that is not what I mean by it."

"What sort of terms?"

He heard the interest in her voice and he moved a step or two closer as if to take her into his confidence. "Stay until I can find a replacement for you. I would consider it a personal kindness. Not that you owe me any favors. But still, I ask it."

"You have Sam and Carlos."

"They are good clowns but they are supporting characters and neither one is your equal. It will take time to reshape the clown acts and there will have to be another person added. If you will stay, I will take on young Johnny—your fiancé. He could be a great help with the horses. You remember the equestrian parade I've been planning for the grand entrance? The Waldheims will need help with it. He is quite remarkable with horses, they assure me." He paused to give her time to absorb what he had said. "Naturally, the two of you would have your own wagon once you are married."

He moved beneath the lamp and sat on a trunk. "If you would stay through the summer, I could manage after that. Think of it: San Francisco and the nation's centennial. That's what I'm worried about, to tell the truth. You know my hopes for this summer. We simply won't make the impact I want, not without you."

"We could have our own wagon?" Amanda was calculating the risks and the possible rewards. Fresh from a celebrated stand in San Francisco, it would be easy to get employment with another show.

"Of course."

"I'll have to talk it over with Johnny."

"Naturally, I'll abide by your decision. But please tell him how much this means to me. Just until the end of August, that's all I ask. You will have five months' wages in your pockets, both of you. I'll pay him what I pay you." It was extravagant, but it would be a small price to pay if it gave him time to change her mind.

"You would do that for me?"

"Of course. All I have ever wanted was your happiness."

Amanda searched his face and she saw no deceit, only hope. "Thank you," she said, and her gratitude was genuine. Hachaliah had done much for her over the years; he had never refused her anything, and his generosity now touched her deeply. "I'll talk to Johnny. I'm not saying we'll accept, but thank you for the offer." Her voice caught in her throat and she was surprised to find tears filling her eyes. "I thought you would hate me," she whispered.

"How could I hate you? Here now." He offered her a silk handkerchief. She dabbed at her eyes as he put a comforting arm around her.

"Thank you," she said again. She stood on tiptoes and touched her lips to his cheek. His other arm went around

her and he drew her close against him, lowering his head
to seek her lips with his own. She drew back.

"No, Hachaliah."

"You still want me, don't you."

"Let me go."

"I couldn't stand to lose you. And you couldn't stand to
go."

Amanda's happiness vanished. "Please, Hachaliah." His
grip tightened ever so slightly. Encumbered by the violin
case she could not break free. He tried once more to kiss
her but she twisted her head and avoided him and he did
not insist. Instead, he smiled.

"Did you think I could simply let you walk away?"

"It was all to get me back, wasn't it?"

"My offer? Yes, to get you back for the show. For the
summer. Everything I said is the truth. But I knew there
was more that you didn't want to leave behind." His
hands moved on her back, one dropping down to hold her
hips against his. "Come along for the summer. Bring your
young man. Marry him if you like, but of course there's
really no need for that. Have your *affaire de coeur*. And
when you tire of him—"

"No!" Without thinking, Amanda swung the violin case
with all her might. It caught Tatum full on the side of the
face, breaking the skin and raising a bloody welt on his
cheek. He lifted a hand to ward off another blow and she
broke free, running without looking, and found herself
stopped by the confines of the stall.

Tatum touched his cheek and saw blood on his fingers.
"You shouldn't have done that."

The tone of his voice chilled Amanda. "I didn't mean to
hurt you. I just wanted you to let me go."

"Yes. When you wanted me to hold you, I held you,
and now you want me to let you go as easily as that. You

never once thought about what I want. A young man comes along and catches your fancy and you think you can leave me behind without a second thought. Tell me, is he a better lover than I?''

"It's not like that with him!" She was genuinely shocked by his question. Her time in the Indian village had changed her. She felt purified of all her past mistakes, but now Hachaliah had brought them to life once more.

He smiled knowingly. "Ah I see. You're playing the virgin for him. How clever. But what would he think if he knew that you have warmed my bed all these years? Would he marry you then?"

"You won't tell him because if you do I'll say you forced me into it from the beginning." There was a dangerous glint in Tatum's eye but she felt a sudden reckless bravado. He couldn't control her anymore. And if she provoked him to hurt her, so much the better. Her friends would take revenge on him and they would quit his employ, and then she wouldn't have to leave them at all. Instead it would be Hachaliah who was left with nothing! "That's not all I'll say," she taunted him. "I'll tell everyone that the reason I ran away the other day is because I told you I was breaking it off and you raped me! And they'll believe me because they're my friends!" As she spoke the final words she swung the fiddle case again, hoping to take him by surprise, but he was on his guard. One hand seized her arm in mid-air and he tore the case from her grasp with the other. He flung it aside carelessly. It struck the post at the corner of the stall and popped open, sending the instrument flying. There was a discord of protest from the strings as the fragile neck hit the floor and snapped.

"I hate you! I hate you!" Amanda clawed at Tatum's face and drew blood before he could capture her hands and imprison them in one of his own. Quite calmly he drew back his free hand and struck her aside the head with a closed fist. She reeled and fell, but he jerked her upright and struck her again, then flung her against the back of the stall where she fell in a heap on a mound of straw. Her skirt and petticoats were crumpled around her stockinged thighs. He could see the garters that supported the silk hose.

He knelt beside her. As she raised her head and looked up uncomprehendingly he hit her full in the face and smiled at the terror that flared in her eyes. He resisted the urge to hit her again. He would take his revenge in a more satisfying way. She was groggy from the blows and stilled by fear, and she did not resist as he raised her skirts up about her waist.

When he arose a short time later, he was no longer smiling. Amanda made no move to get up. Her eyes were open but they did not follow his movements as he rearranged her clothing and covered her with her coat. They merely stared.

Tatum glanced around nervously, suddenly aware of what would happen if someone should come into the barn now, and what would certainly happen when what he had done was known. He had imagined that she would yield at the last moment, that some of her resistance was feigned, as she had feigned it to please him so many times before. But she had yielded only because he had brutally overpowered her, and the savagery her refusal had brought out in him frightened him now. He dusted himself off and straightened his clothing, his mind searching in near panic for a way to avoid retribution for his sins.

He paced back and forth within the light, glancing occasionally at the girl, and then suddenly he paused, for he had **hit upon** a desperate plan by which he might escape punishment and still keep what he wanted most of all.

"Stay here," he told her with more authority than he felt, and he took the lamp with him to the barn door, where he extinguished it before stepping outside. As he crossed the yard to the house he forced a mask of calm on his expression and his bearing.

In the saloon the music was in full swing and the floor was crowded with dancers. Tatum moved among the people purposefully, pausing only for a moment here and there to exchange a word. He gave the impression that he was on some small errand, nothing of great importance, just a nuisance to be gotten out of the way before he could enjoy this last night of celebration. He noted Johnny Smoker dancing with Lisa Putnam, enjoying himself thoroughly, and then he spied Kinnean across the room. The one-armed man had a glass in his hand and his eyes were fixed on Hardeman, who was leaning against the bar watching the dancers. As Tatum approached, Kinnean tossed down the last of his drink and got to his feet, his face set and hard. He checked the holstered pistol at his hip and started for Hardeman but Tatum blocked his way, taking him by the arm and turning him aside, speaking low and urgently in his ear.

CHAPTER NINE

"I can't see a thing movin' out there, sir." Corporal Atherton squatted beside Whitcomb in the shelter of a small pine tree. They were alone on a low ridge overlooking the plains, awaiting the return of the three men sent out the afternoon before to scout old Fort Reno. The sky was covered with clouds that dropped occasional flurries of snow, and dusk was falling rapidly. In front of them the land was rolling and barren; behind them, beyond the shallow valley where the rest of the men were camped, the foothills rose. Whitcomb could see the campsite because he knew where to look for it, but it was in good shelter and the smoke from the fire could not be seen at all.

As the Lost Platoon drew near the Powder and old Fort Reno, Whitcomb had first thought to make straight for the abandoned post, but it was fifteen miles or more beyond the protection of the foothills and some instinct had cautioned him against such a direct course. He had remembered then the story Crook had told him about being lost in the Oregon country. *We have not been given instincts merely to confuse us*, the general had said. *We should never ignore them entirely.* And so Whitcomb had obeyed his instincts. When he judged that he was as close to Reno as he could get without exposing his men on the open plains, he had given the three strongest horses to Corporal McCaslin and Privates Gray and Heiss, and had sent them to scout the fort. They had more than thirty miles to cover and they had been gone for just over a day. If they didn't return soon they might not find the small campsite in the dark.

Whitcomb prayed they would bring help. If any part of Crook's command remained at the fort, McCaslin would bring some men and horses back with him to assist the lost remnant of E Troop to the army encampment, and by midnight Corwin could be in a doctor's hands. Surgeon Munn's assistant, Dr. Ridgely, had returned to Reno with the supply train, taking with him the wounded beef herder. Ridgely was to set up tents and prepare to treat further wounded when Crook returned to the wagons. But ten days had passed since the battle and there was no telling where Crook and the supply train might be by now.

"How are the men?" Whitcomb asked out of habit. Little had changed. The men survived. Atherton had just come from the camp to relieve him on watch, but Whitcomb had chosen to remain until the scouts returned.

"Private Rogers cut off 'is bad toe, sir."

This gave Whitcomb a jolt. "He did it himself?"

"Luttner and Donnelly 'elped 'im. Rogers said 'e didn't feel a thing. 'e done a good enough job of it, sir. 'e says the walkin' will be easier now."

"How was Major Corwin when you left him?"

"Not good, sir. That leg is killin' 'im. We could cut away some more of the dead flesh but we can't make a proper job of it, not without a saw. 'e needs a doctor's care and bed rest and hot food, and with all that 'e may die anyway.''

The report was no worse than Whitcomb expected. On the day following the amputation, Corwin's pulse had been so faint, his breathing so shallow, that Whitcomb had not dared to move him at all. The next morning Corwin had seemed somewhat stronger and was briefly conscious. ''Why aren't we under way?'' he had asked. Whitcomb had explained that he was afraid the strain of travel would prove too much for Corwin, but Corwin brushed the notion aside. ''Carry on, Mr. Reb,'' he had said. ''Don't delay on my account.'' And so they had resumed the march, but the going was slow. Corwin groaned at every jounce of his travois and several times they had stopped to let him rest. Whitcomb had left Corwin's tending to Atherton and the others at first, afraid that the sight of the stump would make him sick again. That was what he had told himself, but his deeper fear was that the crude butchery would prove to be in vain, and when he dared to look at Corwin's leg again he saw that his fear was justified. The flesh was cracked and oozing where the stump had been cauterized and the end of the stump was livid. He had not needed to see the sober expressions of the non-commissioned officers to know that Corwin's condition was worsening. The wounded officer's lucid moments were few and far between now and he no longer sang songs of the sea.

Whitcomb found himself nodding and he rose to have another look for the scouting party. His stomach was tight with hunger but he did not look forward to his evening ration of horsemeat. Early the day before, he had shot an antelope, a bit of long-range luck that had earned him a cheer from the men. The beast was winter-poor and they had devoured it at a single sitting. Whitcomb had felt sick after eating so much and had almost vomited, and the lean antelope had seemed to give him very little energy the next day. The beast had no fat, Dupré had said. But it was tasty. It would have been better to hoard it and spread it out among the meals of horsemeat. After antelope, horsemeat was even less palatable than before.

Part of the landscape before him moved. He thought at first that his eyes were playing tricks on him in the failing light, but the moving shadows resolved themselves into three mounted men ascending the gentle slope. He waited long enough to be sure the figures were his own soldiers and then he said "Here they come" to Atherton and he started down to meet the scouts.

"There's no one there, sorr," were the first words McCaslin said. "The wagons are gone." He and his men dismounted wearily.

Whitcomb tried to hide his disappointment. When he saw the scouts returning alone he had guessed what they had found, but having his guess confirmed left him feeling helpless and alone. "Did they go north or south?" he asked.

"I can't say, sorr. We left the horses in a draw and Private Gray and meself walked the last mile or two. We got close enough to see there was nobody there and we was about to go have a look at the tracks when we saw a party of Indians on horseback. Six of them, there was. They come ridin' from the south. They rode around the fort and then went down into the river bottom. Makin' camp for the night, I reckoned, and I thought it best not to risk bein' seen, sorr."

Whitcomb nodded his approval. So his instincts had been right. If he had taken the little column to the fort they might have been caught out in the open. Even half a dozen Indians could pose a serious threat to the weakened force. "Well, we've got to go on to Fetterman," he said. "That's all that really matters. Come on now, let's get you to a fire and a meal.''

He ushered the others ahead of him, with Atherton in the lead and himself bringing up the rear. Could we have gotten here sooner? he wondered. If he had pushed the men harder, or if Corwin were hale and still in command. . . . There was no use thinking about it. The Lost Platoon had made the best progress possible, given Corwin's wound and the harsh winter weather, which had returned with a vengeance after a brief mild spell. After the wound cost them a day, the weather had cost them the better part of another. On the first day of marching after the amputation they had come upon a recent camp by the banks of a tiny stream, and by the oval sleeping shelters the campers had made, Dupré had guessed it was a small party of Indians. After that the soldiers had kept a renewed watch in all directions. They had seen no further signs of hostiles but they had nearly succumbed to a far more obvious danger. In mid-afternoon it had begun to snow. The platoon had crossed one small watercourse that offered fair shelter, but they had passed it by, hoping to make a few more miles before dark, and then the squall had hit them. They were on a barren plateau, far from any cover or wood or water, and within the space of a few moments the swirling snow reduced visibility to a handful of yards and the men were forced to hold on to a stirrup or a comrade's shoulder to keep together. By good fortune the squall passed after a quarter of an hour but the experience had frightened Whitcomb badly. When the column came on another creek where the steep banks and clumps of brush offered shelter and firewood, he ordered them to make camp, and there they had stayed for most of the following day as the storm continued. They had butchered a second horse and kept close to the fire, eating and sleeping. When the sky finally began to clear in mid-afternoon, they had set out once more and made just five miles before dusk, camping that night by a stream they took to be the south fork of Crazy Woman.

But they had done well yesterday. By Sergeant Dupré's estimate they had covered more than fifteen miles. The days of enforced rest had made the men impatient, and fortified by the antelope, which Whitcomb had shot just at dawn and which they had cooked and eaten at once, they had marched with a will all day.

Whitcomb noticed that Private Gray had dropped back and fallen into step beside him. "Those Indians you saw, were they a war party?"

"There were too few to be a war party, sir. A scouting party, I should think." The cultured Virginia cadences of Gray's speech were incongruous in the rough-clothed and bearded figure.

"I imagine General Crook resupplied himself and took the wagons with him when he returned up-country."

"Well, he did have some wounded, sir," Gray offered. "He may well have sent some of the wagons back to Fort Fetterman to carry the wounded and bring more supplies to a new rendezvous. That's what I would have done."

"And what would you do if you were in command of this force, Private Gray?"

"It's your command, sir, not mine."

"And my first, as you are well aware."

"There is a first time for everyone, sir. I am not sure it is any easier to be promoted to command by departmental orders than to have it thrust on you like this. You'll manage, sir. You have done well for us."

Whitcomb shook his head. "There are times when I'm scarcely able to think. I feel like a blind man."

"Every commander knows that feeling, sir."

"Just now, for instance, I have no idea at all what to do next. We have to make for Fetterman, but if there are more hostiles about . . ." He left the sentence unfinished. He wasn't afraid to reveal his uncertainties to Gray. Gray knew what it was to command.

"I shouldn't think there are many, sir. My guess is now that they have been attacked they will gather in strength and keep well to the north. The scouts we saw may have followed the supply train to Fort Fetterman, if that's where it went, and they'll be keeping watch for reinforcements. We can't be certain, but I imagine they'll keep close to the road." Gray walked in silence for a moment and then he said, "Do you remember on our first few days of march, sir, when we first left Fort Fetterman, there was a ridge on our left? It had pine trees along the top."

"I remember it." The ridge ran parallel to the wagon road, five or ten miles to the west, most of the way from Fetterman to the Big Horns.

"Well, sir, if we kept to the west of that ridge it would take us straight to the Platte, very close to Fetterman."

"Thank you, Captain."

"I am no longer a captain, sir, and have no wish to be one." Gray touched the brim of his cap and increased his pace to overtake the others, who were a dozen yards ahead.

At the campsite Corwin was awake and calling for Whitcomb. "Why have we stopped, Mr. Reb?" he demanded as Whitcomb approached the litter.

"It's nighttime, sir. We have good shelter here. Have you had something to eat?"

"We've got to press on! Press on! We've got no time to dawdle."

"The men are in no condition to march at night, sir."

"Laggards and malingerers, that's what they are. By

God, back in the war we had *men* in the army." Corwin
lay back in his robes. "Why am I so tired? When I catch
up on my rest I'll show the lot of you. Twenty miles a
day. Thirty." His voice trailed off and his eyes closed,
and Whitcomb heaved a silent sigh of relief. It was not the
first occasion on which Corwin had given orders that made
no sense. Whitcomb wondered for the hundredth time
what he would do if a real confrontation developed between him and the wounded officer. Thus far he had
maintained a pretense that Corwin was in command whenever he was conscious, but if Corwin gave an order that
endangered the men, he would have to oppose him openly
and risk a charge of insubordination or worse.

He joined the men at the fire and accepted the plate
Donnelly offered him, feeling their eyes follow him as he
sat on a small log. They had heard McCaslin's news and
they were awaiting his orders, awaiting reassurance that
their young leader was still willing to lead.

"We're going on to Fetterman," he said. "We'll follow
west of the pine ridge, out of sight of the wagon road in
case the hostiles are watching it. Each man walks half an
hour and then rides, except you, Rogers. You ride from
now on. We'll be there in three days."

"Thirty miles a day, sir?" someone asked.

"The going will be easier out on the plains. We'll make
it."

In the morning he woke them at first light. An inch of
new snow had accumulated on their robes and blankets
during the night and the sky was still gray with clouds.
Whitcomb wanted a cup of coffee but there was no coffee
anymore. They had drunk the last of it three days before,
during the storm.

After a few mouthfuls of roasted horsemeat for breakfast
and more put in their pockets for noontime, the men

formed in line without complaint and started off to the southeast. They marched in a column of twos, half mounted and half on foot, a man walking beside each horse to steady the rider if he fell asleep.

They had gone scarcely a mile when Corwin began to moan loudly. The column halted while Atherton and Dupré knelt beside the travois. Neither spoke as Whitcomb joined them.

"What can we do for him?" he demanded.

"Nothing, sair."

Corwin's eyes opened. "Report, Mr. Reb." He looked straight at Whitcomb and seemed to know him, but Whitcomb could no longer tell when Corwin was thinking clearly.

"We're going on to Fetterman, sir. There was no one at Fort Reno."

"Are we on the road?"

"We're keeping somewhat to the west, sir. Corporal McCaslin saw Indian scouts on the road yesterday. We'll follow a course parallel to the road until we reach the Platte."

Corwin looked at Dupré and Atherton. "By God, he's not stupid, is he?" He laughed. It was a rasping, ugly sound. "He's got a head on his shoulders all right. Carry on, Mr. Reb. And wake me when we get there. By God, I want to see Teddy Egan's face when he sees us pull in looking like this. They'll bring out the band to pipe us home!" He closed his eyes, still chuckling, and he made no complaint when the travois began to move once more.

Whitcomb took a position behind the travois, to keep an eye on Corwin. Just when he thought Corwin had his wits about him he said something like that, about Teddy Egan and a brass band welcoming them to Fetterman. Egan was still with Crook, wherever that was, and there would be no band for a bunch of stragglers who had been cut off during the battle and had missed the rest of the campaign.

New snow began to fall, small round pellets that lodged against every ridgelet and obstacle. Whitcomb knew by looking at them how they would feel on his face and what sound they would make underfoot. In four weeks he had become an authority on snow in all its variations.

He felt the air turn colder as the wind picked up and he realized that his field of view had shrunk to a quarter mile. The clouds had descended and the snowfall was thickening. Was there no end to winter here? In Virginia the dogwood would be in bloom.

We're like cattle, he thought, drifting before the wind. But he was almost glad for the wind. On the warm days the men wanted to rest in the sun at noontime. Today they would eat on the march and keep putting one foot in front of the other until he called a halt at dusk. Then they would cook more horsemeat and fall into a sleep close to death. Not too close, please God. I don't want to lose them.

McCaslin swayed in the saddle and jerked his head up at the sound of laughter. He saw Whitcomb walking nearby with an eerie grin cracking the dried skin of his face. His sandy beard had not grown thick enough in a month of campaigning to hide that golden skin.

"Caught you, by God, McCaslin!" Whitcomb laughed again. "I never thought I would catch you dozing off."

"I beg your pahrdon, sorr."

"No need, Mac. No need. I was beginning to think you weren't human."

"Oh, I'm human enough, sorr. I'd be on me toes all right if I could walk. It's this ridin' that sends me off."

"All right, Mac. Dismount. And keep an eye out when

there's anything to see.'' He moved off up the column, leaving McCaslin to bring up the rear.

McCaslin swung stiffly off the horse and handed the reins to Gwynn. "You ride for a while, Gwynn lad. And don't be fallin' off and breakin' yer head."

Freed of the animal, he shrugged the cumbersome carbine sling off his shoulder and reversed it so he could carry the weight on the other side for a while. He swung his arms to warm himself and did a little Irish jig as he walked along. He hummed the tune off-key to himself, allowing the dance to turn him around, as he had seen the men dancing in the comforting little pubs that seemed to have been sprinkled across the Irish countryside by benevolent leprechauns. How often his mother had sent him for a bucket of beer, or to bring his dad home, and he had always lingered as long as he could, watching the men dance and listening to the fiddle. Happy music it was. No other race knew so many tunes that could lift a man's spirits.

The snow stopped and the wind picked up and here and there a little sunshine shone through the clouds. McCaslin danced in circles with his hands on his hips. Ahead of him the men marched with heads hung down. They were approaching a river. What would it be now? The Powder or one of its forks. The Middle Fork, it should be. And a sad puny stream it was. He hopped in a circle, surveying the countryside. Nothing moved, except the horsemen coming from up the river, riding on the far— Here now, what's this? Horsemen? Lord help us if it's Indians.

"Mr. Whitcomb, sorr! There's riders comin'! Look there!"

CHAPTER TEN

"If we don't rest 'em soon, these horses will play out."
Fisk got no reply from Tatum and he didn't dare repeat
himself. Since the fugitives had left Putnam's Park, Tatum's mood had been as dark as the night, and when dawn
greeted them in the broad belt of foothills east of the
mountains, the blackness had lingered on in the circus
master.

They were seven, carried on six horses. Amanda rode
with Tatum, seated before him. Her eyes were open but
she took little notice of what went on around her. Fisk
rode beside Kinnean in the lead while Tanner and Morton
and Johansen brought up the rear. The wagon drivers
looked back over their shoulders often, but there had been
no sign of pursuit. Around them the foothills were rough
and broken, like rubble cast aside after the Big Horns were
formed. The country was sparsely wooded in patches and
here and there a splash of red sandstone enlivened the
otherwise drab surroundings. In such a landscape, a small
group of horsemen was insignificant; with new snow be-

ginning to fall, their tracks would soon be covered and the riders would disappear into the vastness.

Tatum had chosen his escort with care, selecting men whose self-interest would override any other loyalties. He had spoken to Kinnean and Kinnean had talked with Fisk; Fisk had found Tanner and whispered in his ear; Tanner had passed the word to Johansen, who had brought Morton along. One by one they had slipped out of the saloon, and when they were all in the barn Tatum had promised them double wages to help him spirit the girl away in the night. He had offered no reasons and permitted no questions. When Tanner asked what he had done, to leave all he had worked for behind, Tatum had silenced him with a curt "Take it or leave it," and he had made it clear that those staying behind could expect no pay at all.

They had saddled the horses and left the settlement under cover of darkness with the gay music from the saloon following them on the still air. Amanda had come willingly enough, or at least she had made no move to resist. There was an ugly bruise on her cheek, but no one had dared to question Tatum about that. If the men knew the full truth of what had caused his flight, they might abandon him even now.

"Are you warm enough, my dear?" He spoke low in Amanda's ear, wanting to comfort her, as if with his concern he might undo what he had done. He had decided against giving her a mount of her own, lest she try to run. The white stallion could easily bear the extra weight. "We'll both be safe and warm before long," he told her. In two days they would reach the old Oregon Trail; in another two, Rawlins; and there he and Amanda would entrain for the east.

He had left a great deal behind him. The hoped-for triumph in San Francisco had been abandoned along with the rest of his plans and the circus that had taken him years to build, but in the end he had run rather than face the Old Testament vengeance that was typical of frontier justice. A rope over a tree limb would be his reward, and for what? For losing his temper with a girl who had given herself willingly to him at the age of sixteen? He cursed his own failure of control.

Once the deed was done he had seen immediately that his choices were few. To flee alone and vanish back in the States? Amanda would tell what he had done and retribution might find him even there. Violated womanhood stirred almost as much outrage in the settled regions of the land as it did here in the territories, where white women were still scarce and hence valued all the more highly. But it was not fear of the long arm of the law that had decided Tatum against that course.

He could not give up Amanda.

When his wife died he had been certain that he would never love another woman as much, but he had been wrong. Amanda had needed his love and he had given it, innocently at first and then more urgently, as his own need grew, until now he was willing to part with everything else he owned before letting her go.

Helena Tatum had hoped for children of her own, but not until her best performing years were behind her, and so she had become like a second mother to the Spencers' only child. She had encouraged Amanda's instruction in clowning and the other circus arts that struck her childish fancy. After the horrible fire, Hachaliah had taken the orphaned girl under his wing in large part because she had been Helena's favorite, and he had sought through her to recapture some of his wife's affection, which she had given to Amanda so freely and which was now lost to both of them forever. Amanda's dependence on him helped to fill that void, and when his time of mourning was past he did not seek to remarry. He and Amanda were a little family by then, content to be by themselves within the larger family of the circus.

Then Amanda had changed everything, and in the new state of things, he had found his love for her growing beyond all bounds. From the first he was faithful, but she was true to him only for a time. She had learned how to tease him with her suitors and her occasional *affaires,* and he knew he must suffer in silence or lose her. Losing her was what he feared above all. He knew the pain of loss and would not bear it again. And so he put up with her teasing, secure in the belief that she would always return to him. But in Putnam's Park she had sought to betray him completely and his temper had snapped at last, at great cost to both of them.

Even so, he would rise from the ashes of his former hopes, carrying her with him. With new backing he would form a smaller show around exquisite equestrian demonstrations and an act of pantomime and clowning that would match any other in the world. He would add other acts as they came to his attention, but each would be outstanding, and in time the name of Hachaliah Tatum would stand above them all, just as he had always planned. All this was possible still, if Amanda came to her senses and refused to accuse her benefactor. Back at Putnam's Park they would know nothing, only that the girl had vanished and Tatum with her. They would suspect the worst, but without her words to damn him they could never prove their fears. Amanda would recover in time and she would find herself far from the boy she had thought to marry, far from the protection of old and new friends. Once again Tatum would be her only shield against a frightening world and she would turn to the comfort he offered. Together they would start anew.

There might be a brief scandal over the manner in which he had abandoned his former employees, but it would be a scandal of rumor, not of proven deeds, and it would not persist for long.

"We'll walk the horses for a bit," Kinnean said, dismounting. He started off again at once, leading his horse, his derby hat pulled low to protect his eyes from the snow, his long buffalo coat brushing the ground as he walked. The others dismounted and followed him. Tatum helped Amanda down and took her arm to guide her along.

"Gonta storm before long," said Fisk, casting a glance over his shoulder at the back trail and the sky. "We might better find a place to wait it out." His head preceded him as he walked, moving from side to side like a badger's, as if he was looking for a hole.

"We keep going," Kinnean stated flatly. "The snow will cover our trail." It was he who guided the way, not Fisk. During the weeks in Putnam's Park he had talked with Julius Ingram and Harry Wo to learn the lay of the land, and he was sure of his course. Since leaving the park the band of riders had followed the river trail of the Putnam Cutoff, retracing the path the circus wagons had taken into the mountains a month before. A few miles below the park the creek had joined the Middle Fork of the Powder, which would lead them to the plains. There they would turn south, making straight for the Oregon Trail and the railroad beyond.

Kinnean's one regret was that he had been denied the chance to stand up to Hardeman and learn once and for all if the shot that had broken his Winchester had been intended for the gun all along. But Tatum had paid him well to forgo his revenge. Kinnean hadn't settled for the double wages that had bought the other men. To conduct Tatum and Amanda to safety he had demanded and received two hundred dollars in gold. It was enough to buy the new start he had been promising himself since the war, when the loss of his arm had destroyed his army career in mid-stride and sent him westward to seek new opportunities. His loss was no handicap when it came to handling firearms and he had even been a peace officer once or twice, but for the most part the larger settlements wanted a man with two arms for the job, and so he had taught himself to handle a deck of cards and he had made his way by gambling. He had moved from one boomtown to the next, most recently following the rush of prospectors to the Black Hills, but by the time Hachaliah Tatum and his circus came along he had been ready to move on. Gambling was a way to get by but it wasn't the life he wanted. Someday he would find an enterprise at which a one-armed man could excel and until then he would keep looking. Just now Tatum had provided the means. When they reached the Union Pacific, Kinnean would sell his horse and replace the stock on his Winchester, and then he would take the train to California. Maybe there he would find what he was looking for.

For half an hour the six men led the horses and then at Kinnean's command they remounted. The snow thickened and flew at them from all directions for a time before thinning again to reveal the bottoms of the clouds, lower than before, here and there trailing long skirts of grayish white, the patches of falling snow as clearly defined as summer rainstorms.

Where the river ran through a narrow cut, the trail left the course of the stream and rose atop a small ridge. From this vantage point Kinnean stopped to look back the way they had come. He remained motionless for so long that the others turned to discover what kept him and then they too saw what he was watching. A mile or two back up the trail, dark spots moved against the only slightly less dark background of the mountains.

"You said they couldn't trail us at night!" Tanner protested. His deep voice came from somewhere within the curls of his beard as the huge head turned to face Kinnean.

"I said they'd have a hard time of it," Kinnean corrected him. "That boy lived with the Cheyenne and Hardeman's got twenty years of reading sign."

"Let's get moving!" Tom Johansen urged, reining his horse around. He was the youngest of the men and suddenly he wished he had never come.

"You stay put!" Kinnean's voice was full of menace. "A man sitting still might as well be a rock or a tree at this range. They'll drop out of sight soon enough. Then we'll move quick. It might be we'll give them the slip."

"They've stopped," said Fisk.

"Looking for sign."

The moving dots were motionless now. One horseman dismounted, followed by a second. Soon they were off again, the two figures on foot leading the way. Before long they passed out of sight behind an intervening hill.

"All right now. Keep in single file behind me." Kinnean started off without waiting for a reply, with Tatum close behind him. He led away from the trail, keeping to the low ridges that were blown almost bare by the wind, where the riders left scarcely any tracks on the hard ground. When he had gone a few hundred yards from the river he turned to follow its course, keeping always to the windswept areas and the rocks, and when he reached flat ground he increased the pace to a lope.

The snow returned, protecting the fugitive band from distant eyes. Kinnean looked back and then ahead. They were nearing the edge of the foothills, but even out on the plains the country was ridged and rolling and cut with gullies, and a man could rarely see more than a mile or two. Between that and the cover afforded by the snow, they might shake off the pursuers or at least keep ahead of them until dark, when it would be easy work to vanish into the night. But if the pursuers overtook them . . . Kinnean shrugged inwardly. What happened to Hachaliah Tatum was of little consequence to him. He would get Tatum and the girl safely away if he could, but if not, he would have the satisfaction of an overdue reckoning with Chris Hardeman.

The band rode in silence, each of them looking back often. As they passed over the last hill before entering on the rough grasslands that stretched away to the east, they paused beyond the crest. Behind them the land was arrayed in a series of ascending steps and any movement would be easy to see.

"There they are," said Tatum when only a few minutes had passed.

Kinnean nodded. "Still on our trail. We'll have to move faster."

"Runnin' ain't the way," said Fisk. "We got to make a stand."

Kinnean looked about, considering the possibility. An ambush might kill or wound enough of the pursuers to eliminate any further obstacle to the fugitives' escape. The cover here was sparse, but if the horses and the girl were kept well out of sight it could work. Maybe in the river bottom—

"Jesus God in Heaven!" Johansen was not looking at the pursuing riders. He pointed off to the northwest, where horsemen were emerging from a draw—fifteen, twenty, twenty-five or more.

Kinnean felt a chill as he saw what they were.

"Well?" Tatum demanded, but it was Fisk that answered him.

"Indians!" He gathered his horse's reins to flee, but Kinnean held out a hand.

"Keep still!" he barked. "They'll see the others before they see us. Maybe they'll go after them."

It was true; the Indians were on a course that would bring them on top of the riders from Putnam's Park.

"They've seen them!" Tanner shouted needlessly. The Indians were kicking their mounts into a run, swerving to head straight for the pursuers. But now the whites saw the Indians and they too changed direction, not running from the Indians but moving toward them, arms raised in greeting.

"Damn the luck!" Kinnean swore. "It must be that bunch the Putnam woman knows."

"Lord God, they come to help 'em chase us!" said Johansen, his face white with cold and fear.

"Let's get going." Kinnean reined around and led the way, urging his horse into a run. The thought of an ambush here was hopeless now, with the strength of the pursuing party increased fourfold. Flight was the only chance. If the snow would just keep up they still might get away.

But the snow thinned and then it stopped entirely, and a shaft of sunlight bathed the plains to the southeast. The wind gusted strongly now, pushing the low clouds along. The fugitives rode hard, careless of their tired horses, looking back often, expecting at any moment to see the force of whites and Indians reach the last ridge and spy their quarry in the distance.

"There's more of 'em!" Fisk shouted, jerking his horse up short. He pointed to the front, where a small group of riders was moving slowly toward the river.

"They're not Indians," Kinnean said, struggling to still his nervous horse.

"More from the settlement?" Tatum wondered aloud.

Kinnean tried to count the new party but they were over half a mile away and he could make out only that nine or ten were mounted and the rest afoot. They moved like men on a long journey, plodding slowly, as if they lacked the strength to keep up a faster pace. They were armed, each man carrying a rifle in his hands or over his shoulder, some of those pointing muzzle down, the way a cavalryman carried—

"They're soldiers!" Kinnean exclaimed.

As Lisa approached the Indians she saw that it was Sun Horse himself who led the band. The headman sat straight in the saddle with the bearing of a younger man and he held a flintlock rifle in his hands. He was flanked by Standing Eagle and Little Hand; Walks Bent Over rode beside the war leader. By the looks of it, they had brought every warrior in the Sun Band.

Hardeman and Johnny had stayed back on the fugitives' trail, but Bat and Julius and the four circus men followed Lisa to greet the reinforcements. She spurred her horse out in front of the others, needing the sudden gallop to free herself from the strained tedium of long hours spent tracking in the cold and dark. She raised her Winchester over her head in greeting and reined to a halt as the Indians reached her. Her horse panted and snorted, prancing about. She was very glad to see these feathered men, all clothed in their hides and furs, but as they slowed and swirled around her she recognized a white face in their midst. It was Hutch, watching her warily, sitting astride his mule, Old Joe, and she understood now how the Indians had come to be here. She frowned and tried to adopt a stern expression but she could not find it in her heart to be angry with the youth. She had told him to remain behind when the pursuers set out on Tatum's trail, despite the young man's pleading that he be allowed to come along. With herself and Julius gone from Putnam's Park, there were only Harry and Hutch left to care for the settlement and the cattle; Lisa had feared the pursuit might keep her away for days and so she had ordered Hutch to stay. But he had disobeyed her and she was glad.

"It seems you have a mind of your own." She favored him with a welcoming smile.

"Yes, ma'am!" He grinned from ear to ear, certain now that she did not intend to scold him. It had taken all his nerve to ride over to the Indian village alone in the dark, but he had suspected that Sun Horse would want to know of Amanda's plight. He had been scared half to death by the sudden appearance of the Sioux sentry on the trail, but once the scout had recognized the white youth he had taken him at once to Sun Horse and the old man had lost no time in rousing the village and mounting a war party.

The others from the settlement posse had reached the Indians now, Chalmers towering over the rest as he and the three Waldheims shook hands all around while Bat conveyed in words and signs what little there was to tell of the night's pursuit. Hutch thought of the settlement whites as a posse even though there were no lawmen among them. These men had the same intensity of purpose he had seen as a small child back in "Bloody Kansas" during the late years of the Rebellion, when honest citizens had banded together to protect themselves from Indians, guerrillas and Confederate raiders, who robbed and burned and sometimes carried off young women against their will, or so Hutch had heard. In the posse from Putnam's Park there was no doubt that Amanda had been taken against her will, not after the sight of Johnny Smoker holding up her busted fiddle in front of the hushed saloon.

Johnny had been on the dance floor as soon as the music began, dancing first with Miss Lisa and then with the other women one by one, seeming bound and determined to dance with all of them before the night was done. He had even danced with Maria, bringing her close to the bandstand so she could give Hutch a wink and a smile. She had promised to meet Hutch later for a private farewell. Hutch wasn't sure just how long it was after that when the musicians grew impatient with waiting for Amanda to join them and asked Johnny to go find her. Johnny had returned in what seemed like no time at all, bursting through the kitchen door holding Amanda's fiddle up by the neck, the broken remains of the body dangling by the gut strings. A shocked silence had spread through the room, bringing the music to a ragged halt, and into the sudden quiet Johnny had said, "She's gone. Tatum's gone too."

Things had moved swiftly then. Hardeman and Johnny had gone off to the barn with Bat and Julius right behind them. Miss Lisa had run upstairs to change into her riding clothes, leaving Chalmers and Joe Kitchen to control the circus performers, who were all clamoring to go along, and to choose the few that might be of some use. Hutch had caught up with Miss Lisa in the barn but she had told him to stay behind, trying to make him feel better by saying that someone had to take care of the ranch while she was away.

Bat rode up to Hutch and looked him up and down. "Your ma know you run to fetch redskins when you need help?"

Hutch feared for a moment that he might be scolded after all, but then he saw the mischief in Bat's eyes and he got the joke. He laughed aloud, and it seemed like more than enough reward for passing half the night with his heart in his mouth.

A quarter mile to the south, Hardeman and Johnny were still searching for sign. Once he saw that the warriors were from the Sun Band, Hardeman didn't give the riders a second glance. He was glad of their presence, but there was no time to waste. A new storm was brewing. When it hit, the snow and wind would fill in the tracks left by Tatum and his men. The pursuers would have to close on their quarry soon or lose them.

Johnny dismounted and moved forward on foot, leading his horse across an expanse of windswept ground that was strewn with pieces of shale. From the moment the little band started out on Tatum's trail, Johnny had placed himself in front of the others and no one had questioned his right to lead the chase. Through the dark hours before dawn he had pushed ahead as fast as he dared, close-mouthed and grim all the while. Sometimes he had dismounted to feel the trail with his bare hands, but he had made good time, especially at the start, knowing Tatum and his men would have to keep to the river trail at least until it reached the foothills. At first light Johnny had lost the tracks where the wind had wiped them away, and only then had he turned to Hardeman for help. Together they had cast about as the light brightened, but it was Johnny who found the trail again and since then he had not lost it. Hardeman judged that he himself could not have made better progress if he had followed the tracks alone.

"There." Johnny pointed, finding the scrape made by a shod hoof on frozen ground almost as soon as Hardeman's eyes had settled on the faint mark. The youth remounted and rode forward, bending low in the saddle. His pace quickened as he looked to the front and saw where recent tracks crossed a small drift of snow. Beyond, the ground was covered in white once more and the trail was plainly visible.

Johnny urged his horse into a trot and Hardeman kept pace with him, wondering at the boy's control. Despite his anguished concern for Amanda, Johnny had never once panicked, nor had he forgotten that a man who kept his horse to a steady pace all day would soon overtake another who had gotten off to a faster start.

Hoofbeats came from behind them and Hardeman turned to see the rest of the pursuers, Indians and whites, strung out in a long line behind Sun Horse and Walks Bent Over. As the old chief drew abreast of him, Hardeman made a sign of greeting.

"*Hau*, Christopher," said Sun Horse, and he reined in beside the white man.

Walks Bent Over moved ahead of them but he saw the intensity with which Johnny followed the trail and he kept behind the young man. Like Hardeman, he watched for any signs Johnny might miss and allowed the youth to keep the lead. Ahead, the land fell away toward the Middle Fork.

Lisa and Bat Putnam made their way to the front of the pack, followed closely by Julius. Behind them came the quartet of circus men. Chalmers rode a dapple-gray Shire gelding of enormous proportions and Papa Waldheim was mounted on a sturdy bay stallion. By now even the impulsive Waldheims knew that they must adjust their pace to that of the tracker.

Chalmers was heartened by the new strength of the band. Until now the pursuers had numbered only nine, the number kept small so they would not be hindered by men unfamiliar with the demands of what could be a long and arduous ride, but through the night and into the chill grayness of the stormy morning, Chalmers had grown increasingly concerned about what might happen when the fugitives were overtaken. The outcome of a gun battle between the two groups, so evenly matched, was far from certain, and Amanda would be put in danger if it came to an armed confrontation. Now, with the Indians along, Tatum might see that his situation was hopeless and surrender without a fight.

Chalmers felt personally to blame for Amanda's predicament. When she had run away from Putnam's Park, and after Lisa had brought word that the girl was safe in the Indian village, he and Joe Kitchen and Papa Waldheim had met in his wagon and they had talked over their suspicions that some action of Tatum's must have caused her to flee. "Maybe now's the time for her to get out from under his wing, but she might need some help," Joe had said. "Yes, but how far are ve villing to go?" Papa Waldheim had responded, and Joe had been the first to declare himself. "You fellers make up your own minds, but I'll tell you what. As sure as folks've got to eat, they'll pay me to cook. And they'll pay to see the Waldheim boys do their tricks and to see Alfred here wrap an iron bar around his neck like it was a silk ribbon. It don't matter who runs the show. Oh, Tatum's a great one for getting the show on the road, but he ain't the only one. If I get the boot for standing by Amanda, I won't go hungry for long, and neither will you." Chalmers and Papa Waldheim had immediately declared themselves in accord with these sentiments, and so they had spoken with the other performers by ones and twos, and Lydia had talked with the women, and by the time Amanda and Johnny returned, the performing artists were prepared to form a protective phalanx around the young clown at the first sign of trouble. Chalmers had helped Harry Wo move an extra bed into Lisa's bedroom so Amanda could sleep safely with her there, and he and the others had resolved always to keep Amanda within view until she had gone to bed each night, but Tatum's contrite welcome to the girl and his expression of good wishes had lulled their fears; the high-spirited celebration had made them careless and in the end all their resolutions and good intentions had been worthless.

The riders plunged down a slope to the riverbank. Even unpracticed eyes could follow the trail here.

"If he keeps to the Middle Fork he'll come out of the foothills soon," Lisa said. "He could make good time on the old wagon road."

"So could we," said Julius. "We'd catch him in a couple of hours out there. Even a dude like Tatum won't make that kind of mistake."

"They turn south, they'll come on the South Fork," said Bat. "She twists like a snake but she'll lead 'em straight to the Oregon road. It's a fair little valley too. Give 'em some cover for quite a ways."

Ahead of them, where the river passed through a narrow cut and the trail climbed a rise, Johnny halted by a cluster of tracks and motioned those behind him to stay back. He rode in a broad arc until he found where the fugitives had turned off the main trail. His eyes met Hardeman's. "They've seen us." He set off again, following the tracks with new urgency now. Hardeman had to kick his horse into a fast trot to keep up. Within moments Lisa Putnam overtook him and fell in beside him, where she had been throughout most of the night.

Back in the settlement she had reached the barn before Hardeman had finished saddling the horse he had picked at random from the horse pasture, a chestnut gelding. He had taken one look at her riding garb and the Winchester in her hand, and he had tried to dissuade her from coming along. "Lisa, you can't—" was all he got out before she had cut him off. "Can you ride all day and night if you have to?" she demanded. "Can you shoot a rifle with that bad arm? I can do both, Mr. Hardeman!" A quarter of an hour later the nine riders were on the trail and making for the river canyon. Hardeman and Lisa had spoken only rarely since then. Once or twice he had addressed her as Lisa, but each time she had called him Mr. Hardeman in reply and he had fallen back on his former habit of using her surname. Her manner toward him was the same as it might have been if their intimacy of three nights before had never happened, but still she kept close to him.

The band of pursuers rode in silence, slowing where Johnny had to search out the tracks on bare, frozen ground, increasing their pace where the trail was preserved in patches of snow. The tracks were fresher now.

The snow thinned and stopped and the clouds parted to admit a few rays of sunshine to the country below. Just beyond the last of the foothills the trail turned suddenly again, crossing the Middle Fork to its south bank. Hereabouts the stream flowed for the most part in a narrow channel with banks eight or ten feet high, but the fugitives had found a crossing where the banks were crumbled and low. As the pursuers gained the far bank they scanned the countryside, but nothing moved.

"They're runnin' lickety-split along here," Julius observed with his eyes on the tracks. "Must of spooked when they seen us comin'. I cain't see why they'd keep on like this. They'd do better back in the foothill country. They ever shook us off the trail back there, they could go to ground and lose us for good."

For more than half a mile the tracks led straight as an arrow along the bank of the stream, the fugitives' horses running in line, and then suddenly the trail doubled back, descended a steep bank to the river, and vanished in the water. Johnny crossed the stream and searched the far side, but he found nothing.

Walks Bent Over made signs to indicate horsemen going downstream, hiding their tracks in the water. Johnny understood at once and started off along the far shore, while the hunchbacked Indian advanced on the southern bank. Sooner or later Tatum and his men would have to leave the water.

Sun Horse glanced at Standing Eagle and Little Hand and he made a few signs, motioning them forward along the banks. They obeyed him at once, Little Hand crossing the stream and gaining the top of the bank there, while Standing Eagle galloped off on the near side. Together they would move out in advance of the trackers to see if swift riders might find an obvious trail leaving the river.

The main body of pursuers advanced more slowly behind Johnny Smoker and Walks Bent Over, who watched for signs a man traveling fast on horseback might miss, but before they had gone another half mile Standing Eagle came back in sight, riding like the wind. He made broad signs as he approached and then he swung off toward the southeast, beckoning the others to follow him. In an instant the warriors were off, with Walks Bent Over in the lead and the whites close on their heels. To the rear, Johnny Smoker was already across the river and gaining rapidly on the pack.

"I knew it!" Bat exulted. He had guessed right. Somewhere up ahead Tatum's bunch had left the water and made a run for the South Fork and the shelter of the river bottom there, hoping to throw the pursuers off the scent, but they had failed.

Bat reveled in the thrill of the chase and the sight of the riders around him, whites and Indians together, just like the old days. They were all racing hell-for-leather, eager to close the gap. Standing Eagle led them over one rise and then another, and there was Little Hand waiting for them. He had followed the fugitives' trail from the Middle Fork and now he pointed to the south and led the way. When Bat reached the trail he saw that once more the fugitives had ridden in line, one man leading and the rest following. Why did they take such care to keep in single file? It was an Indian trick, not a white man's, and everyone knew how many men had run off with Tatum, so what was the point?

"How far to the South Fork?" Hardeman called to Bat as he and Johnny Smoker drew abreast of the mountain man.

"A few miles, I reckon. I ain't much of a one fer white man's distance. But I'll tell you what. We'll be there in a jiffy." Bat grinned. " 'Bout the time that hits us." He jerked a thumb back over his shoulder. A gray wall of clouds was bearing down on the pursuers from behind, pushed along by the wind, which howled past their ears and whipped the horses' tails about their haunches even as they tried to outrun it. To the west, the mountains were completely hidden. The storm was coming on fast. Even so, the trail was fresh and they wouldn't lose it now. Soon Silk-Hat Tatum and his bunch would be brought to bay and all the questions would be answered, and until then the chase was the thing. It brought Bat to mind of other pursuits long past, like the one on the Green when a large party of trappers and friendly Snakes had wakened one morning to find all their horses gone; it had taken four days, but they had got the horses back and taught the thieving Crows a lesson too.

"Shinin' times!" he said to himself, and he began to tell himself the story under his breath.

"Where in hell have they got to?" Julius wondered

aloud, riding nearby. "We oughta catch sight of 'em 'long about now."

"Gone to ground, mebbe," Bat offered, and he put his memories aside to concentrate on the fresh tracks before him. He was a woolly-headed old coot, never content to take what the moment had to offer, always mooning about some time gone by, one he remembered as better. They hadn't all been good times, and that was truth. He knew what it meant to be cold and hungry and a whisker away from death. But he had lived each day and gone on to the next, and that was what he would do now, just get through the day and take it as it came. By the look of things there would be some doin's before nightfall.

He reined his horse back to a trot and drew aside from the pack, looking around warily. When your quarry disappeared, you might be the quarry before you knew it.

Ahead, the trail followed a shallow gully down to the bottom of a dry wash. Beyond the wash the land rolled away to the southeast where the tops of a few trees revealed the course of the Powder's southern fork a mile or two distant. It was a bleak landscape, almost devoid of vegetation, and Bat recalled with longing the pleasant, wooded hills and the lush grass of the lower Powder valley where he had been so recently. Even in winter the northern country seemed rich and fertile compared with this. Let the *washichun* have the country here if he wanted it. It was little enough to give away if there could be a chance for peace.

Fifty yards ahead of Bat, Hardeman and Johnny were in the forefront as the pursuers entered the dry wash. Hardeman kept his eyes on the tracks, still in a narrow file like those of a party of Indians, who rode that way when they wished to conceal their true numbers. In the bottom of the wash there was a bare patch of sand and a hoofprint clean and sharp, one of the horses showing a cleat much like an army winter shoe . . .

He looked up suddenly. To the right, the wash curved and twisted away into higher ground, and there was movement along its rim.

"Look out!" he cried, too late.

A crashing volley of gunfire came from up the gentle slope, where clouds of gray-white smoke puffed out along the lip of the wash to reveal the ambushers' position. A horse screamed and in that same moment Little Hand flew backward off his mount, arms flung wide and the rifle falling from his hand; he was dead before he hit the ground.

Hardeman had swerved his horse to one side as he shouted out his warning and he heard two rifle balls miss him by inches, bracketing him. He cursed himself for not realizing sooner what the single-file trail meant. The fugitives had been reinforced! But who had joined them, and how many were there?

A second volley chased the pursuers as they wheeled and scattered, running for safety. Hardeman saw Lisa Putnam riding close in front of him and his first concern left him, but the ambush had taken its toll. Hutch's mule lay on the ground, kicking in its death throes, while the youth scampered away on foot, picked up now by Willy Waldheim. Another horse hobbled in circles, whinnying from pain and fear. In the bottom of the wash the crumpled form of Little Hand lay still. Ten yards to Hardeman's left, Johann Waldheim reeled in the saddle, clutching his side, but he still had control of his mount. Nearby, a young Indian held a wounded arm as he rode.

Hardeman realized that there had been no more gunfire from the ambushers since the second volley and he reined in to look back. Up the slope, the landscape was motionless, devoid of life. The ambushers were keeping low.

Sun Horse and Standing Eagle joined Hardeman, followed by Johnny and Lisa, and the others began to regroup around them. Of the wounds, Johann Waldheim's was the most serious, but already his father and brother were tending him. "I will be all right," he said, waving off the looks of concern cast in his direction.

Hutch was winded but not hurt, and Willy's horse could carry the two of them, at least for now. A young Lakota had caught Little Hand's pony after his own mount was hit. No one was left afoot.

Higher on the slope, Bat Putnam was off his horse and kneeling on the ground, and he fired now at the ambushers' position. Some of the Lakota warriors moved off, circling the wash.

"Keep an eye out for the girl!" Hardeman shouted after Standing Eagle, who galloped away to lead the surround. The ambushers would have to move soon or they would be trapped.

"Where did they get so many guns?" Lisa wondered aloud, just as Hardeman heard distant hoofbeats.

"They're pulling out!" he cried, and he led the way back up the slope toward the battleground.

"There!" Julius pointed and Hardeman saw the riders then, streaming out of a far bend in the wash and over the crest of the low ridge, running off toward the distant river. He counted eight horses. Many of the riders were doubled up, but there was no mistaking the way they rode with the Springfields in their hands. They were soldiers. One man calmly flipped up his trapdoor breech and reloaded his piece at a full gallop, but Hardeman saw no sign of Tatum's white horse, nor any glimpse of Amanda.

Were the soldiers alone? If they were Crook's men, where was the rest of the command?

A few shots from the Indians chased the last of the troopers out of sight, and Standing Eagle kicked his pony out in front of the rest, shouting his war cry. Bat Putnam remounted his horse and joined the pursuit.

Lisa swerved her horse close to Hardeman. "Those are soldiers! We can't fight them!"

Hardeman himself had fought the bluecoats not so long ago, perhaps these very men, but he knew she was right. Tatum must have come upon the troopers and told them some tale to enlist them in his defense. He and his men had probably gone on ahead with the girl. The task now was to get within hailing range of the cavalrymen and tell them the true state of affairs.

"Bat!" he called out, and the mountain man reined back a little. Sun Horse was riding by his son-in-law and it was to the aged headman that Hardeman directed himself. "You'll have to hold back your young men once we get in range! I'll try to make the soldiers parley. They won't side with Tatum once they know what he's done."

" 'Tain't gonna be easy," Bat said. "Not with Little Hand lyin' cold back there."

Sun Horse spoke briefly in Lakota.

"Sun Horse says he understands. You'll get yer chance to make the soldier boys talk turkey. He'll keep back the warriors."

The pursuers were cresting the ridge now. The land sloped away before them and they could see the clump of soldiers half a mile ahead of them and riding hard for the South Fork of the Powder. Sun Horse moved out in front of the whites, urging his horse after the foremost warriors. He raised a hand and shouted out; some of the Lakota looked back and slowed their mounts, but beyond them, out of earshot, a single horseman rode, and he was gaining on the troopers.

"Just like Eagle," said Bat. "Runnin' fer the glory. I'll fetch him back." And he was off in pursuit.

Bat delighted in the ease with which the little mare increased her pace. In no time at all he overtook Sun Horse and the warriors and passed them by. Far to the front, a shaft of sunlight shone bright on the land beyond the river, serving as a beacon for the fleeing soldiers, but now the golden rays paled and died away as if a giant hand had squeezed the wick of a lamp between two fingers and snuffed the flame. A gust of wind from behind nearly lifted Bat's winter cap of skunk fur from his head. He clamped it down tighter and pulled up the hood of his capote, looking back over his shoulder. The rest of the pursuers were strung out over a quarter mile, blown like tumbleweeds before the gale, the horses' feet scarcely seeming to touch the ground. Behind them the gray wall of the oncoming storm loomed nearer, building higher and darker as it advanced. It was as if the earlier storm that had welcomed the pipe carriers home and all the clouds and winds and snow showers of recent days were no more than forerunners of the tempest that was sweeping down on the riders now, caroming off the buttress of the Big Horns and rolling out over the plains, perfectly indifferent to the puny creatures in its path.

On and on the little mare ran and Bat was glad he had thought to feed her some oats in Putnam's Park the evening before. A few days' rest and a bucketful of oats and she was up to silk hats and bluecoats today. Once again he recalled other full-tilt gallops made in flight and pursuit and during the hunt. How many times in his years with the trappers and the Lakota had he reveled in the simple pleasure of being borne pell-mell across the prairie by a willing horse? This was the life! And by a miracle, it seemed the good times weren't over yet. Just a few days ago he had thought to leave the Sun Band for good, but the change in Sun Horse had put a stop to that! High spirits had filled the village ever since the headman had broken his fast. The camp was alive with talk and laughter again, dogs barking and fighting over bones, children running everywhere, everyone feeling the good strength of *pte*. Women worked with fleshers to scrape the hides and make badly needed robes and winter moccasins, sinew was stripped for thread, hooves boiled for glue, and once again life had meaning and purpose. True, there was still a dark cloud or two hanging around. No one knew what had become of Crook's soldier boys, and Hears Twice was still keeping to himself, listening for God knows what; Sun Horse had told him he could quit, but the prophet had said, "There is something I must hear," and since then not another word had passed his lips. But Bat wouldn't let that kind of thing discourage him now. Who could tell what the old coot might hear? Voices from the spirit world, no doubt, and sounds of things to come, but meantime there was life to be lived! Just when Bat had thought the Lakota life was going belly up the way the fur trade had done, there was old Sun Horse, full of piss and vinegar and presiding over his people as if he saw nothing but an untroubled future for the Lakota, one generation after another free to come along and live in the same way. Bat knew it couldn't be so, but at least it might last a while longer.

Anger rose within him. Why in damnation did it have to end at all? Why should he have to quit such a glorious life just to give way to the greediest race that ever set foot on the earth? The best part of being a free man was deciding how you wanted to live and sticking with it, and now that freedom was to be denied him—and denied to the Lakota and the Shahíyela and all their friends and enemies as well—just because some politicking yahoos half a continent away couldn't let a few thousand Indians alone! *Politicians!* They wanted something so bad they'd push and shove and stab each other in the back to get it, and anyone who got in the way better look out. They had some notion, something so strong it pushed them along and pushed the Sioux and all the other people of the mountains aside without a by-your-leave. What was so wrong with leaving folks in peace?! He should stick with the Lakota just to spite the damn *washíchun*. . . .

"By God I will!" he shouted, and looked around to see if anyone were close enough to hear. Behind him, the rest of the pursuers were far away.

Could it be as simple as that? The bursting joy deep within him told him that it could. He felt all his worries leave him and he whooped at the top of his lungs.

Had there ever been a bigger fool on God's green earth than John Batson Putnam? The blockhead idjit oughta be horsewhipped for thinking all that time that he would have to leave the Lakota just because their glory days were ending! Which race deserved his loyalty now most of all? Hadn't these people welcomed him as no whites would ever welcome an Indian in their midst? He would never find peace among the whites! Not for him, that kind of existence! Far better a life, even a reservation life, among the people he loved than living alone with Penelope among the *washíchun*, who would accept neither one of them!

For thirty years the Lakota had given him everything they had to give, including acceptance as one of their own, and above all they had given him a life that more than made up for the loss of the trapping days. And what had he given back in return for all that? Not a thing. Oh, he had hunted and fought and done all the things expected of a man among the Lakota, but he owed a special debt that remained unpaid. Well by God he had something to give. He was a white man and he could push every bit as hard and be just as stubborn as any white man ever born. He knew how to parley and how to strike a bargain. He could talk to *washíchun* or Injun and speak his mind, and he knew how to make a fool come to bait. Maybe Sun Horse was right after all; maybe there was a way to talk this war to an end, and if there was, Bat Putnam would sit in council and win something for his people. If not the whole Powder River country then a piece of it. Just a piece to hold on to and live proud, and show folks what it meant to be Lakota and by God the freest people on earth!

He looked around and he saw the world all fresh and clean and new, as if he had been delivered to this spot from his mother's womb. Ahead of him was the river, close now, and the storm was fast overtaking him from behind; all around, the plains lay brown and frozen beneath their thin layer of white, and to Bat it was a world as full of life and promise as any he had ever seen.

"Hókahe!" he shouted. He gained a little on Standing Eagle as the mare plunged down a bank and onto the flat of the riverbed. Out ahead, the soldiers disappeared around a bend where a low bluff jutted into the stream. Moments later, Standing Eagle cut close under the bluff and vanished after them, only to reappear an instant later, doubling back as gunfire came from somewhere out of sight. Some of the soldiers had held back to lay for him, but once again they had let fly too soon. They should have let Eagle get on by them and waited for the rest of the pursuers to come in sight. As it was, they had done nothing but give away their position. They'd fall back now and find a new place to fight.

"Wait up, Eagle!" Bat shouted. But Standing Eagle had guessed the same thing and he was already racing off around the bluff again.

They had both guessed wrong. Again there was a burst of gunfire and this time Standing Eagle's horse staggered and fell, throwing him to the ground as bullets kicked up dirt around him. Without hesitation he jumped to his feet and sprinted for the channel of the shallow stream, where a two-foot bank would give him some protection. He fell, dropping his rifle, and Bat feared he had been hit, but he was up in an instant and diving for the bank, where he vanished as more shots chased after him.

Bat reined in as he neared the bluff, keeping out of sight of the soldiers while he plotted his next move. He laughed aloud to see his brother-in-law's gun abandoned in the snow. There's a pretty fix, he thought. Unarmed and pinned down and left it to me to save his bacon. And glad to do it when all was said and done. There was much about Standing Eagle that Bat didn't care for—his stubborn pride, and the satisfaction he could take in an enemy's pain, like that soldier back at Two Moons' camp. But among his own people he was a good enough father and husband and an outstanding warrior, and you couldn't ask a man to be perfect. Eagle was a bullheaded son of a bitch but you had to give it to him, he was a man.

The first of the pursuers were almost upon him and the troopers were still throwing lead at the creek bank where Eagle was hiding. Well, he'd leave it to the rest of them to set the soldier boys straight or run 'em off. Just now he had something to do. You didn't leave your brother pinned down under the guns of the enemy; not if you were a man of the Lakota.

"Get set, Eagle!" he shouted, and he jammed his heels into the mare's flanks. He felt the wind in his face and

behind him he heard a six-gun booming. That would be
Hardeman getting into action, making the troopers keep
their heads down. There were answering shots from the
cavalry carbines and a bullet struck the ground in front of
the galloping mare. Bat grinned. Didn't reckon they'd
plumb forget about Eagle and me. He kept his eyes on the
riverbank, seeking some movement. There! Eagle was
peering over the edge, getting set to rise up.

Bat steadied the Pennsylvania rifle with his right hand,
aiming behind him. We'll show them soldier boys they
best mind their manners. He saw the troopers aiming at
him and then the rifle jumped and the cloud of smoke
whipped away, and the soldiers ducked. He was at the
riverbank now and he guided the mare straight along the
edge, reaching down a hand to grab Eagle and swing him
up behind.

Get ready, Eagle, 'cause I ain't stoppin' to chitchat. . . .
There. That's more like it. Get that hand ready now. . . .

Bat felt Standing Eagle's hand touch his own, and then
the world turned upside down.

A mighty fist slammed into his chest and suddenly he
was flat on his back staring up at the sky, feeling a
creeping numbness that competed for his attention with a
hard knot of pain located nowhere and everywhere within
him. He heard an upsurge of firing, and horses running
away. The soldier boys pulling out at last, he guessed, but
it didn't interest him much. He felt the wind on his cheek
and a few flakes of snow, but he wasn't cold. He didn't
feel much of anything.

Bat smiled where he lay. Fifty years in the mountains
and they finally got me plumb center. Might pull through
and then again I might not. Be a shame to go under now,
just when I seen which way my stick floats, but a sight
worse to go before, thinkin' I'd of lived out my days with

the *washíchun*. Better to go like this. You live yer life and it's got to end. Only the mountains live forever, they say. Hooraw fer the mountains!

He coughed, and choked on something warm in his throat.

Hell of a fix. Still, I picked the life I wanted, just like my brother Jed. . . .

Now there's food fer thought. D'you suppose that's all there was to that confounded dyin' grin? Just knowin' he'd picked his life each step of the way like a free man? What else is there, when you get right down to it? A man takes his pick of the trails in front of him, not tryin' to figure what makes sense and what don't, just pickin' the one that feels right to him. Why Jed, you sneaky son of a bitch, you saw it all along! And here I reckoned you just couldn't make up your mind. Sure, I stuck to the Sioux after the fur trade while you wandered all over creation, but you picked yer life just as sure as I did. You tried one thing and another but it was all the same life, and you died a happy man! You seen a sight more'n I did, I reckon, but I ain't done so bad. I seen the elephant, and that's truth! Even seen a dancin' bear.

He tried to laugh, but although he felt the mirth deep within him he had lost the power to express it.

He made out Standing Eagle bending over him. Howdy, Eagle, where'd you spring from? He wanted to say the words, but his lips wouldn't move and his throat made no sound. Standing Eagle was talking, but Bat couldn't hear him.

He closed his eyes and saw Penelope's face. I'd like to have another dance with her, he thought. He heard music then, double-fiddle music like it was back at the Rendez-vous on Horse Creek in— Which year was it now? The time them two fiddles played so good? It seemed he was moving to the music and he opened his eyes to see where it came from, but he saw only the sky, and Standing Eagle looking down on him with a somber expression.

So long, Eagle. Y'r an ornery bastard, but you know how to live, 'n' so do I.

CHAPTER ELEVEN

"There he is, sair!" Dupré had been riding in the lead as the troopers raced up the river, but he swung around now to join Whitcomb, who was bringing up the rear with Corporal McCaslin. Dupré pointed through the falling snow and Whitcomb made out a clump of cottonwoods a few hundred yards ahead, an unusual sight in the otherwise treeless riverbed. The thicket stood on a small island near the eastern bank of the stream; sluggish water flowed on both sides of it. A figure stood at the tip of the island, waving the soldiers onward. It was Corporal Atherton, who had gone on ahead with Corwin and the civilians.

Whitcomb looked over his shoulder but no pursuers were in sight. The return of the snow had been providential, beginning just as the soldiers withdrew from the second ambush. A handful of shrieking warriors had chased them closely for a time, but they had fallen back.

"Into the water!" He motioned the men to the left. The tired horses, most of them carrying double, splashed into the stream and slowed their pace to a trot. There was no need to make things any easier than necessary for the band of Indians and renegades; they would slow even further when they lost the tracks here and that would give Whitcomb a few more moments to prepare for them. He would need every second.

He surveyed the little island as he drew near it. The patch of trees was small, but it could provide adequate cover for a few dozen men. He wished he had a few dozen.

"Sergeant Dupré, post the men within the trees. I want most of them facing downstream, but send one or two to keep an eye on our rear. When the first Indians come in sight I want a lively fire to drive them back. Make them think twice about coming into range again. Understood?"

"Understood, sair."

As Dupré led the men onto the island, already giving orders for their disposition, Whitcomb reined in beside Corporal Atherton.

"Report, Corporal. How's the major?"

"Bearin' up quite well, sir, all things considered."

"And the civilians?"

"All present and accounted for, sir. None the worse for wear. Exceptin' the girl, that is. She 'asn't said a word. We've been 'ere about 'alf an hour, I should say. I might 'ave gone on a bit, but as you see, sir, there ain't much cover. I thought the trees would do well enough. We've built a fire, figurin' the Indians would find us soon enough with or without it."

Whitcomb turned his head to check the direction of the

wind. It was blowing from the north. The Indians wouldn't smell the smoke unless they passed the island by, and there was scant hope of that. "Well done, Corporal. We have a great deal to thank you for."

When Hachaliah Tatum and his party had met the soldiers on the Middle Fork and told their fearful tale, Whitcomb had seen at once that some way would have to be found to transport Corwin on horseback. With the wounded officer on a travois there was no hope of outrunning the marauders that were following Tatum. It had been Corporal Atherton who provided the solution to the problem. In record time he had rigged what he called a "pole harness" to carry Corwin and his litter. He had seen such a device used in the British cavalry to transport the wounded when speed was vital. Using carbine slings and other pieces of belting, Atherton suspended the litter between two horses, each with a rider to guide him, for the harness was fragile and makeshift at best. Two stout willow poles, one attached to the throatlatch buckles and the other to the rearmost equipment ring on the McClellan saddles, connected the horses and kept them a set distance apart. The poles served both to keep the horses moving in tandem and to prevent them from coming so close to each other that they might crush the wounded man between their flanks. With Corwin loaded in the precarious conveyance, Whitcomb had sent Atherton and four privates with Tatum and his men to make as fast as they could for the South Fork, while the rest of the Lost Platoon followed more slowly behind them, serving as a rear guard. The two ambushes had been intended as much to delay the pursuers as to reduce their numbers, for Whitcomb had instructed Atherton to find some defensive position where the platoon might hope to hold off the attackers until nightfall. Atherton had chosen the wooded island, and it would have to do.

Whitcomb looked back downstream. He could see half a mile or more through the falling snow, but there was no sign of movement there. The pursuers had become more cautious. Twice burned, they were twice shy. They would not rush into a third ambush, but in a short while they would discover the stronghold. Without the civilians to think of, Whitcomb and his men might have continued to run, fighting delaying actions where possible, but they could not run for long with most of the men riding double. Better to stand and fight on ground of their own choosing, and this way Tatum's group would have a better chance.

Atherton led Whitcomb in among the trees to where the civilians were gathered by a small fire. Corwin lay close to the blaze, swaddled in his robes. He appeared to be resting comfortably.

Whitcomb wasted no time in preliminaries. "You had better go now, Mr. Tatum. Quickly, please. We'll hold them here as long as we can."

"Go?" The circus owner was taken aback. "I don't understand." His men held their horses' reins tightly, looking fearfully around, all but the one-armed man, who watched Whitcomb thoughtfully.

"If you go now and ride hard, there's a good chance you'll get clean away," Whitcomb explained. "But you must start now, under cover of the snow." He looked at the girl, wondering if she would ever recover from the brutality she had suffered. "If they take her again, she won't live through it," he said.

"He's right, Tatum," said the one-armed man. "If you want to get away, do what he says."

"This way if you please, sir." Atherton addressed Tatum. "There's an opening through 'ere. Lead the 'orses in the water as far as you dare before mounting. You'll go quieter that way and leave no trail."

Tatum extended a hand to Whitcomb. "Thank you, sir."

"Good luck." Whitcomb watched them go, the girl walking docilely beside Tatum. It was a shocking story, the small circus attacked and the girl brutally ravaged by the hostiles before Tatum and his handful of survivors had managed to rescue her. All the more shocking was the presence of renegade whites among the attacking party. That Indians should do such a thing was to be expected, but that white men could take part. . . . Whitcomb said a silent prayer that the girl would get safely away.

The four soldiers who had accompanied Atherton on his flight were holding the platoon's horses near the fire. They were the men with the worst frostbite. Two of them, Luttner and a small red-haired man named Oswald, could barely handle a rifle. With frostbite, the worst pain occurred when the flesh first thawed. But even if there had been no permanent damage, the affected part was very sensitive for a long time thereafter, and grew painful again when exposed to the slightest cold.

"How's the foot, Rogers?"

"Oh, not so bad today, sir." Rogers grinned. "I do better on horseback, though."

As Rogers spoke there were shots from the woods at the downstream end of the island, one first and then another, followed by a short fusillade. Whitcomb ran through the trees until he found Dupré and McCaslin.

"They 'ave withdrawn, sair," said Dupré. "We fired as they came in range."

Downstream, Whitcomb could see no movement in the riverbed.

"They didn't fire back atall, sorr," said McCaslin. "Just skedaddled."

"They'll dismount and come along on foot," Whitcomb

guessed. The renegades would approach the wooded island cautiously, and when they were sure the soldiers were there they would try to surround it.

"How much ammunition have we left?"

"Twenty or thirty rounds per man, sorr. When we got here."

Whitcomb calculated rapidly. Four-hundred-odd rounds, if Rogers and the others had the same. Not enough for the kind of defense he had planned. He felt like an idiot for not inquiring sooner about the ammunition. He had hoped to keep up a brisk fire to hold the renegades back and with luck prevent them from completely surrounding the troopers' position before dusk. But dusk was still hours away.

He looked around, assessing his position. To the west the river bottom was broad and the banks on that side were low, but close on the eastern side of the island the bank rose sharply to a rocky ridge. From its rim, the attackers could fire down into the trees. But if the soldiers were no longer on the island when the enemy arrived . . .

Overhead the sky was dark. The storm would get worse before it abated. Snow was falling thickly now. Whitcomb looked downstream; a squall was approaching, whipping the fresh snow up from the ground and reducing visibility there to a handful of yards.

"Sergeant, I want you to take four men and build up the fire as high as you can with deadwood. Corporal, fetch the pickets from the far end of the island and pick up Major Corwin and the horses on your way back. I'll be waiting for you on the east bank. You have two minutes."

"Sair, what do you—"

"Just follow your orders, Sergeant. Now. At once!"

"Yes, sair!"

As Dupré and McCaslin hastened off to obey, Whitcomb gathered the remaining men and brought them to the island's eastern shore. Moments later they were joined by McCaslin. Donnelly and Gray were with him, carrying Corwin's litter, and close behind them came Dupré and his fire detail, followed by the horse handlers. Whitcomb could see a rising blaze through the trees. "Good work," he said. He waited then, and the men waited with him, none daring to ask what he planned, and when the squall hit the island, filling the air with blinding flakes, he led the men and horses across the stream and up the rocky slope, fearful all the while that the protecting curtain would part and expose them to the renegades' fire. But no shots chased them and they were fully concealed in new positions atop the rise when the squall finally passed. He had placed Corwin and the horse handlers in a sheltered position on the lee side of the rim and the rest of the men along its crest, behind rocks and boulders that offered fair cover from enemy eyes but little from the weather. Upstream there was no sign of Tatum's little band and downstream the attackers had not yet come in sight.

Whitcomb ordered the men not to fire except on his command, and he dared to feel a glimmer of hope. It was not a position he wished to hold for long; here too he could be outflanked by the larger force, but here at least he held the high ground and he had regained the element of surprise. If his daring move worked, the troopers could be back in the shelter of the trees within the hour. The enemy would see the fire and approach the island, and when they discovered that it was deserted they would find the tracks leading across the river. They would think the soldiers had run, but when they massed to follow the trail once more, the Lost Platoon would be waiting. This time the ambush would succeed. With luck they might kill half of the attackers with a single volley and drive off the rest. Once it was dark, the soldiers would slip away.

Unless the surviving renegades pressed the attack and forced the troopers to expend their precious ammunition. Unless their new position were discovered too soon. Unless something else happened that he hadn't foreseen.

He chided himself for letting his hopes run away with him. Live through the next hour and then the one after that. If E Troop's Lost Platoon met its fate here, it would become a legend in the frontier cavalry. Separated from the command, the soldiers' remains discovered a hundred miles from the battle, perhaps after years of searching, and whose were the bones scattered around the platoon's last stronghold? What a mystery that would be!

Whitcomb grinned in spite of himself. He hadn't done too badly.

"Leftenant, sir. The major's awake. 'e's askin' for you." Atherton had crawled up the ridge close behind Whitcomb.

Whitcomb nodded and called softly to the nearest trooper. "Private Gray! I'll be down with Major Corwin. Tell Sergeant Dupré to send for me if anything moves out there."

But when he reached Corwin and the horses he found Dupré squatting beside the wounded officer.

"I need you on the line, Sergeant," said Whitcomb.

"I sent for him, Mr. Reb. This won't take long." Corwin's voice was barely a whisper. He was calm and alert, but very pale. It seemed to Whitcomb that the dark circles around the lieutenant's eyes had deepened noticeably within the past few hours. He fervently hoped Corwin wouldn't give any senseless orders. He hadn't the time for a confrontation now.

"I hope you're feeling better, sir."

Corwin brushed the question aside with a wave of his hand. "Report, Ham. What's our situation?"

"We encountered a party of civilians, sir. Six men and a young lady, pursued by hostiles and renegade whites. I've sent them on ahead while we hold the Indians here. We're on the South Fork of the Powder, as best we can tell. There are twenty-five or thirty in the attacking party. We've killed at least two."

"From bad to worse, eh?" Corwin seemed almost to be amused.

"We're in a good defensive position on high ground and the renegades don't know we're here. We're going to hit them hard and drive them off. After dark we'll get away."

Corwin said nothing for a time. He seemed to be lost in thought. Then he looked at Dupré and Whitcomb in turn. "I want the truth now. Have I been raving?"

Dupré glanced at Whitcomb.

"Raving? No, sir. Well, the fact is, yes, sir. You haven't made much sense at times. You were singing sea shanties."

Corwin made a grimace that was supposed to be a smile. "I'm not surprised. Only tunes I could ever carry worth a damn." He reached out and touched Dupré's knee. "You wouldn't have a little brandy left, would you, Armand?"

"I am sorry, sair. It is gone."

Corwin cackled. "God, what a calamity!" He was racked by a sudden spasm of coughing. Atherton helped Whitcomb and Dupré turn him on his side. They muffled the coughs with the robes until he fell silent at last and lay back, gasping.

Corwin tried to speak but he was unable, and so he motioned them to wait. He breathed with difficulty for a time, wondering if he was doing the right thing. Should he try to hold on a little longer? No. He couldn't take the risk. Each time he lapsed into unconsciousness there was no telling how long it would last or what crises might arise while he was out cold, and if he had been raving—well, the moment had come. He had done all he could to prepare Whitcomb for command, but back at Fetterman he had never dreamed the young officer would have to stand on his own so soon. He had assumed it would be a matter of years, not weeks. Even so, he had known from the start that he would have to bring his new second lieutenant along quickly if Whitcomb were to survive his first campaign and come through it without endangering the men. Like most shavetails, he had been too eager to prove himself. His chase after the beef herd had revealed a boyish recklessness that needed to be curbed, and so Corwin had fallen back on a method he had employed to train his subordinates during the war, when young officers had learned their craft in battle and died if they learned too slowly. He had been a cold and demanding superior. He had treated Whitcomb like a schoolboy, holding him back until he was champing at the bit, just praying for some chance to show what he could do if he were turned loose. And then suddenly Corwin had let him go. Just as he had hoped, Whitcomb had taken the new responsibility well, keeping his recklessness in check because he was so determined that Corwin should find no fault with him. After the platoon was cut off in the battle, Corwin had tightened the reins again, accusing Whitcomb of wanting command precisely to plant the idea in his mind. But if Corwin had passed the mantle too soon, Whitcomb would have feared it and his fear might have led him into dangerous mistakes. Now, with his troop commander worse than useless, the young officer was almost ready to risk a charge of insubordination just to have the matter settled and done with.

He was a good lad. He would do his best, but would it be enough?

"Dupré, I want you to witness this order. You too, Atherton."

"The major isn't himself, Sergeant," Whitcomb began, but Corwin cut him off.

"Shut up, Mr. Reb! You're still taking orders here." He fumbled beneath the robes. "My damned sword. I can't find my sword." He wanted to give his saber to Whitcomb.

"It's back at Fetterman, sir. We left them there." Whitcomb glanced meaningfully at Dupré. Surely by now the first sergeant could see that Corwin had lost touch with his surroundings. Maybe it would be best simply to tell him he was no longer in command and hadn't been for some time.

"Good thing too." Corwin ceased his fumblings. "Useless piece of trash." A fevered light flickered in his eyes. "You should have seen us in the war, Ham. A saber charge! God, what a sight! It'd scare the balls off Tamerlane!"

Corwin had risen part-way up on his elbows but Atherton gently pressed him back. "Don't be strainin' yourself, sir."

Whitcomb cleared his throat. "Major, there's something I must say. In view of your condition I think it's best if I—"

"Dammit, Ham, will you let me finish!" Corwin lay back and fixed Dupré with his gaze. "You're a witness, Armand. This is official." The eyes, almost lifeless now, moved to Whitcomb. "Lieutenant Whitcomb, I'm placing you in charge of the troop, what's left of it. In my present state I'm not fit to command." The eyes closed. "That's all. Carry on."

"Sergeant! Lieutenant, sorr!" Private Gwynn came scrambling down the slope. "They're comin'! And they're showin' a white flag."

When Whitcomb reached the rim he found a place between Private Gray and Corporal McCaslin. The snow had thinned and a mist was beginning to rise from the water of the river as the air turned colder. The mixed band of Indians and whites was approaching at a walk in the river bottom. Two men, a bearded white man and a tall Negro, were well out in front of the rest. Tied to the barrel of the Negro's rifle was a piece of white cloth, which he waved back and forth slowly as he rode.

"It may be a trick," Whitcomb said to no one in particular. He moved along the line, ordering the men to pick a target and wait for his command to fire.

The two riders halted when they were fifty yards from the island. "Hello in the trees!" the white man called out. "We want to speak to the officer in charge!"

Dupré glanced at Whitcomb, but Whitcomb motioned him to be patient. To reply now would give away their position. He waited until the main party of pursuers came to a stop.

"Bloody hell!" exclaimed Corporal Atherton. "Look at the size of that one, sir."

Prominent in the front rank of the pursuers was a giant of a man on an immense dapple-gray horse. Whitcomb had noticed the man back at the ambush in the dry wash. He wore no hat and was cloaked in a purple cape. It was neither the costume nor the mount of a marauding renegade.

"If they want to talk, I'll talk with them," Whitcomb said. "The rest of you hold on your man and keep out of sight. Range to the main party, about one hundred yards, wouldn't you say, Sergeant?"

"Make it eighty, sair."

"Range eighty yards, and remember you're firing downhill.'' He cupped his hands to his mouth and turned up-stream, hoping his voice would seem to come from everywhere and nowhere. "Who are you?" he demanded.

The two riders turned toward the ridge. They had placed his voice. It was the Negro who replied. "Regimental Sergeant Major Julius Ingram! Formerly of the Ninth Cavalry!" Farther downstream the Indians and whites shifted in their saddles and looked about, wondering if there might be other soldiers in hidden positions around them.

Whitcomb was peering at the man beside the Negro. Beneath his brown oilskin, one arm was in a sling. "I know that man! He was in the battle. He tried to get to Colonel Reynolds, but he was shot by Mills's men." He cupped his hands and shouted again. "Identify the man beside you!"

The white man answered for himself. "Christopher Hardeman! Special scout for General Crook! Who the hell are you?"

"He wasn't one of our scouts, sorr," McCaslin said. "I knew 'em all."

"There was talk of a man sent on ahead of the command," said Private Gray. "Some kind of peace emissary, I think."

Whitcomb shook his head. "I don't like it. I won't violate a flag of truce, but if those Indians move any closer—"

"Oh for the love of God, boys! I've gone 'round the bend. I can't be seein' what I'm seein'!" Private Gwynn was pointing downstream. Approaching along the river-bed, following the trail of the soldiers and their tormentors, was a new band of thirty or more horsemen, and in their midst lumbered a huge elephant with a small man perched atop his shoulders.

Whitcomb stared for a long moment, trying to make

sense of what he saw. The two parties in the river bottom had spied each other now and there were shouts of greeting from the Indians and whites below the ridge. The elephant broke into a headlong run and raised his trunk. The sound of his trumpeting filled the valley.

"Hold your fire," Whitcomb said with a calm he did not feel. He rose to his feet and started down the slope toward the river.

CHAPTER TWELVE

Joe Kitchen and Lisa were the last to arrive on the scene, and already the peace was made. The circus men were clustered on the near side of the stream with Rama standing placidly in their midst, while on the far bank Julius and Hardeman were talking with three soldiers. Other troopers were still descending from the rocky ridge, leading their horses, gawking and pointing at the elephant.

The Indians had not lingered long near the soldiers. Sun Horse and four of his men were talking nearby, but the rest of the Lakota were moving off upriver, beyond the island, searching both banks for tracks. Seen through the rising river mists they resembled wraiths. Lisa made out the hatted figure of Johnny Smoker among them. Nowhere did she see any sign of Tatum and his men or the missing girl.

Alfred Chalmers rode forth to meet the two riders, and as he approached, his eyes were on Lisa. He seemed to be searching for something to say, some way to console her, but she spoke first. "She isn't here?"

He shook his head. "Apparently Mr. Tatum and his men were sent on ahead while the soldiers stayed back to delay us. He told them the Indians had destroyed the circus and violated Amanda. He said the rest of us were renegades who took part in the attack. They had no reason not to believe him."

Lisa had imagined that there would be some such explanation for the soldiers' actions. As always, Tatum's smooth talk had served him well.

"We had to come, Alfred," said Joe Kitchen. "I tried to hold them back, but they wouldn't stay there doing nothing." The second band of riders had left Putnam's Park scarcely an hour after the first. Unable to dissuade them, Joe had ridden in the lead. Ben Long and one of the wranglers had some experience at following sign and they had managed to keep on the trail, which was freshly tracked by Lisa and Hardeman and the others who had gone after Tatum.

"I understand, Joseph. But you know we can't go on with all these men. Many of them aren't even armed."

"I know. Just coming this far will satisfy most of them. They'll feel like they done some good. Monty and Ben will take them back."

Lisa moved her horse a few paces off. She would leave it to the men to make arrangements for getting on with the chase and sending the rest back to Putnam's Park. Such deliberations were beyond her abilities just now.

She had stayed with her uncle's body for a time, and the reinforcements from the circus had come upon her there, squatting on her haunches like an Indian with her arms wrapped around her knees, rocking slowly back and forth, oblivious to the chill wind. When the men saw who it was that she watched over, Joe Kitchen had waved the rest of them up the river while he stayed behind. He had said nothing, but he took the reins from her hand and led her horse a short distance away where he held it with his own, waiting patiently. The wind had blown Bat Putnam's gray hair in his face and Lisa had reached out to brush it back. She had felt the unnatural stiffness of the flesh and she had realized that what lay before her was no longer the uncle she loved. It was a corpse, a lifeless remnant. It had seemed less important then that the body would remain unattended for a while, and she had left it after covering the face with the hood of the Hudson's Bay capote.

The men with Sun Horse moved off toward the little island now and he came to join her. When he reached her side he took her hands between his own. Walks Bent Over and Johnny Smoker would find the trail again soon, he told her. The Strange-Animal Man's horses were tired, and he would not be too far ahead. Meantime, the four Lakota warriors that stayed behind would make pony drags from the cottonwood brush on the island for the men who had died. The bodies would be taken to the Sun Band's village, and when the warriors returned, the burial scaffolds would be made and the ceremonies performed. Lisa nodded in reply, not trusting herself to speak.

On the far side of the stream the talk was ending. Julius mounted his horse and made his way back across the river. Hutch joined him as he reached the bank and walked beside him as he rode up to Lisa. The black man stopped close on her upwind side, as if he thought the wind were the source of her grief and he might shield her from it. He held out his hand and she took it in one of her own, feeling his strength and the comfort he offered.

"Miss Lisa?" Hutch spoke in a voice so quiet she could barely hear it. "I just wanted to say I'm sorry. He was a fine man. It kinda made me feel like I knowed your pa, knowing him."

She saw the heartfelt sorrow in his look and she turned suddenly away, blinking hard and choking back the lump that rose in her throat. She was prepared to bear her own pain, but the pain of others threatened to tear her spirit asunder. Why was it so? It had been the same when her father died. She hadn't cried for him until she saw the tears in Ling Wo's eyes.

"Miss Putnam?"

She turned to find Hardeman approaching her, leading his horse by the reins. A young soldier was with him.

"This is Lieutenant Whitcomb. He and his men were separated from General Crook's command at the battle on the Powder. They've had a hard time of it since then."

The young man did not seem old enough to be an officer, scarcely old enough to be a soldier at all. Lisa saw that he was exhausted and her first impulse was to ask him if he and his men had eaten today, but she kept silent.

Across the river, the last two troopers were coming down from the ridge, carrying a litter between them.

"Miss Putnam," said Whitcomb, "I am told that the old fellow who died . . . the one who . . ." He was standing stiffly before her, not meeting her eyes. "I'm told he was your uncle, ma'am. You have my sincere apologies and my deepest condolences, although I am sure they count for very little in the face of your loss."

Lisa could feel no anger toward this youth with the

sparse sandy beard. Lies and deception had killed her uncle and it didn't matter who had pulled the trigger.

"It wasn't your fault, Lieutenant. It was no one's fault. Except Mr. Tatum's."

"You're very kind to say so, ma'am."

"What about Amanda? How was she?"

"She was somewhat bruised about the face. And she didn't speak at all. Not a word in the entire time she was with us."

Lisa looked at Hardeman.

"There's no sense worrying about what might be," he said. "When we get her back we'll find out what happened. Right now Lieutenant Whitcomb's men need some food and a place to rest. Some of them have frostbite and his troop commander lost a leg. They'll have to go back to Putnam's Park with the circus men."

"Of course." Lisa was glad of a chance to help others in need and put aside her own loss. She turned to Julius. "You could go with them. If there are wounded—"

"I'll do what I can when we've got Amanda back safe." He would not leave Lisa's side. Not now.

Lisa hesitated and then she spoke to Whitcomb. "We'll be home as soon as we can when it's over. Until then my cook and her husband will do everything they can for you."

Another soldier joined Whitcomb now, a stocky man with a drooping mustache and a thick beard.

"This is First Sergeant Dupré." Dupré touched his cap. "I'll send him with the men. One of my corporals and I will ride with you."

"It ain't your fight, Lieutenant." Julius's voice was hard. He had fought off an impulse to come to attention in the young officer's presence, and recognizing Whitcomb as a Southerner had made him wary. But Whitcomb had been the first to rise from cover, the first to walk down to parley, and now he was the first to refuse an offer of food and shelter until the business at hand was completed.

"I have an account to settle with Mr. Tatum, Sergeant Major," Whitcomb said. "It's a matter of honor."

Julius heard the controlled anger in the young man's tone and he understood. Tatum had hidden behind the soldiers' guns and then he had left them to their fate in order to save his own skin. And but for Tatum's lies Bat Putnam would still be alive. Lisa had put it right when she said there was no one to blame but Tatum "We best be getting along then," he said.

Dupré spoke softly in Whitcomb's ear for a moment and Whitcomb seemed to slump a little, but he drew himself up as he faced Lisa again.

"I have just been told that our commanding officer is dead. With your permission, Miss Putnam, I'll arrange to have him transported to your ranch. I can't leave him in this place. I hope you understand."

"We have a small graveyard in Putnam's Park," Lisa said gently. "You're welcome to bury him there."

Whitcomb touched the brim of his cap and made a slight bow before turning away. The soldiers were crossing the river now, the litter carriers coming last of all. There too the face was covered. Why do we cover the faces of the dead? Lisa wondered. We're afraid of death, most of us. But not all. Not the Putnam men, it seemed. Her uncle had gone willingly somehow, as her father had gone. Like his brother Jed, Bat had been smiling, and remembering that smile lessened Lisa's pain.

As the litter carriers climbed the riverbank, encumbered by their awkward burden, the man in front slipped in the snow and mud and dropped to one knee. The body rolled half off the litter and was kept from falling only by the quick action of the man at the rear, who lowered his end to keep the litter level. The robe slipped off the upper part of the body, revealing the face. The skin was gray and waxen and the eyes were closed. Only the reddish-brown beard was lifelike.

Lisa touched her heels to her horse and rode the few yards to the river's edge, staring at the dead man as if in a trance. The litter bearers gained the top of the bank and set the litter on the ground. Whitcomb knelt beside the body and regarded it somberly for several moments before drawing the robe back into place.

"What was his name?" It seemed to Lisa that someone else had spoken, although the voice was her own.

"Hmm?" Whitcomb looked up. "Oh. Corwin, Miss Putnam. Brevet Major Francis Corwin."

"Lisa?"

She turned at the sound of Julius's voice to see him looking at her strangely. Hutch and Hardeman and Sun Horse were watching her as well; beyond them Joe Kitchen and Chalmers had been joined by the Waldheims and their eyes too were on her. She saw the concern on every face and her vision blurred. She was unable to speak, scarcely able to think, suffocated by a burden of numbing grief that was suddenly unbearable.

She kicked her horse so hard that he snorted in surprise as he leaped ahead on command, dashing among the other riders, nearly colliding with one or two. She guided him upriver, past the cottonwood island, urging him into a headlong run, needing to leave the senseless death behind her, wanting the wind strong in her face and the sensation of being fully alive that only a horse in full flight could give her. The tears ran down her face and dried there, making numb trails until they ceased to flow.

She did not know how long she rode, but it seemed that

hardly any time had passed when she saw the Indians ahead of her. She galloped past the surprised warriors and only when she reached Johnny Smoker and Walks Bent Over did she slow to a trot, following close behind them. They had found the trail. The fugitives' tracks were plain to see in the new snow.

Standing Eagle left the main body of Indians and came to ride beside her. He had mounted Bat's bay mare after his own horse was shot from under him by the soldiers. He nodded grimly. "Won't be long now. We'll settle the score for ol' Bat and Little Hand both. He died good, Bat did. Died tryin' to save me. I guess you know that."

It unnerved Lisa to hear the trappers' English so like her uncle's coming from the mouth of the war leader, and she replied in Lakota. "He would be pleased to hear his brother say he died well."

Standing Eagle said nothing more and they rode together in silence until Hardeman and Sun Horse overtook them as the rest of the pursuers caught up and closed ranks with the Indians. Standing Eagle moved forward then, joining Johnny and Walks Bent Over in the lead, and Hardeman took the warrior's place by Lisa's side. He rode close to her, but not crowding, and she was grateful for his company, as she had been throughout the night. An eternity ago, during the music and dancing of the evening before, Bat Putnam had told her of Hardeman's willingness to remain with Sun Horse for a time, and to help if he were asked. Learning this had made Lisa feel that she and the scout were allies once more, at least insofar as the fate of the Sun Band was concerned, and this in turn had made it possible to set her other feelings aside and allow herself the comfort of his presence during the long pursuit.

Lieutenant Whitcomb and his corporal, a slight man with a sharp nose, fell in place beside Lisa and Hardeman, and Hutch was right behind them, mounted on a horse borrowed from one of the circus men who was returning to Putnam's Park. Farther to the rear, there were more than a dozen circus whites among the pursuers now. Sam Higgins and Carlos were there, both armed. The last to overtake the band were Rama and Chatur. The mahout smiled broadly when some of the Lakota looked back in wonder at the behemoth on their trail. The elephant's lumbering pace was more than adequate to keep up with the horses at anything but a full gallop.

Ahead, the river valley deepened. The stream itself twisted and turned, following a winding course in the broad bottom. The hills on either side were dull and barren, dotted with stunted sagebrush and clumps of struggling grass on the flatter places, while the steep slopes were utterly bare save for a thin covering of snow.

As the leaders entered a long straight portion of the valley they increased their pace, glancing only occasionally at the tracks, which ignored the wanderings of the stream and made straight for the small canyon mouth where the valley narrowed abruptly a quarter mile ahead.

To the west the clouds were breaking. The air had become clear and much colder behind the departing storm and the wind had dropped, as if it had spent all its energy during the violent squalls of midday and needed time to catch its breath.

"Be dark in a few hours," Hardeman observed.

Julius nodded. "We don't catch 'em by then, they'll be long gone come daylight."

"Johnny'll track 'em all night if he has to," Hutch protested. "I never seen the like of his trackin'." He was grim and serious, suddenly older. He mourned the loss of his mule, but Bat Putnam's death had overwhelmed any such considerations for now. Like the others, Hutch had but a single goal, a single determination: that the pursuit should be brought to a successful conclusion.

Twenty paces ahead, Johnny and Walks Bent Over rode on either side of the fugitives' trail. The hoofprints were more closely spaced than they had been where they first emerged from the river.

"They're slowin', sorr," McCaslin said to Whitcomb. "Havin' a bit o' rest for the horses. P'raps he thinks we're all spillin' our guts out back yonder." He glanced at Lisa. "Beg pahrdon, mum. I've grown unaccustomed to the presence of a lady."

The corporal's thick brogue and pleasant manner cheered Lisa and she was surprised to find herself smiling.

The trackers were entering the canyon now and suddenly Johnny Smoker held up a hand and pointed straight ahead. As those behind him rounded a slight bend in the narrow passage, they saw horsemen barely a hundred yards away, moving at a walk. Prominent among them was a tall white stallion bearing a large man and a smaller figure seated before him in the saddle.

Walks Bent Over made a peremptory motion to silence the pursuers and he and Johnny led the way at a quick trot, following the soft sand and snow close to the riverbank, hoping to close the distance still further before they were discovered. But some noise reached the ears of the fugitives, or perhaps one of their horses gave the alarm, for as one they turned, and seeing the pursuing force so close behind them, they sprang forward at a run and raced off around the next curve in the meandering river's course.

At once the pursuers kicked their horses forward. The Indians whooped with glee and their shouts echoed between the low walls of the canyon. The whites rode in grim silence. There could be no doubt about the outcome now. The quarry would be driven to ground and then all that would remain was to see how it would end—sensibly or with more futile dying.

When the pursuers rounded the next bend they saw that they were gaining on the fugitives. Tatum's men looked back often and one threw a wild shot over his shoulder. Closer and closer the pursuers came, spurred on by their certain victory. Suddenly the figure on the white horse flung out an arm, and in a final desperate sprint he led his men to a jumble of rocks and boulders at the bottom of a high, sloping bluff that was heavily eroded and rounded at the top, affording no rim from which the attackers might shoot or even see into the hiding place below. The little band vanished among the rocks and the pursuers were forced to double back and take shelter behind a curve in the canyon wall as a few shots boomed out from the stronghold. There was a scattering of rocks at the base of the wall, fewer and smaller than those that formed the bulwarks of Tatum's hideout, but adequate to provide safe vantage points from which to survey the short stretch of canyon where the fugitives had taken cover. As the others dismounted, Chatur and Rama arrived on the scene. Leaving the elephant well to the rear, the mahout came forward on foot.

"It's a fair position," Whitcomb said, looking out on the rocky redoubt. The river curved close to the base of the bluff in a channel half a dozen feet lower than the general level of the canyon floor. With the stream serving as a moat to protect their front and the rounded slope guaranteeing their rear, the fugitives had only to defend themselves against approach from either side.

Sun Horse and Standing Eagle had been talking softly, and now the war leader spoke to four of his warriors, motioning up the canyon. At once they remounted their horses and guided them down the bank to the stream. In an instant they were across and running along the far bank, passing in front of Tatum's stronghold and drawing a few harmless shots as they flew by and disappeared around the next bend in the canyon, where they would take position to prevent escape in that direction.

"Nicely done, sir," Whitcomb muttered, meaning the words for Sun Horse but never for a moment suspecting that the old savage understood him.

"Thank you," said Sun Horse.

Whitcomb was beyond being surprised. Finding himself riding with a band of wild Sioux in pursuit of a kidnapped white girl had exhausted his last measure of that emotion. It was yet another undreamed-of event added to a long list of such experiences he had accumulated in the past month. Together they constituted a second lifetime, equal in breadth and depth to the twenty-two years that had preceded it, and he was certain that nothing would ever surprise him again.

"So, perhaps a few of us should go there too," said Papa Waldheim. "Villy? Johann, you stay." Leaving his wounded son behind, the elder Waldheim remounted. He led Willy down the bank where the Indians had gone before and the two men raced along in the warriors' tracks. At a shouted command from Papa Waldheim, they gripped their saddle horns, dropped off the near side, bounded up and over the horses' backs, then bounced up again and regained their seats as they disappeared from sight to the delighted howls of praise from the Indians.

"Gunther is always the showman," said Chalmers with a wry smile.

"Dangerous bit of tomfoolery, if you ask me," said Joe Kitchen.

"Perhaps not. By, ah, thumbing our noses at Mr. Tatum, so to speak, we make it plain that we have the upper hand. It will give him something to think about."

"He'll see we've got the upper hand," Hardeman agreed. "He'll also see that we can't shoot in there as long as he's got the girl."

Joe Kitchen pointed to the riverbank below the fugitives' redoubt. "We could get pretty close to him down there."

Hardeman shook his head. "We don't want to force his move. Give him some time to think. He'll see he's got no way out and he'll try to bargain with us."

As if he had heard Hardeman's words, Tatum shouted from among the rocks and his silk hat was briefly visible. "Hardeman! Miss Putnam! Can you hear me?"

"We can hear you!" Hardeman replied.

"Let us go or we'll kill the girl!"

"Kill the girl and you've got nothing left to bargain with!"

There was a long silence. Alfred Chalmers cleared his throat. "He is a desperate man. I would not trust Amanda's safety to him. He knows he's lost everything."

"Give him a few more minutes," said Julius. "Pretty quick he'll figure out that his only way out of here is to give us the girl."

"The fact is," Joe Kitchen said, "we don't know just what he's done."

"At the very least he has kidnapped Amanda and caused the deaths of two men today." Lisa's voice was cold. "We can't let him go."

"Not with Amanda." Johnny had scarcely spoken since the pursuit began. The others looked at him now.

"That's the choice," said Hardeman. "We want Amanda, we might have to turn Tatum loose."

Chalmers spoke without hesitation. "We must do what's best for Amanda, whatever has the best chance of freeing her." The circus men nodded in agreement.

Hardeman looked at Lisa and after a moment's delay she too nodded her assent. Nothing could bring back her uncle now. Her first thought must be for the living.

"Tatum!" Hardeman called up the canyon. "Let the girl go and you can ride out of here!"

"We're staying put until the Indians clear out!" another voice replied, and a shot in the attackers' general direction emphasized the point.

"That's Tom Johansen," said Joe Kitchen. "He's got a holy terror of Injuns."

"First we ride out of here!" Tatum shouted. "Then we'll let Amanda go when we're safely away!"

"I was afraid it would come to that," said Whitcomb. "They're not the sort of men to trust simple promises. Once we have the girl back there's nothing to prevent us from doing as we like with them."

Hardeman nodded. "And if we let them ride out of here, Tatum's got no reason to keep his word and let Amanda go."

"It's a Mexican standoff," said Julius.

"We've got to break it somehow," said Lisa.

There was a short silence and then Joe Kitchen spoke. "We can hold them here all night if we have to. Come morning they'll be cold and hungry. It could be they'll be more willing to take our word by then."

"I'm not waiting for morning," said Johnny, addressing himself to Hardeman. "I'll go down under the bank past the rocks to where the river's closest to the bluff. A bunch of men working up close won't do any good, but I might alone. You do something to get Tatum's attention and I'll see if I can't get in there."

Hardeman thought it over and finally nodded. He could see no other way to break the stalemate and Johnny already had his mind made up. "It could work. But you be careful. If they see you too soon they might hurt the girl."

Johnny shook his head. "If they hurt her, they've got nothing left. You said so yourself. Besides, they won't see me." He turned to the others. "Somebody give me a gun."

Lisa drew a pistol from beneath her goatskin jacket and Johnny accepted it without a word. It was the same Remington Army .44 he had carried on the day Amanda was lost. He opened his blanket overcoat and stuffed the gun in his belt the way Hardeman carried his Colt, and then he clambered down into the river channel and began working his way forward under cover of the bank, crouching low.

"We better figure a sure way to keep those fellers watching us," Joe Kitchen said.

"I have an idea that might help," said Lieutenant Whitcomb. "We might even get the girl back without any trouble, but they would still have to trust us. Even if they don't agree, we'll certainly get their attention." He began to explain his plan.

Unnoticed by the others, Chatur left them and returned to Rama. He mounted to the elephant's shoulders and started off down the canyon, urging the beast into a rambling run that quickly took him around a bend and out of sight of the whites and Indians. A few moments more brought elephant and mahout to the mouth of the canyon. There Chatur turned Rama away from the river and guided him up the gentle slopes that led to the canyon's rim, where the land was rocky and rolling on either side of the small gorge. Beast and master made their way back along the heights until Chatur judged that he was above the fugitives' rocky stronghold. He could not see the redoubt, but he knew within a few yards where it was located, by the curve of the river below and the configuration of the canyon wall across the way, which he had noted carefully before setting out. He placed the bull where he wanted him and then descended to the ground and proceeded along the canyon's rim on foot for another hundred yards or more until he came to a place where the canyon's lip was sharp and jutted out over the river, affording him a view of Tatum's hiding place. He could see five men crouched together, watching the attackers' position. To their rear, among the largest rocks at the base of the bluff itself, were the horses and two more human figures. Chatur was not sure he would be able to help Amanda, but should the opportunity arise he was prepared to do what he could.

Below, in the scene the mahout could make out only in miniature, a heated argument was taking place.

"We've got to bargain!" insisted Jack Fisk. "There's no chance we'll get away with the girl. She's our ticket out."

"Listen to me!" Tatum ordered for what seemed to be the dozenth time. "We're going to get out of here and we're taking the girl with us. As long as we have her, they won't touch us."

"I ain't going out there to be cut up by those damned Indians!" said Johansen. "I seen what they do to a person."

"Tell them to pull the Injuns back," suggested Tanner in his slow, methodical way. "Then we promise to turn the girl loose once we get out'n the canyon. Nothin' says we gotta do it."

"Yah, sure, and nothing says the damned Indians won't be waiting," argued Johansen. "They'll promise to pull them back, and who's to say the Indians won't just keep out of sight all up and down the canyon? I ain't going out there, not me."

They had stated and restated their fears and positions since being trapped among the rocks, and now they fell silent, eyeing one another more like beasts than men. Fisk's overcoat was raccoon, but his sharp badger eyes moved back and forth from Tatum to Kinnean as he wondered which he should obey if a time came to choose. Tom Johansen, for all his fair appearance and lanky height, was a frightened ferret in a blanket coat. Tanner, bearlike, was the largest, but Henry Kinnean was the most forceful figure, stocky and solid in his buffalo coat. He took no part in the dispute. Like a buffalo he listened and watched, certain in his own power, moving very little except to keep potential dangers in sight. When he moved it would be suddenly and with great purpose.

Only the circus master, silk-hatted and wrapped in his blue cloak, was unmistakably a product of civilized regions, yet his temper was as short as any and his condition the most desperate of all, for he lived under a threat that menaced none of the others. If he were forced to give up Amanda in order to buy his release, Kinnean and the rest would gain their freedom at no cost to themselves, while Hachaliah Tatum, who had already sacrificed everything else in order to keep the girl, would lose his last treasure.

He looked around, seeking some hitherto unseen avenue by which he might flee, but while his present position was well suited to defense, it offered few opportunities for escape. Close against the cliff stood a group of boulders taller than a man; among them, out of sight of the others, Morton watched over Amanda and the horses. Around this central hideaway an irregular ring of smaller stones formed a natural fortification behind which Tatum and the rest were crouched. Beyond the ring, rocks of varying sizes were scattered for a dozen yards in every direction. On the upstream side they extended to the very edge of the river where it curved close to the bluff; a man on hands and knees might gain the channel unseen, but upstream there were Indians waiting.

Tatum wondered how soon the others would crack and force him to surrender. They had been up all night and none had eaten since the evening before. Kinnean had appropriated a few cuts of buffalo from the meat shed outside the barn in Putnam's Park, but there had been no time since then to stop for cooking and here there was no firewood. The men were hungry and tired and their desperation would focus on Tatum when they saw that only he had a motive for escaping without giving up Amanda.

"I'll tell you one thing," said Tanner. "I ain't handing over that girl so long as they got us pinned down like ducks in a washtub."

"Don't be an idiot!" Tatum snapped. "No one's suggesting we should do anything that stupid."

Tanner turned to face the circus master. "Who are you calling stupid?"

"Quiet." Kinnean held up a hand. From the pursuers' position came a new voice.

"Mr. Tatum! This is Lieutenant Whitcomb!"

"That explains how they caught up with us so quick," said Kinnean. "They got to those soldiers and told them the truth."

"You mean we're fighting the army now too?" Johansen's fearfulness increased. He gave the impression of one whose final moments were tolling away and only the manner of his dying remained to be determined.

"Tatum!" came Whitcomb's voice again. "If you'll surrender to me and release the girl, I promise you safe-conduct to Fort Fetterman!"

The fugitives looked at one another. "It's a chance," said Fisk.

"By golly, it is!" Tom Johansen brightened at the

possibility of a reprieve. "You think we better take it, Mr. Tatum?"

Tatum hesitated and Kinnean answered the youth in his stead, his voice full of scorn. "You want to explain to the post commandant at Fetterman why we got those soldiers into a fight with a bunch of settlers?" Johansen's face fell.

"I hadn't thought of that," Fisk admitted.

"This is Lisa Putnam!" came a woman's voice from down the canyon. "I give you my word that if you surrender to us and release Amanda unharmed, you'll be free to go with Lieutenant Whitcomb."

"Seems there oughta be some way we could use that lieutenant to get clear of the Indians," said Tanner.

Hachaliah Tatum was thinking hard. Even with Lisa Putnam's promise of safe passage, formidable problems remained, considerations that were unknown to his hirelings. In extremity, he would let Amanda go to save his own life, but to release her unharmed—well, there was the rub. She was bruised a bit and shocked into a stupor from which it seemed nothing would arouse her, but as long as her present condition persisted, the real injury would not be known. Could he risk it? Even if it came to giving her up he could not do so on Whitcomb's terms. The soldiers were in no condition to set out directly for Fetterman. Whitcomb would want to see to his injured and afford them some time to recover their strength, and Putnam's Park was the logical place to do those things. If Tatum were there when Amanda was returned to her friends, she might come to herself and reveal what he had done to her, and then all promises would be meaningless.

The perils surrounding him seemed to increase with each passing moment. If there were a way to escape them and still keep Amanda, he would have to hit on it soon.

"Lieutenant Whitcomb!" he called. "Perhaps we can

reach a compromise! Surely you see that we can't surrender the girl while we're trapped like this. Let us ride away and you can come with us. Just you, while the others wait here. Ride with us for a mile or two and we'll give you the girl." Even as he proposed it, Tatum knew the offer would be refused. One man alone with the fugitives could easily be overpowered and the bargain broken. Lacking a more promising course, he was stalling for time.

"It's no good, Tatum!" came the reply, in Hardeman's voice. "The girl stays here! We're coming out to get her. You meet us halfway and we'll escort you out of the canyon. Sun Horse will take his Indians downstream while you get away." As he spoke, the scout rose from cover and stepped into plain view at the base of the canyon wall where the river curved out of sight downstream. Whitcomb, Julius Ingram and Lisa Putnam joined him. There was movement behind them as the Indians withdrew. Hardeman and his companions started forward. Only Lisa Putnam carried a weapon in view, a Winchester carbine held in the crook of her right arm. Behind the quartet came the boy Hutch, leading half a dozen horses.

"You tell them yes or I will, Tatum," Fisk threatened, made bold by his master's indecision. "We're not all of us going to risk our necks to help you keep that girl."

"Whatever you're going to do, make up your mind," said Kinnean quietly. He withdrew his pistol from its holster and checked his load, smiling slightly, as if he was enjoying Tatum's quandary. While he watched Tatum and the others watched the approaching party, a movement on the upstream edge of the redoubt went unobserved. Except by Amanda.

Back among the boulders, Thaddeus Morton was peering through a narrow gap in the rocks, listening to the others talk. He held the horses' reins in his hand and paid no attention to the girl, who sat on a small rock behind him. She hadn't made a move on her own since leaving Putnam's Park, and like Tatum, Morton assumed she was scarcely aware of what went on around her. Like Tatum, he was wrong.

Amanda had acquiesced in her abduction because she was unable to do otherwise. Hachaliah was her protector, but who would protect her from him? No one, it seemed. He had beaten her and no one came to the rescue; he had taken his way with her despite her efforts to resist. He was the strongest of all and so she had gone with him, powerless to resist him further. When she first saw the soldiers she had felt a flicker of hope, but Hachaliah had bent them easily to his will and her hope had vanished. Now she felt it return. A flash of movement at the edge of the stream caught her eye. Morton didn't notice it, nor did the others. She could hear their voices still, arguing about what to do. "Make up your mind," said Kinnean, but Hachaliah didn't answer. Upstream, among the rocks close to the water, everything was still, and then something moved again. A figure passed from one rock to the next, then to the next, coming closer. It stopped and cautiously raised its head.

It was Johnny Smoker.

Amanda's hope grew strong, but she was fearful as well. When Johnny learned what Hachaliah had done to her, would he still want her? She felt soiled and ashamed, as she had felt during the long night and through the day, but the sight of Johnny reawakened her courage. If he could rescue her, if he could somehow vanquish Hachaliah, then he would become her new protector and they could go forward together, leaving the past behind.

Johnny raised his eyebrows in a silent question. Amanda looked at Morton. His back was to her and all his attention was on something happening downstream. She turned back to Johnny and nodded. His head vanished and a moment later he reappeared, slipping from rock to rock, moving more rapidly now, making no sound as he approached. He reached the boulders and for a moment he was gone from Amanda's sight. When he stepped into view he held a pistol in his hand. He gave her a quick smile, then crossed the small space among the boulders as quietly as a cloud and brought the pistol down hard on Morton's head. He caught the man as he fell unconscious and took the horses' reins from his hand.

"All right, Tatum!" Chris Hardeman's voice came from surprisingly near at hand. Johnny looked between the boulders as Morton had done and saw that he would never have a better moment to act. Fifteen feet away, Tatum and his men were hidden behind their rocks, watching Chris, Lisa, Julius and Lieutenant Whitcomb, who stood on the flat land of the canyon bottom midway between the fugitives' retreat and the place where the pursuers had first taken cover. Now, while her kidnappers' attention was occupied, Amanda might be snatched from their grasp; Tatum would be helpless without his hostage and he could be made to answer for what he had done.

"We'll wait here for two minutes!" Chris called out. "Then we'll let you think about it overnight."

"I'm goin' out there!" Jack Fisk told Tatum. "You do what you like."

"Hold on." Kinnean's pistol shifted in Fisk's direction. "We go together or not at all. What's it to be, Tatum?"

Johnny waited no longer. Moving quickly, he looped each horse's reins around the saddle horn of the next animal until all six were tied in a row, with Tatum's white stallion in the lead. He led the stallion to an opening between two boulders on the upstream side of the redoubt and slapped him on the rump. The stallion trotted off, taking the others with him, their hooves clattering on the smaller stones.

"The horses are loose!" came a shout.

Johnny seized Amanda by the hand. He motioned her to keep low and he led her in the opposite direction, downstream, out from among the boulders and through the rocks at the base of the bluff. He caught a glimpse of Chris and the others and he waved, and at that moment the alarm was sounded behind him.

"He's got the girl!" A shot boomed out and the bullet glanced off a rock by Johnny's head, spraying him with chips. One struck his cheek and he felt the blood begin to flow. There were more shots from behind, but there was firing from the bottomland as well; no longer afraid of endangering Amanda, Chris and the others were shooting at the fugitives.

"Come on!" Johnny let go of Amanda's hand. On his hands and knees he led her along for a few more yards until there was no cover ahead. He pushed her to the ground behind the last substantial rock and protected her body with his own. Bullets from Tatum's men flew overhead, striking the rocks and the face of the bluff, but the pursuers' covering fire intensified now as the circus men in the background joined the fray. The firing from Tatum's men dwindled. By raising his head, Johnny could look out on the scene. Hutch was running to the rear with the horses; Chris and Lisa and Julius and Whitcomb had made for the river when the shooting began and they had taken cover beneath the bank. Now and then one or another would appear briefly to fire at the fugitives, but they couldn't expose themselves for long without attracting return fire. It was a new and more dangerous standoff.

Johnny looked back the way he and Amanda had come. Before long Tatum or one of the others would crawl along the same route and then Johnny would be forced to shoot a man for the first time in his life or allow not only Amanda but himself as well to be taken captive.

Help from an unexpected quarter spared him the decision and broke the stalemate with sudden finality. High up on his cliff, Chatur had seen Johnny make his way into the rocky stronghold. He had seen him overcome Morton and turn the horses loose, and lead Amanda off through the rocks. Had the pair gotten clean away, Chatur might have taken no action at all, for what he planned to do would have uncertain results. But when he saw Johnny and Amanda pinned down by the outburst of gunfire, he threw caution to the winds. Putting two fingers to his lips, he let out a shrill whistle that echoed in the canyon. Before leaving the river bottom, he had noted that rocks of all sizes dotted the face of the bluff above Tatum's hideout, some just revealed, some standing out, awaiting only a few more rains before they too would roll to the bottom. As he had hoped, there were more rocks at the crest of the slope, several quite large. He had placed Rama behind a boulder nearly as tall as Chatur himself, and as he heard the signal now, the elephant put his massive forehead and tusks against the boulder and pushed. The rock was still embedded in the ground but it could not stand against the strength of the huge pachyderm, and at Rama's second lunge it broke loose and rolled, quickly gathering speed, striking other rocks and knocking them loose as it bounded down the slope.

Those in the hideout heard Chatur's whistle, then a brief silence, and then a sudden clattering from above. They looked up to see a cascade of rocks and stones rushing down upon them. Among the boulders, Morton was just coming to his senses. The blow to his head had been partially cushioned by his felt hat and he had been unconscious for only a few moments, but he was still groggy and confused. He saw that the girl and the horses were gone. A sound caused him to look up and he saw an enormous rock plummeting down as if it were falling from the sky itself. It was the last thing he ever knew.

Unaware of Morton's fate, the others rose from cover like quail flushed from a thicket. Johansen ran in blind panic, not looking where he was going, glancing back fearfully over his shoulder. Suddenly the ground disappeared from beneath his feet. He plunged headlong into the river and sat up in the shallow water, gasping for breath, only to find himself looking into the muzzle of a Colt .45 revolver in the hand of Hamilton Whitcomb.

His comrades were less foolish. Tanner sprinted off upstream. Kinnean too had the good sense to run not away from the impending menace but at right angles to its path. He might have run upstream or down, but even in choosing his direction he kept his wits about him. It was he who had seen Johnny Smoker leading Amanda away and he who had fired first, shooting not to kill but only to pin the couple down, for he had realized at once that without a hostage he and the others would be at the mercy of the attackers, both whites and Indians. His urge for self-preservation moved him to sudden action when he saw the falling rocks, but he wished to survive the day as well as the moment, and so when he ran he went downstream, keeping as much as possible within the shelter of those rocks already on the ground, making for the place where he had last seen the young man and the girl.

Two others were close on his heels. Hachaliah Tatum, finding himself suddenly robbed of both Amanda and the horses, had realized in that instant that a point had been reached beyond which his plans and calculations were useless, and so he had turned to Kinnean, whose less refined skills might yet assure his survival. Fisk, although he would admit it to no one, had long recognized Kinnean as his superior, and like Tatum, he followed him instinctively now, seeking protection in the one-armed man's shadow. The three ran with all their might, as if speed itself could protect them from any danger, but they were often within the attackers' view and the gunfire redoubled around them. Suddenly Fisk cried out and fell, clutching his leg. Tatum ducked down behind a rock, but Kinnean kept on toward his goal, bending low, leaping smaller rocks and dodging around the larger ones. A bullet tugged at the skirt of his buffalo coat and another nipped at his bowler hat, but he had his quarry in sight.

"Run!" Johnny shouted, pushing Amanda out into the open. He had kept her with him until now, fearful that a stray bullet might find her if she ran, but he would not let her be taken captive again. She took to her heels without further urging and Johnny turned to protect her retreat. Kinnean came into sight a dozen feet away and dropped into a crouch, smiling as he brought his pistol to bear on the youth. Johnny raised his gun, but he saw that the one-armed man had no further interest in Amanda and he found in that moment that he was not prepared to take another man's life simply to save his own. He lowered the gun and Kinnean's smile broadened.

All around them, others were in motion. Those who had held Tatum and his men under siege were taking advantage of the fugitives' sudden confusion, and they converged from all sides now, each intent on his own purpose.

Amanda's appearance was the event Sun Horse had been waiting for. When the other Lakotas withdrew at his command, he had mounted his horse and remained behind, watching from the shadow of the canyon wall. Since the night before, when the white youth from the settlement had come to the Sun Band's village to tell that the clown girl was in danger, Sun Horse had hoped for a chance to save her. His power had returned to him as a result of her coming together with the One Who Stands Between the Worlds and he owed her a great debt, but he felt that there was something unfinished, something still to be done. Even without such a feeling he would have come gladly to Amanda's aid; his grandson had chosen her for his wife and Sun Horse was personally fond of her, but the nagging sense of incompletion had lent a special urgency to the chase. When he saw the two young people move among the rocks he had tightened his knees to prepare his horse for action, and when Amanda ran into the open, he started toward her, his horse reaching a gallop in a few steps, racing past the Strange-Animal Men, who were only then rising from cover to run forward. From upstream came the whoops of the four Lakotas that had guarded the way there, as they rode forth now to take part in the fight. Sun Horse heard shots on every side and he saw one man fall in the river, but he held to his course and at the last moment Amanda saw him coming and held out her arms to him.

Even as Sun Horse made his move, Hardeman and Lisa and Julius were out of the riverbed and running for the stronghold. With Tatum's men routed by the falling rocks, there was no opposing fire, but at any moment the fugitives might regroup. Fisk had disappeared from view after he fell and there was no sign of Tatum. Only Kinnean was in sight, his head and shoulders just visible near the base of the bluff, and it was for him that Hardeman ran, but Julius had a different goal. He had seen Tanner dart off upstream and saw where he took cover again, and he intended to surprise the teamster before he could pose any further threat, but his concern for Amanda was more im-

mediate, and he hesitated at the edge of the rocks, pausing
to see that Sun Horse picked her up safely. The old man
wheeled the horse in a sharp turn as he came even with the
girl, bringing the animal's body between her and Tatum's
men. He leaned over to gather her in his arms, and at that
moment a movement in the corner of Julius's eye caught
the black man's attention. From behind a rock a few yards
away Jack Fisk rose on one knee, raising a pistol in Sun
Horse's direction. As Julius turned to confront the danger
he saw a second figure, farther away. It was Tanner, and
the rifle in his hands was coming to bear on Julius.

There was no time for decision. The Starr Army .44 in
Julius's hand bucked once and Fisk pitched over, uttering
a soft groan. Julius pivoted, thumbing the hammer back,
and as he fired a second time, he felt a red-hot poker stab
him in the left arm with enough force to spin him around
and throw him to the ground. He heard the report of
Tanner's rifle as he fell, and saw the puff of smoke from
the barrel. He hit the ground rolling and came to rest in a
prone position with his gun at the ready, but Tanner had
dropped from sight. Hardeman was almost in the rocks and
Lisa was running after him, and farther away Sun Horse
galloped off with Amanda before him in the saddle, both
of them apparently unhurt. Julius was cheered by the sight.
But what had happened to Tanner? he wondered.

Tanner was dead. Lisa had seen the danger to Julius and
she had fired as he did. Like his shot, hers was true. Both
bullets struck the bearded man at the same moment and
Lisa knew from the way Tanner fell that he would offer no
more trouble. She wanted to stop and help Julius but she
saw him roll and take aim again and she kept on after
Hardeman. Until Kinnean and Tatum were accounted for
and Johnny Smoker safe, the fight would not be over.

Kinnean didn't intend that it should end as Lisa hoped.

Only moments had passed since Amanda ran for safety. From his vantage point in the rocks he had watched the ensuing events without taking part. He had seen Tanner die, Julius Ingram wounded, Fisk shot for a second time and maybe dead too, and the girl whisked away by the old Indian, and through it all he had kept his gun steady on Johnny Smoker. The youth offered him his sole chance to escape. When the gunplay ended there would be a stalemate once more if Kinnean still had a hostage. But there was something else he wanted, something he had put off for too long, and if he had to choose between escape and fulfilling that old obligation, he didn't know what he would do.

"Drop it, Kinnean."

Moving very slowly, Kinnean rose to his feet. Hardeman was a few yards to his right, crouched in the same stance he had assumed in the sudden gunplay back in Putnam's Park on the day the circus arrived, but the scout had only one hand today and he preferred to shoot with two. They were evenly matched, two one-armed men. Hardeman's Colt was aimed at Kinnean's midsection. Twenty feet behind Hardeman, Lisa Putnam came to a stop, holding her Winchester at waist level. It too was pointed at Kinnean. The circus men had reached the rocks now and they halted when they saw the motionless figures with guns trained. From down the canyon came a rush of hoofbeats, and the band of Sioux warriors swept into view, recalled by the firing. They drew near, saw the standoff, and reined in their ponies. Suddenly the canyon was quiet.

To the onlookers it seemed that there was stillness and then there was motion, with no transition from one to the other. Kinnean's gun leaped toward Hardeman, the two pistols spurted flame with a thunderous roar, and stillness returned.

Kinnean lay on the ground, his eyes open but unseeing. Smoke curled from the muzzle of Lisa's carbine as well as Hardeman's Colt. Johnny Smoker straightened up, looking down at the body. The gun that Lisa had loaned him was still in his hand, unfired.

"Johnny!" Amanda came running headlong from the background, where Sun Horse had set her down, but she slowed when she saw that Johnny was all right. He moved to meet her and when he reached her he touched the bruise on her cheek with his free hand.

"Are you all right?" he asked, and she nodded, her hurts forgotten. She was moved beyond words to find him returned to her unharmed.

"Chris." Lisa spoke softly but even the Indians across the river heard her, and they saw what she saw. A half-dozen paces to Hardeman's left, Hachaliah Tatum had risen from behind a rock. He was holding his nickel-plated Colt and his desperate eyes swept the gathering as if searching for a target.

Johnny stepped protectively in front of Amanda.

Hardeman's gun moved in a short arc and found Tatum. The hammer came back with an audible click and the muzzle trembled almost imperceptibly.

Tatum blanched. "Don't shoot, Hardeman. Look, here's my gun." He lowered the hammer gently and tossed the gun into the snow.

Hardeman remained as he was and the moment lengthened, and then slowly, like a man in a daze, he lowered the gun and dropped the hammer back to half cock. He felt the anger leave him, the trembling rage that overtook him whenever another man forced him to kill. There had been no need for Kinnean to die, and the senseless death sickened him. Why had the man challenged him? Over an incident that was a month in the past? There had been more to it than that. He had seen Kinnean's expression just before he made his move, and he had recognized the look of a man who didn't care if he lived or died. The look reminded Hardeman of Hickok's, that day in Cheyenne not so long ago. "I've done my scouting," Hickok had said, and he seemed to be saying that the times had passed him by. Was that how Kinnean had felt today—like a man who saw no place for himself in the coming scheme of things? Fifty years before, he might have been a trapper like the Putnams; not so long ago he might have been a scout like Hickok, like Hardeman himself. But he was a younger man; a violent man who hadn't found a way to live as he wanted to live, beyond the edge of civilization, where he would carry the whole weight of his life and death on his own shoulders, sharing it with no one. Lacking sufficient reason to live, he had chosen to die.

Hardeman looked at the crumpled figure in the buffalo coat. Kinnean's bowler hat had rolled a short distance in the snow and come to rest. The snow on the crown was melting, leaving tiny drops of water, perfectly round. Soon they would freeze. The warmth of a man's life was ebbing from the hat as it ebbed from his body.

Hardeman turned away from the corpse, unwilling to look at it any longer. There had been too much dying today. He walked through the onlookers as if they were so many trees and he let the Colt drop from his hand. He was tired and his shoulder hurt. He wanted to sleep until he could forget the dying, but the memory of Kinnean's visage was before him still and he knew he would never forget it, for he saw himself reflected there as if in a looking glass. He was not so different—always searching, never satisfied. He had better find his own reason for living soon, someplace where there were few opportunities to kill or be killed.

Lisa and the others watched him go. Behind them, believing he was unnoticed, Tatum took a step forward and reached for his gun. Here in the wilderness, far from the places where he belonged, he had been stripped of all his possessions. He was powerless even to save himself now that his last pawn had been taken, and like a wounded animal he lashed out in desperation, directing all his anger at the one who had brought him to this end.

But there were two in the crowd who had not forgotten the circus master.

Seven years of traveling with Chris Hardeman had trained Johnny to be wary when Chris turned his back on danger. He was not aware that he had kept watch, but he saw Tatum move and he saw in his eyes the willingness to kill that marked a dangerous man. A moment before, faced by Chris's gun, that willingness had been absent, but now that his enemy's back was turned, Tatum sought revenge for his humiliation.

Johnny raised his gun and the weapon felt strangely familiar in his hand. As a child of the Cheyenne he had handled pistols and been instructed in their use by the men, before his dream. Since then he had seen Chris shoot a pistol countless times, both during long hours of practice in remote places where the shooting would not be heard, and on the rare occasions when Chris had drawn in self-defense. Johnny had always watched the movements carefully, acquiring the feeling of gunmanship without the actual experience, and the position he adopted now was a near-perfect imitation of Hardeman's two-handed shooting stance. His thumb drew back the hammer as the sights came into view and he felt his finger tighten on the trigger, but he hesitated. Tatum was not aiming at Chris. He was turning, his eyes on Johnny, it seemed. Johnny was surprised and the surprise delayed him, but only for an instant. Something moved on his left, someone approaching as if to stop him from shooting. He pulled the trigger.

It was Amanda who moved toward Johnny, but not to prevent him from shooting. She had kept her eyes on Tatum ever since the moment he appeared; she had seen the malice in his gaze when he looked at her and she feared what he still might do. He had nothing more to lose, except his life. She knew he would try to hurt her, and when he moved to pick up his gun, she was certain he hoped to inflict the greatest hurt of all. He was going to shoot Johnny!

She had to stop him! Johnny had saved her life once already, and today he had risked his own to save her again. He was the source of her strength. Near him, her courage had returned. He was her example and her hope, and she would do anything to protect him!

Hardeman's gun lay at her feet where he had dropped it as he passed by. She bent and scooped it up, fumbling to grasp it with her heavy gloves. Already Hachaliah's gun was in his hand and he was bringing it to bear. Amanda struggled to draw back the hammer of Hardeman's Colt, but the mainspring was strong and her small thumb was too weak to bend it. She tried to use both thumbs, but as she shifted her grip the gun slipped from her fingers and fell, and there was no more time.

Moving with all the grace she displayed on the tightrope, Amanda stepped forward to place herself in front of Johnny. She felt light on her feet. Her eyes met Hachaliah's and she saw his triumph, but it was a mean emotion and no match for her own. Johnny would live and the greater triumph would be hers, for in the act of saving him she knew, if only for a moment, the joy of an unselfish love.

Two shots blended into one, and as Johnny's bullet struck Tatum in the chest, Amanda met the other, which Tatum had intended for her all along.

LISA PUTNAM'S JOURNAL

Sunday, April 2nd. 6:40 a.m.

Today the circus and the cavalry are off, and with their departure I will feel that we are done with healing the wounded and burying the dead. The account of the pursuit that I wrote in these pages two days ago has helped me to move beyond the dreadful events of that day, but I am still living from moment to moment.

Lt. Whitcomb and his men will conduct the circus to Fort Fetterman, and with the present uncertain state of things he believes the army will provide them an escort to the railroad at Rawlins.

Yesterday Sun Horse came to the park with Blackbird. The boy is able to sit a horse but I believe his leg still pains him considerably. They brought eight horses which they presented as a gift to Lt. Whitcomb, much to his astonishment. Thus all his men will be mounted when they leave here today, and Lt. Whitcomb has seen at least one instance (two, counting the Indians' aid in our ill-fated attempt to rescue Amanda) in which the "hostiles" have acted to promote brotherhood between the races. It was Sun Horse's visit that gave me the idea for the letter to General Crook. I have written it this morning and I will give it to Lt. Whitcomb before he leaves. In it I have told the general of our friendship with Sun Horse and much more, and I dare to hope this may help protect Sun Horse and his people through whatever is to come.

Almost to a man the soldiers have found opportunities to take me aside and express their personal sorrow for Uncle Bat's death. They have been solicitous and kind, and I cannot regard them as my enemies. Their health is much improved. The sight of a potato is a miracle to them, and the somewhat monotonous meals we have been able to offer them have been proclaimed unqualified culinary delights. They have all gained weight and recovered good color in their four days here, and they have helped with calving, those that have experience in such matters, while the rest of the able-bodied have assisted in many small ways with the ranch work and done what they could to prepare the circus for its journey. From their ranks the burial detail was drawn. They interred their fallen commander with such military honors as they could muster, after which we read a few words over Mr. Tatum, Kinnean, Tanner and Morton. For all our bitter feelings toward these men we felt compelled to give them a Christian burial, and we brought them home to spare ourselves the delay of burying them where they fell. Mr. Fisk and Tom Johansen will be taken to Fort Fetterman, where, I imagine, Mr. Fisk's wounds will require further tending. Neither Fisk nor young Tom could shed any light on what transpired between Mr. Tatum and Amanda before he abducted her, and I believe they are ignorant of those events. Whatever crimes Hachaliah Tatum may have com-

mitted, they died with him, and no charges will be brought against his henchmen.

Amanda is on the knoll with my parents. Johnny allowed Julius and Mr. Chalmers and Hutch and Chatur to assist him in preparing the grave. After the service there, which was attended by everyone in the settlement, Johnny and Mr. Hardeman gathered their few belongings and went to join the Sun Band. How long they will remain there, and whether we shall see them again, I do not know.

Do you who read these pages live in a gentler time? Is violent death a stranger to your experience? I hope so. But whatever manner of life you lead, you will eventually know the necessity for grief. On the way home, the moments I found most difficult were when I looked into Johnny's face. Somehow I was more deeply wounded by his sorrow than my own. It seems only natural to me that Uncle Bat should risk his life to save a friend, but over and over again in my mind's eye I see the step Amanda took to place herself in front of Johnny. I saw her face at that moment and it stays with me as clearly as a portrait. She was as calm as if she were performing before a rapt audience. She was serene.

CHAPTER THIRTEEN

The sun shone brightly over the eastern ridge and the morning was springlike as the circus prepared to leave. The yard had been churned into a sea of mud by wheels and hooves and booted feet as the wagons were put in line.

"We're gonta miss you folks," Julius said as he shook Joe Kitchen's hand. The Negro's left arm was bound in a sling.

"What will you do now?" Lisa asked Chalmers. Lydia stood with the Englishman, hugging his arm. Her eyes were red-rimmed, and wet with tears. Already the others had said their goodbyes to Lisa and Julius and taken their places in the wagons. Not far away, Hutch stood at Rama's side, talking with Chatur, who was atop the elephant's shoulders. Maria Abbruzzi approached Hutch and took his hand. The small band of cavalry was formed in a column of twos at the head of the caravan.

"We hope to keep our engagements in Salt Lake City and San Francisco," Chalmers replied. "After that, I am not certain."

"Soon as we get to a telegraph, we'll wire Colonel Hyde," Joe Kitchen explained. "He's the money man in 'Frisco. We still got a circus here, and a good one. If he'll put up the place, we'll put up the show."

"There is some talk that we might try to keep the show together and manage it ourselves," Chalmers added, and Lydia nodded hopefully.

"Amanda would like that," Lisa said.

Chalmers was quiet for a moment. "She would, wouldn't she. Then we will have to do our best to make it so."

Lieutenant Whitcomb trotted back from the head of his troop. "Mr. Chalmers? We're ready if you are."

"At your pleasure, Leftenant." Chalmers turned to Harry Wo, who had stood by silently throughout the farewells. "I relinquish my arm-wrestling crown to you, my friend. You are champion once more."

Harry made a slight bow and shook the giant's hand. "You and me, we know who the real champ is." He gave Chalmers a wink.

Chalmers retrieved Lydia from Lisa's arms, where the Gypsy woman had sought comfort for a last time as she allowed her tears to flow freely once more. He helped her to the seat of the lead wagon before climbing up beside her and taking the reins.

Whitcomb cantered to the front of the column and raised a hand over his head, dropping it forward as he took his place beside First Sergeant Dupré. "Forward!" he called, and it struck him that it was the first time he had used the gesture and the command, which he had practiced over and over in front of the looking glass in his room at West Point. He had always imagined that there would be a full-strength troop behind him, the men smart in their field uniforms, with weapons at matching angles over their shoulders, the column of fours starting off in precise step across a landscape of cactus and dust under a bright sun, with the guidons fluttering in the breeze and perhaps even the regimental band along to provide marching music. He had thrilled to the image then, but now he felt no particular emotion.

He could not imagine their return to Fetterman. Fetterman was something that existed only in a dream, a hazy memory from a previous life. This was all that was real—Dupré and McCaslin and his handful of men, and this valley where the Lost Platoon had found escape from Purgatory. Here they had been forgiven their sins; neither whites nor Indians had held them to blame for the deaths they had caused, perhaps because they too had lost one of their own. They were healed now, and their spirits restored. When they left this place behind, everything would be discovered anew.

Whitcomb wondered if he would ever absorb everything he had learned on his first campaign. Just when he was certain he could never be surprised again, Sun Horse had come with his gift of horses, and Whitcomb had been struck speechless once more. Had the old chief done it merely to speed the soldiers from his land or had he been motivated by nobler feelings? In acting to save the girl, it seemed he had been moved by simple human compassion; could it be that he felt a similar compassion for his enemies when he found them in distress? If so, what other feelings might he harbor that neither white soldiers nor politicians dreamed could exist in a savage heart? "Tell Three Stars the horses are for him," Sun Horse had said. "Tell him the Sun Band wants peace."

Perhaps everything Whitcomb had learned could be reduced to a single lesson—that the common wisdom about the conflict on the frontier was woefully inadequate preparation for experiencing it firsthand. The realities were far more complex. He felt that he might try for the rest of his life to learn about the western regions and their aboriginal inhabitants and still know only a fragment of the truth. Even so, he would try. What had General Crook said? *Over the years our instincts become tempered by experience.* Whitcomb had followed his instincts and he had survived thus far, and given the opportunity and the time, he would hone those instincts and temper them with the wisdom of experience. He would learn what he could of the Indians and their land, and with luck he might have a hand in bringing the conflict to an end.

The caravan was nearing the bend in the road where the stand of pines sheltered the settlement's little graveyard. Whitcomb's eyes found Corwin's marker, set apart from the rest. He could not read the lettering but he knew what it said, for he had chosen the words himself.

Bvt. Major Francis Corwin
Co. E, 3rd U.S. Cavalry
Died 28 March, 1876

Laid to rest by his men,
who owe him their lives.

Julius Ingram had promised to whittle the edges of the lettering in his spare moments, so it would still be legible when the paint faded.

"Eyes right!" Whitcomb ordered, and he held a salute while the troop rode past the grave.

Lisa and Julius watched the caravan pull away from the settlement and then they turned and strolled together to the corral fence, where Harry and Hutch were harnessing the work horses to the hay sled. Feeding the cattle had been delayed past its usual hour so everyone could be on hand for the farewells.

Lisa wore her riding clothes. Soon she would ride through the meadow to look over the calves but just now she felt no urgency to be on her way. For the first time in a long time there was no urgency about anything.

Ling Wo stepped out of the kitchen entryway and came toward the corral, and Lisa realized that the five of them were the only ones left in the settlement. We're six now, she corrected herself. Ling carried little Jed in her arms. Jedediah Batson Wo had been born on the night after Amanda and Bat Putnam died. The birth had been long but not difficult, and was attended by Greta Waldheim and Lydia. When Lisa and the others returned on the following day, having spent the night beside the trail when darkness overtook them on the way home, they found Ling in the kitchen proudly nursing her son while Harry and Ben Long prepared dinner. The soldiers and circus men had arrived late the evening before, bringing word of Bat's death, but the news that Amanda too had died occasioned a new round of grieving, and in the midst of their woe, circus and settlement folk alike had found themselves visiting the newborn infant in a stream; they wished to touch and hold him, and he was a comfort to them all.

The proud father had waited until the next morning to take Lisa aside and impart to her his thoughts about his son's birth. "My son is American," he had announced. "I wish to become a citizen some day, but my son is born American and I am proud for him. My people have a long history. Many thousand years. The Chinese people are a great people, but that life was not good for me. I am not a man to bow to others. I am a proud man. The Christian God says it is a bad thing to be proud. If my son follows the Christian God he may come to believe that. But I am a proud man. I have done something that is not possible for most Chinese men: I have begun a new life. You made that possible, you and your father. I will teach my son to honor you, not by bowing, but in the American way, as one friend honors another. The life you have given to me, I will give to my son. He is American, and today I am proud for him.''

Suspecting that Harry must have rehearsed his speech carefully did not lessen its effect on Lisa, and in sharing his joy she began the process of healing her sorrow.

"Don't know how I can cook just for us," Ling said now, rocking the infant gently in her arms. He was sound asleep, wrapped in a woolen baby blanket that had been Lisa's.

"I reckon to get hungry three times a day, just like before," Julius said. He peered at the sleeping infant. "Don't let that child take a chill." He walked off toward the barn to find some work a one-armed man could do. Tanner's bullet had shattered one of the bones in Julius's forearm. Sun Horse had treated the wound at the scene and Corporal Atherton and Sergeant Dupré had inspected it later. Atherton had told Lisa privately that he doubted the colored man would regain full use of the arm.

Harry and Hutch were done harnessing the team. Ling joined her husband and they talked softly. In the meadow the cows were bawling, but they would be fed soon enough. Harry reached within the folds of little Jed's blanket and stroked his son's face.

"It's so quiet," Lisa said to no one. In the pigpen the pigs were snorting happily, reveling in the mud. The geese waddled into the yard in a group, making small sounds to themselves, the first time this year that they had ventured so far from the springpond. In the willows, blackbirds chattered. The pigs, the geese, the birds, all were normal sounds of the valley in springtime, but Lisa noticed them now for the first time. There had been other sounds here recently, other voices filling the silence; she had grown accustomed to them, and suddenly they were gone.

In a few days the strange caravan would be at Fort Fetterman. In another week the circus could be on the Pacific shore.

She wondered how soon her letter would reach General Crook. Lieutenant Whitcomb's parting words before he mounted his horse had made it easy for her to ask the favor of him.

"My men and I are in your debt, Miss Putnam," he had said. "I wish there were some way we could repay you."

"There is something," she had said, taking the letter from the pocket of her coat. "You can give this letter to General Crook. Before you attacked that village, Sitting Bull and Crazy Horse had agreed to a peace plan; if they may keep some of this country and have an agency here, there need be no more fighting. I have told the general what I know of the plan and begged him to consider it. I have also told him about Sun Horse. He has influence with the other chiefs. He could be a great help in making peace."

Whitcomb had shown no surprise. "I'll see that the general gets the letter, ma'am. And I will tell him what happened here, including Sun Horse's part in it. My report will include the gift of the horses, and your own generous assistance. Mr. Hardeman also told me of the peace plan in some detail. He asked me to set it before the general myself. Your letter will help me do that. Mr. Hardeman offered to act as an intermediary with the hostiles, if the general should want to use him in that capacity."

It was the first Lisa had heard of Hardeman's message to Crook and the offer to serve as go-between. She wondered if it meant he intended to stay with the Sun Band even after they left their winter valley, but Whitcomb had said nothing more and she had not dared to ask.

Still he wanted peace and he would work for it if he could. And after that, what?

The caravan had reached the stand of pines by the graveyard. As the soldiers rounded the bend in the road, their faces were turned toward the graves.

Lisa had asked Lieutenant Whitcomb to tell her about Major Corwin and he had poured out the story, all unsuspecting. He told her how Corwin had saved them in the battle, getting them away safely and starting them on the trail south, and he told her what he knew of Corwin's career before the present campaign. When he was done, she had asked a question.

"Was he married?"

"Yes, ma'am. He had a wife and daughter. The girl's name was Elizabeth, I believe. They died in Arizona."

And so Lisa had learned what her own fate might have been, but for the grace of God and her own stubbornness. Whitcomb hadn't told her how Corwin's wife had died, nor had she told him that Boots Corwin was the young lieutenant with tired eyes who had ridden into Putnam's Park and into her life in the summer of her twenty-fifth year. It was his eyes that had first caught her interest, and the way he concealed his wound that won her heart. It was a wound of the spirit, not the body, inflicted in no single moment but over the course of two years in a Confederate prison, his career held in limbo while his more fortunate comrades were promoted beyond him and went on to win victories and make names for themselves. Lisa had healed his wound and she had rejoiced to see the change in him, but she had refused his offer of marriage and stayed behind in Putnam's Park, tied to the land.

She felt once more the shock and grief that had nearly overcome her down on the Powder's south fork, when she had first recognized Corwin's body. She turned suddenly away from the sight of the graveyard and the pines and the caravan growing smaller in the distance, thinking to go to her parents' graves to seek the comfort she often took in that place, but she had forgotten the new marker there. A broken violin leaned against the fresh wooden cross. Julius had put Amanda's fiddle on the grave before breakfast, when he thought no one was watching.

Lisa felt a sudden rage. Everywhere around her there were reminders of death! She had had too much of death! It was life she wanted! She wanted to seize it with both hands and wring from it every drop of pleasure and work and satisfaction, all the sheer *living* it contained! And above all she wanted to share it. Eight years after Boots Corwin rode out of her life she had found another man. Like the first, she had healed him in a time of need, and like the first he had risen from her arms and left her. Even before he left she had felt betrayed, remembering Corwin, but she knew she had only herself to blame. By restoring his strength she had made it all the more likely that he would leave, and she refused to use tricks to hold him. In a way it was easier for her this time; she gave no thought to leaving the land. It might be taken from her by events beyond her control, but she would stay as long as she could. If a war forced her to abandon her home, she would go. But only when that ragged piece of deerskin marked with Indian pictographs and Jedediah Putnam's name became worthless. Only when her sole remaining patrimony was what she carried in her breast, the rest gone to become part of the public domain, to be homesteaded and cut up and fenced and squabbled over. Until then she would cling to her home and her life the way the Indians clung to theirs.

She stomped through the mud to the barn and saddled her horse, and as she led him back out into the sunshine she saw the valley anew, and remembered the lines of poetry her father had given her on her twenty-first birthday. *Of thee, O earth, are my bone and sinew made; to thee, O sun, I am brother. Here I have my habitat. I am of thee.*

Perhaps Boots Corwin might still be alive if he had left the army and stayed in this place. It was a life-giving place. Here a man could prove himself and find his true rewards, as her father had done. And Jed Putnam had returned as much to the little valley as he took from it. It had more to give! Would no man ever have the sense to stay?!

She mounted the horse, her jaw set and her expression hard. Some day a man would come, and if none did she would still take her satisfaction from this life, together with Julius and Harry and Ling and any others that chose to accept what Putnam's Park offered.

"Miss Lisa?"

Hutch was approaching her. Behind him, Harry was waiting on the sled.

"There's somethin' I been wantin' to say," the boy began, coming to a stop beside her and looking at his feet. "Everything kept gettin' in the way of it, and now's as good a time as any, I guess. When I first come here, you and me just talked about me workin' through the winter, but I'll be stayin' on a while, if you'll have me." He looked up hopefully, awaiting a reply.

Lisa's anger left her and she blinked to clear a film of water that came suddenly to her eyes, despite the lack of wind. She managed a smile. "I'd like that."

Hutch smiled too, and then he said, "Well, those cows are pretty hungry. I guess we better get 'em fed." His proprietary concern both amused Lisa and touched her. She had wished for a man with the sense to stay in Putnam's Park and one had come to her. He was young, and he was not the man who would share her life, but he was willing to stay, and by his simple expression of that willingness he made it possible for Lisa to believe that winter would finally end and spring would come, and after that there would be summer and fall and another winter, and then another spring and more new calves being born, all waiting in store for her.

Her horse snorted and shied as Rufus the house cat came racing out of the barn with a barn cat in hot pursuit. Rufus had been gone from the Big House all night, hunting in the dark. His emergence from hibernation was a sure sign of spring.

Lisa touched her heels to the horse's flanks and trotted out of the yard ahead of the hay sled. When she reached the wagon road she urged the horse into a canter. She felt the wind in her face and smelled the scent of the pines and the sunshine in the air. She wanted to get back to the house in time to make something special for the midday meal. Buffalo and potatoes were wearing a bit thin. She wanted something festive, so her crew wouldn't feel the letdown of being left so alone. The peaches, that was it! She had saved a tin of peaches. She would make a cobbler. And this afternoon she and Hutch would move the new calves out of the heifer lot. He would enjoy that.

The caravan had reached the foot of the valley. One by one the wagons entered the gap and then they were gone.

LISA PUTNAM'S JOURNAL

Friday, April 28th. 6:15 a.m.

I have been irregular of late about my writing. After the fateful events of last month, it has been comforting that recent weeks have been so ordinary, offering so little of note to write about.

The weather continues cool and the grass is greening slowly. I would think that in another week the cattle could fend for themselves, although at this rate it will be a while longer before we put them out of the park, unless the sun shines more than has been his habit of late. All in all we have not done badly this year once the early bouts of scours were over. The calves are doing well and the absence of any runts strengthens my belief in our breeding program. Julius and I have decided to buy a few new bulls this year and begin increasing the proportion of Shorthorn blood in the herd. It occurs to me that a time may come when we will want to eliminate the Longhorn strain altogether. We are going to have a look at Hereford stock

333

when next one or the other of us has a chance to get to Cheyenne.

We fed the cattle double yesterday and this morning Julius and Hutch and I are going to say goodbye to the Sun Band. Day before yesterday I got up my courage and rode over the hill, which is how I learned that they would be departing for the north country today. Mr. Hardeman took me to see Uncle Bat's resting place. He seemed to know the way very well. It is on a high place overlooking the valley, within sight of the village. Little Hand's scaffold stands nearby. Bat's mare was killed and placed beneath him and his old rifle lies beside him, together with all the things he might need in his final journey. By now I imagine he has made his way to the spirit trail "beyond the pines." Surely after so many years with the Lakotas, his spirit will be admitted to their afterlife. It is a happy place, they say, where the grass is always green and the game plenty, and one sees all the relatives and friends who have gone before. I have come to believe in it almost literally, and although I am aware that it makes no sense at all, whenever I imagine Uncle Bat arriving there, I see my father waiting to greet him.

What with my visit to the camp and our ride together, Mr. Hardeman and I spent several hours in company with each other, but we spoke little. He and Sun Horse were very much at ease together. Johnny Smoker was quiet and reserved with me once more, but he appears to have found a new tranquillity. Twice orphaned by violence and denied his first love by that same agency, he seems to accept death as part of the natural order of things, against which it is futile to protest.

There has been no further sign of General Crook, nor has Sun Horse heard any word from the northern bands. It is as if the earth had opened and swallowed them all,

soldiers and Sioux, save for the Sun Band. Sun Horse and
his people continue in high spirits. The great change in
them gives me as many new worries as it relieves, but I
have no cause for complaint. I got what I hoped for. They
will remain at liberty, at least for now, and so long as they
are free there is hope.

CHAPTER FOURTEEN

The Sun Band was already starting off down the valley as
the three riders drew near the Lakota campsite. Most of the
people were walking beside the pony drags that bore all
their possessions. They went at a leisurely pace, the horses
pausing here and there to crop the tender shoots of new
grass. Children and dogs raced up and down the caravan.

The day was cool and gray, the air still. In the woods
the snowbanks lingered, but they were smaller than those
in Putnam's Park and the grass here was greener.

Hard-packed circles of bare ground marked the ring
where the tipis had stood all winter. Beyond the ring a
small group of people and horses awaited the riders. Lisa
made out Hardeman among them, and Johnny Smoker.

Two days before, Hardeman's left arm had still been supported in a sling but today it hung free. Sun Horse was there with Standing Eagle and Penelope beside him. Blackbird held the horses, all but two. Lisa had given Hardeman the chestnut gelding he had ridden during the chase after Tatum and his men. Together with Hardeman's pack horse it was picketed nearby, saddled and packed for traveling.

A single lodge remained standing in the old camp circle. As the riders passed near, a figure rose from the buffalo robe in front of the entrance. *"Hau,* Julius!" Hears Twice called out cheerfully. "Come and smoke!" Behind him, Mist stepped out of the lodge to see the riders.

"Looks like he ain't goin' with the rest," Julius observed, and he spoke to Hears Twice in Lakota, saying he would return in a short while, once he had bid farewell to those who waited beyond the camp.

Sun Horse greeted the black man as he dismounted and inquired at once about the condition of his shattered forearm, reaching within the sling to feel it. Julius replied that the bone needed more time to heal but the wound no longer bothered him. The old Indian gently probed the arm with his fingers and only when he was satisfied that Julius felt no pain did he nod and turn to Lisa, smiling broadly.

"Ho, chunkshí," he said, taking both her hands in his own as always. Lisa smiled wanly, unable to speak. Hello, daughter, he had said, and she realized that having Sun Horse leave her now, if only for the summer, was like losing her last relative in the world. But it cheered her today, as it had two days earlier, to see how well he looked. He seemed to have grown younger in the past two months. In that time the circus had come and gone, a war had begun and many had died, both far to the north in Two Moons' village and on the plains below Putnam's Park,

and yet somewhere in these events, or despite them, Sun Horse had found an irrepressible joy.

"We do not come to this place again," he said, surprising Lisa both by his pronouncement and the fact that he spoke it in English. "Too close to the wagon road; too close to the soldier forts. Too easy for bluecoats to find us here. We go north to hunt. In the great council I will speak for peace. Next winter we stay there." He made a gesture to the north, the movement of his hand suggesting a country far away.

"I tried to make him see this is a good place for him," Hardeman said. "The army knows he gave horses to the soldiers and I told that lieutenant he'll speak for peace to the other headmen. No matter what happens to the other bands, he'd be safer here, out of the way." He looked at Sun Horse. He had made the same argument often in recent days, but he knew Sun Horse would not change his mind. "He's a stubborn old man and I told him so. He won't budge."

"We are Lakota," Sun Horse said. "Now we will live in the hoop of the nation. The hoop must be strong in bad times. It will need the strength of the Sun Band."

He spoke the simple words patiently to Hardeman, and Lisa realized that these two men understood each other perfectly. A bond of friendship had grown between them in a few short weeks, and they both seemed to take comfort from it despite their disagreements.

Penelope had stood silently by during this exchange and Lisa turned to her now, holding out her arms to her uncle's widow. Penelope ran into the offered embrace and the two women held each other for a long time, Lisa taking as much comfort as she gave. Sun Horse's news had numbed her. The sorrow would come later, and regret for all that was ending here today. When the embrace ended at last,

Penelope kissed Lisa quickly on the cheek, observing the white custom, then turned and ran to her horse.

"I'll be saying goodbye too," said Johnny, offering Lisa his hand. "I'm grateful for all your kindness."

"You're going with them," she said, not as a question. From the disposition of the horses she had guessed that Johnny would go with the Indians while Hardeman went off alone. Somehow she wasn't surprised. She held Johnny's hand for a moment, then took him in her arms and hugged him tightly.

"I reckoned you'd be goin' off one way or another," Hutch said to Johnny when Lisa released him. "I'm glad I had the chance to know you."

"You keep up with the roping. You'll be a top hand in no time." They shook hands, and a general round of hand shaking commenced, in which Lisa and Julius and Hutch each shook hands with Standing Eagle and Blackbird and then with Johnny and Sun Horse again, and it seemed as if the leave-taking might go on for some considerable time. No one was willing to break it off until Standing Eagle took his horse from Blackbird and said a few words in Lakota to his father, gesturing toward the retreating village, which was nearing the lake at the lower end of the valley.

Hardeman stood apart, having already made his goodbyes. Always before he had been the one to ride away, never one of those who stayed behind, but for the first time in his life he was in no hurry to be gone. It seemed to him that he was surrounded by people, both living and dead, who could make up their minds with confident certainty about matters that would surely affect the rest of their lives, while he himself had no notion which way he would ride when he left this place, nor where he might spend the night. He felt like a stranger in such company.

Hawk Chaser and Kinnean had chosen death; so had Bat Putnam, or even if he didn't choose it, he had accepted it. Sun Horse had turned his back on what was likely his last chance to go peacefully to Dakota and he looked happy about it. And when Hardeman and Johnny had been in the Lakota village for only a few days, Johnny had announced that he was staying with the Sun Band. He hadn't said that Amanda's death had turned his life upside down in the blink of an eye, nor had he put in words the simple fact that with the Sun Band he would be among people who knew of his loss and understood it. Sun Horse himself had helped Johnny build the pony drag that had carried Amanda's body back to Putnam's Park, and the wound her death had made upon the old man was plain to see. He and many others in the band had set great store by the clown girl, for reasons known only to themselves, and they shared Johnny's grief. In the white world, even with Hardeman, he would bear that grief alone. Maybe that was a good enough reason by itself for staying with the Indians, but Johnny had other reasons too, ones he had been more willing to talk about. His earlier conviction that he belonged in the white world seemed to him like no more than a passing fancy now, he had said, the selfish choice of a young man who wanted to remain footloose forever. And there was no chance he would change his mind again, for Sun Horse had told him at last the full import of his dream. "With the Sioux I have the power to help the people," he had told Hardeman. "That's what Sun Horse says anyway. That's what the dream said. Maybe it's true and maybe not. I'd like it to be so."

And so the dream had recaptured the boy in the end, and Hardeman knew better than to fight it, although he had plenty of misgivings about Johnny's choice. Some time ago he had resolved to be as good a teacher for Johnny as

Jed Putnam had been for him, turning him loose to try his luck in the world when he was ready to go. The resolve had been easy to keep when he thought Johnny would be safe with Amanda in the white man's world, but he couldn't go back on it now just because the boy might face danger with the Sioux. He reminded himself once again that Johnny was a boy no longer, but a man.

A man does what he must. It is for other men to understand and accept. Bat Putnam had taught him that.

Johnny and the Lakotas were mounted. Johnny met Hardeman's eyes but he said nothing. They had come to terms with this parting in their own fashion. Not being men much given to speaking their feelings, they had spent the last month recalling the years they had been together, sometimes talking far into the night over Sun Horse's lodge fire, acknowledging the value of their companionship with each memory brought alive in the retelling.

Lisa stood close to Sun Horse, looking up at him. "If you ever come back, the valley will be here."

Sun Horse smiled at Lisa and shook his head. "A power brought me here. Now it takes me away." He looked around the valley, savoring the comfort of it for a last time, remembering the way it had looked in his vision. He would not see it again with the grasses tall and the flowers blooming. From this place he had watched the steady approach of the whites, had seen the impending collision of the two worlds. He had been given the power to understand the *washíchun,* and at last he had fulfilled the promise. In the time that remained to him he must act on what he knew, and so he must leave the watching place behind.

He spoke a few words of Lakota to Standing Eagle. The war leader drew a rolled piece of deerskin from his robe and passed it to Sun Horse. The headman glanced at Hardeman and gestured around the valley with the scroll.

"This is a good place. I do not want the *washíchun* to cut the earth or make fences here. I want someone to take care of this place." He held out the scroll.

Hardeman hesitated, but the brown arm remained outstretched, insistent. Hardeman took the scroll and unrolled it. He held it at arm's length and looked it up and down. The top half was covered with Indian pictographs. The first drawing showed a man—a Sioux, by the feather in his hair and the choker around his neck. Above the man's head was a sun and a horse galloping. These things were connected to the man by a thin line. They represented his name: Sun Horse. The man handed something to another figure with a hat. A white man. There were some trees and a circle of tipis, and a stream flowing to a lake. More drawings followed. Below, in carefully lettered English, the scroll proclaimed: *Sun Horse gives the valley of the Sun Band to the whiteman scout, Christopher Hardeman.*

Numb with surprise, Hardeman handed the hide to Lisa.

"The one that died writ it fer y'," Standing Eagle explained.

"He means Bat," Johnny added, smiling.

"That's truth," said the war leader. "He reckoned you knew poor bull from fat cow. Said you knew good pasture when you seen it and savvied some about cattle. This child don't know such. Don't aim to." He looked Hardeman up and down. "Dunno if'n he had you pegged right. Hope so." He turned and rode away, followed by Penelope and Blackbird.

With a last smile at Lisa, Sun Horse reined around and rode off after his son and daughter and grandson.

"Now hold on there," said Hardeman.

"I'll be seeing you," Johnny said, and he too rode away.

"I reckon I'll go and set a spell with Hears Twice,"

Julius announced. He turned to Hutch. "You want to seddown and smoke a pipe with a wild Sioux Indian, boy?"

"Sure thing!"

As the two of them led their horses away, Lisa looked from Sun Horse's departing figure back to the deerhide document. Sun Horse had planned the gift over a month ago! Bat had known of it, but he had not had time to tell her. He had written the deed before his death, just as he had written a similar deed long ago.

She passed the hide back to Hardeman. He inspected it again, holding it gingerly, as if it were alive and might do him harm. Slowly he rolled it up, looking down the valley.

Lisa followed his gaze. The five riders had broken into a lope to overtake the rest of the band. At the foot of the valley, beyond the lake, the main body of Indians was entering the trees. The horsemen reached the end of the column and two of them stopped. One raised a hand in a last farewell before riding out of sight.

Lisa and Hardeman stood for a long time, regarding the empty valley. Finally Lisa spoke.

"We both have worthless deeds now, Mr. Hardeman. Do you think we will keep our land?" She looked at him and he turned to face her, but he made no reply. Instead he gazed upon her as if seeing her for the first time. She met his gaze and she saw that there was a change in him. Like Sun Horse, he too seemed suddenly younger. And then she realized with a shock what had wrought the change. The searching look had left him. In its place was an expression of calm and contentment.

CHAPTER FIFTEEN

Ham Whitcomb emerged from the post trader's store and started off toward the parade ground, keeping to the grassy areas and avoiding the muddy paths. He already wore the high moccasins he would wear during the campaign and he had just purchased a pair of buckskin pants to complete his outfit. Immediately on arriving at Fetterman he had sought out the scouts and inquired about the most practical garb for a summer campaign. "We jest follows the example o' the deer, General," Hank Hewitt had told him. "They wear their skin, 'n' so do we." After six weeks of garrison life at Fort D. A. Russell, Whitcomb was glad to be back at Fetterman and free to adopt whatever clothing he chose as Crook's enlarged command prepared to take to the field once more.

It was mid-morning on the twenty-eighth of May. The day was bright but cool, and a stiff wind held the flag out straight from the flagpole. Whitcomb enjoyed the sunshine, which had been in short supply throughout the long, cold spring.

On every side there was purposeful activity as the command prepared to set out on the morrow. It was a far cry from the dejected post Whitcomb and the Lost Platoon had found on their return from Putnam's Park. They had been astonished to learn that the rest of Crook's column had arrived back at Fetterman two weeks before them and was already dispersed to the various posts of the department, having fought no more engagements after the battle on the Powder. The arrival of Whitcomb and his men had caused quite a stir and set the telegraph lines humming, for they had been given up for dead. The presence with them of the traveling circus had also occasioned great interest, and Mr. Chalmers and his colleagues had given an impromptu performance for the post by way of thanks for the escort that Colonel Chambers, the post commandant, had insisted on providing for their journey to the railroad.

"Ham!"

Whitcomb turned to see John Bourke hurrying toward him. Bourke's thigh-length field blouse was unbuttoned and his boots were caked with mud. He held a packet of papers in one hand.

"Hello, John! You look as if you've been on campaign already."

Bourke grinned. "I've been traveling with General Crook, which is much the same thing. How have you been?" He pumped Whitcomb's hand with enthusiasm.

The two men had seen each other once since the March campaign, when Crook and his aide had stopped at Fort Russell. Bourke had obtained an audience with Crook for his friend, who had delivered to the general the messages from Hardeman and Lisa Putnam. Since then Whitcomb had remained at his post and he had little new to tell as he and Bourke exchanged recent news now. Bourke, in the meanwhile, had accompanied Crook on a journey to the

Sioux reservation agencies in an attempt to recruit Sioux and Cheyenne scouts for the summer campaign. The attempt had failed due to a strong reluctance on the part of the agency Indians to take the field against their wild brethren, and Crook had been discouraged to find conditions on the reservation bad and getting worse.

"There's damn little food, Ham," Bourke said. "It's no wonder they'll risk sneaking off. At least in the Powder River country they may find some game. The hostiles have been reinforced, there's no doubt of that. We may have a lively time of it." He lowered his voice as a squad of men passed near. "How are you getting along with Sutorius?"

Whitcomb shrugged. "He's not much like Boots Corwin." Captain Alexander Sutorius had been released from his sobering confinement at Fort D. A. Russell and returned to command of Company E. In the absence of a new first lieutenant, Whitcomb was second-in-command.

"He has almost as much experience," Bourke said. "He's a good man if he stays clear of John Barleycorn. You should get along with him well enough in the field."

Whitcomb nodded. "I intend to."

"By the way, you might like to know that Anson Mills's report says that Corwin transferred command to you before he died, nothing more. You did a fine job, Ham. I mean that with all my heart. We're all proud of you. Oh, and a copy of Grant's letter has been put in your record. Crook saw to that."

Whitcomb was startled by the news. He had stated clearly in his report that he had assumed command on his own responsibility, well before Corwin had seen fit to pass the torch. The report was part of the permanent record, but the fact that Mills, Whitcomb's battalion commander, had chosen to overlook the insubordinate action meant it would almost certainly be forgotten. The deliberate omission would not have been possible without the good will of Dupré, McCaslin and Atherton, all of whom had made verbal reports to Mills on the Lost Platoon's adventures. The faith in him displayed by such worthy men made Whitcomb feel that he had been handed an additional burden of responsibility. As for the letter Bourke had mentioned, President Grant had written to General Crook after the campaign, referring to Whitcomb's feat in admiring terms. The retreat of the Lost Platoon had come to the President's attention in the newspapers, where it had been briefly celebrated. Whitcomb was well aware that such notice might accrue to his benefit, but he was embarrassed by all the praise, and especially that from Bourke, eight years his senior and a recipient of the Medal of Honor.

"I'll be glad to be on campaign again," Whitcomb said. "At least it will mean an end to all this fuss."

"Don't be bashful, old man!" Bourke exclaimed. "Opportunity knocked and you answered. You pulled a miracle out of your hat and saved half of E Troop."

"At the time, all I wanted to do was save my skin, believe me."

"And you did such a good job of it that you brought the men back with you and a train of circus wagons to boot. You should have seen the eyes pop in Omaha when we heard that story!" Bourke laughed, and Whitcomb laughed with him. "Between you and me," Bourke went on, "the general would have liked to promote you first lieutenant, but there was no way to do it. Length of service and all that. You understand. Still, you've made quite a name for yourself in a short time." He glanced at the packet in his hand. "Well, I've got to go. Morning dispatches for the general. Oh, I almost forgot." He dug in the pocket of his blouse. "There was a mail pouch late yesterday. I was looking through it and I found this." He handed Whitcomb a folded letter. "I'll see you tomorrow. We'll have more chance to talk once we're on the trail."

Bourke set off at a trot for the headquarters building where Crook had his temporary office, leaving Whitcomb staring at the letter. It was addressed in his father's handwriting. He opened it and read:

> *My dear son,*
> *I have received a letter from the Yankee*
> *general who calls himself the president. As*
> *you may well imagine, the opinions of Yankee*
> *generals count for very little with me, but*
> *from what he tells me, you have acquitted*
> *yourself with honor. In war there is no*
> *higher duty, next to following orders and*
> *gaining the victory, than caring for your*
> *men and bringing them safely out of danger.*
> *It seems that fortune has tested you and you*
> *have met the challenge. I am proud of you,*
> *my boy.*

It was signed, "Affectionately, your father."

"Lieutenant Whitcomb!"

Sergeant Dupré was waving to him from the post gates. The first sergeant's mustache was waxed once again, the points curling jauntily upward. "The troop is ready for inspection, sair! Captain Sutorius requests your presence."

Whitcomb placed the letter in his breast pocket and buttoned it carefully. "Coming, Sergeant."

"Ah, Mr. Bourke." Crook looked up as Bourke entered. The general's black-and-white border collie lay on the floor in front of his desk. The dog opened one eye and his tail thumped the floor at the sight of Bourke.

"Morning dispatches, sir."

"Anything significant?"

Bourke opened the packet and selected a telegram from the top of the pile. "The Gros Ventres told their agent that they were robbed of all their guns and powder when they went south of the Yellowstone to visit the Sioux."

"That means they traded the guns away."

Bourke turned to the next dispatch. "There are reports that another one hundred and fifty Sioux are not to be found at their usual camping place near the Red Cloud Agency. The agent claims they have gone hunting on the Missouri."

Crook snorted and scowled. "Where there is no game whatsoever. We know that and he knows it. I would like to pack all those agents in a wagon and bring them along with us. If there is to be more fighting, I would like them to see what their greed and incompetence have caused! It need not have come to this, you know." He accepted the sheaf of papers from Bourke's hand and began to leaf through them, his face clouded by a lingering frown.

Bourke remained discreetly silent. Ever since returning from the Dakota reservation, Crook's mood had been darker than usual, and he had ample cause for his anger. Rations at the agencies remained woefully inadequate, despite the general's frequent protests both to the agents and Washington City. There were persistent rumors of large bands moving west to join the hostiles, and while the command was off on its late-winter campaign, new scandals in the nation's capital had thwarted the army's hope of regaining control of Indian affairs. Secretary of War William Belknap had been accused of accepting a bribe of twenty-four thousand dollars to appoint a man named C. P. March to the position of post trader at Fort Sill, Indian Territory. Belknap had resigned in the face of certain impeachment, and "Belknapism" had been coined by the newspapers as a synonym for taking bribes. Congress had decided that the War Department was no more fit than Interior to manage the aborigines, and it had struck down the attempt to return the Indian Bureau to the army. On the frontier, Indian activities had increased as the spring advanced. Throughout April and May there had been nearly continuous raiding all along the far-flung borders of the Powder River country, until no one but large forces of armed troops could travel safely in these regions.

Crook held up a sheet of yellow foolscap. "Did you see this? It's the latest figures on the desertions."

Bourke nodded, withholding comment. Crook leaned back in his chair, regarding his aide thoughtfully. "I would be grateful to have your impression of the troops' morale, as compared with the start of our last campaign."

Bourke shook his head. "Not so good, sir. But it's better now that we're here and ready to go. The men will settle down. That's the impression I get."

Crook considered this for a moment, nodded, and returned to his reading.

Bourke hoped he had not been optimistic about the future behavior of the men. They had lost a great deal of faith in their leaders. Following the announcement of the new campaign there had been desertions from posts throughout the department. At the battle on the Powder, not only had part of E Troop been cut off as Reynolds' force withdrew, but the bodies of the dead had been left behind. Persistent rumors that a man had fallen alive into the hands of the enemy had not helped matters. The soldiers were reluctant to serve under officers that abandoned their men, living or dead, to the savage mercies of the Indians. Ironically, only one man, Private Donnelly, had deserted from E Troop itself, a fact that Bourke attributed to Whitcomb's standing with the men and his presence as second-in-command. Ham Whitcomb had emerged from his first campaign with a shining reputation, while heads far more exalted than his rolled about him. Colonel Reynolds and Captain Moore had been formally charged with misbehavior before the enemy, Moore for his failure to prevent the Indians from leaving the village and taking the high ground, and Reynolds because as the expedition's commander he shared responsibility for that failure and others as well, including the disordered withdrawal. The two men were absent from the reorganized command and would be tried by court-martial later in the year. Whatever the outcome, their careers would surely suffer. Captain Henry Noyes had also been charged; he had been tried at Fort D. A. Russell in April and found guilty of conduct to the prejudice of good order and discipline, a lesser offense. It seemed that he had unsaddled his troop during the battle and permitted the men to eat lunch. He was sentenced to be reprimanded by the department commander, but Crook had been lenient. Noting Noyes's excellent Civil War record, he had declined to make a formal reprimand and had placed him in command of five troops of Second Cavalry for the summer campaign, an action of which Bourke heartily approved. Detailed by Reynolds to capture the Indians' horse herd, Noyes had perhaps shown an error in judgment by remaining in the rear while the battle raged, but his testimony and that of others had made it clear that he had not intended to shirk his duty. Fortunately for him, General Crook was a fair man. He would hold any officer or enlisted man to account for a serious offense, but he reserved the harshest condemnation for failures at the level of overall command, where he believed the greatest responsibility lay.

Crook was nearing the bottom of the pile of dispatches.

Bourke took a paper from his pocket and held it in his hands. Crook noticed the movement and looked up. "What's that you've got there?" he inquired.

"I was saving the best news for last, sir. Teddy Egan's done it again. He drove off six hundred warriors on the Black Hills road. He got there just as the Indians were attacking a party of miners and sent them running with just his own troop!"

"And of course those miners should never be allowed into the hills in the first place," Crook said with a trace of bitterness. "If there could be a worse example to the Sioux not to trust us, it is our conduct there. Within what is properly their land we are robbing them daily. No wonder their mood is ugly." He was incensed that troops he could have put to better use elsewhere were compelled to protect the miners on the Black Hills road, men whose presence and every action worsened the chance for peace.

Bourke leaned across the desk and leafed through the papers, plucking one from the pile. "You saw this one, sir? The raids have lessened in Nebraska and along the Platte. Surely that's good news."

"Possibly." Crook hoped it meant that the raiders were moving north, along with the six hundred Egan had encountered. He pulled his beard, one tail of the fork and then the other, as he reread another telegram. "Terry and Gibbon confirm their departures. That's something, anyway. Terry left Fort Lincoln on the seventeenth, and Gibbon is en route from Fort Shaw to Fort Ellis." He looked up at his aide. "Mr. Bourke, will you be so good as to find Colonel Royall and the chief of scouts and inform them that I will see them here at five o'clock this afternoon?"

"Sir."

Bourke saluted and left him. Crook leaned back in his

chair and put his feet on the desk. It was a minor errand and not the sort he usually gave to Bourke. It could have waited until later, but he wished to be alone to think. Tomorrow he would be in the field, where action was everything, and this time he would succeed come hell or high water.

Three months ago he had hoped to end the war before the advent of spring. Now, under conditions far more favorable to the Indians, he faced a stronger enemy, thanks to the bungling of distant bureaucrats. "The Indian agents will never induce the hostiles to come in and surrender while the people at the agencies are starving!" Crook had informed Sheridan when the division commander had visited Omaha in April. "They can't even keep the Indians they have!" Sheridan had suggested that the reports of agency Indians making off to join the hostiles were exaggerated. "They have no horses," Sheridan had said. The policy of denying horses to the reservation Sioux was his, supporting his oft-expressed opinion that a Sioux on foot was a Sioux no longer. "The hostiles have plenty of horses," Crook had replied bitterly, "including twenty-three of mine."

The loss of the cavalry horses still rankled him. They had been stolen away from Reynolds' force on the night after the battle, along with the Indian ponies recovered by the hostiles. Reynolds had failed to post an adequate guard despite the obvious presence of the angry Indians, who had pursued him all the way to Lodgepole Creek. It was another failing for which Reynolds would be called to account, but at bottom Crook knew that he himself was responsible for the failure of the campaign. There was no doubt that it had been a failure, despite the trumpetings of success in the newspapers. "Crazy Horse's Village Attacked!" they had proclaimed. "One Hundred Lodges

Destroyed! Hostiles Routed!'' The papers had not said that the spirit of the hostiles remained strong and that the identification of the village was in doubt. Grouard admitted he had identified it as Crazy Horse's because of the presence of the Oglala lodges and some horses in the pony herd that he recognized as belonging to He Dog, Crazy Horse's good friend. He claimed to have seen one of Crazy Horse's favorite ponies too, but Little Bat Garnier had hunted with Crazy Horse and knew him well. He said if the Oglala had been there he would surely have been in the forefront of the fighting, but Little Bat had seen him nowhere. He said too that many of the hostiles were Cheyenne, not Sioux. Hardeman and the Putnam woman had told Lieutenant Whitcomb that the village was that of Two Moons, a peaceful Cheyenne. If that was true, and the Cheyenne now considered themselves at war, then Crook's fears of a renewed Indian alliance were realized.

If only he himself had commanded the attack force. . . . But he had given the opportunity to J. J. Reynolds, and Reynolds had failed him. If Moore had managed to hold the bluffs, Reynolds might have seen the wisdom of holding the village. By all accounts the Indian camp could have fed and sheltered the entire command until the arrival of summer and beyond! Reynolds' orders had been to strike the hostiles and destroy their shelter and supplies, but it was the job of a commander in the field to think for himself and to seize whatever opportunities came his way. Choosing to hold the village would have been within Reynolds' authority. Instead he had burned the village, and by that and his other actions he had guaranteed that the entire expedition would be forced to withdraw ignominiously from the country, leaving the field to the Indians.

Crook and the pack train had reached the rendezvous at Lodgepole Creek at noon of the eighteenth to find half the

Indian horse herd already recovered by the hostiles and the spirit of Reynolds' men at low ebb. Their hunger and fatigue were to be expected, but many were without top-coats and gloves, these articles having been laid aside when the battle began and never recovered in the retreat, and sixty of the men were suffering from frostbite. Sixty cases of frostbite, after sixteen days of arduous marching without a single occurrence! Dr. Munn and Steward Bryan had done their best to alleviate the suffering, but with limited success.

With supplies short and so many men unfit for battle, Crook had had no choice but to continue south along the Powder to Fort Reno, pursued by bands of hostiles who fired into the night camps, once again convinced they were lords of the intermountain west. To prevent them from recovering the remaining horses, Crook had ordered the Indian ponies shot. At Reno he had given brief consider-ation to resupplying his able-bodied men and turning back, but reports from Lieutenant Bourke and Surgeon Munn had persuaded him of the futility of such an attempt. The injured would need a strong escort to assure their safe arrival at Fetterman, and the loss of part of Company E had been a blow to morale. There was a deep unease among the men, Bourke had reported. They no longer trusted their officers. Crook could not restructure his com-mand in the field and so he had bowed to the inevitable and returned to Fetterman.

Court-martialing Reynolds was a necessary evil, but it could not erase the greater evil that had already been done. With the retreat of the soldiers and the recovery of their horses, the hostiles no doubt felt that they had won the day. Now, armed with the new weapons for which by all accounts they had been eagerly trading all spring, and strengthened by new arrivals from the agencies, they would be hot to prove their mettle against any soldiers that dared to enter their domain. The end result of the March campaign, then, had been to increase not only the Indians' will to fight, but their capacity to do so as well.

Crook had planned his strategy accordingly, but it was based on his own reading of the savage mind and so was fraught with dangers. This was the time of year when the Indians customarily grouped together to hunt and dance their savage dances, and he assumed that this year would be no different. With the coming of the warm months the hostiles would move north to gather in the lower reaches of their Powder River stronghold. There they would council to discuss the events of the spring and plan what to do. Emboldened by their "victory" over Colonel Reynolds, would they be confident enough to go about their summer hunt as usual? Crook sincerely hoped so, for based on his guesswork and assumptions, he had taken a tremendous risk in order to bring the strongest possible force into the field. He had stripped bare the posts throughout his command, and left them garrisoned with skeleton guards of infantry. Every able-bodied cavalryman in the Department of the Platte was here at Fetterman, nine hundred of them, and two hundred and fifty infantry. There were twelve hundred horses and three hundred thousand rounds of ammunition. Without the need to carry forage for the animals, without the cumbersome clothing and extra bedding demanded by a winter campaign, his men were at long last on a truly equal footing with their foe. How Terry's and Gibbon's forces were outfitted, he did not know, but his own men were prepared to live off the land. Oh, he had supplies in profusion now. Two hundred teamsters and packers; a thousand mules; a small beef herd at Sheridan's insistence; six hundred thousand pounds of varied provisions. But unlike the March campaign, he could leave it all behind if the occasion demanded. Not just for two weeks but indefinitely, and he was prepared to do just that.

If his assumptions were wrong, what then? If the hostiles had not regrouped in the north, if they remained scattered in small bands and if the raiders that had appeared everywhere in droves during the past two months were merely lurking in the hills and planning their next attack, they would find easy pickings along the Platte and George Crook would bear the blame. But if his calculations were right, the Indians would be surprised in the heart of their buffalo country by the three columns that would soon converge from Dakota and Montana and Fort Fetterman. If Terry and Gibbon did their share, the effect of the combined forces could be overpowering.

Crook picked up the report of Terry's and Gibbon's departures from their respective forts and read it again to reassure himself that both commanders were truly in the field. He had sent a request for this confirmation two days before and it had arrived in time. Neither man had set foot on the trail in March, although Colonel Brisbin, of Gibbon's command, had ventured as far as Fort Pease to evacuate the garrison there, which had been under constant attack by the hostiles. The weather had been too severe for an extended campaign, Terry had said later. Crook snorted. The weather had not been too severe for his troops of the Second and Third Cavalry. At least the others were on the move now. And Custer was riding with Terry after all, although as his subordinate. As Crook had expected, Custer's testimony before the House committee investigating corruption in Indian affairs had aroused President Grant's fury, and until the eleventh hour it had appeared that Grant would keep the Boy General from joining the campaign. In the end, Custer had written to the President personally, begging that he be spared the disgrace of seeing his regiment march without him. Terry, Sheridan, and Sherman himself had endorsed the request, and Grant, ever the old soldier, had relented. Custer would be hot for the smell of powder now and anxious to redeem himself.

At first Crook had thought the split command was lunacy. Once he and Terry and Gibbon were all in the field, communication among them would be next to impossible until—if and when—they joined forces. But at least the orders left him free, answerable only to himself, and now he saw that they suited him perfectly. The others might weary of the campaign if it failed to produce spectacular victories, but he would keep at it. He had learned long ago that when there was a difficult task to be done, he had better prepare to do it himself without depending overmuch on others, and it was with this in mind that he had taken the risk and assembled here the largest force he could muster. This time he would not leave the field without obtaining a resolution. He would continue through the summer and into autumn and winter if need be, and in time the Indians would submit.

That was how the war must end. Before there could be any hope of a lasting peace, the white man must feel he had won the victory. Nothing less would satisfy him. There could be no parleys, no negotiated settlement that seemed to condone or justify the intransigence of the hostiles. All the recent events—the constant raiding, the fevered newspaper reports of every incident, every rumor, the uproar over the Black Hills gold and the demands that something "be done" about the Indians—had created a climate in which there could be only one outcome: there must be a surrender. There might be a single big battle or a series of small ones, but sooner or later the hostiles must yield to the military force and then the public attention would turn elsewhere. The Indians, now pacified, would be forgotten, as they were always forgotten once the alarums of war died away. And that was when Crook might achieve what he had sought all along, a just peace for the Sioux, with fair terms and promises kept, resulting in benefits to both peoples. "It is absurd to speak of keeping faith with Indians," Phil Sheridan had proclaimed more than once, but Crook knew that Sheridan was fatally wrong. Only by keeping faith could the peace endure, and even without that practical consideration, honor would permit no other course.

The campaign would be long and hard. If there were no swift victory the nation would soon tire of reports from the battleground, and when the final surrender came, the public would embrace any terms that brought a secure peace. Crook no longer believed there was any chance for the Sioux to retain their "sacred" Black Hills; the gold was too important. But with that plum secured for the white man, Sitting Bull and Crazy Horse might be able to keep some of the land they cherished almost as much, along the Powder River.

Outside, a bugle sounded recall-from-drill and Crook got to his feet. He would take his midday meal in the officers' mess today. He needed to feel the tension and high spirits that always attended the start of a campaign.

Seeing his master moving about, the dog arose, his tail wagging in anticipation of a walk through the post. Crook bent to stroke the collie's silken ears, daring to enjoy the hope that his plan might succeed. For what seemed the hundredth time he reviewed in his mind the peace terms that Whitcomb had brought him. There were no flaws, no impossibilities. In Hardeman's message and Elizabeth Putnam's there were the seeds of a fruitful peace. The Congress would never approve such terms now, but if a Powder River reservation could be hidden in the terms of surrender so none could call it a concession to the unreconstructed hostiles, it was a possibility. In the general relief at obtaining a final peace with the Sioux, the Congress might be magnanimous in victory and the certain objections of the Indian Bureau overcome.

Crook would do all he could to obtain such a result. But first there must be a surrender.

CHAPTER SIXTEEN

The water shimmered in the stream and the air shimmered in the rising heat of the day. The great encampment crowded the banks of the Greasy Grass. Gathered in the thousands, the Lakota rejoiced in their power.

Sun Horse sat atop a low hill overlooking the river and the camp. He had come there before sunrise, to pray to the morning star as it ushered in the light. The morning was well along now and the buffalo robe that had warmed him in the chilly dawn was spread on the ground. He sat upon it cross-legged, wearing only a loin cover, giving himself to the heat of the sun. The feeling pleased him so much that he lay back and closed his eyes, letting the sun bathe him from the front and feeling its warmth rise from the earth and the *pte* hide beneath him.

After so much cold and gray and wet, the weather had turned warm at last. The Moon of Fat Calves was waning now, but still rounded. When it was young the snows had come again for a last time before *Okaga*, the power of the south, had finally triumphed, driving *Waziya* back to the north and bringing an outpouring of new life from the soft earth that had been cleansed by the healing snows. Already the grass stood nearly to a man's knees and the hills were covered with flowers.

Sun Horse felt the growing power flow through his body, warming him, and he heard the sounds of the great camp below him in the river bottom—the horses stamping and whickering, children and dogs playing joyfully, many voices making a humming along the banks where the grass grew thick and sweet. The sounds were full of life and he sat up again to look upon what he heard. Clusters of lodges dotted the banks as far as he could see. He spread his arms to embrace the encampment but he could not contain it all. It was too huge. Around the bends upstream and down, there were more lodges, and still more people arrived each day and their horses joined the almost numberless herds that raised great clouds of dust when they went to water.

All during the warming moons the Lakota and their allies had been on the move, drawing together in numbers even the oldest ones had never seen before. From the reservations they came, moving north and west to the streams that fed the Yellowstone, to join the ones already there. The Sun Dance had been held on the Rosebud, and Sun Horse had danced with the others. For two days he had danced beneath the open framework of the Sun Dance lodge, pulling a buffalo skull by thongs tied through slits in his chest muscles, and all the while he had prayed his thanks to *pte* and to *Wakán Tanka*, who gave the greatest of the four-leggeds as a gift to man. It had been good for the people to see the Sun Dance conducted in the old way, with great ceremony. It had made them strong. For a time the wounds in Sun Horse's chest had pained him, but they were already healing. Now, with the sun full on his chest, the wounds were only two spots that felt warmer than the rest, with no pain. Now as then, he gave himself to the sun and the sun healed him.

When the Sun Dance had ended, the grass on the Rosebud was already exhausted by the pony herds, and so the people had moved here to the Greasy Grass, where the council would be held.

All seven council fires of the *Títonwan*, the western Lakota, were here. There were Two Kettles and Blackfeet-Lakota and Burnt Thighs, No Bows led by Spotted Eagle and Minneconjou under Touch the Clouds and Fast Bull and young Hump. The Sun Band was camped with the Hunkpapa, close by the people of Sitting Bull and Gall and Black Moon and Crow King. The names of the famous men were spoken throughout the camp as the people watched the building of the immense council lodge where the leaders would soon gather, but the name mentioned most of all was spoken quietly, for Crazy Horse shunned praise. He led all the Oglala now, and others looked to him as well. In the Moon of Shedding Ponies, the month the whites called May, the Oglala had made their Strange Man a new kind of chief, a headman for leading in peace as well as war, and they gave the position for life. The new honor was not something to be taken away as the Big Bellies had taken his shirt. The people had rejoiced at this choice, and the news carriers had spread the word far and wide, even to the people at the agencies. Crazy Horse leads us all! they said, and from all sides the bands had come.

Far away in the wooded lands where the sun rose, the eastern Lakota had heard of the council and they too had come, the *Iháŋktonwan* and even some of the *Isáŋyati*, those who said Dakota instead of Lakota, the ones who survived the war in the year 1862. They were poor people now, called No Clothes by some, but they were led by the legendary Inkpaduta, a great man whose people had been brought to nothing by the whites. He still walked tall and proud and would take a seat high in the council.

Here and there among the Lakota camps were a few lodges of Arapaho, and many Shahíyela, those of Little Wolf and Old Bear and Two Moons joined now by Dull Knife's people and other smaller bands.

Truly the power to grow shone brightly on the Lakota and their friends. They grew in many ways, but they grew strongest of all for war. Throughout the spring they had traded with neighboring tribes for guns, even with their enemies, the Crows and the hated Blackfeet. Relatives from the agencies had brought the guns a friendly agent let them have for hunting, and the halfbreed traders' sons had managed to bring some more. There were many of the back-loading kind and a few of the many-shooting kind too, and powder and lead, enough for every man who needed them. Throughout the encampment the men cleaned the guns and sharpened their knives, and around the lodge fires it was the young men of the Shahíyela who spoke strongest of all for fighting the whites. Until the soldiers struck Two Moons and his people, the Shahíyela had been at peace with the whites, and they were still angry at the whiteman's treachery. We whipped Three Stars and drove him away! the young men said. If he comes back, we will whip him again!

Long Hair will come, some of those from the agencies said.

We know Long Hair! said the Lakotas who had fought him on the Yellowstone two snows past when he came there to make an iron road. There was no iron road yet!

We know him too, said the Shahíyela, remembering the Washita and those who had died there, and they looked at the one they had called Little Warrior in his childhood, before his dream took him back to the white world for a time. The white youth accompanied Sun Horse everywhere now, as did the old man's other grandson, Blackbird. These three were silent when others talked of war, but their silence was lost in a storm of angry words.

Long Hair will not find us sleeping again! the Shahíyela said, and around them the howls of approval grew deafening.

Sun Horse sighed as he looked at the encampment, so peaceful in the morning sunshine. Hardeman had warned that the people would feel invincible gathered together like this, and he had been right.

Off to the southwest, the Snowy Mountains, the range called Big Horns by the whites, stood snow-capped and beautiful against the clear blue sky. Far away in the southern foothills lay Sun Horse's vision-valley, his winter home for so long, but he would not see it again. It belonged to Hardeman now. It was not so much the land itself that had been Sun Horse's parting gift to the scout; by giving the land he had assured that Hardeman would have companionship. It was not good that a man should live alone. Or a woman. Men and women needed one another, and among the whites, who had no tribe to sustain them, they needed one another all the more. Hardeman and Lisaputnam would care for the land and they would remember the friendship that had grown there between Lakota and *washíchun*.

Sun Horse missed Hears Twice as well. The old prophet had been a good friend for many years. Once Sun Horse had found the answers to his dilemma and ceased his fast, he had spoken with Hears Twice. Having asked the prophet to use his power to help the people, Sun Horse could not simply tell his friend that there was no further need to listen for the voices of the spirit world, but he had told Hears Twice that he had decided what the band should do, and the seer had seemed happy. "I am glad you have found your power again," Hears Twice had said. "I was afraid for you when you would not eat." Then the old man had touched his ear. "There is something I must hear," he said, and he had continued his silent vigil, keeping to himself, listening still. On the day before the Sun Band left the winter valley he had come to Sun Horse and told him what he heard. "There is big trouble coming. A big fight. The people win, but I hear no victory, no peace. I hear only the sound of tears falling. I hear buffalo gone away, Lakota gone away, everything gone." Here he had passed one palm across the other in the sign that meant *rubbed out.* "I will go to the agency at Red Cloud," he had added, brightening somewhat. "I will live with old friends and smoke the pipe. We will talk about times long ago before the whiteman came. It is good to smoke with old friends."

The spirits had told Hears Twice what was to come, but Sun Horse already knew.

By now Hears Twice and Mist would be on the Dakota reservation, learning what life would be like for all the Lakota in times to come, but before that day arrived for Sun Horse, he had much to do.

His long years of watching from the small valley had not been in vain. He had perceived the true nature of the whites, but he feared the knowledge he had gained, and so he had looked away, pretending it was incomplete. What was worse, he had misunderstood his own power! For so many years he had sought a pathway to peace with the whites, all in vain! That was not his power at all. To understand the *washícun*, yes. To lead his people, yes; and in time he would lead his people to live beside the whites; but it was not his power to force the *washíchun* into a peace that was contrary to their own nature! Once the whites began fighting, they kept on until the enemy surrendered. That was their nature, and Sun Horse knew that a man could not betray his true nature, neither *washíchun* nor Lakota. In the end, the Lakota would have to yield to the numberless foe.

From the start, Hardeman had spoken the truth. Even before he went off with the pipe carriers he had said that the Sun Band would have to submit to the will of the whites, and when he came back he had said the same thing. That evening, when the pipe carriers had eaten and the whites were gone and everyone else was asleep, Sun Horse had finally admitted to himself the truth of the white scout's words, for in his heart he had always known it was so.

Washíchun, a people not at peace with themselves. Uncertain of their own great power, they must conquer others to feel strong.

Confronting this immutable fact, Sun Horse had been led to a dreadful conclusion. He had despaired, and from his despair had come the answer to his prayers.

The conclusion was one not even Hardeman saw: not only would the whites demand that the Lakota lay down their arms and live in confinement, *they would demand a surrender of the spirit as well!*

The whites looked at the Lakota and they did not see men like themselves; they saw the feathers and the paint, the symbols on the tipis, the songs and dancing, the way of life so different from their own. They feared what was different, and so they would try to change it until they feared it no longer. When the Lakota surrendered, the whites would destroy the old way of life. They would take away the weapons and the horses, they would end the hunting; they would destroy all the symbols, seeking in this way to destroy the spirit.

Could the spirit survive without the symbols? If not, then the hoop of the world would be broken; the people would lose touch with the good red road of spiritual understanding and the tree of life would wither. And yet on that fateful night, sitting in his lodge with the storm howling outside, despairing at the thought of the old life ending, Sun Horse had felt a sudden hope.

Look beyond the symbol! Sees Beyond had commanded him when the Snowblind Moon was round and bright, yet until the night of the pipe carriers' return he had not seen just how far beyond he would have to look.

Was not the Lakota way of life itself one all-embracing symbol? The graceful lodges of buffalo hide, the rituals of childhood and manhood, the vision quests, the songs, the dances, the offerings to the spirits, the ceremonies, the prayers—all were part of a great symbol that contained the Lakota spirit. Yet the spirit did not live in the symbol! It was in the hearts of the people, and there it might be preserved!

The people would need a new kind of leader, one who could nurture the spirit and keep it well even when the old way of life was gone. The trail ahead would be long and difficult and Sun Horse knew he would not see its end. He was too old. He could start the people on the new path, but who . . . ?

In that same moment, even as he asked the question, he

had seen the answer there before his eyes, in the sleeping form of his grandson Blackbird.

"I want to understand the *washíchun*," the boy had said earlier that evening, and, "There is so much to learn about being a man." "You are the future of the people," Sun Horse had said, little dreaming as he spoke just how true those words might be! The boy was greatly changed by his first brush with war and death. He had fought the whites and survived. Now he wished to understand them, and to shoulder the burdens of manhood. He was prepared to become a man of the people! But with the innate wisdom of youth he had recognized the greatest threat to his learning. In the onrushing flood of *washíchun* he saw the one power that could deny him the time he needed. "I was angry with the whites," he had said, "because it seemed they would change the world before I could become a man."

He must have the time! But how to give it to him? Sun Horse had wondered. In two moons, no more than three, the bluecoats would return, yet it would take years for the boy to learn all he would need to know! He must learn every aspect of the old life; he must experience the strength of the Lakota way and know the meaning of all the symbols; only then could he look beyond these things and comprehend the essence of the Lakota spirit, which was all he could hope to save when the day of surrender came.

How could that day be put off for long enough? Sun Horse's despair had threatened to return, but then he had smelled the meat in the lodge and felt his hunger strong within him. And once again the answer to his question had come to him, so simple, so obvious.

Pte, the gift of life for the Lakota. The greatest of the four-leggeds, the greatest gift of *Wakán Tanka*. *Pte*, the strength to live in the Lakota way.

The clown girl had run away and Sun Horse's white grandson had found her. The young man had been led by a spirit animal and the girl had seen *pte*. With the coming together of these two, a power had come to help the Sun Band: the power of *pte*. Had the buffalo returned just so the people could go to Dakota and surrender? No! They had returned so the people could continue living in the Lakota way! In an instant, Sun Horse's confidence had been restored to him and he saw his pathway open before him: Blackbird, the future of the people; to give him time to learn, live in the Lakota way for as long as possible, so it would become ingrained in him, so the spirit would persist when the old ways had been destroyed by the whites!

Flee the whites! the blackbirds had told his grandson before the fight at Two Moons' village. They had spoken wisely and Sun Horse would obey.

Thus it was that he had left his vision-valley behind forever. It was too close to the soldier forts and the wagon road, this was true, but he had left it for another reason as well. The Lakota life was not tied to a place; it was something the people carried with them wherever they might go. From now on the band would live on the move, wintering wherever winter found them, and this too would be a lesson for Blackbird to learn. Sun Horse had brought the people here to the Greasy Grass in order that they should grow strong in the hoop of the nation. In the council he would still speak for peace, but he would not advise surrender. The old life is good for us, he would say; we must keep to it for as long as we can. When the council was done, the Sun Band would go on the summer hunt with Sun Horse's cousin Sitting Bull. After the hunt they might stay with the Hunkpapa war man or go off on their own. Sun Horse would decide when the time came. Above all they would stay away from the whites, away from the fighting, if it came. For as long as possible they would live at peace, without surrender, in the Lakota way. And all the time Blackbird would be learning.

Already the youth had taken more steps on the path to manhood. In the Moon of Shedding Ponies he had gone with his father on a raid against the *Kanghí*. He had stolen horses and left them at the lodge of Yellow Leaf's uncle, Hawk Chaser's brother, with whom the girl and her mother now lived. The horses had been accepted and gifts exchanged. After the great council a new lodge would be built in the Sun Band's camp circle for the two young people.

Sun Horse had encouraged Standing Eagle to instruct Blackbird in the skills of a warrior, but against a traditional enemy, not against the whites. It was good that the boy should spend some time with his father, but not too much. Standing Eagle was a great warrior, a strong man, but he would cling to the old ways so long as he drew breath. He would fight the *washíchun* before the end. He would die rather than surrender. All to preserve a symbol. He could not see beyond the symbol, but perhaps his son could, given time. The boy should respect his father and learn from him, but Blackbird would learn from others as well, men who would teach him what it meant to be a man of the people. Here too his instruction was moving ahead. Before the Sun Dance Blackbird had been taken into the Raven Owners warrior society of the Oglala; there were both Oglala and Hunkpapa in the Sun Band and the society had a lodge there. Crazy Horse himself had spoken for the boy in the ceremony. Blackbird had returned to his grandfather's lodge swollen with pride, but also humbled and awed that the light-haired man of the Oglala should do such a thing for him.

Sun Horse had encouraged this step too, asking the

favor of Crazy Horse privately. It was true that Blackbird was still young for marriage and the rigors of a warrior's training, but there was little time. The *washíchun* were an impatient people.

Sun Horse stretched his legs out straight before him and leaned back against his hands. Today his joints and muscles were those of a younger man. The sun had soothed away his aches and pains. Overhead, the blinding orb was nearing the zenith. The day was hot, but it was not uncomfortable. Sun Horse preferred the warm weather. The winter had been long and cold and full of worry. Even his worries were banished by the sun. He was strong again as a leader should be strong, confident in the direction he led his people. In the time that remained, he and Sees Beyond and the others they chose would teach Blackbird everything they knew, moving the boy along fast, hastening his way to manhood, training him to lead, guiding him to see beyond the symbols to the very heart of the Lakota spirit. Blackbird would learn without knowing he was taught, for he was eager to know everything, and in time he would lead without seeming to lead, perhaps even without knowing he was a leader. The *washíchun* would always single out a leader and break his power, but Blackbird would be a new kind of leader, a guardian of the Lakota spirit. As the old-man chiefs kept the coals of the village fire on the journey from one camping place to the next, so it would be Blackbird's task to keep the glow of the Lakota spirit alive during the journey through the troubled times ahead, so that one day the fire might be rekindled for all men to see.

The camp had grown quiet in the heat of the day. A figure moved among the Sun Band lodges and Sun Horse recognized his white grandson by his hat and coat. Like Lodgepole, the youth would keep some habits of the white race, but he was Lakota now, Lakota-by-choice. The mov-

ing figure stopped and raised a hand toward the hill where
Sun Horse sat. Sun Horse waved in reply and got to his
feet with fluid ease. He made broad signs, telling the
young man to wait for him, and then he gathered up his
buffalo robe and started down the hill, enjoying the feeling
of the warm earth beneath his feet. He liked to walk
barefoot on the Mother Earth in the spring when she was
soft like the flesh of a woman.

The thought caused a stirring in his loins. Last night he
had enjoyed both his wives, going from Elk Calf's robes to
Sings His Daughter in the middle of the night. From the
old to the young.

Sun Horse chuckled as he walked. Even in his lovemaking he saw symbols for the path he had chosen. From the
old to the young. From Sun Horse to Blackbird the power
would pass, the power to lead the people from the old way
to a new one among the whites. As man planted his seed
in woman, so Sun Horse would plant knowledge in Blackbird, seeds that would grow slowly. Only long after Sun
Horse was placed on his scaffold and offered to the winds
and the sky would the seeds bring forth new life.

Below, in the camp, his other grandson awaited him in
the shade of a cottonwood. He would have to choose a
name for the young man now that he was Lakota. And
before long he should have a wife.

A pain returned, and the smile faded from Sun Horse's
face. Had it been necessary for the clown girl to die? He
did not know. The answers to such questions were *wakán*,
a mystery. He had grieved for her, but even then he had
seen that her dying was the final gift, the act that led his
white grandson to step between the worlds once more,
joining the Lakota as Sitting Bull had foreseen long ago,
and so assuring that Sun Horse and his people would
remain connected to the white world, as they had been

ever since Lodgepole joined the band more than thirty snows ago. As Lodgepole and his brother had shared their knowledge of the *washíchun* with Sun Horse, so Sun Horse's white grandson would share his knowledge with Blackbird. And he would share something even more valuable—the strength of the warrior who declines to fight. That was the lesson Blackbird must learn above all, how to keep his strength within him. For to fight the whites was to fight the whirlwind.

Sun Horse was nearing the bottom of the slope. As he walked he felt the warmth of the day and the softness of the earth underfoot, and the great power of the encampment that was spread along the winding banks of the Greasy Grass, the stream the whites called Little Big Horn. Embraced by the hoop of the nation, he felt his own power strong within him. Would he succeed? Would there be enough time for Blackbird to learn it all? Would the spirit survive? Sun Horse shook his head. He was not one of those who saw the future. His power was to lead his people in this world. He had chosen his course and he would lead his people as best he could. For now he was content.

As the Moon of Fat Calves grew slender, Three Stars returned, seeking the hostiles. They met him on the Rosebud and they fought him, and left him there to lick his wounds. And on the Greasy Grass the soldier chief Long Hair found the great encampment, the hoop of the Lakota nation raised for the last time. Long Hair struck the camp, and he died.

But the triumph of these victories vanished like the wind in the buffalo grass. Again and again the soldiers came and one by one the bands surrendered. When the leaves had fallen once and turned yellow to fall again, Crazy Horse, the strange man who had brought such hope to all the Lakota, was dead, and Sitting Buffalo Bull took his tipis, those of the Sun Band among them, and moved across the invisible line into Grandmother Land, and stayed there for many years. In the end even these came to the agencies and surrendered, to live there among old friends, to talk and smoke and remember the days when buffalo covered the prairie.

HISTORICAL NOTE

It has been my intention to place my fictional characters against a background that is as historically accurate as research and one man's fallible understanding can make it. The fragments of history of the American West presented in *The Snowblind Moon*—the fur trade, the westward migration, the incidents in the Indian wars—are all factually accurate, as informed readers will recognize. Historical personages are not portrayed in times and places where they were not actually present.

Secretary Chandler's letter to Indian Commissioner Smith, reproduced at the start of the narrative, is in fact the document that initiated the process of confining the last free-roaming Sioux on the Dakota reservation.

Chris Hardeman and Johnny Smoker, Jed, Bat and Lisa Putnam and the other inhabitants of Putnam's Park, as well as the park itself and the Putnam Cutoff, are all products of my imagination.

Hachaliah Tatum and his circus and all its personnel are fictional as well, but the appearance of such a troupe in the intermountain West at this time is well within the scope of historical events, as are the individual acts and animals that make up Tatum's Combined Shows. By 1876 the circus was a familiar American entertainment, and many small circuses had toured the frontier states and territories, both by rail and wagon. Several shows, some including elephants, had visited remote regions before this date.

The Sun Band and all its people are fictional. The names of other Indians and bands, and their locations in the tale, are accurate. The council at Two Moons' village at which Crazy Horse and Sitting Bull are present is an invention, but the proximity of the bands at that time is factual, and it is not impossible that these men might have met within the time period of the novel.

General Crook's campaign of March 1876 occurred as related and has not been altered in any significant respect save one: with the exception of Captain Alexander Sutorius, who did in fact miss the campaign because he was confined at Fort D. A. Russell for chronic drunkenness, and Private Peter Dowdy, who was killed in the battle of March 17, the officers and men of Company E, Third Cavalry, are fictional, as is the separation of the "Lost Platoon" from the troop at the end of the battle and its separate retreat to Fort Fetterman. Company E, Third Cavalry, was indeed one of the companies on the campaign, along with the others named in the story, and the fictional characters are not intended to represent any of the real men who served in that troop. Apart from this liberty, the names of officers and men in the command, including scouts and packers, are factual. Robert Strahorn, who wrote for the *Rocky Mountain News* under the pen name Alter Ego, was with Crook once again for the summer campaign, which left Fort Fetterman on May 29.

The reader may have noticed inconsistencies of rank in

references to certain officers. This is in keeping with the confusion that was caused by the existence of brevet ranks. In theory, an officer was entitled always to be addressed by his highest brevet rank, but contemporary accounts make it clear that this practice was not consistently observed. Both Crook himself, in his autobiography, and John Bourke in his invaluable memoir, *On the Border with Crook,* refer to officers variously by their brevet and permanent ranks.

The narrative of the battle of March 17 is based on the accounts of men who fought on both sides. Each of the six companies under Reynolds' command moved independently before and during the battle and I have simplified their movements somewhat in the interest of clarity, but the broad movements related in the story are generally accurate, especially as they would have been perceived by the characters with whom the reader enters and participates in the battle. Captain Moore did fail to prevent the Indians from leaving the village and gaining the high ground, in part through no fault of his own due to the rugged and unfamiliar terrain. Although the withdrawal from the field was ordered well in advance and took nearly two hours to execute, it seemed quite sudden to those on the line of battle; the cavalry dead were in fact left behind, and Bourke says it "was rumored among the men, one of our poor soldiers fell alive into the enemy's hands and was cut limb from limb."

The soldier found alive and unharmed in the village and subsequently tortured by Little Hand is an invention.

Warriors from the village pursued Reynolds and recaptured a majority of their horses. With the soldiers on the run, the Indians regarded the action as a victory, and the news of this event played its part in encouraging agency bands to return to the Powder River country for the summer gathering. The Cheyenne, hitherto at peace with the whites (Secretary Chandler's order applied only to the hostile Sioux), regarded the attack as utterly unprovoked, and they now joined the Sioux in preparing for war. Throughout the spring the allied tribes made extraordinary efforts to obtain new weapons by purchase and trade. Thus the Reynolds attack was in large part responsible both for the number of Indians at the great encampment on the Little Big Horn and their high degree of preparedness.

Crook fought an inconclusive engagement with a large force from the allied tribes on the Rosebud on June 17, eight days before the Custer battle. He remained in the field throughout the summer and autumn, and obtained a considerable victory at Slim Buttes in September. The forces that defeated the Cheyenne under Dull Knife in November were under Crook's command. He left the field for the winter, sending those of his scouts who knew the hostile headmen to try once more to persuade them to come in peacefully. As an inducement, Crook promised that if they would surrender, he would do everything in his power to obtain for them a permanent home in the Powder River country and an agency there. On May 6, 1877, Crazy Horse, the last hope of the hostiles, surrendered with nearly nine hundred people and seventeen hundred horses. He was in the custody of authorities at Fort Robinson, Nebraska, when he was killed on September 5 of the same year.

With the peace secured at last, Crook kept his promise to the Indians. He argued forcefully for an agency on the Yellowstone, at the mouth of the Tongue, and a reservation in that portion of the Powder River country, but his efforts were in vain, as were many similar efforts made by other military men before and after Crook on behalf of the plains Indians. In the end, with all the Sioux confined on the Dakota reservation and certain to remain there, Crook wrote to the headmen at Pine Ridge expressing regret for his failure.

(The Pine Ridge Agency was established after the last battles of the Sioux wars and thus does not appear on the map. It was just above the Nebraska-Dakota border, north of the Red Cloud and Spotted Tail Agencies. It replaced those agencies, eliminating the last sanctioned camping grounds for the Sioux beyond the borders of the Dakota reservation.)

ACKNOWLEDGMENTS

I am indebted to the following people, who generously contributed their time and expertise and thereby did much to assure the historical accuracy of *The Snowblind Moon:* Marie T. Capps, Map and Manuscript Librarian at the United States Military Academy Library, West Point, New York; Catherine T. Engel, Reference Librarian, Colorado Historical Society, Denver, Colorado; Neil Mangum, Historian, Custer Battlefield National Monument, Montana. Special thanks are due to B. Byron Price, Director of the Panhandle-Plains Historical Museum, Canyon, Texas, who read the sections concerning the frontier army and made many valuable suggestions, and to my friends John and Elaine Barlow and Melody Harding of the Bar Cross Ranch, Cora, Wyoming, and Pete and Holly Cameron of Game Hill Ranch, Bondurant, Wyoming, without whose kindness and hospitality I would know even less about the care and raising of beef cattle.

I am particularly grateful to Dr. Bernard A. Hoehner of San Francisco State University, San Francisco, California, for his invaluable advice in matters pertaining to Lakota language and culture as they appear in the novel. (A *Sihásapa*-Lakota, Dr. Hoehner was given the named Jerked With Arrow in his youth, and is now also known as Grass among his people.)

In including some Lakota words and phrases in a work intended for a general readership I have chosen to disregard certain conventions commonly employed in writing Lakota; I have used no linguistic symbols other than the acute accent and have adopted spellings intended to make something close to proper pronunciation as easy as possible for those with no previous knowledge of the language. These decisions were mine alone. I hope persons familiar with Lakota will forgive these simplifications.

Naturally, any remaining historical errors in *The Snowblind Moon*, whether of fact or interpretation, are my sole responsibility.

John Byrne Cooke
Jackson Hole, Wyoming

ABOUT THE AUTHOR

John Byrne Cooke was born in New York City in 1940. He was graduated from Harvard College and has worked as a musician, filmmaker, rock and roll road-manager, screenwriter and amateur cowboy. He has lived on both the East and West coasts and now resides in Jackson Hole, Wyoming. *The Snowblind Moon* is his first novel.

THE
SNOWBLIND
MOON
JOHN BYRNE COOKE

"An epic canvas created with sure, masterful strokes. Bravo!"
—John Jakes

"*The Snowblind Moon* is an intensely readable story."
—The Washington Post

"An epic tale . . . lyrically beautiful."
—Los Angeles Times Book Review